CAROL MARINELLI

UNLOCKING THE SURGEON'S HEART

BY
JESSICA MATTHEWS

MILLS
BOON

HERS FOR ONE NIGHT ONLY?

BY
CAROL MARINELLI

First published in Great Britain 2012
by Mills & Boon, an imprint of Harlequin (UK) Limited.
Harlequin (UK) Limited, Eton House, 18-24 Paradise Road,
Richmond, Surrey TW9 1SR

© Carol Marinelli 2012

ISBN: 978 0 263 89177 5

Harlequin (UK) policy is to use papers that are natural, renewable
and recyclable products and made from wood grown in sustainable
forests. The logging and manufacturing process conform to the
legal environmental regulations of the country of origin.

Printed and bound in Spain
by Blackprint CPI, Barcelona

Carol Marinelli recently filled in a form where she was asked for her job title and was thrilled, after all these years, to be able to put down her answer as 'writer'. Then it asked what Carol did for relaxation. After chewing her pen for a moment Carol put down the truth—'writing'. The third question asked—'What are your hobbies?' Well, not wanting to look obsessed or, worse still, boring, she crossed the fingers on her free hand and answered 'swimming and tennis'. But, given that the chlorine in the pool does terrible things to her highlights, and the closest she's got to a tennis racket in the last couple of years is watching the Australian Open, I'm sure you can guess the real answer!

CHAPTER ONE

'YOU'RE far too available.' Bridgette didn't really know how to respond when her friend Jasmine's sympathy finally ran out. After all, she knew that Jasmine was right. 'It's me and Vince's leaving do and you won't come out *in case* your sister needs a babysitter.'

'You know it's not as simple as that,' Bridgette said.

'But it *is* as simple as that.' Jasmine was determined to stand firm this time. Her boyfriend, Vince, was a paediatric intern at the large Melbourne hospital where Bridgette had, until recently, worked, and he was heading off for a year to do relief work overseas. At what felt like the last minute the rather dizzy Jasmine had decided to join him for three months, and after a lot of paperwork and frantic applications, finally tonight there was a gathering to see them both off. 'You've put everything on hold for Courtney, you've given up a job you love so you can do agency and be more flexible— you've done everything you can to support her and look at where it's got you.'

Jasmine knew that she was being harsh, but she wanted Bridgette to cry, damn it, wanted her friend to admit the truth—that living like this was agony, that something had to give. But Bridgette refused to cry, insisting instead that she was coping—that she didn't mind doing agency work, that she loved looking after Courtney's son, Harry. 'Come out, then,' Jasmine challenged. 'If everything's as fine as you say, you deserve a night out—you haven't had one in ages. I want you there—we all want to see you. Everyone will be there…'

'What if…?' Bridgette stopped herself from saying it. She was exhausted from going over the what-ifs.

'Stop hiding behind Harry,' Jasmine said.

'I'm not.'

'Yes, you are. I know you've been hurt, but you need to put it behind you.'

And it stung, but, then, the truth often did and, yes, Bridgette conceded, maybe she was using Harry as a bit of an excuse so as not to get out there. 'Okay!' Bridgette took a deep breath and nodded. 'You're on.'

'You're coming?' Jasmine grinned.

'Looks like it.'

So instead of sitting at home, Bridgette sat in the hairdresser's and had some dark foils added to her mousey-brown hair. They made her skin look paler and her sludgy-grey eyes just a bit darker, it seemed, and with Jasmine's endless encouragement she had a wax and her nails done too and, for good measure, crammed in a little shopping.

Bridgette's bedroom was in chaos, not that Jasmine cared a bit, as they fought over mirror space and added another layer of mascara. It was a hot, humid night and already Bridgette was sweating. Her face would be shining by the time she got there at this rate, so she climbed over two laundry baskets to open her bedroom window and then attempted to find her shoes. 'I must tidy up in here.' Bridgette searched for her high-heeled sandals.

Her bedroom had once been tidy—but when Harry had been born Courtney had moved in and Bridgette's two-bedroom flat had never quite recovered from housing three—actually, four at times if you counted Paul. Her love life hadn't recovered either!

Bridgette found her sandals and leant against the wall as she put them on. She surveyed the large boxes of shelves she had bought online that would hopefully help her organise things. 'I want to get these shelves put up. Dad said he'd come around and find the studs in the wall, whatever they are…'

Jasmine bit her tongue—Maurice had been saying that for months. The last thing Bridgette needed tonight was to have her parents criticised but, honestly, two more unhelpful, inflexible people you could not meet. Maurice and Betty Joyce just closed their eyes to the chaos their youngest daughter created and left it all for Bridgette to sort out.

'How do you feel?' Jasmine asked as, dressed in a guilty purchase, make-up done and high heels on, Bridgette surveyed herself in the mirror.

'Twenty-six.' Bridgette grinned at her own reflection, liking, for once, what she saw. Gone was the exhausted woman from earlier—instead she literally glowed and not with sweat either. No, it was the sheer silver dress she had bought that did the most amazing things to her rather curvy figure, and the heavenly new blusher that had wiped away the last remnants of fatigue in just a few glittery, peachy strokes.

'And single,' Jasmine nudged.

'Staying single,' Bridgette said. 'The last thing I want is a relationship.'

'Doesn't have to be a relationship,' Jasmine replied, but gave in with a small laugh. 'It does with you, though.' She looked at her friend. 'Paul was a complete bastard, you know.'

'I know.' She did not want to talk about it.

'Better to find out now than later.'

'I know that,' Bridgette snapped. She *so* did not want to talk about it—she didn't even want to think about it tonight—but thankfully Jasmine had other things on her mind.

'Ooh, I wonder if Dominic will be there. He's sex on legs, that guy…' Even though she was blissfully happy with Vince, Jasmine still raved about the paediatric locum registrar, Dominic Mansfield.

'You're just about to fly off to Africa with your boyfriend.' Bridgette grinned. 'Should you be noticing such things?'

'I can still look.' Jasmine sighed. 'Honestly, you can't help looking when Dominic's around—he's gorgeous. He just doesn't belong in our hospital. He should be on some glamorous soap or something… Anyway, I was thinking of him more for you.'

'Liar. From what you've told me about Dominic, he's not the *relationship* kind.'

'Well, he must have been at some point—he was engaged before he came to Melbourne. Mind you, he wouldn't do for you at all. He hardly speaks. He's quite arrogant really,' Jasmine mused. 'Anyway, enough about all that. Look at you.' She smiled at her friend in the mirror. 'Gorgeous, single, no commitments… You're allowed to have fun, you know.'

Except Bridgette did have commitments, even if no one could really understand them. It was those commitments that had her double-check that she had her phone in her bag. She didn't feel completely single—more she felt like a single mum with her child away on an access visit. Courtney and Harry had lived with her for a year and it had ended badly, and though she spoke little to Courtney now, she was an extremely regular babysitter.

She missed him tonight.

But, she reminded herself, he wasn't hers to miss.

Still, it was nice to be out and to catch up with everyone. They all put in some money for drinks, but unfortunately it was Jasmine who chose the wine and it was certainly a case of quantity over quality. Bridgette took a sip—she was far from a wine snob, but it really was awful and she sat on one drink all night.

'When are you coming back to us?' was the cry from her ex-colleagues.

'I'm not sure,' Bridgette responded. 'Soon, I hope.'

Yes, it was a good night; it just wasn't the same as it once had been.

She wasn't one of them any more.

She had no idea who they were talking about when they moaned about someone called Rita—how she took over in a birth, how much her voice grated. There had been a big drama last week apparently, which they were now discussing, of which Bridgette knew nothing. Slipping her phone out of her bag, she checked it, relieved to see that there were no calls, but even though she wasn't needed, even though she had nowhere else to be right now, the night was over for her.

She wasn't a midwife any more, or at best she was an occasional one—she went wherever the agency sent her. Bridgette was about to say goodbye to Jasmine, to make a discreet exit, when she was thwarted by some late arrivals, whom Jasmine marched her over to, insisting that she say hello.

'This is Rita, the new unit manager.' Jasmine introduced the two women. 'And, Rita, this is Bridgette Joyce. She used to work with us. We're trying to persuade her to come back. And this is…' He really needed no introduction, because Bridgette looked over and fell into very black eyes. The man stood apart from the rest and looked a bit out of place in the rather tacky bar, and, yes, he was as completely stunning as Jasmine had described. His black hair was worn just a little bit long and swept backwards to reveal a face that was exquisite. He was tall, slim and wearing black trousers and a fitted white shirt. He was, quite simply, divine. 'This is Dominic,' Jasmine introduced, 'our locum paediatrician.'

He didn't look like a paediatrician—oh, she knew she shouldn't label people so, but as he nodded and said hello he didn't look in the least like a man who was used to dealing with children. Jasmine was right—he should be on a soap, playing the part of a pretend doctor, or… She imagined him more a surgeon, a cosmetic surgeon perhaps, at some exclusive private practice.

'Can I get anyone a drink?' He was very smooth and polite, and there was no hint of an accent, but with such dark looks she wondered if his forebears were Italian perhaps, maybe Greek. He must have caught her staring, and when he saw that she didn't have a glass, he spoke directly to her. 'Bridgette, can I get you anything?'

'Not for me, thanks, I'm—' She was just about to say that she was leaving when Jasmine interrupted her.

'You don't need to buy a drink, Dominic. We've got loads.' Jasmine toddled over to their loud table and poured him a glass of vinegary wine and one for

Bridgette too, and then handed them over. 'Come on.' Jasmine pushed, determined her friend would unwind. 'Drink up, Bridgette.'

He was terribly polite because he accepted it graciously and took a sip of the drink and managed not to wince. But as Bridgette took a tiny sip, she did catch his eye, and there was a hint of a shared smile, if it could even be called that.

'It's good that you could make it, Dominic.' Vince came over. He had just today finished his paediatric rotation, and Bridgette had worked with him on Maternity for a while before she'd left. 'I know that it hasn't been a great day.'

She watched as Dominic gave a brief nod, gave practically nothing back to that line of conversation—instead, he changed the subject. 'So,' he asked, 'when do you fly?'

'Monday night,' Vince said, and spoke a little about the project he was joining.

'Well,' said Dominic, 'all the best with it.'

He really didn't waste words, did he? Bridgette thought as Jasmine polished her cupid's bow and happily took Vince's hand and wandered off, leaving Bridgette alone with him and trying not to show just how awkward she felt.

'Careful,' she said as his glass moved to his lips. 'Remember how bad it tastes.'

She was rewarded with the glimpse of a smile.

'Do you want me to get you something else?'

Yikes, she hadn't been fishing for drinks. 'No, no…' Bridgette shook her head. 'Jasmine would be offended. I'm fine. I was just…' Joking, she didn't add, trying to make conversation. Gorgeous he might be to look at but he really didn't say very much. 'You're at the hospital, then?' Bridgette asked.

'Just as a fill-in,' Dominic said. 'I've got a consultant's position starting in a couple of weeks in Sydney.' He named a rather impressive hospital and that just about summed him up, Bridgette decided—rather impressive and very, very temporary.

'Your family is there?'

'That's right,' he said, but didn't elaborate. 'You work on Maternity?' Dominic frowned, because he couldn't place her.

'I used to,' Bridgette explained. 'I left six months ago. I've been doing agency…'

'Why?'

It was a very direct question, one she wasn't quite expecting, one she wasn't really sure how to answer.

'The hours are more flexible,' she said, 'the money's better…' And it was the truth, but only a shred of it, because she missed her old job very badly. She'd just been accepted as a clinical nurse specialist when she'd left. She adored everything about midwifery, and now she went wherever the agency sent her. As she was qualified as a general nurse, she could find herself in nursing homes, on spinal units, sometimes in psych. She just worked and got on with it, but she missed doing what she loved the most.

He really didn't need to hear it, so back on went the smile she'd been wearing all night. 'And it means that I get to go out on a Saturday night.' The moment she said them, she wanted those words back, wished she could retrieve them. She knew that she sounded like some sort of party girl, especially with what came next.

'I can see it has benefits,' Dominic said, and she

swore he glanced down at the hand that was holding the glass, and for a dizzy moment she realised she was being appraised. 'If you have a young family.'

'Er, no.' Oh, help, she *was* being appraised. He was looking at her, the same way she might look at shoes in a window and tick off her mental list of preferences—too flat, too high, nice colour, shame about the bow. Wrong girl, she wanted to say to him, I'm lace-up-shoe boring.

'You don't have children?'

'No,' she said, and something twisted inside, because if she told him about Harry she would surely burst into tears. She could just imagine Dominic's gorgeous face sort of sliding into horrified boredom if the newly foiled, for once groomed woman beside him told him she felt as if her guts were being torn, that right now, right this very minute, she was having great difficulty not pulling out her phone to check if there had been a text or a call from Courtney. Right now she wanted to drive past where her sister was living with her friend Louise and make sure that there wasn't a wild party raging. She scrambled for something to say, anything to say, and of course she again said the wrong thing.

'Sorry that you had a bad day.' She watched his jaw tighten a fraction, knew, given his job, that it was a stupid thing to say, especially when her words tumbled out in a bright and breezy voice. But the false smile she had plastered on all night seemed to be infusing her brain somehow, she was so incredibly out of practice with anything remotely social.

He gave her the same brief nod that he had given Vince, then a very brief smile and very smoothly excused himself.

'Told you!' Jasmine was over in a flash the minute he was gone. 'Oh, my God, you were talking for ages.'

'For two minutes.'

'That's ages for him!' Jasmine breathed. 'He hardly says a word to anyone.'

'Jasmine!' She rolled her eyes at her friend. 'You can stop this very moment.' Bridgette let out a small gurgle of laughter. 'I think I've just been assessed as to my suitability for a one-nighter. Honestly, he's shameless... He asked if I had children and everything. Maybe he's worried I've got stretch marks and a baggy vagina.'

It was midwife-speak, and as she made Jasmine laugh, she laughed herself. The two women really laughed for the first time in a long, long time, and it was so good for Bridgette to be with her friend before she jetted off, because Jasmine had helped her through this difficult time. She didn't want to be a misery at her friends' leaving do, so she kept up the conversation a little. They giggled about lithe, toned bodies and the temptresses who would surely writhe on his white rug in his undoubtedly immaculate city apartment. It *was* a white rug, they decided, laughing, for a man like Dominic was surely far too tasteful for animal prints. And he'd make you a cocktail on arrival, for this was the first-class lounge of one-night stands, and on and on they went... Yes, it was so good to laugh.

Dominic could hear her laughter as he spoke with a colleague, as again he was offered yet more supposed consolation for a 'bad day'. He wished that people would just say nothing, wished he could simply forget.

It had been a... He searched for the expletive to best describe his day, chose it, but knew if he voiced it he might just be asked to leave, which wouldn't be so bad, but, no, he took a mouthful of vinegar and grimaced as it met the acid in his stomach.

He hated his job.

Was great at it.

Hated it.

Loved it.

Did it.

He played ping-pong in his mind with a ball that broke with every hit.

He wanted that hard ball tonight, one that bounced back on every smash, one that didn't crumple if you hammered it.

He wanted to be the doctor who offered better answers.

Today he had seen the dominos falling, had scrambled to stop them, had done everything to reset them, but still they'd fallen—click, click, click—racing faster than he could halt them till he'd known absolutely what was coming and had loathed that he'd been the only one who could see it.

'Where there's life there's hope' had been offered several times.

Actually, no, he wanted to say as he'd stared at another batch of blood results and read off the poisons that had filled this tiny body.

'There is hope, though...' the parents had begged, and he had refused to flinch at the frantic eyes that had scanned his face as he'd delivered news.

He loved hope, he craved hope and had searched so hard for it today, but he also knew when hope was gone, said it before others would. Unlike others, he faced the inevitable—because it was either cardiac massage and all lights blazing, or a cuddle without the tubes at the end.

Yes, it came down to that.

Yes, it had been a XXXX of a day.

He had sat with the parents till ten p.m. and then entered a bar that was too bright, stood with company that was too loud and tasted wine that could dissolve an olive, and hated that he missed her. How could you miss a woman you didn't even like? He hated that she'd ring tonight and that he might be tempted to go back. That in two weeks' time he'd see her. Shouldn't he be over Arabella by now? Maybe it was just because he had had a 'bad day'. Not that he and Arabella had ever really spoken about work—oh, they'd discussed their career paths of course, but never the day-to-day details. They'd never talked about days such as this, Dominic mused.

Then he had seen her—Bridgette. In a silver dress and with a very wide smile, with gorgeous nails and polished hair, she had drawn his eye. Yet on inspection there was more behind that polished façade than he cared to explore, more than he needed tonight.

He *had* been checking for a wedding ring.

What no one understood was that he preferred to find one.

Married women were less complicated, knew the rules from the start, for they had so much more to lose than he did.

Bridgette was complicated.

He'd read her, because he read women well. He could see the hurt behind those grey eyes, could see the effort that went into her bright smile. She was complicated and he didn't need it. But, on the way down to her ring finger, he'd noticed very pale skin and a tapestry of freckles, and he'd wondered where the freckles stopped, had wondered far too many things.

He didn't need an ounce of emotion tonight, not one more piece, which was why he had excused himself and walked away. But perhaps he'd left gut instinct in his car tonight, the radar warning that had told him to keep his distance dimmed a fraction as he looked over to where she stood, laughing with her friend.

'Hey, Dominic…' He heard a low, seductive voice and turned to the pretty blonde who stood before him, a nurse who worked in Theatre and one whose husband seemed to be perpetually away. 'So brilliant to see you tonight.' He looked into eyes that were blue and glittered with open invitation, saw the ring on her finger and the spray tan on her arm on the way down. 'I just finished a late shift. Wasn't sure I'd make it.'

'Are you on tomorrow?' someone asked.

'No,' she answered. 'And I've got the weekend to myself. Geoff's away.' Her eyes flicked to his and Dominic met her gaze, went to take another sip of his drink and then, remembering how it tasted, changed his mind, and he changed his mind about something else too—he couldn't stomach the taste of fake tan tonight.

Then he heard Bridgette laughing, looked over and ignored his inner radar, managed to convince himself that he had read her wrong.

He knew now what Bridgette's middle name was.

Escape.

'People are talking about going for something to eat…' Vince came over and snaked his arm around Jasmine, and they shared a kiss as Bridgette stood, pretending not to feel awkward—actually, not so awkward now that she and Jasmine had had such a laugh. She wasn't going out to dinner, or to a club, but at least she and Jasmine had had some fun—but then the waitress came over and handed her a glass.

'For me?' Bridgette frowned.

'He said to be discreet.' The waitress nodded her head in Dominic's direction. 'I'll get rid of your other glass.'

Double yikes!

She glanced over to black eyes that were waiting to meet hers.

Wrong girl, she wanted to semaphore back—so very, very wrong for you, Dominic, she wanted to signal. It took me weeks to have sex with Paul, I mean weeks, and you're only here for two. And I don't think I'm very good at it anyway. At least he hinted at that when we broke up. But Bridgette didn't have any flags handy and wouldn't know what to do if she had them anyway, so she couldn't spell it out; she only had her eyes and they held his.

She lifted the glass of temptation he offered and the wine slipped onto her tongue and down her throat. It tasted delicious—cold and expensive and not at all what she was used to.

She felt her cheeks burn as she dragged her eyes from him and back to her friend and tried to focus on what Jasmine was saying—something about Mexican, and a night that would never end. She sipped her champagne that was far too nice, far too moreish, and Bridgette knew she had to get out of there. 'Not for me,' she said to Jasmine, feeling the scald of his eyes on her shoulder as she spoke. 'Honestly, Jasmine...' She didn't need to make excuses with her friend.

'I know.' Jasmine smiled. 'It really is great that you came out.'

It had been. Bridgette was relieved that she'd made it this far for her friend and also rather relieved to escape from the very suave Dominic—he was so out of her league and she also knew they were flirting. Dominic had the completely wrong impression of her—he thought she worked agency for the money and flexibility, so that she could choose her shifts at whim and party hard on a Saturday night.

If only he knew the truth.

Still, he was terribly nice.

Not nice, she corrected. Not *nice* nice, more toe-curlingly sexy and a dangerous nice. Still, no one was leaving. Instead he had made his way over, the music seemed to thud low in her stomach and for a bizarre moment as he joined them she thought he was about to lean over and kiss her.

Just like that, in front of everyone.

And just like that, in front of everyone, she had the ridiculous feeling that she'd comply.

It was safer to leave, to thank him for the drink, to say she wasn't hungry, to hitch up her bag and get the hell out of there, to ignore the dangerous dance in her mind.

'I'll see you on Monday,' she said to Jasmine.

'You can help me pack!'

The group sort of moved out of the bar as she did and walked towards the Mexican restaurant. There had been a burst of summer rain but it hadn't cleared the air. Instead it was muggy, the damp night air clinging to her cheeks, to her legs and arms as her eyes scanned the street for a taxi.

'Are you sure you don't want something to eat?' Dominic asked.

And she should say no—she really should walk away now, Bridgette told herself. She didn't even like Mexican food, but he was gorgeous and it had been ages since there had been even a hint of a flirt. And she was twenty-six and maybe just a bit flattered that someone as sophisticated as he was was paying her attention. Her wounded ego could certainly use the massage and she'd just checked her phone and things seemed fine, so Bridgette took a deep breath and forced back that smile.

'Sounds great.'

'Good,' he replied, except she was confused, because he then said goodbye to Vince and Jasmine as Bridgette stood on the pavement, blinking as the group all bundled into a restaurant and just the two of them remained. Then he turned and smiled. 'Let's get something to eat, then.'

'I thought…' She didn't finish her sentence, because he aimed his keys at a car, a very nice car, which lit up in response, and she glanced at her phone again and there wasn't a single message.

Her chariot awaited.

She climbed in the car and sank into the leather and held her breath as Dominic walked around to the driver's side.

She didn't do things like this.

Ever.

But there was a part of her that didn't want to say goodnight.

A part of her that didn't want to go back to an empty flat and worry about Harry.

They drove though the city; he blasted on the air-conditioner and it was bliss to feel the cool air on her cheeks. They drove in silence until his phone rang and she glanced to the dashboard where it sat in its little charger and the name 'Arabella' flashed up on his screen. Instead of making an excuse, he turned for a brief second and rolled his eyes. 'Here we go.'

'Sorry?'

'The maudlin Saturday night phone call,' Dominic said, grinding the gears. 'How much she misses me, how she didn't mean it like that...'

The phone went black.

'Your ex?'

'Yep.' He glanced over to her. 'You can answer it if she rings again.' He flashed her a smile, a devilish smile that had her stomach flip. 'Tell her we're in bed—that might just silence her.'

'Er, no!' She grinned. 'I don't do things like that.'

On both counts.

'Were you serious?' she asked, because she couldn't really imagine him serious about anyone. Mind you, Jasmine had said they'd been engaged.

'Engaged,' he said. 'For a whole four weeks.'

And he pulled his foot back from the accelerator because he realised he was driving too fast, but he hated the phone calls, hated that sometimes he was tempted to answer, to slip back into life as he once had known it.

And end up like his parents, Dominic reminded himself.

He'd lived through their hellish divorce as a teenager, had seen their perfect life crumble, and had no intention of emulating it. With Arabella he had taken his time. They had been together for two years and he thought he had chosen well—gorgeous, career-minded and she didn't want children. In fact, it had turned out, she didn't want anything that was less than perfect.

'You're driving too fast.' Her voice broke into his thoughts. 'I don't make a very good passenger.' She smiled. 'I think I'm a bit of a control freak.'

He slowed down, the car swishing through the damp city streets, and then they turned into the Arts Centre car park. Walking through it, she could hear her heels ringing on the cement, and even though it was her town, it was Dominic who knew where he was going—it had been ages since she had been in the heart of the city. She didn't feel out of place in her silver dress. The theatres were spilling out and there were people everywhere dressed to the nines and heading for a late dinner.

She found herself by a river—looking out on it from behind glass. She was at a table, with candles and silver and huge purple menus and a man she was quite sure she couldn't handle. He'd been joking in the car about telling his ex they were in bed, she knew it, but not really—she knew that too.

'What do you want to eat?'

Bridgette wasn't that hungry—she felt a little bit sick, in fact—but she looked through the menu and tried to make up her mind.

'I…' She didn't have the energy to sit through a meal. Really, she ought to tell him now, that the night would not be ending as he was undoubtedly expecting. 'I'm not very hungry…'

'We can get dessert and coffee if you want.'

'I wouldn't mind the cheese platter.'

'Start at the end.' He gave her a smile and placed the order—water for him and cognac for her, he suggested, and, heaven help her, the waiter asked if she wanted it warmed.

'Dominic...' She took a deep breath as their platter arrived, a gorgeous platter of rich cheeses and fruits. 'I think—'

'I think we just ought to enjoy,' he interrupted.

'No.' Bridgette gulped. 'I mean...' She watched as he smeared cheese on a cracker and offered it to her.

'I don't like blue cheese.'

'Then you haven't had a good one.'

He wasn't wrong there!

He took a bite instead and her hand shook as she reached for the knife, tasted something she was quite sure she didn't like and found out it was, in fact, amazing.

'Told you.'

'You did.' She looked at the platter, at the grapes and dates, like some lush oil painting, and she knew the dance that was being played and the flirting and the seduction that was to come, and it terrified her. 'I don't think I should be here...' She scrabbled in her bag, would pay the bill, knew that she must end this.

'Bridgette.' He wasn't a bastard—he really wasn't. Yes, he'd been playing the field since his engagement had ended, and, yes, he had every intention of continuing to do so, but he only played with those who were happy with the rules, and he knew now for sure that she wasn't. 'It's cheese.'

She lifted troubled eyes to his.

'No, it isn't—it's the ride home after.'

He liked her. He hadn't wanted emotion tonight, and yet she made him smile as a tear washed away the last of her foundation and he could see freckles on her nose.

'Bridgette, it's cheese and conversation.' He took her hand, and she started to tell him he didn't want just cheese and conversation, oh, no, she knew it very well. She told him she wasn't the girl in the silver dress who partied and he held her hand as she babbled about zebra-print rugs, no white ones, and cocktails. 'Bridgette.' He was incredibly close to adoring her, to leaning over and kissing her right now. 'It's cheese and conversation and then I'll take you home.' He looked at her mouth and he was honest. 'Maybe just one kiss goodnight.'

Oh, but she wanted her kiss.

Just one.

'That leads nowhere,' she said.

'That leads nowhere,' he assured her.

'We're not suited,' she said, and was incredibly grateful that he nodded.

'We're completely incompatible,' Dominic agreed.

'And I'm sorry if I've misled you…'

'You didn't.' He was very magnanimous, smearing more cheese and this time handing it to her, no, wait, feeding her, and it wasn't so much seductive as nice. 'I *let* myself be misled,' he said, and he handed her her cognac. 'I knew from the start you were nice.' He gave her a smile. 'And you are, Bridgette.'

'So are you.'

'Oh, no,' he assured her. 'I'm not.'

CHAPTER TWO

IT FELT so good to feel so good and it was as if they both knew that they didn't have long. It was terribly hard to explain it, but now that there wasn't sex on the menu, now they'd cleared that out of the way, they could relax and just be.

For a little while.

She took a sip of cognac and it burnt all the way down, a delicious burn.

'Nice?' Dominic asked.

'Too nice,' she admitted.

And he hadn't wanted conversation, or emotion, but he was laughing, talking, sharing, and that XXXX of a day melted away with her smile.

So they worked the menu backwards and ordered dessert, chocolate soufflé for Bridgette and watermelon and mint sorbet for him. As he sampled his dish, Bridgette wanted a taste—not a spoonful, more a taste of his cool, watermelon-and-mint-flavoured tongue—and she flushed a little as he offered her the spoon.

'Want some?' Dominic said.

She shook her head, asked instead about his work, and he told her a bit about his plans for his career, and she told him about the lack of plans for hers.

'You love midwifery, though?' Dominic checked.

'I am hoping to go back to it.' Bridgette nodded. 'It's just been a bit of a complicated year...' She didn't elaborate and she was glad that he didn't push. Yes, she loved midwifery, she answered, loved babies.

'You want your own?' He asked the same question that everyone did when they heard her job.

'One day maybe...' Bridgette gave a vague shrug. Had he asked a couple of years ago she'd have told him that she wanted millions, couldn't wait to have babies of her own. Only now she simply couldn't see it. She couldn't imagine a place or a time where it might happen, couldn't imagine really trusting a man again. She didn't tell him that of course—that wasn't what tonight was about. Instead she gave a vague nod. 'I think so. You?' she asked, and he admitted that he shuddered at the very thought.

'You're a paediatrician.' Bridgette laughed.

'Doesn't mean I have to want my own. Anyway,' he added, 'I know what can go wrong.' He shook his head and was very definite. 'Nope, not for me.' He told her that he had a brother, Chris, when Bridgette said she had a sister, Courtney. Neither mentioned Arabella or Paul, and Bridgette certainly didn't mention Harry.

Tonight it was just about them.

And then they ordered coffee and talked some more.

And then another coffee.

And the waiters yawned, and Dominic and Bridgette looked around the restaurant and realised it was just the two of them left.

And it was over too soon, Bridgette thought as he paid the bill and they left. It was as if they were trying to cram so much into one night; almost as if it was understood that this really should deserve longer. It was like a plane trip alongside a wonderful companion: you knew you would be friends, more than friends perhaps, if you had more time, but you were both heading off to different lives. He to further his career and then back to his life in Sydney,

She to, no doubt, more of the same.

Except they had these few hours together and neither wanted them to end.

They walked along the river and to the bridge, leant over it and looked into the water, and still they spoke, about silly things, about music and videos and movies they had watched or that they thought the other really should see. He was nothing like the man she had assumed he was when they had been introduced in the bar—he was insightful and funny and amazing company. In fact, nothing at all like the remote, aloof man that Jasmine had described.

And she was nothing like he'd expected either when they had been introduced. Dominic was very careful about the women he dated in Melbourne; he had no interest in settling down, not even for a few weeks. Occasionally he got it wrong, and it would end in tears a few days later. Not his of course—it was always the women who wanted more than he was prepared to give, and Dominic had decided he was never giving that part of himself again. But there was a strange regret in the air as he drove her home—a rare regret for Dominic—because here was a woman he actually wouldn't mind getting to know a little more, one who might get him over those last stubborn, lingering remnants of Arabella.

He'd been joking about Bridgette answering the phone.

Sort of.

Actually, it wasn't such a bad idea. He couldn't face going back to Sydney while there was still weakness, didn't want to slip back into the picture-perfect life that had been prescribed to him since birth.

And it was strange because had they met at the start of his stay here, he was sure, quite sure, time would have moved more slowly. Now, though, it seemed that the beach road that led to her home, a road he was quite positive usually took a good fifteen minutes, seemed to be almost over in eight minutes and still they were talking, still they were laughing, as the car gobbled up their time.

'You should watch it.' She was talking about something on the internet, something she had found incredibly funny. 'Tonight when you get in.' She glanced at the clock on the dashboard and saw that it was almost two. 'I mean, this morning.'

'You watch it too.' He grinned. 'We can watch simultaneously…' His fingers tightened on the wheel and he ordered his mind not to voice the sudden direction it had taken—thankfully those thoughts went unsaid and unheard.

'I can't get on the internet,' Bridgette grumbled, trying desperately not to think similar thoughts. 'I've got a virus.' She swung her face to him. 'My computer, I mean, not…' What was wrong with her mouth? Bridgette thought as she turned her burning face to look out of the window. Why did everything lead to sex with him? 'Anyway,' she said, 'you should watch it.'

There was a roundabout coming up, the last roundabout, Bridgette knew, before her home, and it felt like her last chance at crazy, their last chance. And, yes, it was two a.m., but it could have been two p.m.; it was just a day that was running out and they wanted to chase it. She stole a look over at his delectable profile and to the olive hands that gripped the steering-wheel—it would be like leaving the cinema in the middle of the best movie ever without a hope of finding out the end. And she wanted more detail, wanted to know how it felt to be made love to by a man like him. She'd been truthful when she'd spoken to Jasmine—a relationship was the very last thing that she wanted now. Maybe this way had merit... '*We* should watch it.'

'Your computer's not working,' he pointed out.

'Yours is.' The flick of the indicator signalling right was about half the speed of her heart.

'Bridgette...' He wasn't a bastard—he was incredibly, incredibly nice, because they went three times round the roundabout as he made very sure.

'I don't want you to regret...' He was completely honest. 'I leave in two weeks.'

'I won't regret it.' She'd firmly decided that she wouldn't. 'After much consideration I have decided I would very much regret it if I didn't.' She gave him a smile. 'I want my night.'

She did. And he was lovely, because he did not gun the car home. It was so much nicer than she would ever be able to properly remember, but she knew for many nights she would try.

She wanted to be able to hold on to the moment when he turned and told her that he couldn't wait till they got all the way back to the city for the one kiss they had previously agreed to. She wanted to remember how they stopped at a lookout, gazed out at the bay, leant against his bonnet and watched the glittering view, and it felt as if time was suspended. She wanted to bottle it somehow, because she wasn't angry with Courtney at that moment, or worried for Harry. For the first time in ages she had a tiny glimpse of calm, of peace, a moment where she felt all was well.

Well, not calm, but it was a different sort of stress from the one she was used to as he moved his face to hers. Very nicely he kissed her, even if she was terribly nervous. He let her be nervous as he kissed her—till the pleats in her mind unfurled. It was a kiss that had been building all night, a kiss she had wanted since their introduction, and his mouth told her he had wanted the same.

'I was going to stay for one drink...' His mouth was at her ear, his body pressed into hers.

'I was just leaving,' she admitted as his face came back to view.

'And now look at us.'

So nice was that kiss that he did it again.

'You smell fantastic.' She was glad, to be honest, to have only him on her mind. He smelt as expensive as he looked and he tasted divine. She would never take this dress to the dry cleaner's, she thought as his scent wrapped around them, and his mouth was at her neck and under her hair. He was dragging in the last breaths of the perfume she had squirted on before going out and soaking in the scent of the salon's rich shampoo and the warm fragrance of woman.

'So do you,' he said.

'You taste fantastic,' Bridgette said. She was the one going back for more now.

'You too.'

And he liked the weight of responsibility that cloaked

him as he pressed her against the bonnet and his hands inched down to a silver hem. He could feel her soft thighs and wanted to lift her dress, but he wanted to know if her legs too were freckled, so he ended the kiss. He wanted more for her than that, more for himself than that.

Just tonight, Dominic assured himself as she did the same.

'What?' He caught her looking at him as they headed for his home, and grinned.

'Nothing.' She smiled back.

'Go on, say what you're thinking.'

'Okay.' So she did. 'You don't look like a paediatrician.'

'What is a paediatrician supposed to look like?'

'I don't know,' Bridgette admitted. 'Okay, you don't *seem* like a paediatrician.' She couldn't really explain it, but he laughed.

They laughed.

And when she told him that she imagined him more a cosmetic surgeon, with some exclusive private practice, his laugh turned wry. 'You're mistaking me for my father.'

'I don't think so,' Bridgette said.

And he pulled her towards him, because it was easier than thinking, easier than admitting he wasn't so sure of her verdict, that lately he seemed to be turning more and more into his father, the man he respected least.

It was three o'clock and she felt as if they were both trying to escape morning.

There wasn't a frantic kiss through the front door—instead the energy that swirled was more patient.

It was a gorgeous energy that waited as he made

her coffee and she went to the bathroom and he had the computer on when she returned. They did actually watch it together.

'I showed this to Jasmine—' there were tears rolling down her face, but from laughter '—and she didn't think it was funny.'

And he was laughing too, more than he ever had. He hadn't had a night like this in ages—in fact, he couldn't recall one ever.

Okay, she would try to remember the details, how he didn't cringe when she pretended his desk was a piano; instead he sang.

It was the most complicated thing to explain—that she could sing to him, that, worse, he could take the mug that was the microphone and do the same to her!

'We should be ashamed of ourselves.' She admired their reflection in the computer as they took a photo.

'Very ashamed,' he agreed.

She thought he was like this, Dominic realised, that this was how his usual one-night stands went. Didn't she understand that this was as rare for him as it was for her? He hadn't been like this even with Arabella.

He didn't just want anyone tonight; he wanted her.

It was an acute want that tired now of being patient and so too did hers. As their mouths met on time and together, he kissed her to the back of the sofa. It felt so seamless, so right, because not for a second did Bridgette think, Now he's going to kiss me. One moment they were laughing and the next they were kissing. It was a transition that was as simple as that.

It was his mouth and his taste and the slide of his tongue.

It was her mouth and a kiss that didn't taste of plastic, that tasted of her tongue, and he kissed her and she curled into it. She loved the feel of his mouth and the roam of his hands and the way her body was craving his—it was a kiss that was potent, everything a kiss could be, distilled into one delicious dose.

He took off her dress, because he wanted to see *her*, not the woman in silver, and his eyes roamed. They roamed as he took off her bra and he answered his earlier question because her freckles stopped only where her bikini would be. There were two unfreckled triangles that wanted his mouth, but he talked to her as well and what she didn't know was how rare that was.

He left control behind and was out of his mind.

He wanted her in France, he told her as he licked her nipple.

Topless and naked on the beach beside him, and new freckles on her breasts. She closed her eyes and she could smell the sun oil, could feel the heat from the sun that shone in France and the coolness of his tongue on sunburnt nipples. He pressed her into the couch and she pressed back to him.

She was lying down and could feel him hard against her and she didn't think twice, just slid his zipper down.

She could hear her own moan as she held him and he lifted his head.

'We're not going to make it to the bedroom, are we?'

'Not a hope,' she admitted.

Was this what it was like?

To be free.

To be irresponsible.

More, please, she wanted to sob, because she wanted to live on the edge for ever, never wanted this night to end.

She wanted this man who took off his trousers and kept condoms in his wallet, and it didn't offend her—she already knew what he was like, after all.

'Bastard.' She grinned.

And he knew her too.

'Sorry,' he said. In their own language he apologised for the cad that he was and told her that he wasn't being one tonight.

This was different.

So different that he sat her up.

Sank to his knees on the edge of the sofa.

And pulled her bottom towards him.

'Let's get rid of these.' He was shameless. He dispensed with anything awkward, just slid her panties down, and she did remember staring up at the ceiling as his tongue slid up a pale, freckled thigh that didn't taste of fake tan and then he dived right in. As he licked and teased and tasted she would remember for ever thinking, Is this me?

And she was grateful for his experience, for his skill, for the mastery of his tongue, because it was a whole new world and tonight she got to step into it.

'Relax,' he said, when she forgot to for a moment.

So she did, just closed her eyes and gave in to it.

'Where's the rug?' she asked as he slid her to the floor.

'No rug,' he said.

He maybe should get one, was her last semi-coherent thought, because the carpet burnt in her back as he moved inside her, a lovely burn, and then it was his turn to sample the carpet for he toppled her over, still deep inside her, and she was on top.

Don't look down.

It wasn't even a semi-coherent thought; it was more a familiar warning that echoed in her head.

Don't look down—but she did, she looked down from the tightrope that recently she'd been walking.

She glimpsed black eyes that were open as she closed hers and came, and he watched her expression, felt her abandon, and then his eyes closed as he came too. Yes, feeling those last bucks deep inside her she looked down and it didn't daunt her, didn't terrify. It exhilarated her as greedily he pulled her head down and kissed her.

'It's morning,' he said as they moved to the bedroom, the first sunlight starting.

Better still as she closed her eyes to the new day, there was no regret.

CHAPTER THREE

It was like waking up to an adult Christmas.

The perfect morning, Bridgette thought as she stretched out in the wrinkled bed.

She must have slept through the alarm on her phone and he must have got up, for there was the smell of coffee in the air. If she thought there might be a little bit of embarrassment, that they both might be feeling a touch awkward this morning, she was wrong.

'Morning.' Dominic was delighted by her company, which was rare for him. He had the best job in the world to deal with situations such as this—in fact, since in Melbourne, he had a permanent alarm call set for eight a.m. at weekends. He would answer the phone to the recorded message, talk for a brief moment, and then hang up and apologise to the woman in his bed. He would explain that something had come up at work and that he had no choice but to go in.

It was a back-up plan that he often used, but he didn't want to use it today. Today he'd woken up before his alarm call and had headed out to the kitchen, made two coffees and remembered from last night that she took sugar. He thought about breakfast in bed and perhaps another walk to the river, to share it in daylight this time. Sunday stretched out before him like a long, luxurious yawn, a gorgeous pause in his busy schedule.

'What time is it?' Bridgette yawned too.

'Almost eight.' He climbed back into bed and he was delicious. 'I was thinking...' He looked down at where she lay. 'Do you want to go out somewhere nice for breakfast?'

'In a silver dress?' Bridgette grinned. 'And high heels?'

'Okay,' he said. 'Then I guess we've no option but to spend the day in bed.' She reached for her coffee and, as she always did when Harry wasn't with her, she reached for her phone to check for messages. Then she saw that it wasn't turned on and a knot of dread tightened in her stomach as she pressed the button.

'Is everything okay?'

'Sure.' Only it wasn't. She hadn't charged her phone yesterday; with Jasmine arriving and going out she hadn't thought to plug it in. Her phone could have been off for hours—anything could have happened and she wouldn't even know. She took a sip of her coffee and tried to calm herself down. Told herself she was being ridiculous, that she had to stop worrying herself sick, but it wasn't quite so easy and after a moment she turned and forced a smile. 'As much as I'd love to spend the day in bed, I really am going to have to get home.'

'Everything okay?' He checked again, because he could sense the change in her. One moment ago she'd been yawning and stretching; now she was as jumpy as a cat.

'Of course,' Bridgette said. 'I've just got a lot on...'

She saw the flash of confusion in his eyes and it could have irritated her—in fact, she wanted it to irritate her. After all, why shouldn't she have a busy day planned? Why should he just assume that she'd want a day with him? But that didn't work, because somehow last night had not been as casual as she was now making it out to be. It needed to be, Bridgette reminded herself as she turned away from his black eyes—she felt far safer with their one-night rule, far safer not trusting him. 'I'll get a taxi,' she said as she climbed out of bed and found her crumpled dress and then realised she'd have to go through the apartment to locate her underwear.

'Don't be ridiculous—I'll drive you home,' Dominic said, and he lay there as she padded out. He could hear her as she pulled on her panties and bra, and he tried not to think about last night and the wonderful time they'd had. Not just the sex, but before that, lying on the sofa watching clips on the computer, or the car ride home.

It wasn't usually him getting sentimental. Normally it was entirely the other way round.

'You really don't have to give me a lift.' She stood at the door, dressed now and holding her shoes in her hand, last night's mascara smudged beneath her eyes, her hair wild and curly, and he wanted her back in his bed. 'It's no problem to get a taxi.'

'I'll get my keys.'

And she averted her eyes as he climbed out of the bed, as he did the same walk as her and located his clothes all crumpled on the floor. She wished the balloon would pop and he'd look awful all messed and unshaven. She could smell them in the room and the computer was still on and their photo was there on the screen and *how* they'd been smiling.

'Bridgette…' He so wasn't used to this. 'You haven't even had your coffee.'

'I really do need to get back.'

'Sure.'

And talking was incredibly awkward, especially at the roundabout.

She wanted the indicator on, wanted him to turn the car around and take them back to bed, and, yes, she could maybe tell him about Harry.

About Courtney.

About the whole sorry mess.

End the dream badly.

After all, he was only here for two weeks, and even if he hadn't been, she could hardly expect someone as glamorous and gorgeous as him to understand.

She didn't want him to understand, she didn't want him to know, so instead she blew out a breath and let the sat nav lead him to her door.

'Good luck in Sydney.' She really was terrible at this one-night thing.

'Bridgette.' He had broken so many rules for her and he did it again. 'I know that you're busy today, but maybe…'

'Hey!' She forced a smile, dragged it up from her guts and slathered it on her face and turned to him. 'We're not suited, remember?'

'Completely incompatible.' He forced a smile too.

He gave her a kiss but could sense her distraction.

She climbed out of the car and she didn't say good-bye because she couldn't bear to, didn't turn around because she knew she'd head back to his arms, to his car, to escape.

But she couldn't escape the niggle in her stomach

that told her things were less than fine and it niggled louder as she made a half-hearted attempt at cleaning her room. By midday her answer came.

'Can you have Harry tonight?'

'I can't,' Bridgette said. 'I'm on an early shift in the morning…' Then she closed her eyes. She had reported her sister a couple of months ago to social services and finally voiced her concerns. Oh, there was nothing specific, but she could not simply stand by and do nothing. Since she'd asked Courtney to leave her flat, things had become increasingly chaotic and in the end she'd felt she had no choice but to speak out. Not to Jasmine or her friends—she didn't want to burden them. Instead she had spoken to people who might help. Her concerns had been taken seriously, and anger had ripped through her family that she could do such a thing. Sour grapes, Courtney had called it, because of what had happened between her and Paul. And then Courtney had admitted that, yes, she did like to party, she was only eighteen, after all, but never when Harry was around. She always made sure that Harry was taken care of.

By Bridgette.

And as she stood holding the phone, Bridgette didn't want to find out what might happen if she didn't say yes.

'I'll ring the agency,' Bridgette said. 'See if I can change to a late shift.'

Even if it was awkward talking to her sister when she dropped him off, Bridgette really was delighted to see Harry. At eighteen months he grew more gorgeous each day. His long blond curls fell in ringlets now and he had huge grey eyes like his aunt's.

Courtney had been a late baby for Maurice and Betty. Bridgette delivered babies to many so-called older women, but it was as if her parents had been old for ever—and they had struggled with the wilful Courtney from day one. It had been Bridgette who had practically brought her up, dealing with the angst and the crises that always seemed to surround Courtney, as her parents happily tuned out and carried on with their routines.

It had been Bridgette who had told them that their sixteen-year-old daughter was pregnant, Bridgette who had held Courtney's hand in the delivery room, Bridgette who had breathed with hope when Courtney, besotted with her new baby, had told Harry that she'd always be there for him.

'And I'll always be there for you,' Bridgette had said to her sister.

And Courtney was taking full advantage of that.

By seven, when Harry had had supper and been bathed, dressed in mint-green pyjamas, one of the many pairs Bridgette kept for him, and she had patted him off to sleep, she heard a car pulling up outside. She heard an expensive engine turning off, and then the sound of shoes on the steps outside her ground-floor flat, and she knew that it was him, even before she peeked through the blinds.

There was a loud ring of the bell and the noise made Harry cry.

And as Dominic stood on the step, there was his answer as to why she'd had to dash off that morning.

He waited a suitable moment, and Bridgette waited a moment too, rubbing Harry's back, telling him to go back to sleep, ignoring the bell. They were both quietly relieved when she didn't answer the door.

Still, last night had meant many things to Bridgette— and it wasn't all about the suave locum. Seeing her old colleagues, hearing about the midwifery unit, she'd realised just how much she was missing her old life. She knew somehow she had to get it back.

It was a curious thing that helped.

When Harry woke up at eleven and refused to go back to sleep, she held him as she checked her work sheet for the week. She was hoping that Courtney would be back tomorrow in time for her to get to her late shift when an e-mail pinged into her inbox.

No subject. No message. Just an attachment.

She had no idea how Dominic had got her e-mail address, no idea at all, but she didn't dwell on it, just opened the attachment.

It didn't upset her to see it. In fact, it made her smile. She had no regrets for that night and the photo of them together proved it. The photo, not just of him but of herself smiling and happy, did more than sustain her—it inspired her.

'Harry Joyce,' she said to the serious face of her nephew. 'Your aunty Bridgette needs to get a life.'

And she *would* get one, Bridgette decided, carefully deleting Dominic's e-mail address so she didn't succumb, like Arabella, in the middle of the night. The photo, though, became her new screensaver.

CHAPTER FOUR

'HE'LL be fine.'

It was six-thirty a.m. on Monday morning and Bridgette's guilt didn't lift as she handed a very sleepy Harry over to Mary, whom she had been introduced to last week. 'It seems mean, waking him so early,' Bridgette said.

'Well, you start work early.' Mary had the same lovely Irish brogue as Bridgette's granny had had and was very motherly and practical. 'Is his mum picking him up?'

'No, it's just me for the next few days,' Bridgette explained. 'She's got laryngitis, so I'm looking after Harry for a while.'

'Now, I know you'll want to see him during your breaks and things, but I really would suggest that for the first week or two, you don't pop down. He will think you're there to take him home and will just get upset.' She gave Bridgette a nice smile. 'Which will upset you and you'll not get your work done for worrying. Maybe ring down if you want to know how he is, and of course if there are any problems and we need you, I'll be the first to let you know.' Holding Harry, Mary walked

Bridgette to the door and gave her a little squeeze on the shoulder. 'You're doing grand.'

Oh, she wanted Mary to take her back to some mystical kitchen to sit at the table and drink tea for hours, for Mary to feed her advice about toddlers and tell her that everything was okay, was going to be okay, that Harry was fine.

Would be fine.

It felt strange to be back in her regular uniform, walking towards Maternity. Strange, but nice. It had been a busy month. She was so glad for that photo—their one night together had caused something of an awakening for Bridgette, had shown her just how much she was missing and had been the motivation to really sort her life out as best she could. She had been to the social-work department at the hospital she had once worked in and taken some much-needed advice. They suggested daycare and allocated Harry a place. At first Courtney had resisted. After all, she had said, she didn't work, but Bridgette stood firm—relieved that there would be more people looking out for Harry. She was especially glad that she had held her ground when the day before she started her new job, Courtney had come down with a severe throat infection and asked if Bridgette could step in for a few days.

Bridgette's interview with Rita had been long and rather difficult. Rita wasn't at all keen to make exceptions. She would do her best to give Bridgette early shifts but, no, she couldn't guarantee that was all she would get, and certainly, Rita said, she wanted all her staff to do regular stints on nights.

It all seemed a little impossible, but somehow Bridgette knew she had to make it work and get through things one day at a time—and today would be a good day, Bridgette decided as she entered the familiar unit, the smell and sound of babies in the air. This was where she belonged. She made herself a coffee to take into the long handover. Bridgette was hoping to be put into Labour and Delivery—she really wanted to immerse herself in a birth on her first day back.

'You're nice and early.' Rita was sitting at the computer, all busy and efficient and preparing for the day. 'Actually, that helps. It's been a very busy night, a busy weekend apparently. I've got a nurse who has to leave at seven. She's looking after a rather difficult case— would you mind taking handover from her and getting started?'

'Of course.' Bridgette was delighted. It often happened this way, and it would be lovely to get stuck into a labour on her first day back. She took a gulp of her coffee and tipped the rest down the sink, rinsed her cup and then headed off towards Labour and Delivery.

'No, it's room three where I want you to take over— twenty-four weeks with pre-eclampsia. They're having trouble getting her blood pressure back down.'

Okay, so she wasn't going to witness a birth this morning, but still, it was nice to be back using her midwifery brain. 'Hi, there, Heather.' She smiled at the familiar face. The room was quite crowded. Dr Hudson, the obstetrician, was there with the anaesthetist, and the anxious father was holding his wife's hand. The woman's face was flushed and she looked very drowsy. Thankfully, she was probably oblivious to all the activity going on.

'It's so good to see you.' Heather motioned to head

to the door and they stepped just a little outside. 'I've got to get away at seven.'

'Is that why it's good to see me?' Bridgette smiled.

'No, it's just good to see you back, good to have someone on the ball taking over as well. I'm worried about this one. Her name is Carla. She came up from Emergency yesterday evening.' Heather gave Bridgette a detailed rundown, showing her all the drugs that had been used overnight in an attempt to bring Carla's blood pressure down. 'We thought we had it under control at four a.m., but at six it spiked again.' Bridgette grimaced when she saw the figures. 'Obviously, they were hoping for a few more days at the very least. She's supposed to be having a more detailed scan this morning. They were estimating twenty-four weeks and three days.' That was very early. Every day spent in the womb at this stage was precious and vital and would increase the baby's chance of survival.

The parents wanted active treatment and the mother had been given steroids yesterday to mature the baby's lungs in case of premature delivery, but even so, to deliver at this stage would be dire indeed. 'She's just been given an epidural,' Heather explained, 'and they're fiddling with her medications through that as well. They're doing everything they can to get her blood pressure down.' It just didn't seem to be working, though. The only true cure for pre-eclampsia was delivery. Carla's vital signs meant that her life was in danger. She was at risk of a stroke or seizures and a whole host of complications if she didn't stabilise soon—even death. 'They were just talking about transferring her over to Intensive Care, but I think Dr Hudson now wants to go ahead and deliver. The paediatrician was just in…he's warned them what to expect, but at that stage we were still hoping for a couple more days, even to get her to twenty-five weeks.'

It wasn't going to happen.

'I hate leaving her…'

'I know,' Bridgette said.

'Dillan starts at a new school today.' Bridgette knew Heather's son had had trouble with bullying and it sounded as if today was a whole new start for him too. 'Or I wouldn't dash off.'

'You need to get home.'

The monitors were beeping and Heather and Bridgette walked back in.

'Carla…' Heather roused the dozing woman. 'This is Bridgette. She's going to be taking care of you today, and I'll be back to take care of you tonight.'

The alarms were really going off now. The appalling numbers that the monitors were showing meant the difficult decision would have to be made. Bridgette knew that Heather was torn. She'd been with Carla all night and at any moment now Carla was going to be rushed over to Theatre for an emergency Caesarean. 'Go,' Bridgette mouthed, because if Heather didn't leave soon, she would surely end up staying, and Dillan needed his mum today.

'Let Theatre know we're coming over,' Dr Hudson said to Bridgette, 'and we need the crash team from NICU. I'll tell the parents.'

Bridgette dashed out and informed Rita, the smooth wheels of the emergency routine snapping into place. Five minutes to seven on a Monday was not the best time. Staff were leaving, staff were starting, the weekend team was exhausted, the corridors busy as they moved the bed over to the maternity theatres.

'Okay.' Bridgette smiled at the terrified father, whom Dr Hudson had agreed could be present for the birth. 'Here's where you get changed.' She gave him some scrubs, a hat and some covers for his shoes. 'I'm going to go and get changed too and then I'll come back for you and take you in.'

Really, her presence at this birth was somewhat supernumerary. For a normal Caesarean section she would be receiving the baby; however, the NICU team was arriving and setting up, preparing their equipment for this very tiny baby, so Bridgette concentrated on the parents. Frank, the husband, wanted to film the birth, and Bridgette helped him to work out where to stand so that he wouldn't get in the way. She understood his need to document every minute of this little baby's life.

'It's all happening so fast...' Carla, though groggy, was clearly terrified, because now that the decision had been made, things were moving along with haste.

'We're just making sure we've got everything ready for your baby,' Bridgette explained as Dr Hudson came in. The anaesthetist had topped up the epidural and the operation would soon be starting.

'We're just waiting on...' Kelly, one of NICU team called out, when asked if they were ready, and then her voice trailed off. 'No problem. Dr Mansfield is here.'

Bridgette looked up and straight into those familiar black eyes, eyes that she stared at each day on her computer, except they didn't smile back at her now. She tore her gaze away from him and back to her patient. She completely halted her thoughts, gave all her attention to her patient, because the operation had started, the incision made at seven-eighteen, and just a few moments later a tiny baby was delivered.

'She's beautiful,' Bridgette told Carla. 'She's moving.' She was, her red, spindly limbs flailing with indignation at her premature entry to the world.

'She's not crying,' Jenny said.

'She is.' There was a very feeble cry and her face was grimacing. Frank was standing back, filming their tiny daughter. Bridgette watched the activity and for the first time she took a proper look at Dominic.

He needed to shave, his face was grim with concentration and he looked exhausted. Bridgette remembered Rita saying that it had been a very busy weekend, and this emergency had come right at the tail end of his on-call shift.

'Can I see her?' Carla asked, but already the team was moving the baby and she was whisked past. Carla got only a very brief glimpse.

'They're taking her into another area,' Bridgette explained, as the team moved away, 'and then she'll be taken up to the NICU.'

'Can I go with her?' Frank asked. 'Can I watch? I won't get in the way. I just want to see what they're doing.'

'I'll go and find out.'

Bridgette walked into the resuscitation area, where the baby would be stabilised as much as possible before being moved to NICU. Even though she had seen premature babies, now and for evermore the sight of something so small and so fragile and so completely tiny took her breath away. Bridgette loved big, fat babies, little scrawny ones too, but a scrap like this made her heart flutter in silent panic.

'She's a little fighter.' Kelly came over. 'We're going to move her up in a couple of minutes.'

'Dad wants to know if he can come and watch. He's promised not to get in the way. He just wants to see what's happening.'

'Not yet,' Dominic called over. 'I'll talk to him as soon as I can.'

'Tell him to stay with his wife for now,' Kelly suggested. 'I'll come and fetch him when Dominic is ready to talk to him.'

Kelly was as good as her word, and by the time Carla had been moved to Recovery, Kelly appeared, holding some new photos of their tiny daughter, which she handed to Mum and explained a little of what was going on. 'The doctors are still with her, but Dominic said if I bring Frank up he'll try to come out to speak with him. He'll come down and talk to you a bit later.'

It was a busy morning. Carla spent a long time in Recovery before being transferred back to the maternity unit, but even there she still required very close observation as her vital signs would take a while to stabilise after the birth. Carla was still very sick and of course wanted more information about her baby, whom they'd named Francesca. Frank had seen her very briefly and was now back with his wife and clearly a little impatient about the lack of news.

'Mary from daycare is on the phone for you.' Nandita, the ward clerk, popped a head around the door and handed Bridgette the phone.

'Nothing to worry about at all' came Mary's reassuring voice as Bridgette stepped out into the corridor. 'I'm just about to head off for lunch and I thought I'd let you know how well he's gone today. He's found a stack of bricks, which amused him for most of the morning.'

'Thanks so much for letting me know.'

'He's heading for an afternoon nap now. Anyway, you can get on with your day without fretting about him.' Bridgette felt a wave of guilt when she realised she hadn't even had time to worry about Harry and how he was doing on his first day at crèche and a wave of sadness too when she found out that, no, neither had Courtney rung to find out.

'Hi, Carla.' She gave the phone to Nandita, and as she walked back into her patient's room she heard Dominic's voice. If he had looked tired that morning then he looked exhausted now. 'Hi, Frank.' He shook the other man's hand. 'Sorry that it's taken so long to come and speak with you. I've been very busy with your daughter and another child who was delivered yesterday. I wanted to take the time to have a proper talk with you both.' He sat down next to the bed. 'Carla, you'll remember I spoke with you yesterday.' He didn't bog them down with too much detail. Apparently yesterday he had explained the risks of such a premature delivery and he didn't terrify them all over again. He told them their daughter's condition was extremely serious, but there was some good news. 'She seems a little further on than first estimated. I'd put her well into twenty-five weeks, which, though it's just a few days' difference, actually increases the survival rates quite dramatically. She's got size on her side too,' Dominic explained. 'Even though she's tiny, she is a little bit bigger than we would expect at twenty-five weeks, and she's had the benefit of the steroids we gave yesterday. She's a vigorous little thing, and she's doing absolutely as well as can be expected.'

'When can I see her?' Carla asked.

'I spoke to Dr Hudson before I came down, and as much as we know you want to see your daughter, you're not well enough at the moment.'

'What if...?' Poor Carla didn't even want to voice it, so Dominic did.

'If her condition deteriorates, we'll sort something out and do our best to get you up there.' He glanced over at Bridgette and so too did Carla.

'Of course we will,' she said.

'But right now the best you can do for your baby is to rest and get well yourself.' He answered a few more questions and then turned to Frank. 'You should be able to see her for a little while now. I've told them to expect you.'

'I'll get Nandita to walk you up,' Bridgette offered.

'Lunch?' Rita suggested as Bridgette walked over to speak with Nandita. 'Emma will take over from you.'

It was a late lunch, and as Bridgette hadn't had a coffee break, it was a sheer relief to slip off her shoes and just relax for a few moments. Well, at least it was until Dominic came in and sat on the couch opposite and unwrapped a roll. He gave her a brief nod but did not make any attempt at conversation, instead choosing to read a newspaper. It was Bridgette who tried to tackle the uncomfortable silence.

'I thought you were in Sydney.'

'It didn't work out.' He carried on reading the paper for a moment and then finally elaborated a touch. 'The professor I would be working under was taken ill and has gone on long-term sick leave—I didn't really care for his replacement, so I'm just waiting till something

I want comes up, or the professor returns. I'm here for a few more weeks.'

He sounded very austere, such a contrast to the easy conversations they had once shared. He didn't say anything else, didn't even read his paper, just sat and ate his roll.

Couldn't he have done that on NICU or on the paed ward? Bridgette thought, stirring her yoghurt. If he was going to sit there all silent and brooding, couldn't he do it somewhere else? Surely it was already awkward enough?

For Dominic, in that moment, it wasn't awkward, not in the least. He was too busy concentrating on not closing his eyes. Fatigue seeped through him. He'd had maybe six hours' sleep the entire weekend and he just wanted to go home and crash. Thank goodness for Rita, who had noticed his pallor and given him a spare cold patient lunch and suggested that he take five minutes before he saw the baby he had come down to examine, as well as speaking with Frank and Carla. Rebecca, his intern, came in. Bridgette recognised her from that morning, and then a couple of other colleagues too, which should have broken the tension, but instead Dominic ignored everyone and made no attempt to join in with the chitchat.

And later, he didn't look up when she had no choice but to sit and join him at the nurses' station to write up her notes before going home.

He told, rather than asked, Rebecca to take some further bloods on a baby born over the weekend, and then when one of the midwives asked if he'd mind taking a look at some drug orders, holding out the prescription chart to him, he didn't take it. Rather rudely, Bridgette thought, he didn't even look up.

'Is it a patient of mine?'

'No, it's a new delivery.'

He just carried on writing his own notes. 'Then you need to ring the doctor on call.'

The midwife rolled her eyes and left them to it, and the silence simmered uncomfortably between them, or at least it was uncomfortable for Bridgette.

'I'm sorry this is awkward.' She tried to broach it, to go ahead and say what was surely on both their minds, to somehow ease the tension, because the Dominic she had seen today was nothing like the man she had met, and she certainly didn't want to cause any problems at work. 'Had I known you were still working here, I wouldn't have…' Her voice trailed off—it seemed rather stupid to say that she'd never have taken the job, that she wouldn't have come back to the unit she loved. But had she known he would be here for a little while more, there might have been a delay in her return—with Jasmine being away she was completely out of the loop as to what was going on at work.

'Awkward?' Dominic frowned as he carried on writing. 'Why would it be awkward?' And then he shook his head. 'Are you referring to…?' He looked over and waited till her skin was burning, till there was no question that, yes, she was referring to that night. 'Bridgette, it was months ago.' She swallowed, because it was actually just a few weeks; she'd counted them. 'We shared one night together.' How easily he dismissed it, relegated it, reduced it to a long-ago event that had meant nothing—something so trivial that it didn't even merit a moment's reflection. Except she was quite sure that wasn't true.

'Thanks for the e-mail,' she said, to prove it had been more than that, that he had come back to her door, had later that night sent her a photo, yet he frowned as if trying to place it and then he had the nerve to give a wry laugh.

'Oh, that!'

'You got my e-mail address?'

'On some stupid group one from Vince and…' He gave a shrug, clearly couldn't remember Jasmine's name. 'Just clearing out my inbox, Bridgette.' She felt like a stalker, some mad, obsessed woman, and he clearly must be thinking the same. 'It was one night— hardly something to base your career path on. Don't give it another thought. There really is no problem.'

'Good.'

'And as for awkward, it's not in the least. This is how I am at work.' And then he corrected himself. 'This is how I am—ask anyone.' He gave a very thin smile. 'I'm not exactly known for small talk. It has nothing to do with what took place. It really is forgotten.'

And over the next few days he proved his point. She saw that Dr Dominic Mansfield *was* cool and distant with everyone. He was mainly polite, sometimes dismissive, and just never particularly friendly. There was an autonomous air to him that wasn't, Bridgette realised, solely reserved for her. Not that she should mind—nothing had shifted her heart. She was still way too raw to contemplate a relationship. And the patients, or rather their parents, didn't seem to mind the directness of his words in the least. In fact, as Bridgette wheeled Carla up later in the week for a visit with her newborn, Carla admitted it was Dr Mansfield's opinion she sought the most about her daughter.

'I don't want a doctor who tries to spare my feelings,' Carla said as they waited for the lift. 'He tells it like it is, which Frank and I appreciate.

'Mind you…' she smiled as Bridgette wheeled her in '…he's not exactly chatty. Gorgeous to look at he may be, but you wouldn't want to be stuck in a lift with him.' Whether she agreed or not, Bridgette smiled back, pleased to see her patient's humour returning, along with colour to her cheeks. It really had been a hellish ride for Carla. It had been four days until she had been well enough to see her baby, and there was still, for Francesca, a long road ahead.

'Carla.' Dominic gave a nod to the patient as Bridgette wheeled her over.

'Is everything okay?' Carla asked, anxious to see him standing by Francesca's incubator.

'She's had a good morning, by all reports,' Dominic said. 'I'm just checking in.'

He gave Bridgette the briefest nod of acknowledgement then moved on to the next incubator. He wasn't, she now realised, being rude or dismissive towards her. It was the way Dominic was to everyone.

It hurt more than she had time to allocate to it. Her days were so busy, and more and more Courtney was asking her to have Harry. It was hard trying to achieve some sort of routine and work full-time with a toddler— a toddler who worryingly didn't toddle very much, one who seemed far happier to sit with his building blocks, happier in his own world than hers. But sometimes at night, when all she should do was close her eyes and get some much-needed sleep, it was then that Bridgette's mind wandered. It was on those occasions that she re-alised not so much what she'd lost but more what she'd been privy to that night.

A side to Dominic that was rare indeed.

CHAPTER FIVE

'HARRY!' Bridgette gave him a wide smile but Harry didn't look up. He was engrossed with the pile of bricks in front of him. 'How has he been today?' Bridgette asked.

'Busy building!' Mary answered. 'He loves his bricks.'

Bridgette saw her own fingers clench around the pen as she signed Harry out for the day, saw the white of her knuckles as her brain tightened just a fraction, wondering if Mary's comment was friendly chatter or a more professional observation. She was being paranoid, Bridgette told herself, seeing problems where there were surely none, but as she picked up Harry she wished, and not for the first time, that Harry was just a little bit more pleased to see her, a little more receptive.

There couldn't be something wrong with him. It wasn't just for selfish reasons that she panicked at the thought—it was Courtney's reaction that troubled Bridgette, or rather Courtney's lack of reaction towards her son. Her sister wasn't exactly coping now, let alone if her son had special needs.

Special needs.

It was the first time that she had actually said it, even

if only in her mind, and instantly she shoved it aside because there was just so much to deal with at the moment. She had so many things to contend with, without adding the unthinkable to the pile. But she had to approach it.

'How do you think he's doing?' she asked Mary.

'Grand.' She beamed. 'Mind, he does have a bit of a temper—' she tickled him under the chin '—if one of the other littlies knocks over his bricks.'

'What about his talking?' Bridgette looked at Mary, who just smiled at Harry.

'He's not much of a talker,' Mary said, 'but, then, he's just been here a couple of weeks and is still settling in so maybe he's a bit shy. If you're concerned, though…' Mary was lovely, but she told Bridgette what she already knew, that maybe his mum should take him to his GP if she was worried that he wasn't reaching his milestones.

'How is Mum?' Mary asked, because, despite Courtney collecting him a couple of times, it mainly fell to Bridgette.

'She's okay,' Bridgette answered. 'Though I'll be bringing Harry in for the next couple of days. She's got some job interviews lined up in Bendigo and is staying there with friends for a few nights.'

'Bendigo!' Mary's eyebrows rose. 'That's a good few hours away.'

'Well, it's early days,' Bridgette said, 'but it's good that she's looking for work.'

Bridgette had mixed feelings. Yes, she wanted her sister to get a job and to make a fresh start, but the thought of her, or rather Harry, so far away had Bridgette in a spin. She was doing her best not to dwell on it as she left the crèche.

'Excuse me!' She heard the irritation in the man's

voice as she, a woman who wasn't looking where she was going, collided with him as she walked out of the daycare centre. And then Dominic looked down, saw who he was talking to, saw who she was holding, and she was quite sure that he frowned as he gazed into Harry's eyes. Eyes that were exactly the same sludgy grey as hers, and though he quickly moved his features to impassive and gave her a very brief nod, she could feel the tension. They walked down a long corridor, Bridgette several steps behind him. As he headed out through the ambulance bay and turned left, it was clear they were both heading for the car park.

She should have managed to avoid him, given that she now walked incredibly slowly, but one of the security guards halted him and they spoke for a moment. No matter how Bridgette dawdled, no matter how hard she tried not to catch up, the security guard gave him a cheery farewell at the very second Bridgette walked past and, like it or not, for a moment or two there was no choice but to fall in step alongside him.

'Is that why you had to dash off?'

It was the first time he acknowledged he even *recalled* the details of that night, that morning, the slice of time when things had felt more than right.

'I should have explained…' She really didn't know what to say, what could she say. 'I didn't know how…' She still didn't. Should she plead, 'I'm his aunt. He's not my responsibility'? Harry was, he was solid in her arms—and whether Harry understood her words or not, he certainly did not need to be present as she defended her reasons for not telling this man of his existence. Instead she walked to her car that, unlike his, which lit up like a Christmas tree the second he approached, needed keys. Bridgette had to scrabble in her bag for them, with Harry, who was becoming increasingly heavy, but she was too nervous to put him down in the middle of a car park. He was, she realised, just too precious to let go.

As Dominic's sleek silver car slid past her, she deliberately did not look up, did not want to remember the night he'd driven her to heaven then returned her home again.

She was very close to crying, and that Harry did not need, but finally she found her keys and unlocked the car, opening the windows to let it cool down before she put Harry in.

'Here we go.' The car still felt like a sauna but she strapped Harry in, climbed into the seat and looked in the rear-vision mirror at his wispy curls and serious grey eyes. She gave him a very nice smile. 'You're ruining my love life, Harry!'

CHAPTER SIX

'Wow!' Bridgette walked into the delivery room, where Maria was pacing. 'I turn my back for five minutes...' She smiled at Maria, who had progressed rapidly in the past half hour.

'I was worried you wouldn't make it back,' Maria said.

'I'm sorry I had to dash off.' Harry had been a touch grizzly this morning when she'd dropped him off and had, half an hour ago, thrown the most spectacular temper tantrum, bad enough for Mary to call her on the ward and for Bridgette to take an early coffee break.

'I know what it's like,' Maria said. 'I've got three of my own.'

'Four soon,' Bridgette said, and Maria smiled.

'I can't wait to meet her.'

'Neither can I,' Bridgette admitted. It was, so far, turning out to be a gorgeous labour—especially as it was one that could have been labelled 'difficult' because the testing and scans had revealed that Maria and Tony's baby had Trisomy 21. The diagnosis, Maria had told Bridgette, had caused intense upset between both families—Spanish passion combined with pointless accusations and blame had caused a lot of tension and heartache indeed. Maria and Tony, however, once they had got over the initial shock, had researched as much as they could, and had even met with a local support group who ran a regular playgroup.

'It took away a lot of the fear,' Maria had explained, when Bridgette admitted her. 'Seeing other Down's syndrome babies and toddlers and their parents coping so well. We're so looking forward to having our baby. I just wish our families would stop with the grief.'

So upset was Maria with the response of her family that she hadn't even wanted them to know that she had gone into labour, but with three other small children to care for she'd had no choice but to tell them. And now two anxious families were sitting in the maternity waiting room. Still, Maria was doing beautifully and was helped so much by her husband's unwavering support. He rubbed her back where she indicated, stopped talking when she simply raised a hand. They had their own private language and were working to deliver their daughter as a team.

'How are things?' Rita popped her head around the door. 'The family just asked for an update.'

'It's all going well,' Bridgette said.

'Tell them it will be born when it's good and ready,' Maria snapped, and then breathed through another contraction. She was suddenly savage. 'You'd think they were preparing for a funeral more than a birth!' She let out an expletive or three in Spanish and Tony grimaced, then she told him *exactly* what she thought of Abuela.

'Grandmother,' Tony translated with a smile when Bridgette winked at him. 'My mother.' He rolled his eyes. 'She does a lot for us, but she can be a bit too much at times, though she means well.' He rubbed his wife's back as Maria said a little more of what she thought about her mother-in-law. 'Maria always does this when…' And Bridgette smiled, knew as Tony did, what was coming. Maria leant against the bed, her face changing to a familiar grimace.

'I want to push.'

'That's good,' Bridgette cheered.

'Come on, Tony,' she said and they both helped Maria up onto the bed. 'I'm just going to let Dr Hudson know—'

'No need.' Dr Hudson came in.

'How's she doing?' Rita popped her head around the door again and Bridgette gritted her teeth, while trying not to let Maria see.

'Can we get the paediatrician down?' The obstetrician's tone was a little brusque and Bridgette saw the flare of panic in Maria's eyes.

'It's fine, Maria,' Bridgette reassured her as Rita went to make the call. 'The fact Dr Hudson wants the paediatrician to come down means that you're getting close now and it won't be long till your baby's born.'

'The paediatrician is on his way,' Rita called over the intercom. 'I'll come in and give you a hand in a moment.'

Bridgette watched as Maria's eyes closed; as she dipped into her own private world and just tried to block the gathering crowd out. She had wanted the birth to be as low-key and as relaxed as possible, and had three other births with which to compare, but because of the possible health complications, more staff would be present with this one. Though potentially necessary, it just compounded things for Maria.

'Have you got everything ready?' Rita bustled into the room. 'Dominic is just a couple of minutes away.'

Bridgette felt incredibly confident with Dominic. He was an amazing doctor and very astute. However, for Maria, perhaps it was not the best combination of staff. Dr Hudson believed in planning for every eventuality—*every* eventuality—and Rita was one of those high-energy people who somehow didn't soothe. Now Dominic, a rather aloof paediatrician, was being added to the mix, except... 'Dominic Mansfield?' Tony looked over at Bridgette. 'Is that the paediatrician who's coming?' When Bridgette nodded, Tony hugged his wife. 'That's good news, Maria.'

'Bridgette?' Rita was checking and double-checking everything Bridgette had already done. 'Have you got the—?'

'*Shut up!*' roared Maria, just as Dominic came into the room.

For once Bridgette was grateful for his silence. He gave Tony a nod as Maria quietly laboured. Dominic took off his jacket and headed to the sink to wash his hands and then tied on a plastic apron.

'Big breath, Maria,' Bridgette said gently. 'Come on, another one...' The birth was imminent. 'And then push until Dr Hudson tells you to stop.' Maria was very good at this. There was grim concentration on her face as she bore down and Bridgette held her leg, relaying Dr Hudson's gruff instructions but in more encouraging tones. 'Don't push now. Just breathe. The head's out.'

The baby didn't even require another push. She slithered out into Dr Hudson's hands, where Rita was waiting to cut the cord and whisk the baby off for examination.

'Up onto Mum's stomach,' Dominic said. 'Tony can cut the cord.' Bridgette silently cheered as his calm, authoritative voice slowed the haste.

'Do you want the baby moved over for examination?' Rita checked when, again, she didn't need to. It had been a very beautiful birth, and Bridgette was especially thrilled that Dominic seemed in no rush to whisk the baby off and examine her—instead, he just quietly observed.

The little girl was small and Bridgette placed a towel over her, rubbing her to stimulate her, but she felt very calm with Dominic's stoic presence so close.

As the baby took her first breaths, Dominic called Tony over and the cord was cut—and Bridgette felt a blink of tears because the birth Maria had wanted so badly for her baby was happening.

'I can examine her here,' Dominic said, when Rita checked again if he wanted the baby moved over. And he did. He checked the little baby's muscle tone and her palate and listened to her heart for a long time. He told Maria he would perform a more comprehensive examination in a little while. 'But for now I'll let you enjoy her.'

There really was a lot to enjoy. She peered up at her mum, her almond-shaped eyes huge and gorgeous; she was very alert, and even though she let out a few little cries, she was easily comforted by Maria.

'Do you want me to let your family know?' Rita asked, and Bridgette's jaw tightened. She could understand the conversation that had been held at Jasmine's leaving do now. Rita really did try and take over.

'They'll want to come in,' Maria said. 'I just don't

want...' She held her baby closely. 'I want it to be a cele-bration, the same as it was with my others.'

'It will be,' Dominic said. 'They just haven't met her yet.'

'She wants to feed,' Maria said, as her daughter fran-tically searched for her breast.

'Let her.'

'You said they'd scan her first,' Maria said, because, though detailed prenatal scans had not shown anything, the nature of the syndrome meant the little girl was at risk of a heart defect and would need to be checked by a paediatric cardiologist soon after birth, but Dominic was clearly happy with his findings.

'She's looking great,' he said, quietly observing, and the baby did latch on, but Bridgette helped with the po-sitioning.

It was one of those births that confirmed her voca-tion—there was no greater gift than watching a new life come into the world, and today's so-called diffi-cult birth had been made especially wonderful by the calm presence of Dominic. Again he had surprised her. He wasn't particularly effusive or gushing, he was so much *more* than that, and he was everything this little family needed today.

Dominic stayed and wrote up his notes while the little girl fed and Bridgette watched for any signs that the baby was having trouble sucking and swallowing but she was doing very well. 'Dominic said that breast feeding might be more difficult than with the others...' Maria looked down at her daughter, who was tiring, so Bridgette suggested she take her off now.

'She's doing an awful lot right,' Bridgette said,

checking the babe and then filling in her own notes. 'She's cried, pooed, wee'd and fed.'

Dominic came over. 'You remember I said that I'd take her up to NICU for a little while after she was born,' he said. 'I want that scan done. Everything looks good,' he reassured the parents, 'but I just want her thoroughly checked. Hopefully she'll be back down with you soon.'

Maria nodded and then took a deep breath. 'Can you bring in my family first?' Her eyes went to her husband's. 'If they start, I want you to…'

'We'll be here,' Bridgette said. 'You won't have to say a thing. I'm very good at bringing up excuses as to why people have to leave. If you start getting upset, or you've just had enough, you just have to let me know.' They worked out a little code, and she gave Tony a smile as he walked out. Dominic, she noted, instead of heading out to the desk, was sitting on a couch in the corner of the room, finishing his notes—a quiet, unobtrusive presence that was welcome.

Maria and Tony set the tone, but Bridgette's heart did go out to the family. They were trying to be brave, to not be upset, but there was so much tension, so many questions as they all peered at the newest member of the clan. Then Maria's three-year-old, Roman, climbed up on the bed and gazed at his sister, kissing her on the forehead, and the old *abuela* laughed.

Dominic came over and checked the baby briefly again, more for the family's benefit, or rather Maria's, Bridgette rightly guessed, because the questions they had been asking Maria were aimed at him now.

'She's doing very, very well,' he said, and answered more of their questions and told them that, yes, the prenatal diagnosis was correct. Yes, shortly there would be further testing, but for now she was doing perfectly. And then Bridgette blinked as he chatted with the *abuela* in what appeared to be fluid Spanish for a moment. *'Sí, ella es perfecta...'*

'We're going to move her up now.' Kelly from NICU had come down just as all the cameras came out.

'Photo with *el medico*,' the *abuela* said.

'We really ought to get moving.' Dominic was reluctant, but then obliged, and it struck Bridgette that though of course he held babies in the course of examining them, he wasn't the type to steal a cuddle.

He held the new infant and gave a smile for the camera and then he looked down at her.

'She's gorgeous, isn't she?' Maria said.

'Oh, I don't do the cute-baby thing,' Dominic answered, 'but, yes, I think I have to agree in this case. You have a very cute baby. Has she got a name?'

'Esperanza,' Maria said.

'Hope!' Dominic smiled.

He popped her back in her cot and at the last minute Tony asked if he might be able to stay with the baby during her tests. When Dominic agreed, the family all followed Dominic, Kelly and the porters in a little procession down the hall.

'He's lovely, isn't he?' Maria said. 'Dominic, I mean. He sort of tells you like it is.'

'He's very good,' Bridgette said, and gave Maria a wink. 'Speaks Spanish too.'

'Abuela was very impressed.' Maria grinned. 'Dominic's mother is Spanish apparently.' She had to find out about him from a patient! 'He's been great. We went to him when we got the amnio back and he told us what to expect. Well, I guess he'd know as his brother has Down's.' She must have seen Bridgette's eyes widen. 'Sorry, maybe I shouldn't have said—it was just that Tony was crying and so was I and it seemed like a disaster when we first found out, but Dominic was terribly patient. He told us what we were feeling was completely normal. We saw him again a couple of weeks ago and we were embarrassed about the scene we'd made, but he said not to give it another thought. It was all very normal, that his mother had been the same.'

They knew nothing about each other, Bridgette realised.

Which had been the point, she remembered.

She really was lousy at one-night stands.

Still, she didn't have time to dwell on it. L and D was busy and she was soon looking after another birth, a first-time mum called Jessica, who was very nervous, as well as keeping an eye on Maria.

Esperanza was gone for about an hour, and her heart test was clear, which was brilliant news, and by the time she was back, Bridgette had just transferred Maria to the ward. Having checked on her next patient, Bridgette was more than ready for lunch.

'What's all this?' Bridgette tried not to care that Dominic was sitting in the staffroom. After all, if he didn't care, why should she? Anyway, Rita was there too and there were other distractions this lunchtime. Instead of plain biscuits the table was heaving with fruit platters, small filled rolls and a spread of cheese.

'Leftovers from the obstetricians' meeting.' Rita gave a wry smile. 'I rescued some for the workers. Enjoy.'

Bridgette selected a roll and a few slivers of fruit. She glanced at the cheese—even though that would usually be her first option, even if it seemed stupid, with Dominic there she chose to give it a miss.

'How's Harry?' Rita asked.

'Better,' Bridgette answered. 'He was just having a bit of a tantrum. He's not in the best of moods today. I'm sorry I had to dash off.'

As annoying and inflexible as she could be, Rita could, Bridgette conceded, also be very nice. 'No problem. It's to be expected in the first weeks at daycare. He'll soon get used to it. The real question is, how is his aunt doing?'

'Trying to get used to it too,' Bridgette admitted. 'But we're getting there.'

Unfortunately Rita's break was soon over and word couldn't yet have got around about the spread on in the staffroom because only Dominic and Bridgette remained. Well, she wasn't going to give up a single minute of the precious break by going back early. Her feet were killing her and she was hungry too, and Jessica, her new patient, was progressing steadily. If Dominic wasn't feeling awkward then why on earth should she be? And if she wanted cheese, why not?

Bridgette stood and refilled her plate with some Cheddar and Brie and a few crackers and went to sit back down, selecting a magazine to read as she did so.

'I thought you liked blue cheese.'

'Maybe.' Bridgette refused to look up, just carried on reading the magazine. She was not going to jump to make conversation just because he suddenly deigned to do so.

'How's Maria?'

'Marvellous.' She refused to be chatty, just because he suddenly was.

'The baby I saw you with yesterday...' Still she did not fill in the spaces. 'He's your nephew?' When still he was met with silence, Dominic pushed a little further. 'Why didn't you just say so?'

'I don't really see that it's relevant,' Bridgette answered, still reading her magazine. 'Had our one-night stand been two years ago and you'd seen me walking out of daycare carrying a mini-Dominic, then, yes, perhaps I'd have had some explaining to do. But I don't.' She smirked with mild pleasure at her choice of words and looked up. She was rather surprised to see that he was smiling—not the Dr Mansfield smile that she had seen occasionally since her return to work but the Dominic smile she had once been privy to.

'I'm sorry about yesterday. I just jumped to conclusions. I saw you with—' he paused for a brief second '—Harry, and I thought that was the reason...' He really felt awkward, Bridgette realised. Despite insisting how easy this was, Dominic seemed to be struggling.

'The reason?' She frowned, because he'd done this to her too, made her blush as she'd revealed that she thought about that night—but Dominic didn't blush in the same way Bridgette had.

'The reason that you went home that morning.'

'Oh, I needed a reason, did I?' She went back to her magazine.

What was it with this woman? She had made it very clear that morning that she didn't want more than their one night. Normally it would have come as a relief to Dominic, an unusual relief because he was not the one working out how to end things.

'Excuse me.' Her phone buzzed in her pocket and

Bridgette pulled it out, taking a deep breath before answering.

'Hi, Mum.'

Why did he have to be here when she took this call? Hopefully he'd choose now to leave, but instead he just sat there.

'I might need a hand a little bit later,' she said to her mother. She'd left a message for her parents earlier in the day, when she'd realised that Harry might not last out the day in crèche and also she wanted to stay longer for Jessica. 'There's a chance that I won't be able to get away for work on time and it would really help if you could pick up Harry at four for me.' She closed her eyes as her mother gave the inevitable reply. 'Yes, I know the crèche doesn't close till six, but he's a bit grizzly today and I don't want to push things—it's been a long day for him.'

Bridgette looked down and realised she was clicking her pen on and off as her mother reeled out her excuses. She could hear the irritation creeping into her own voice as she responded. 'I know Dad's got the dentist but can't he go on his own?' She listened to the train of excuses, to how they would love to help, but how nervous Dad got at the dentist, and if he did need anything done when they got there... 'You mean he's just having a check-up?' Now Bridgette couldn't keep the exasperation from her voice. She really wanted to be there for Jessica and didn't want to be nervously keeping one eye on the clock in case the crèche rang. With a pang that she didn't want to examine, her heart ached for the long day Harry was having. She wanted some back-up, and despite her parents' constant reassurances that they would help, she never seemed to ask at the right time.

'Don't worry about it' Bridgette settled for, and managed a goodbye and then clicked off the phone. Then she couldn't help it—she shot out a little of the frustration that her parents so easily provoked. 'Why can't he go to the dentist by himself?' Bridgette asked as Dominic simply grinned at her exasperation. 'They go shopping together, they do the housework together... I mean, are they joined at the hip? Honestly, they don't do anything by themselves.'

'Breathe.' Dominic grinned and she did as the doctor recommended, but it didn't help and she stamped her feet for a moment and let out a brief 'Aagggh!'

'Better?' Dominic asked.

'A bit.'

Actually, she did feel a bit better. It was nice to have a little moan, to complain, to let some of her exasperation out. Her parents had always been the same—everything revolved around dinner, everything in the house was geared towards six p.m. They were so inflexible, right down to the brand of toothpaste they used, and that was fine, that was how it was, that was how they were, but right now Bridgette needed more hands and their four seemed to make a poor two.

'Have you got no one else who can help?' Dominic asked.

'I miss Jasmine for things like this,' Bridgette admitted. It was nice that they were finally talking but of course now that they were, Rita buzzed and told her Jessica was in transition and it was time for her to go back.

'You might be out by four,' he said, and she shook her head, because Jessica was a first-time mum.

'I doubt it.'

Dominic's phone was ringing as she left, and when he saw that it was his father, he chose not to answer it. Stupid, really, because his father would just ring again in an hour, Dominic thought, and every hour after that, till he could tick it off his to-do list.

He finally took the call at three.

'Hi.'

Dominic rolled his eyes as his father wished him a happy birthday. 'Thanks.' Dominic was being honest when he said that he couldn't talk for long, because he was summoned urgently and headed down to Theatre when paged for a child who was having an allergic reaction in Recovery. There was that theatre nurse, her blue eyes waiting, when he and the anaesthetist had finished discussing the child's care.

'Long shift?' Dominic asked when she yawned, because on certain occasions he did make conversation.

And today was a certain occasion.

It was, after all, his birthday.

'It's been busy.' She nodded.

'Back again in the morning?'

'Yes…though I shouldn't moan. My husband's away so I can just go home and sleep.'

He was always away, Dominic thought.

'What does he do?' He broke one of their rules and he watched her cheeks go pink. There were colleagues around, and they were seemingly just chatting, so of course she had to answer.

'He drives a coach,' Blue Eyes said. 'Overnight, Melbourne to Sydney.'

He gave a nod and walked off, felt a bit sick in the guts really, which wasn't like him, but he thought of the poor bloke driving up and down the freeway as Dominic bonked his wife. No questions asked, no real conversation.

Maybe he was growing up, Dominic thought. He hadn't been with anyone in weeks, not since Bridgette, in fact, though he rapidly shoved that thought out of his mind.

Well, why wouldn't he be growing up? It was his birthday, after all.

And birthdays were supposed to be enjoyed.

Never doubt the power of a woman in labour—Bridgette should really have known better. Jessica was amazing, focused and gritty, and the birth was wonderful, so wonderful that she was still high on adrenaline as she sped down the corridor to daycare.

'Bridgette.' He was walking towards her and this time he nodded *and* said her name—progress indeed!

'Dominic.' She grinned and nodded back at him, ready to keep walking, except he stopped in front of her.

'I was wondering,' Dominic said. 'Would you like to come out tonight? You're right, this is awkward, and I'd really like to clear the air.'

This she hadn't been expecting. 'The air is already clear, Dominic.' Except it wasn't, so Bridgette was a little more honest. 'You were right. Harry is the reason that I didn't want you to come in that first night. My computer didn't have a virus.' She gave a guilty grin. 'Well, it wasn't Harry exactly, more the cot and the stroller and the rather blatant clues that were littered around my flat at the time.' And with Bridgette, he did ask questions, and got some answers. 'I look after my nephew a lot. My sister's really young.' He didn't look away, his eyes never left her face, and she rather wished that they would. 'So!' She gave him a smile as his pager went off and Dominic glanced down at it and then switched it off. 'That's a little bit what my life is like when Harry's with my sister—I'm permanently on call.' Yes, the air had been cleared, and now they could both move on; she truly wasn't expecting what came next.

'Bridgette, would you like to come out tonight?'

She turned around slowly and he looked the same as he had before—completely unreadable. She didn't want a charity dinner, didn't want him taking her out because he'd already asked her. To make things easier for them both she gave him a small smile, shook her head and politely declined. 'That's really nice of you, thanks, but I have to say no—it's hard to get a baby-sitter.' There, she'd given him the out. It was over and done with, and she awaited his polite smile back—it didn't come. Instead he looked at his watch.

'How long does a dental check-up take?' He even smiled. 'Can you try?' He pulled out a card and wrote his mobile-phone number on it and handed it to her. Maybe he read her too well because instead of saying that he would wait to hear if she could make arrangements, he lobbed the ball firmly back into her court. 'I'll pick you up at seven, unless I hear otherwise. Ring me if you can't get a babysitter.'

It was utterly and completely unexpected. She had thought he would run a mile—she'd given him an out, after all.

She wanted him to take it.

Bridgette really did. She just wasn't ready to get back out there and certainly not with Dominic. Still, maybe tonight he would just tell her how impossible it all was; maybe she would receive a long lecture on how they found each other attractive and all that, but how unsuitable they were—yet, remembering just how good they had been, it was very hard to say no.

'Hi, Mum.' It was the second time that day she'd asked her mum for help. 'Is there any chance you and Dad could babysit tonight?'

'You mean have our grandson over?' Betty laughed. 'We'd love to.' As Bridgette blinked in surprise, as she paused just a fraction, her mother filled the gap. 'Though we do have a couple of friends coming over tonight. Old friends of your dad's—remember Eric and Lorna?' Bridgette felt her jaw tense. Her parents insisted they were accommodating, but it was always on their terms—when it suited them. 'Could we maybe do it tomorrow?'

'I've got an invitation to go out tonight, Mum. I'd really like to go.'

'But we've got people over tonight. Tomorrow we can come over to you and stay. It might be easier on Harry.' Yes, it might be easier on Harry, but it certainly wouldn't be easier on her—or Dominic. He was already taking a leap of faith in asking her out. Though he wasn't asking her out, she reminded herself—he simply wanted to clear the air. Still, no doubt he was used to having the door opened by a groomed, glossy beauty who invited him in for a drink as she applied a final layer of lip gloss—somehow she couldn't imagine inflicting her mother and father and Harry on the guy.

'Mum, I haven't had a night out in weeks.' She hadn't, not since that night with Dominic. 'I'm sorry for the short notice. If you can have Harry, that would be great. If not…' If not, then it simply wasn't meant to be, Bridgette decided. If she couldn't get away for one single night without planning it days in advance, she might just as well text Dominic now with the whole truth.

It would be quite a relief to, actually, but after a moment's silence came her mother's rather martyred response. 'Well, make sure you bring a decent change of clothes for him. I want Harry looking smart. I've got Eric and Lorna coming over,' she repeated. 'Have you had his hair cut yet?' Bridgette looked at the mop of blond curls that danced in the afternoon sun as Harry built his bricks and wondered why her mother assumed that Harry's hair was Bridgette's responsibility. His mop of unruly hair was a slight bone of contention between them—Courtney would never think to get a haircut for her son and though at first it had irritated Bridgette, more and more his wild curls suited him. Bridgette was now reluctant to get them cut—she certainly wasn't going to rush out and get a haircut just to appease her parents' guests and, anyway, there wasn't time. 'No, Courtney hasn't had his hair cut, but he's looking beautiful and I've got a gorgeous outfit for him.'

And with Harry dropped off and the quickest bath in history taken, the flat had to be hastily tidied, not that she had any intention of Dominic coming in. She'd be ready and dressed at the door, Bridgette decided, so she had about sixteen minutes to work out a not-so-gorgeous outfit for herself.

There was a grey shift dress at the back of her wardrobe and she had to find her ballet pumps but first she had a quick whiz with hair tongs and her magical blusher.

'Please be late,' she begged as she remembered her

screensaver was of them. Her computer was in the spare bedroom, but in case of earthquake and it was the room they ended up in, she had to change it.

'Please be late,' she said again as she stashed dishes in the cupboard beneath the sink and shovelled piles of building bricks into the corner.

'Please be late,' she said as she opened her bedroom door to get her pumps and was distracted by the shelves she'd been meaning to build and the million-thread-count sheets she'd bought in a sale and had been saving for when the room was painted.

But the bedroom was too untidy to even contemplate bringing him in and, no, her prayers weren't answered.

Bang on seven, she heard the doorbell.

CHAPTER SEVEN

'READY!' Bridgette beamed as she opened the front door and stepped out, because there was no way he was coming in.

'Shoes?' Dominic helpfully suggested just after she closed the door.

'Oh. Yes.' Which meant she had to rummage in her bag for her keys as he stood there. 'They must be in here.'

'Can't the babysitter let you in?'

'He's at my parents',' she said as she rummaged.

'Have you locked yourself out?'

'No, no,' Bridgette said cheerfully. 'I do this all the time—here they are.' She produced them with a 'ta ra!' and she let herself in, which of course meant that she had to let him in too—well, she couldn't really leave him on the doorstep.

'Go through,' she said, because she didn't even want him to get a glimpse of the chaos in the bedroom. 'I'll just be a moment.' Except he didn't go through. He stood in the hallway as she slipped through the smallest crack in the door and then scrambled to find her shoes. She must get more organised. Bridgette knew that, dreamt of the day when she finally had some sort of routine. She'd had a loose one once, before Harry was born, but now the whole flat seemed to have gone to pot.

There they were, under the bed. She grabbed her pumps and sort of limbo-danced around the door so that he wouldn't see inside. 'Sorry about that,' she said. 'Just been a bit of a mad rush.'

'Look, if you're too tired to go out for dinner...'

She gave him a strange look. 'I'm starving,' Bridgette said. 'How could anyone be too tired to eat dinner?'

'I meant...'

'So we're not going out dancing, then,' she teased. 'You're not going to teach me the flamenco.' She was leaning against the wall and putting on her ballet pumps, hardly a provocative move, except it was to him.

'Impressed with my Spanish, were you?'

'No Flamenco Medico?' She pouted and raised her arm and gave a stamp of her foot. Dominic stood there, his black eyes watching and sudden tension in his throat.

'Any chance of a drink?'

'Sure!' She beamed and headed to the kitchen and opened the fridge. 'I've got...' She stared at a jug of cordial, kicked herself for not grabbing some beer or wine, or olives and vermouth to make cocktails, she frantically thought.

'I meant water.'

'Oh, I think I've got some somewhere.' She grinned and turned on the tap. 'Oh, yes, here it is.' Was that a reluctant smile on the edge of his lips? 'Here you go.' She handed him the glass as his phone rang, and because of his job he had no choice but to check it. Bridgette's smile was a wry one as 'Arabella' flashed up on the screen.

'She's hitting the bottle early tonight.'

He laughed. 'It's my birthday.'

'Oh!' It was all she could think of to say and then her brain sort of slid back into functioning. 'Happy birthday,' she said. 'I've got candles but no cake.'

Then the phone rang again and they stood there.

And she was annoyed at his ex, annoyed that he was standing there in her kitchen, and her eyes told him so. 'You really did break her heart, didn't you?'

'Long story,' he said. He didn't want to talk about it, hadn't ever spoken about it, and really he'd rather not now.

'Short version?'

'Come on,' he said, 'the table's booked.'

'You know what?' Bridgette said. 'I'm not very hungry.'

'You just said you were starving.'

'Not enough to sit through five hundred phone calls from your ex.'

'Okay, okay.' He offered a major concession. 'I'll turn it off.'

'No,' she said. 'I'm not doing it any more, putting up with crap.' She was talking about Paul, but she was talking about him too, or rather she was talking about herself—she would not put herself through it again. 'Even if you turn it off, I'll know she's ringing. What's that saying? If a tree falls in a forest, does it make a noise?'

'What?' He was irritated, annoyed, but certainly not with her. 'I've said I'll turn it off, Bridgette. She doesn't usually ring—I never thought when I asked you to come out that it was my birthday. I don't get sentimental, I don't sit remembering last year, blah blah blah.'

'Blah blah blah…' Bridgette said, her voice rising,

irritated and annoyed, and certainly it was with him. 'That's all she was, blah blah blah.' The night was over before it had even started. She really should have left it at one night with him. 'What is it with men?' She stormed past him, completely ready to show him the door, and it was almost a shout that halted her.

'She didn't want my brother and his friends at our engagement party.'

They both stood, in a sort of stunned silence, he for saying it, she that he had.

'He's got Down's,' Dominic said, and she was glad that she knew already. 'He lives in sheltered housing. When I'm there I go over every week and sometimes she came with me. She was great…or I thought she was, then when we were planning the engagement, my dad suggested it might be better if Chris didn't come, Chris and his friends, that we have a separate party for them, and she agreed. "It might be a bit awkward."' He put on a very plummy voice. '"You know, for the other guests. You know how he loves to dance."'

And Bridgette stood there and didn't know what to say.

'I couldn't get past it,' Dominic said, and he'd never discussed this with another person, but now that he'd started, it was as if he couldn't stop. Months of seething anger and hurt for his brother all tumbling out. 'My dad wanted nothing to do with him when he was born, he has nothing to do with him now, and it turned out Arabella didn't want him around either—well, not in the way I thought she would.'

'I'm sorry.' It was all she could say and she could hear the bitterness in his response.

'She keeps saying sorry too—that she didn't mean it

and if we can just go back of course he can come to our party. She claims that she said what she did because she was just trying to get on with my dad, except I heard it and I know that it was meant.' He shook his head. 'You think you know someone...'

And when the phone rang again she decided that she did know what to say, after all.

'Give it to me,' she said, and she answered it and gave him a wink and a smile as she spoke. 'Sorry, Dominic's in bed...' She looked at him, saw him groan out a laugh as she answered Arabella's question. 'So what if it's early? I never said that he was asleep.' And she put down the phone but didn't turn it off. Instead she put her hand to her mouth and started kissing it, making breathy noises. Then she jumped up onto the bench, her bottom knocking over a glass.

'Dominic!' she shrieked.

'Bridgette!' He was folded over laughing as he turned off the phone. 'You're wicked.'

'I can be,' she said.

And he looked at her sitting on the bench all dishevelled and sexy, and thought of the noises she had made and what she had done, and just how far they had come since that night. Her words were like a red rag to a bull—he sort of charged her, right there in the kitchen.

Ferocious was his kiss as he pushed her further up the bench, and frantic was her response as she dragged herself back.

His hands were everywhere, but she was just as bad—tearing at his shirt till the buttons tore, pulling out his belt, and she was delighted that they weren't going to make it to the bedroom again, delighted by her own condom-carrying medico. Except Dominic had other ideas.

'Bed.' He pulled her from the bench. 'This time bed.'

'No.' She pulled at his zipper. 'No, no, no.'

'Yes.' He didn't want the floor again. He was leading her to her room, dragging her more like as she dug her heels in.

'You can't go in there!'

'Why?' He grinned, except he'd already pushed the door open. 'Have you got more babies stashed away that you haven't told...?' He just stopped. She doubted anyone as glamorous as he had seen a really messy bedroom, like a *really* messy one. He looked at the chaos and then at the beauty that had somehow emerged out of it.

'I told you not to go in there!' She thought she'd killed the moment. Honestly, she really thought she had, but something else shifted, something even more breathtaking than before.

'In here now, young lady.' His voice was stern as he pointed, and she licked her lips, she could hardly breathe for the excitement, as she headed to her bedroom. 'You can hardly see the bed,' he scolded as he led her to it. 'I've a good mind...'

Yes, they *were* bad. He did put her over his knee, but she nearly fell off laughing and they wanted each other too much to play games. It was the quickest sex ever, the best sex ever.

Again.

Again, she thought as he speared into her. They were still half-dressed, just mutual in want. She'd wanted him so badly again and now he was inside her.

It was bliss to have him back, to be back, to scream out as he shuddered into her.

Bliss for it already to have been the perfect night and it was only seven-thirty p.m.

To be honest, as she looked over he seemed a bit taken back by what had happened.

'Bridgette...' Please don't say sorry, she thought. 'I had no intention...' He looked at her stricken face. 'I mean...I had a table booked and everything.'

'You're not sorry, then?'

'Sorry?' He looked over to her. 'I couldn't be less sorry, just...' He might even be blushing. 'I did want to talk, to take you out. We could still go...'

'If you can sew on your own buttons!' Bridgette looked at his shirt. 'But first you'd have to find a needle. And thread,' she added after a moment's thought.

They settled for pizza. Bridgette undressed and slid into bed, and there would be time for talking later, for now they filled the gap and her roaring hunger with kissing until the pizza was delivered, and then he undressed and got into bed too.

And they did have that grown-up conversation. It sort of meandered around other conversations, but the new rules were spoken by both of them. It was difficult and awkward at times too, but so much easier naked in bed and eating than at some gorgeous restaurant with others around. They spoke about nothing at first and then about work.

'I don't get close.' Dominic shook his head. 'I'm good at my job. I don't need to be like some politician and hold and cuddle babies to be a good doctor.'

'Never?' she checked.

'Never,' Dominic said. 'Oh, I held little Esperanza,

but that was more for the parents, for the *abuela*, but...'
He *did* try to explain it. 'I said she was cute and, yes,
she is, but they're not going to get a touchy-feely doctor if they are on my list.' He said it and he meant it. 'I
can't do that. I know all that might happen—I can't get
involved and then in a few weeks have to tell them that
the news isn't good.' He was possibly the most honest
person she had met. 'I'll give each patient and their parent or parents one hundred per cent of my medical mind.
You don't have to be involved to have compassion.' It
was too easy to be honest with her, but sometimes the
truth hurt. 'I couldn't do it, Bridgette. I couldn't do this
job if I got too close—so I stay back. It's why I don't
want kids of my own.' He gave her a nudge. 'That's why
I don't get involved with anyone who has kids.'

'I don't have kids.' Bridgette said. 'And I think it
wasn't just the long-term viability of our future you
were thinking about that night...' She nudged him and
he grinned, though she didn't repeat midwife-speak to
him; instead she spoke the truth. 'Here for a good time,
not a long time...and not have the night interrupted with
crying babies.'

'Something like that.'

'Didn't Arabella want kids?'

'God, no,' Dominic said.

The conversation sort of meandered around, but it
led to the same thing.

They both knew it.

'I will be moving back to Sydney.' He was honest.
'It's not just work. It's family and friends.' And she
nodded and took a lovely bite of cheesy dough and then
without chewing took another. She couldn't blame him
for wanting to be with them. She took another bite and

he told her about his brother, that he'd been thirteen when Chris was born. 'To be honest, I was embarrassed—I was a right idiot then. So was my dad,' he said. 'They broke up when he was three. I was doing my final year school exams and all stressed and self-absorbed and Chris would just come in and want to talk and play—drove me crazy.

'He didn't care that I had my chemistry, couldn't give a stuff about everything that was so important to me—except clothes. Even now he likes to look good, does his hair.' Dominic grinned. 'Loves to dance!' He rolled his eyes. 'Loves women…'

'Must be your brother!' Bridgette smiled—a real one.

'When I was doing my exams I'd be totally self-centred, angry, stressed. "What's wrong, Dom?" he'd ask. And I'd tell him and he'd just look at me and then go and get me a drink or bring me something to eat, or try to make me laugh because he didn't get it. You know, I stopped being embarrassed and used to feel sorry for him. My dad didn't have anything to do with him, but then I realised Chris was the one who was happy and feeling sorry for me!'

'We've got it all back to front, you know,' Bridgette admitted.

'He's great. And you're right…' He saw her frown. 'I'm not like a paediatrician. I was like my dad growing up—just me, me, me. Without Chris I would have been a sports doctor on the tennis circuit or something—I would,' he said, and she was quite sure he was right, because he had that edge, that drive, that could take him anywhere. 'I'd certainly have had a smaller nose.'

'What?' She frowned and he grinned. 'My father thought I needed a small procedure. I was to have it in the summer break between school and university. He had it all planned out.' He gave a dark laugh. 'The night before the operation I rang him and told him to go jump.'

'Do you talk now?'

'Of course.' He looked over. 'About nothing, though. He never asks about Chris, never goes in and sees him on his birthday or Christmas, or goes out with him.' He gave her a grin. 'I can still feel him looking at my nose when he speaks to me.'

'He'd be wanting to liposuction litres out of me!' Bridgette laughed and he did too.

Dominic lay and stared up at the ceiling, thought about today—because even if he did his best not to get close to his patients, today he hadn't felt nothing as he'd stood and had that photo taken. He'd been angry—yes, he might have smiled for the camera, but inside a black anger had churned, an anger towards his father.

He'd walked up to NICU and Tony had walked alongside him, had stood with his baby for every test, had beamed so brightly when the good news was confirmed that her heart was fine.

'I'll come back to Maternity with you in case Maria has any questions,' Dominic had said, even though he hadn't had to. He had stood and watched when Tony told his wife the good news and wondered what he'd have been like had he had Tony as a father. He didn't want to think about his father now.

'How long have you been looking after Harry?' he asked instead.

Bridgette gave a tense shrug. 'It's very on and off,' she said.

'You said she was a lot younger…'

'Eighteen,' Bridgette said. He'd been so open and honest, yet she just couldn't bring herself to be so with him. 'I really would rather not talk about it tonight.'

'Fair enough,' Dominic said.

So they ate pizza instead and made love and hoped that things might look a little less complicated in the morning.

They didn't.

'Do you want to go out tonight?' he asked, taking a gulp of the tea she'd made because Bridgette had run out of coffee. 'Or come over?'

'I'd love to, but I truly can't,' she said, because she *couldn't*. 'I've got to pick Harry up.'

'When does his mum get back?'

'Tomorrow,' Bridgette said. 'I think.'

'You think.' Some things he could not ignore. 'Bridgette, you seem to be taking on an awful lot.'

'Well, she's my sister,' Bridgette said, 'and she's looking for flats and daycare. It's better that she has a few days to sort it out herself rather than dragging Harry around with her.'

'Fair enough.'

And he didn't run for the hills.

Instead he gave her a very nice kiss, and then reached in for another, a kiss that was so nice it made her want to cry.

'Have breakfast,' she said to his kiss, trying to think what was in the fridge.

And he was about to say no, that he had to go to work in an hour and all that.

Except he said yes.

He thought of the frothy latte he'd normally be sipping right now.

Instead he watched Bridgette's bottom wiggle as she made pancakes because she didn't have bread.

Watched as she shook some icing sugar over them.

How could you not have bread? she screamed inside.

Or bacon, or fresh tomatoes. She had thrown on her nursing apron—it had two straps with buttons and big pockets in the front. She had ten of them and they were brilliant for cooking—so the fat didn't splat—but she was naked beneath.

'We should be sitting at a table outside a café—' she smiled as he watched her '—or at the window, watching the barista froth our lovely coffees.'

She must have read his mind.

As she brought over two plates of pancakes, where Bridgette was concerned, he crossed the line. 'How long ago did you break up with Paul?'

'Excuse me?' She gave him a very odd look as she came over with breakfast. 'I don't remember discussing him with you.'

'You didn't.' He gave a half-shrug. 'You really don't discuss yourself with me at all, so I've had to resort to other means.' He saw the purse of her lips. 'I didn't just happen across it—I asked Vince for your e-mail address. Guys do talk.' He saw her raise her eyebrows. 'He said there had been a messy break-up, that was all he knew.'

'Well, it wasn't very messy for me.' Bridgette shrugged. 'It might have been a bit messy for him because he suddenly had to find somewhere to live.' She shook her head. She wasn't going there with him. 'It's a long story…'

'Short version,' Dominic said.

'We were together two years,' Bridgette said. 'Great for one of them, great till my sister got depressed and moved in and suddenly there was a baby with colic and…' She gave a tight shrug. 'You get the picture. Anyway, by the time Harry turned one we were over.' She had given the short version, but she did ponder just a little. 'He felt the place had been invaded, that I was never able to go out.' She looked over at him. 'Funny, I'd have understood if it had been his flat.' She gave Dominic a smile but it didn't reach her eyes. He could see the hurt deep in them and knew better than to push.

'I'll see you at work on Monday,' she said as she saw him to the door.

'I'm still here for a while,' Dominic said.

'And then you won't be…'

'It doesn't mean we can't have a nice time.' If it sounded selfish, it wasn't entirely. He wanted to take her out, wanted to know her some more, wanted to spoil her perhaps.

'Like a holiday romance?' Bridgette asked.

'Hardly. I'm working sixty-plus hours a week,' he said to soften his offering, because, yes, a brief romance was the most he could ever commit to. But she hadn't said it with sarcasm. Instead she smiled, because a holiday romance sounded more doable. She certainly wasn't about to let go of her heart and definitely not to a man like him. A holiday romance maybe she could handle.

'I won't always be able to come out… I mean…' Bridgette warned.

'Let's just see.' He kissed the tip of her nose. 'Who knows, maybe your sister will get that job, after all, and move up to Bendigo.'

And you should be very careful what you wish for, Dominic soon realised, because a few days later Courtney did.

CHAPTER EIGHT

AT FIRST it was great. Out had come the silver dress, and he *had* taught her the flamenco—not that he knew how, but they'd had fun working it out.

In fact, with Courtney and Harry away, it had been Dominic who had found himself the one with scheduling problems.

'I'll get back to you within the hour.' There was a small curse of frustration as Dominic put down the phone and pulled out his laptop.

'Problem?' Bridgette asked.

'Mark Evans wants me to cover him till eleven a.m. I'm supposed to be picking up Chris from the airport then.' He pulled the airline page up. Chris had been missing his brother, and with Dominic unable to get away for a while, a compromise had been reached and Chris was coming down to Melbourne for the night. 'I'd say no to Mark except he's done me a lot of favours. I'll see if I can change his flight.'

'You could just ask me,' Bridgette said, unable to see the problem. 'Surely if Chris can fly on his own, he won't mind being met by a friend of his brother's.'

'You sure?'

'It's no big deal.'

To Dominic it was a big deal. Arabella would, he realised, have simply had Chris change his flight, which was maybe a bit unfair on her, because Arabella would have been at work too. Bridgette was, after all, not starting till later. 'What if the flight's delayed? It doesn't leave you much time to get to your shift as it is...'

'Then I'll ring work and explain that I'm delayed. What?' She misread his curious expression. 'You don't think I'd just leave him stranded?'

Chris's flight wasn't delayed. In fact, it landed a full ten minutes early and he had hand luggage only, which left plenty of time for a drink and something to eat at an airport café before she started her late shift. He told her all about his first time flying alone and then they drove back to Dominic's, getting there just as he arrived. There was no denying that the two brothers were pleased to see each other. 'Come over tonight if you want,' Dominic said, 'after your shift. We're just seeing an early movie so we could go out for something to eat if you like?'

'I'll give it a miss, thanks,' Bridgette said. 'I don't want to spoil your party and anyway I'm on an early shift tomorrow.' And he was always defensive around his brother yet not once did he think it was a snub. He knew Bridgette better than that—well, the part of Bridgette that she let him know. And he knew that she wouldn't even try to win points by hanging around to prove she was nothing like Arabella.

She *was* nothing like Arabella.

'See you, Chris.' She gave him a wave. 'Have a great night.'

'See you, Bridgette,' he said. 'Thanks for the cake.

'We went to a café,' Chris explained, when she had gone. 'Is that your girlfriend?'

'She's a friend,' Dominic said.

'Your girlfriend.' Chris grinned.

'Yeah, maybe,' Dominic admitted, 'but it's not as simple as that.' It wasn't and it was too hard to explain to himself let alone Chris.

There was a reason why holidays rarely lasted more than a few weeks—because any longer than that, you can't pretend there are no problems. You can't keep the real world on hold. Perhaps selfishly Dominic had wanted Courtney to leave, wanted to get to know a bit better the woman he had enjoyed dating, but once Chris had gone home, he realised that it wasn't the same Bridgette when Harry wasn't around. Over the next few days she couldn't get hold of Courtney and they were back to the morning after he'd met her—Bridgette constantly checking her phone. There was an anxiety to her that wasn't right.

He wanted the woman he'd found.

But Bridgette had that bright smile on, the one he had seen when they'd first met. She gave it to him the next Friday afternoon at work as she dropped off a new mum for a cuddle with her baby and he gave her his brief work nod back. Then she stopped by the incubator, as she often did, to speak with Carla.

'How are you?' she asked.

'Good today!' Carla smiled. 'Though it all depends on how Francesca is as to how I'm feeling at any moment, but today's been a good day. Do you want a peek?' There were drapes over the incubator and when she peeled them back Bridgette was thrilled by the change in the baby. She was still tiny, but her face was visible now, with far fewer tubes. It had been a precarious journey, it still was, but Francesca was still there, fighting.

'She gave us a fright last week,' Carla said. 'They thought she might need surgery on the Friday, but she settled over the weekend. Every day's a blessing still. I'm getting to hold her now—it's fantastic. Frank and I are fighting to take turns for a cuddle.'

It was lovely to see Francesca doing so well, but Bridgette's mind was on other things as she walked back to the ward, and she didn't hear Dominic till he was at her side.

'Hi.' He fell into step beside her. Not exactly chatty, he never was at work, but today neither was she. 'How's your shift?'

'Long,' she admitted. 'Everything's really quiet— I'm waiting for a baby boom.' She smiled when she saw Mary walking towards them.

'We're missing that little man of yours,' Mary said. 'How is he doing?'

'He's fine,' Bridgette said, expecting Dominic to walk on when she stopped to talk to Mary, but instead he stood there with them. 'I am sorry to have given you such short notice.'

'Hardly your fault.' Mary gave her a smile. 'You'd be missing him too?'

Bridgette gave a nod. 'A bit,' she admitted, 'but they should be home soon for a visit.'

'That's good.' Mary bustled off and Bridgette stood, suddenly awkward.

'Have you heard from her?'

Bridgette shook her head. 'I tried to ring but couldn't get through—I think she's out of credit for her phone.

Right.' She gave a tight smile. 'I'm going to head for home.'

'I should be finished soon,' Dominic said. 'And then I'm back here tomorrow for the weekend.' He gave her a wry grin. 'Some holiday romance.'

'We can go out tonight,' Bridgette offered. 'Or sleep.'

'Nope,' Dominic said, 'we can go out and then...' He gave her that nice private smile. 'Why don't you head over to mine?' he asked, because there were cafés a stone's throw away, unlike Bridgette's flat.

'Sure,' Bridgette said, because she couldn't face pizza again and the flat still hadn't been tidied. The cot was down, but stood taking up half the wall in her spare bedroom, which made it an obstacle course to get to the computer.

Next weekend she was off for four days and she *was* going to sort it.

Bridgette let herself into his flat, and wondered how someone who worked his ridiculous hours managed to keep the place so tidy. Yes, he'd told her he had someone who came in once a week, and she knew he did, but it wasn't just the cleaner, Bridgette knew. He was a tidy person, an ordered person.

Knew what he wanted, where his life was going.

She had a little snoop, to verify her findings. Yes, the dishes were done and stacked in the dishwasher; the lid was on the toothpaste and it was back in its little glass. She peered into the bedroom—okay, it wasn't exactly hospital corners, but the cover had been pulled back up. She wandered back to his lounge and over to his desk.

There was a pile of mail waiting for him, one a very thick envelope, from that exclusive hospital where he wanted to work, but it was too much to think about and she had a shower instead. Then she pulled on a black skirt with a pale grey top, because an awful lot of her clothes seemed to live here now. The outfit would look okay with ballet pumps or high heels—wherever the night might lead.

It was a holiday romance, Bridgette kept telling herself to make sense of it, and summer was coming to an end. The clock would change soon and in a couple of weeks it would be dark by now. She felt as if she were chasing the last fingers of the sun, just knew things were changing. Oh, she'd been blasé with Mary, didn't want to tell anyone what was in the bottom of her heart, that things were building, that at any moment now the phone would ring and it would all have gone to pot.

'Sorry about that...' He came in through the door much later than expected and gave her a very haphazard kiss as he looked at his watch and picked up his mail. He didn't want her to ask what the hold-up had been, didn't want her to know the scare little Francesca had given him just a short while before. He had twelve hours off before a weekend on call and he needed every moment of it, but first... 'I've got to take a phone call.'

'No problem.'

'Hey,' Dominic said when his phone rang promptly at seven-thirty. 'How are you?'

'Good,' Chris said, and got straight to the point. 'When are you coming back to Sydney?' Chris was growing impatient. 'It's been ages since you were here.'

And Dominic took a deep breath and told him the news he hadn't really had time to think about, let alone share with Bridgette. 'I got a phone call today, an—' he didn't want to say too much at this early stage '—I'm coming home for a few days next weekend. We'll go out then.'

'It's been ages.'

'I know,' Dominic said, and he knew how much his brother missed him, but he tried to talk him around, to move the conversation to other things. 'What are you doing tonight?'

'A party,' Chris said, and normally he'd have given him details as to who was going, the music that would be played, what they were eating, but instead he had a question. 'Bridgette *is* your girlfriend, isn't she?'

And normally Dominic would have laughed, would have made Chris laugh with an answer like 'One of them', but instead he hesitated. 'Yes.'

And usually they would have chatted for a bit—until Chris's Friday night kicked off and he was called out to come and join the party, but instead Chris was far from happy and told Dominic that he had to go and then asked another question.

'When are you properly coming back?'

'I've told you—I'm coming back soon for a few days,' Dominic said.

It wasn't, from Chris's gruff farewell, a very good answer.

'Right.' He came out of his room and saw that Bridgette was writing a note. 'Finally… Let's go and get something to eat. I've still got the sound of babies crying ringing in my ears.'

'Actually—' she turned '—my sister just called.' Back on went that smile. 'Things didn't work out in Bendigo and she's back. She's a bit upset and she's asked if I can have Harry tonight. I called and asked my parents, but they're out.'

'Oh.' He tried to be logical. After all, apart from one time in the corridor he'd never even seen Harry, and if her sister was upset, well, she needed to go. And even if more children was the last thing he needed tonight, she really had helped out with Chris and, yes, he did want to see her. 'We can take him out with us.'

'It's nearly eight o'clock,' Bridgette said, though when Harry was with her sister his bedtime was erratic at best.

'It's the Spaniard in me,' Dominic said.

Courtney, Dominic thought as he sat in the passenger seat while Bridgette collected Harry, didn't look that upset. But he said nothing as Bridgette drove. They'd gone out in her car because of baby seats and things, but they drove along to the area near his house and parked. It was cool but still light as they walked. She felt more than a little awkward. Walking along, pushing a stroller on a Friday night with Dominic felt terribly strange.

They sat out in a nice pavement café. They were spoiled for choice, but settled for Spanish and ate tapas. It was a lovely evening, but it was cool, even for summer. For Bridgette it was made extra bearable by one of Dominic's black turtlenecks and a big gas heater blazing above them. It was nice to sit outside and Harry seemed content, especially as Bridgette fed him *crema catalana*. Dominic had suggested it, a sort of cold custard with a caramel top, and Harry was loving his first Spanish dessert, but the mood wasn't as relaxed as it usually was. Dominic was lovely to Harry, there was no question about that, but Bridgette knew this wasn't quite the night he'd had planned.

'So, what's Courtney upset about?' He finally broached the subject

'I didn't really ask.'

'Does she do this a lot?'

Bridgette shot him a glance. 'It's one night, Dominic. I'm sorry for the invasion.' She was brittle in her defence and he assumed she was comparing him with Paul. She changed the subject. 'Have you been to Spain?'

'We used to go there in the summer holidays,' Dominic said. 'Well, their winter,' he clarified, because in Australia summer meant Christmas time. 'My father had a lot of social things on at that time, you know, what with work, so Chris and I would stay with Abuela.'

'And your mum?' Bridgette asked.

Dominic gave her an old-fashioned look, then a wry grin. 'Nope, she stayed here, looking stunning next to Dad. And I spent a year there when I finished school. I still want to go back, maybe work there for a couple of years at some point. It's an amazing place.'

And there were two conversations going on, as she ate thick black olives and fried baby squid, and he dipped bread in the most delicious lime hummus, and Harry, full up on the custard, fell asleep.

'I'd better get him back.'

They walked back along the beach road, a crowded beach full of Friday night fun, except Dominic was pensive. He was trying to remember the world before Chris had come along and Bridgette was for once quiet too.

She drove him back to his place. Harry was still asleep, and she didn't want to wake him up by coming in. Dominic had to be at work tomorrow, so there was no way really he could stay at hers.

And they kissed in the car, but it was different this time.

'Not your usual Friday night,' she said. 'Home by ten, alone!'

He didn't argue—she was, after all, speaking the truth.

CHAPTER NINE

RATHER than change things, the situation brought what was already coming to a head.

Dominic didn't know how best to broach what was on his mind.

He was used to straight talking, but on this Tuesday morning, lying in bed with Bridgette warm and asleep beside him, he didn't know where to start. He'd been putting this discussion off for a couple of days now, which wasn't at all like him.

'Hey, Bridgette.' He turned and rolled into her, felt her sleepy body start to wake, and he was incredibly tempted to forget what had been on his mind a few seconds ago and to concentrate instead on what was on his mind now. 'When do you finish?'

'Mmm…?' She didn't want questions, didn't want to think about anything other than the delicious feel of Dominic behind her. She could feel his mouth nuzzling the back of her neck and she wanted to just sink into the sensations he so readily provided, to let him make love to her, but automatically she reached for the phone that was on her bedside drawer, checked there were no messages she had missed and frowned at how early it was—it wasn't even six a.m.

'It's not even six,' she grumbled, because they hadn't got to bed till one—an evening spent watching movies and eating chocolate, laughing and making love, because neither wanted to talk properly.

'I know that you're off next weekend, but when do you actually finish?'

'I've got a long weekend starting Thursday at three p.m. precisely.' She wriggled at the pleasurable thought. 'I'm not back till Wednesday when I start nights. Why?'

'Just thinking.'

Though he didn't want to think at the moment, it could surely wait for now, Dominic decided, because his hands were at her breasts, and how he loved them, and her stomach and her round bottom. She was the first woman he loved waking up with.

It was a strange admission for him, but he usually loathed chatter in the morning. Arabella had driven him mad then too.

'Do you want coffee?' Arabella would ask every morning.

It was just the most pointless question.

Okay, maybe not for a one-nighter, but two years on, had she really needed to start each day with the same?

He looked at Bridgette's back, at the millions of freckles, and she was the one woman who could make him smile even in her sleep. 'Do you want coffee?' he said to a dozing Bridgette.

'What do you think?' she mumbled, and then… 'What's so funny?' she asked as he laughed and his mouth met her neck.

'Nothing.'

'So what are you lying there thinking about?'

'Nothing.'

'Dominic?'

He hesitated for an interminable second, his lips hovering over her neck and his hand still on her breast. 'I've been invited for an informal interview.' He was back at her neck and kissing it deeply. 'Very informal. It's just a look around…'

'In Sydney?'

Her eyes that had been closed opened then. She'd sort of known this was coming. He'd always said he wanted to work there; they'd been seeing each other just a few short weeks and there had been that envelope she'd peeked at.

'Yep—there's a position coming up, but not till next year. It's all very tentative at this stage—they just want me to come and have a look around, a few introductions…'

'That's good.'

And that wasn't the hard bit.

They both knew it and they lay there in silence.

Like an injury that didn't hurt unless you applied pressure, they'd danced around this issue from day one, avoided it, but they couldn't keep doing that for ever.

'Come with me,' he said. 'We could have a nice weekend. You could use the break before you start nights.'

She didn't want to think about it.

Didn't want to think about him going to Sydney, and there was still something else to discuss. Bridgette knew that, and Dominic knew it too.

There was a conversation to be had but it was easier to turn around, to press her lips into his. 'Bridgette…' Dominic pulled back. 'It would be great.' He gave her a smile. 'I won't inflict my family on you.'

'What?' She tried to smile back. 'You'll put me in some fancy hotel?'

'We'll be staying at my flat,' Dominic said—and there it was, the fact that he owned a flat in Sydney but he was only renting here. He had a cleaner there, coming in weekly to take care of things while he was temporarily away. 'Bridgette, you've known from the start that was where I was going.'

'I know that.'

'It's only an hour's flight away.'

She nodded, because his words made sense, perfect sense—it was just a teeny flight, after all—but her life wasn't geared to hopping on planes.

'Look,' Dominic said, 'let's just have a weekend away. Let's not think about things for a while. I'll book flights. The interview will be a morning at most. I'll see Chris...'

And so badly she wanted to say yes, to say what the hell, and hop onto a plane, to swim in the ocean, shop and see the sights, to stay in the home of the man she adored, but... 'I can't.'

'You've got days off,' Dominic pointed out.

'I really need to sort out my flat.' She did. 'I've been putting it off for ages.'

'I know,' Dominic said. 'Look, why don't I come round a couple of nights in the week and help with those shelves?'

'You!' She actually laughed. 'Will you bring your drill?' She saw his tongue roll in his cheek. 'Bring your stud finder...' she said, and dug him in the ribs. He would be as hopeless as her, Dominic realised. After all, his dad had never been one for DIY—he wouldn't know how to change a washer. But it wasn't the shelves that were the real problem. Yes, it would be so much easier to talk about stud finders, to laugh and to roll into each other as they wanted to, but instead he asked her again.

'If I can't do it—' he had visions of her being knocked unconscious in the night by his handiwork '—then I will get someone in and those shelves will be put up on your return,' he said. 'But it really would be nice to go away.'

'I can't,' she said, because she simply could not bear to be so far away from Harry. Courtney's silence was worrying her and it couldn't be ignored; also, she couldn't bear to get any closer to Dominic. To open up her heart again—especially to a man who would soon be moving away.

'Look, I have to go back this weekend.'

'Go, then!' Bridgette said. 'I'm not stopping you. I'm just saying that I can't come.'

'You could!' he said. He could see the dominos all lined up, so many times he'd halted them from falling, and he was halting them now, because when talking didn't work he tried to kiss sense into her. She could feel her breasts flatten against his chest and the heady male scent of him surrounding her, and she kissed him back ferociously. It was as close as they had come to a row: they were going to have a row in a moment and she truly didn't want one, knew that neither did he. This way was easier, this way was better, this simply had to happen, because somehow they both knew it was the last time.

He kissed her face and her ears, he pushed her knees apart and they were well past condoms now. He slid into her tight warmth, went to the only place she would come with him and she did. They both did.

It was a regretful orgasm, if there was such a thing,

because it meant it was over. It meant they had to climb back out of the place where things were so simple.

'I think a weekend away would be great.' He tried again. He'd heard the first click of the dominos falling and still he was trying to halt them. 'I think we need to get away. Look, if you don't want to go to Sydney...' He didn't want to let down Chris, didn't want to reschedule the interview, but he didn't want things to end here. He wanted to give them a chance. 'We could drive. There's a few places I want to see along the coast...'

'I can't this weekend,' she said. 'I told you, I've got the flat to sort out. Courtney's still upset...'

'Well, when can you?' And he let them fall. 'I want to get away on my days off.' He really did—it had been a helluva weekend at work. He wanted to be as far away from the hospital as possible this next weekend, didn't want to be remotely available, because he knew that if they called, he'd go in. What was he thinking, driving to the coast when he had an interview, letting down Chris? For what? So that they could stay in and wait for her sister to ring?

'Look, I know you help out your sister...' He simply did not understand her. In so many things they were open, there were so many things they discussed, but really he knew so little about her. There was still a streak of hurt in her eyes, still a wall of silence around her. 'But surely you can have a weekend off.'

'Maybe I don't want one,' Bridgette said. 'Maybe I don't want to go up to Sydney and to see the life you'll soon be heading back to.'

'Bridgette...' He was trying to prolong things, not end them. 'I don't get you.'

'You're not supposed to, that's not what we're about.'

It wasn't, she told herself. It was supposed to be just a few short weeks—a break, a romance, that was all. It was better over with now. 'Just go to Sydney,' Bridgette said. 'That's what you want, that's where you've always been heading. Don't try and blame us ending on Harry.'

'I'm not blaming Harry,' Dominic said, and he wasn't. 'I'll admit I was a bit fed up with his aunt on Friday.'

'Sorry to mess up your night.' She so wasn't going to do this again. 'God, you're just like—'

'Don't say it, Bridgette,' Dominic warned, 'because I am nothing like him.' He'd heard a bit about her ex and wasn't about to be compared to Paul. 'I'll tell you one of the differences between him and me. I'd have had this sorted from the start. Your sister's using you, Bridgette.' He looked at her, all tousled and angry, and truly didn't know what this was about.

'Do you think I don't know that?'

'So why do you let her?' He gave an impatient shake of his head. 'Do you know, I think you hide behind Harry. He's your excuse not to go out, not to get away.' Bridgette was right, Sydney *was* where he'd always intended to be—that was his hospital of choice and he wasn't about to have his career dictated to by Courtney.

'I'm going for the interview. I'm flying out on Thursday night. I'll text you the flight times. We'll be back Sunday night.'

'Don't book a ticket for me,' Bridgette said. 'Because I can't go.'

'Yes, you can. And, yes, I am booking for you,' Dominic said. 'So you've plenty time to change your mind.'

He did book the tickets.

But he knew she wouldn't come.

CHAPTER TEN

'SORRY to call you down from NICU.' Rebecca, the accident and emergency registrar, looked up from the notes she was writing. It was four a.m. on Tuesday morning. It had been a long day for Dominic and a very long night on call. After the interviews in Sydney and long walks on the beach with Chris, his head felt as if it was exploding, not that Rebecca could have guessed it. He was his usual practical self. 'I'm trying to stall Mum by saying we're waiting for an X-ray.'

'No problem. What do we know so far?'

'Well, the story is actually quite consistent—Mum heard a bang and found him on the floor. He'd climbed out if his cot, which fits the injury. She said that he was crying by the time she went in to him. It was her reaction that was strange—complete panic, called an ambulance. She was hysterical when she arrived but she's calmed down.'

'Are there any other injuries you can see?'

'A couple of small bruises, an ear infection, he's a bit grubby and there's a bit of nappy rash,' Rebecca said, 'but he is a toddler, after all. Anyway, I'm just not happy and I thought you should take a look.' She handed him the patient card and as Dominic noted the name, as his stomach seemed to twist in on itself, a young woman called from the cubicle.

'How much longer are we going to be waiting here?' She peered out and all Dominic could think was that if he had not recognised the name, it would never have entered his head that this woman was Bridgette's sister. She had straggly dyed blond hair and was much skinnier. Her features were sharper than Bridgette's and even if she wasn't shouting, she was such an angry young thing, so hostile in her actions, so on the edge, that she was, Dominic recognised in an instant, about to explode any moment. 'How much longer till he gets his X-ray or CT or whatever?'

'There's another doctor here to take a look at Harry,' Helga, the charge nurse, calmly answered. 'He'll be in with you shortly—it won't be long.'

'Well, can someone watch him while I get a coffee at least?' Courtney snapped. 'Why can't I take it in the cubicle?'

'You can't take a hot drink—' Helga started, but Dominic interrupted.

'Courtney, why don't you go and get a coffee? Someone will sit with your son while you take a little break.

'Is that okay?' He checked with Helga and she sent in a student nurse, but Rebecca was too sharp not to notice that he had known the name of the patient's mother. 'You know her?' She grimaced as Courtney flounced out, because this sort of thing was always supremely awkward.

'I know his aunt.' Dominic was sparse with his reply but Helga filled in for him.

'Bridgette. She's a midwife on Maternity. She's on

her way. I called her a little while ago—Courtney was in a right panic when she arrived and she asked us to.'

'Okay.' Dominic tried not to think about Bridgette taking that phone call—he had to deal with this without emotion, had to step out and look at the bigger picture. 'I'm going to step aside.' He came to the only decision he could in such a situation. 'I'm going to ring Greg Andrews and ask him to take over the patient, but first I need to take a look at Harry and make sure that there's nothing medically urgent that needs to be dealt with.' His colleague might take a while. He did not engage in further small talk; he did not need to explain his involvement in the case. After all, he was stepping aside. Dominic walked into the cubicle where Harry lay resting in a cot with a student nurse by his side. Rebecca came in with him.

'Good morning, Harry.' He took off his jacket and hung it on the peg and proceeded to wash his hands and then made his way over to the young patient. He looked down into dark grey eyes that stared back at him and they reminded him of Bridgette's. He could see the hurt behind them and Dominic did not try to win a smile. 'I expect you're feeling pretty miserable? Well, I'm just going to take a look at you.' Gently he examined the toddler, looking in his ears for any signs of bleeding, and Harry let him, hardly even blinking as he shone the ophthalmoscope into the back of each eye, not even crying or flinching as Dominic gently examined the tender bruise. Through it all Harry didn't say a word. 'Has he spoken since he came here?' Dominic asked

'Not much—he's asked for a drink.' The curtains opened then and Helga walked in. Behind her was

Bridgette, her face as white as chalk, but she smiled to Harry.

'Hey.' She stroked his little cheek. 'I hear you've been in the wars.' She spoke ever so gently to him, but her eyes were everywhere, lifting the blanket and checking him carefully, even undoing his nappy, and he saw her jaw tighten at the rash.

'How is he?'

'He just gave everyone a fright!' Helga said, but Bridgette's eyes went to Dominic's.

'Could I have a quick word, Bridgette?'

He stepped outside the cubicle and she joined him.

'He's filthy,' Bridgette said. She could feel tears rising up, felt as if she was choking, so angry was she with her sister. 'And he didn't have any rash when I saw him on Friday. I bought loads of cream that she took—'

'Bridgette,' he interrupted, 'I'm handing Harry's care over to a colleague. You will need to tell him all this. It's not appropriate that I'm involved. You understand that?' She gave a brief nod but her attention was diverted by the arrival of her sister, and he watched as Bridgette strode off and practically marched Courtney out towards the waiting room.

'I'll go.' Helga was more than used to confrontations such as this and called to the nurses' station over her shoulder as she followed the two sisters out. 'Just let Security know we might need them.'

And this was what Courtney had reduced her to, Bridgette thought, standing outside the hospital early in the morning, with security guards hovering. But Bridgette was too angry to keep quiet.

'He climbed out of his cot!' Courtney was immediately on the defensive the moment they were outside.

'I didn't know that he climbed. You should have told me.' Maybe it was a good idea that security guards were present because hearing Courtney try to blame her for this had Bridgette's blood boiling.

'He's never once climbed out of the cot when I've had him,' Bridgette answered hotly. 'Mind you, he was probably trying to get out and change his own nappy or make himself a drink, or give himself a wash. You lazy, selfish…' She stopped herself then because if she said any more, it would be way too much. She paused and Helga stepped in, took Courtney inside, and Bridgette stood there hugging her arms around herself tightly, mortified when Dominic came out.

'This has nothing to do with you,' Bridgette said, still angry. 'You've stepped aside.'

'You know I had to.'

She did know that.

'Is this why you couldn't get away?' Dominic asked, and she didn't answer, because a simple yes would have been a lie. 'Bridgette?'

'I don't want to talk about it.'

'You never do,' he pointed out, but now really wasn't the time. 'I know that it doesn't seem like it now,' Dominic said, 'but Harry being admitted might be the best thing that could have happened. Things might get sorted now.'

As an ambulance pulled up she gave a nod, even if she didn't believe it.

'Bridgette, I was actually going to come over and see you today,' Dominic said, and she knew what was coming. 'I didn't want you to hear it from anyone else—I've just given notice. I'm leaving on Saturday.' He chose not to tell her just how impossible the decision had been, but in the end it had surely been the right one—he wanted simple, straightforward, and Bridgette was anything but. He'd opened up to her more than he had with anyone, and yet he realised that, still, despite his question, he knew very little about her and even now she said nothing. 'Anyway, I thought I should tell you myself.'

'Sure.'

'I'd better get up to…' His voice stopped, his stomach tightened, as the ambulance door opened and he met Tony's frantic eyes.

CHAPTER ELEVEN

DOMINIC checked himself, because it should make no difference that it wasn't Esperanza on the stretcher. Instead it was Roman, their three-year-old, and he needed Dominic's help and concentration just as much as his little sister would have. 'Dr Mansfield's here…' Tony was talking reassuringly to his son, who was struggling hard to breathe as they moved him straight into the critical area. 'The doctor who looked after Esperanza. That's good news.'

'He did this last year…' Tony said as Dominic examined him, and Tony explained about his severe asthma. 'He does it a lot, but last year he ended up in Intensive Care.'

'Okay.' Dominic listened to his chest and knew that Roman would probably have to head to Intensive Care again this morning.

Roman took up all of Dominic's morning, but by lunchtime, when he'd spoken to the family and the frantic *abuela*, things were a little calmer.

'While he's still needing hourly nebulisers it's safer that he is here,' Dominic explained, but then it was easier to speak in Spanish, so that Abuela understood. He told them things were steadily improving and would continue to do so.

Tony rang Maria, who was of course frantic, and Dominic spoke to her too.

'You get a taxi home,' Tony said to Abuela, 'and Maria can come in between feeds.'

Writing up his drug sheets, Dominic listened for a moment as they worked out a vague plan of action, heard that Tony would ring his boss and take today off.

'You think he might go to the ward tomorrow?'

'Or this evening.' Dominic nodded.

'I'll stay with him tonight and if you can come in in the morning to be with Roman I can go to work tomorrow,' Tony said to his mother. She rattled the start of twenty questions at him, but Tony broke in.

'We'll deal with that if it happens.'

Dominic headed down to the children's ward. Bridgette wasn't around and neither was Courtney. An extra layer had been added to Harry's cot, in case he was, in fact, a climber, and it stood like a tall cage in the middle of the nursery. He walked in and took off his jacket, washed his hands and then turned round and looked straight into the waiting grey eyes of Harry, who wasn't his patient, he reminded himself.

Harry's head injury wasn't at all serious, but he had been moved up to the children's ward mid-morning. Bridgette knew it was more of a social admission. Maybe she had done rather too good a job of reassuring her parents that it wasn't serious when she rang them, because they didn't dash in. After all, her father had to have a filling that afternoon, so they said they would come in the evening and, with a weary sigh, her mother agreed, yes, they would stop by Bridgette's flat and bring a change of clothes, pyjamas and toiletries.

Bridgette took the opportunity to voice a few of her concerns about his speech delay with the doctor and he gave her a sort of blink when she spoke about Harry's fixation with bricks and that he didn't talk much.

'Has he had his hearing checked?'

'Er, no.'

'He's had a few ear infections, though,' Dr Andrews said, peering through his examination notes. 'We'll get his hearing tested and then he might need an ENT out-patient appointment.'

Later they were interviewed by a social worker, but by dinnertime Courtney had had enough. 'I'm exhausted,' she said. 'I was up all night with him. I think I'll go home and get some sleep.'

'We can put a bed up beside his cot,' a nurse offered.

'I'd never sleep with all the noise,' Courtney said, gave Harry a brief kiss and then she was gone, safe in the knowledge that Bridgette would stay the night. Dominic was on the ward when Bridgette's parents arrived, talking with the charge nurse. She saw him glance up when her mother asked to be shown where Harry was.

'Here, Mum,' Bridgette said as they made their way over, all nervous smiles, slightly incredulous that their grandson was actually here.

'Here's the bits you wanted,' her mum said, handing over a bag.

Bridgette peered into the bag and flinched. 'Did you deliberately choose the ugliest pyjamas I own?' She grinned. 'I'd forgotten that I even had these!' They were orange flannelette, emblazoned with yellow flowers, and had been sent by her granny about five years ago.

'You're lucky I could find anything in *that* room!' Betty said. 'I could barely see the bed.'

Yes, she really must get organised, Bridgette remembered. Somehow she had not got around to it last weekend. She had either been worrying about Harry or mooching over Dominic. Well, Dominic was gone or going and Harry would be sorted, so she would get organised soon.

'So what is he in for?' Maurice asked. 'He looks fine.'

He certainly looked a whole lot better. He'd had a bath and hair wash and had a ton of cream on his bottom. There was just a very small bruise on his head.

'He didn't even need a stitch,' Betty said.

'You know why he's in, Mum.'

'For nappy rash!' Betty wasn't having it.

'Mum… He's getting his hearing tested tomorrow.' They were less than impressed. 'Aren't you going to ask where Courtney is?'

'Getting some well-deserved rest,' Betty hissed. 'She must have had the fright of her life last night.' They didn't stay very long. They fussed over Harry for half an hour or so and it was a very weary Bridgette who tried to get Harry off to sleep.

'How's he doing?' Dominic asked as she stood and rubbed Harry's back.

'Fine,' Bridgette said, and then conceded, as she really wasn't angry with him, 'he's doing great. We're going for a hearing test tomorrow. Dr Andrews said we should check out the basics.' Of course he said nothing. He was his 'at work' Dominic and so he didn't fill in the gaps. 'I thought he was autistic or something.' She gave a small shrug. 'Well, he might be. I mean, if he is, he is…'

'You nurses.'

'You'd be the same,' Bridgette said, 'if he was…' Except Harry wasn't his and he wasn't hers either and it was too hard to voice so she gave him the smile that said keep away.

She washed in the one shower available for parents, an ancient old thing at the edge of the parents' room, and pulled on the awful pyjamas her parents had brought and climbed into the roller bed at seven-thirty p.m., grateful that the lights were already down. But she found out that Courtney was right—it was far too noisy to sleep. When she was woken again by a nurse doing obs around ten and by a baby coughing in the next cot, she wandered down to the parents' room to get a drink and nearly jumped out of her skin to see Dominic sprawled out on a sofa.

He'd changed out of his suit, which was rare for him, and was wearing scrubs, and looked, for once, almost scruffy—unshaven and the hair that fell so neatly wasn't falling at all neatly now.

'Good God.' He peeled open his eyes when she walked in.

'Don't you judge me by my pyjamas,' Bridgette said, heading over to the kitchenette. 'I was just thinking you weren't looking so hot yourself—what happened to that smooth-looking man I met?'

'You did.' Dominic rolled his eyes and sort of heaved himself up. He sat there and she handed him a coffee without asking if he wanted one. 'Thanks.' He looked over at her. 'Bridgette, why didn't you say you were worried about Harry?'

'And worry you too? I haven't been ignoring things. I reported my concerns a few months ago, but I think I might have made things worse. I thought she was on drugs, that that was why she was always disappearing, but they did a screen and she's not. He's always been well looked after. Even now, he's just missed a couple of baths.' It was so terribly hard to explain it. 'They lived with me for nearly nine months, right up till Harry's first birthday.' She missed the frown on Dominic's face. 'And it was me who got up at night, did most of the laundry and bathing and changing. I just somehow know that she isn't coping on her own. Which is why I drop everything when she needs help. I don't really want to test my theories as to what might happen to Harry...'

'You could have told me this.'

'Not really holiday-romance stuff.'

'You've not exactly given us a chance to be anything more.'

'It's not always men who don't want a relationship,' Bridgette said. 'I always knew you were going back to Sydney and that I would stay here. It suited me better to keep it as it was.

'How was your weekend?' she asked, frantically changing the subject. 'How was Chris?'

'Great,' Dominic said. 'It's his twenty-first birthday this weekend, so he's getting all ready for that. Gangster party!' He gave a wry smile. 'I'm flying back up for that.'

'Have fun!' She grinned and didn't add that she'd love to be his moll, and he didn't say that he'd love it if she could be, and then his phone rang.

He checked it but didn't answer and Bridgette stood there, her cheeks darkening as Arabella's image flashed up on the screen.

'Well…' She turned away, tipped her coffee down the sink.

'Bridgette…'

'It doesn't matter anyway.'

Except it did.

He had seen Arabella—she'd found out he was back for the weekend and had come around. He'd opened the door to her and had surprised himself with how little he'd felt.

It would be easier to have felt something, to have gone back to his perfect life and pretend he believed she hadn't meant what she'd said about Chris. Easier than what he was contemplating.

'Bridgette, she came over. We had a coffee.'

'I don't want to hear it.' She really didn't, but she was angry too. It had been the day from hell and was turning into the night from hell too. 'It's been less than a week…' She didn't understand how it was so easy for some people to get over things. She was still desperately trying to get over Paul: not him exactly, more what he had done. And in some arguments you said things that perhaps weren't true, but you said them anyway.

'You're all the bloody same!'

'Hey!' He would not take that. 'I told you, we had coffee.'

'Sure.'

'And I told you, don't ever compare me to him.' He was sick of being compared to a man he hadn't met, a man who had caused her nothing but pain. 'I told you I'd have had this sorted.'

'Sure you would have.'

And in some arguments you said things that perhaps were true, but should never be said. 'And,' Dominic added, regretting it the second he said it, 'I'd never have slept with your sister.'

Her face looked as if it had been dunked in a bucket of bleach, the colour just stripped out of it. 'And you look after her kid—' Dominic could hardly contain the fury he felt on her behalf '—after the way she treated you?'

'How?' She had never been so angry, ashamed that he knew. 'Did Vince tell you? Did Jasmine tell him?' She was mortified. 'Does the whole hospital know?'

'I know,' Dominic said, 'because most people talk about their break-ups, most people share that bit at the start, but instead you keep yourself closed. I worked it out,' he explained. 'Courtney and Paul both happened to move out around Harry's first birthday...'

'Just leave it.'

'Why?'

'Because...' she said. 'I kicked my sister out, which meant I effectively kicked my nephew out, and look what it's been like since then.'

'Bridgette—'

'No.' She did not want his comfort, neither did she want his rationale, nor did she want to stand here and explain to him the hurt. 'Are you going to stay here? Tell me we should fight for Harry?' She just looked at him and gave a mocking laugh. 'You don't want kids of your own, let alone your girlfriend's nephew.' She shook her head. 'Your holiday fling's nephew.'

And he didn't want it, Dominic realised, and did that make him shallow? He did not want the drama that was

Courtney and he did not want a woman who simply refused to talk about what was clearly so important.

'I'm going back,' Bridgette said. 'You can take your phone call now.'

And two minutes later he did.

She knew because she heard the buzz of his phone as she stood in the corridor outside, trying to compose herself enough to head out to the ward.

She heard his low voice through the wall and there was curious relief as she walked away.

She was as lousy at one-night stands as she was at holiday romances.

There was only one guy on her mind right now, and he stood in the cot, waiting patiently for her return.

'Hey, Harry.' She picked him up and gave him a cuddle, and as Dominic walked past she deliberately didn't look up; instead she concentrated on her nephew, pulling back the sheets and laying him down.

It felt far safer hiding behind him.

CHAPTER TWELVE

COURTNEY rang in the morning to see how Harry's night had been and said that she'd be in soon. Bridgette went with Harry for his hearing test and then surprisingly Raymond, the ENT consultant, came and saw him on the ward. 'Glue ear,' Raymond informed her. 'His hearing is significantly down in both ears, which would explain the speech delay. It can make them very miserable. We'll put him on the waiting list for grommets.' It might explain the temper tantrums too, Bridgette thought, kicking herself for overreaction.

By late afternoon, when Courtney still hadn't arrived and Harry was dozing, Bridgette slipped away and up to Maternity, even though she'd rung to explain things. Rita *was* nice and surprisingly understanding.

'We're having a family meeting tomorrow,' Bridgette explained. 'I really am sorry to let you down. I'll do nights just as soon as I can.'

'Don't be sorry—of course you can't work,' Rita said. 'You need to get this sorted.'

Though her family seemed convinced there was nothing to sort, and as Bridgette walked onto the ward, she could see Courtney sitting on the chair beside Harry, all smiles. She was playing the doting mother or 'mother of the year', as Jasmine would have said. Dominic was examining Harry's new neighbor, young Roman, and Bridgette stood and spoke to Tony for a moment. Harry, annoyed that Bridgette wasn't coming straight over, stood up, put up his leg and with two fat fists grabbed the cot, annoyed that with the barrier he couldn't get over it—he was indeed a climber, it was duly noted, not just by the nurses but by Courtney. And Bridgette wondered if she was going mad. Maybe there was nothing wrong with her sister's parenting and she, Bridgette, had been talking nonsense all along.

'Thanks so much for staying last night,' Courtney said. 'I was just completely exhausted. I'd been up all night with him teething. Mum said that that can give them the most terrible rash…and then when he climbed out, when I heard him fall…'

'No problem,' Bridgette said. 'ENT came down and saw him.'

'Yes, the nurse told me,' Courtney said, and rather pointedly unzipped her bag and took out her pyjamas. Brand-new ones, Bridgette noticed. Courtney was very good at cleaning up her act when required. 'You should get some rest, Bridgette.' Courtney looked up and her eyes held a challenge that Bridgette knew she simply couldn't win. 'You look exhausted. I'm sure I'll see you at the family meeting and you will have plenty to say about his nappy rash and that I put him to bed without washing him to Aunty Bridgette's satisfaction.'

Dominic saw Courtney's smirk after Bridgette had kissed Harry and left.

He spoke for a moment with Tony, told him he would see him tomorrow. And Dominic, a man who always stayed late, left early for once and met Bridgette at her car. It wouldn't start, because in her rush to get to see Harry last night, she'd left her lights on.

'Just leave me.' She was crying, furious, enraged, and did not want him to see.

'I'll give you a lift.'

'So I can sort out a flat battery tomorrow! So I can take a bus to the meeting.' She even laughed. 'They'll think I'm the one with the problem. She's in there all kisses and smiles and new pyjamas. She'll be taking him home this time tomorrow.'

'She'll blow herself out soon,' Dominic said.

'And it will start all over again.' She turned the key one last hopeless time and of course nothing happened.

'Come on,' Dominic said. 'I'll take you home.'

They drove for a while in silence. Dominic never carried tissues, but very graciously he gave her the little bit of silk he used to clean his sunglasses. With little other option, she took it.

'I do get it.'

'Sure!'

'No, I really do,' Dominic said. 'For three years after Chris was born it was row after row. My father wanted him gone—he never came out and said it, didn't have the guts, and I can tell you the day it changed, I can tell you the minute it changed.' He snapped his fingers as he drove. 'My mother told him to get out because Chris wasn't going anywhere. She told him if he stayed in *her* home then he followed her rules.' They were at the roundabout and she wanted him to indicate, wanted to go back to his place, but instead he drove straight on. 'She got her fire back.' He even grinned as he remembered his trophy-wife mother suddenly swearing and cursing in Spanish. He remembered the drama as she'd filled his father's suitcases and hurled them out, followed by his golf clubs, as she picked up Chris and walked back in. 'I really want you to listen, Bridgette. You need to think about what you want before you go into that meeting. You will need to sort out what you're prepared to offer or what you're prepared to accept, not for the next week or for the next month but maybe the next seventeen years—you need to do the best for yourself.'

'I'm trying my best.'

'Bridgette, you're not listening to me. My mum could have gone along with Dad—she could have had a far easier life if she hadn't been a single mum bringing up a special-needs child. Chris could have been slotted into a home. Instead he went to one when he was eighteen, to a sheltered home with friends, and my mother did it so that he'd have a life, a real one. She did not want him to have to start over in thirty years or so when she was gone. She thought out everything and that included looking out for herself. What I said was you have to do the best for you—you have to look out for yourself in this...'

Dominic gritted his teeth in frustration as he could see that she didn't understand what he meant and knew that he would have to make things clear. 'The best thing that could happen is that Courtney suddenly becomes responsible and gets well suddenly, becomes responsible and looks after Harry properly—and we both know that's not going to happen. Now, you can run yourself ragged chasing after Courtney, living your life ready to step in, or you can work out the life you want and what you're prepared to do.'

She still didn't get it.

'Bridgette, she could have another baby. She could be pregnant right now!' She closed her eyes. It was something she thought about late at night sometimes, that this could be ongoing, that there could be another Harry, or a little Harriet, or twins. 'Come away with me on Saturday,' he said. 'Come for the weekend, just to see…'

'What about Arabella?'

'What about her?' Dominic said. 'I told her last night the same thing I told her when we had coffee on Saturday. We're through. And I've told her that I'm blocking her from my phone.' He knew he was pushing it, but this time he said it. 'You could be my moll!'

'I've got other things to think about right now.'

'Yes,' he said as he pulled up at her door. 'You do.'

And she didn't ask him in, and neither did he expect her to, but he did pull her into his arms and kiss her.

'Don't…' She pulled her head back.

'It's a kiss.'

'A kiss that's going nowhere,' she said. 'I'm not very good at one-night stands, in case you didn't work it out. And I really think the holiday is over…'

'Why won't you let anyone in?'

'Because I can't stand being hurt again,' Bridgette admitted. 'And you and I…' She was honest. 'Well, it's going to hurt, whatever way you look at it.' And she did open up a bit, said what she'd thought all those days ago. 'My life's not exactly geared to hopping on planes.'

'You only need to hop on one,' Dominic said, and he was offering her the biggest out, an escape far more permanent than her flat.

'Think about it,' he said.

'I can't.'

'Just think about it,' Dominic said. 'Please.'

He wished her all the very best for the next day, then drove down the road and pulled out his phone.

'It's Wednesday,' Chris said. 'Why are you ringing me on a Wednesday?'

'I'm just ringing you,' Dominic said. 'It doesn't only have to be on a Friday.'

'It's about Bridgette?' Chris said, and Dominic couldn't help a wry grin that he was ringing his brother for advice. 'The one with the baby.'

'It's not her baby,' Dominic said, because he'd explained about Harry as they'd walked along the beach.

'But she loves him.'

'Yep.'

'Well, why can't they come and live here?'

'Because it's not going to happen,' Dominic said. 'His mum loves him too.'

'And you can't stay there because you're coming over on Saturday,' Chris reminded him. 'For my birthday.' He heard the silence. 'You said you would.'

'I did.'

'See you on Saturday,' Chris said.

And Dominic did know how Bridgette felt—he was quite sure of that, because he felt it then too, thought of his brother all dressed up with his friends and his disappointment if *he* wasn't there. He thought of Bridgette facing it alone.

'You are coming?' Chris pushed.

'You know I am,' Dominic said. 'I'll see you then.'

'Are you still going to ring me on Friday?' Chris said, because he loathed a change in routine.

'Of course.'

CHAPTER THIRTEEN

'HI, TONY!' Dominic said the next morning. 'Hi, Roman.' He tried not to look at Harry, who was watching him from the next cot. He'd seen all the Joyce family head off to the conference room, Courtney marching in front, the parents, as Bridgette would say, joined at the hip, and an exhausted-looking Bridgette bringing up the rear.

'Is this your last morning?' Tony said, because it was common knowledge now that he was leaving.

'No,' Dominic said. 'I'm on call tonight.'

'Well, if I don't see you I just want to be sure to thank you for everything with Roman and Esperanza and Maria,' Tony said.

'You're very welcome,' Dominic said. 'How are they both doing?'

'They're amazing,' Tony replied. 'Maria's a bit torn of course. She wants to be here more, but she doesn't want to bring Esperanza here…'

'Better not to,' Dominic said. He finished examining Roman and told his father he was pleased with his progress and that hopefully by Monday Roman would be home.

'It will be nice to have a full house again,' Tony

said. 'Thought we couldn't have children—three goes at IVF for the twins, then Roman surprises us and now Esperanza!'

Dominic carried on with his round and tried not to think what was going on in the conference room, tried not to think about the offer he had made last night.

Bridgette couldn't *not* think about it.

She had pondered it all night, had been thinking about it in the car park for the hour she had waited to sort out her battery, and she was feeling neither hopeful nor particularly patient with her family. She sat there and the meeting went backwards and forwards, like some endless round of table tennis, getting nowhere. She listened to Courtney making excuses and promises again, watched her parents, who so badly wanted to believe their youngest daughter's words. She listened to the social worker, who, Bridgette realised, was very willing for Harry's aunt to support her sister—and of course she didn't blame them; but she realised that no one was ever going to tell her that she was doing too much. She had to say it herself.

'This is what I'm prepared to do.' She looked around the room and then at her sister; she took over the bat and slammed out her serve and said it again, but a bit louder this time.

'This is what I'm prepared to do,' she repeated. And when she had the room's attention, she spoke. 'Harry is to attend daycare here at the hospital, whether he's staying with you or being babysat by me—there has to be some consistency in his life. I will pay for his place if that is a concern you have, but he has to be there Monday to Friday from now on.' She looked at the social worker. 'If I can get a place again.'

'I can sort that out.' She nodded. 'We have a couple of places reserved for special allocations.' Bridgette turned to her parents. 'Mum, if I'm on a late shift or working nights and Harry is in my care, for whatever reason, you have to collect him or stay overnight. I can't always work early shifts.'

'You know we do our best!' Betty said. 'Of course we'll pick him up.'

Bridgette looked over at the caseworker, who gave a bit of a nod that told her to go on. 'He's due to have surgery…' She was finding a voice and she knew what to do with it, was grateful for Dominic's advice because she'd heeded it. 'He's on the waiting list for grommets and if that comes up while he's in my care I want to be able to go ahead. I want written permission obtained so that when Harry is in my care, or at any time I'm concerned, I can speak to doctors and I can take him to appointments. And I want—'

'I don't want him in daycare,' Courtney chimed in. 'I've told you—I'm not going anywhere. I decide what treatment he has and who he sees.'

'That's fine.' Bridgette looked at her sister. 'You have every right to refuse what I'm offering. But I can't stand aside any more. If you don't accept my conditions…' It was the hardest thing she would ever say and could only be said if it was meant. Whether he was serious or not, she was incredibly grateful for Dominic's offer last night. 'Then you can deal with it. I'll move to Sydney.'

'Bridgette!' Her mum almost stood up. 'You know you don't mean that.'

'But I do—because I can't live like this. I can't watch Harry being passed around like a parcel. So it's either you accept my terms or I'm moving to Sydney.'

'You said you'd always be there for me.' Courtney started to cry, only this time it didn't move Bridgette. 'You promised…'

'Well, that makes us both liars, then,' Bridgette said. 'Because I can remember you saying exactly the same to Harry the day he was born.'

'Bridgette.' Her mum was trying to be firm, to talk sense into her sensible daughter. 'You know you're not going anywhere. Why Sydney?'

'I've met someone,' Bridgette said. 'And he's from there.' Betty had seen the happy couple, that were back as Bridgette's screensaver, when she'd had a nose in her daughter's spare room, had tutted at the two faces smiling back, and she had a terrible feeling her daughter might actually mean what she was saying.

'You love Courtney…' Maurice broke in.

'I'm not sure if I do,' Bridgette said, and she truly wasn't sure that she did. 'I honestly don't know that I do.'

'You love Harry.' Betty triumphed.

'Yes, I do. So if she wants my help then she can have it, but those are my conditions and she needs to know that any time I think Harry is at risk I will speak up.' She walked out of the meeting because she had nothing left to say. It had to be up to Courtney. She walked over to the ward and saw Harry sitting in his cot, building his bricks. She let down the cot side and held out her arms. She had meant every word she had said in that room, had convinced herself of it last night, but there was a piece of her that was hidden apart, a piece of her that no one must see, because as she picked up her nephew and buried her face in his curls, she knew she could never leave him. They just had to believe that she might.

Dominic watched her cuddling Harry and he wanted to go over, to find out what was happening, but instead he picked up the phone.

It was the longest morning, even though he had plenty to do, but he could not get involved, or be seen to be getting involved, which surely she knew, but still he felt like a bastard.

'Do you want me to give Harry his lunch?' Jennifer, one of the nurses, offered. 'You can go to the canteen, maybe have a little break?'

'I'm fine,' Bridgette said. 'They're still in the meeting. I'll give him his lunch and then—' she took a deep breath '—I'm going home.'

'Jennifer!' Dominic's voice barked across the ward. 'Can you hold on to Harry's lunch for now, please, and keep him nil by mouth until I've spoken to his mum?'

'What's going on?' Bridgette frowned.

'I've no idea,' Jennifer admitted. 'Wait there and I'll find out.' And she went over and spoke to Dominic, but instead of coming back and informing Bridgette, Jennifer headed off to the conference room. The group was just coming out and it was clear that Courtney had been crying but, along with Jennifer, they all headed back inside.

'What's going on?' She went up to him.

'Someone's coming down to speak to his mother.'

'Dominic!' She couldn't believe he'd do this to her.

'I'd go home now if I were you.'

'You know I can't.'

'Yes,' he said. 'You can.' She looked at him, met those lovely black eyes and somehow she trusted him.

'Go home,' he said. 'I'm sure you've got an awful lot to do.' She just stood there. 'Maybe tidy that bedroom, young lady.'

And she trusted him, she really did, but she knew he was leaving tomorrow, knew that right now he was saying goodbye.

'Go,' he said, 'and when she calls, don't come back.' He gave her a small wink. 'You only answer if it's me.'

'I can't do that. I can't just leave him.'

'You can,' he said. 'I'm here.'

CHAPTER FOURTEEN

WHEN her phone rang fifteen minutes later, she was driving, just approaching the roundabout, and she didn't pull over so she could take the call, as she usually would have. She didn't indicate when she saw that it was Courtney and instead she drove straight on.

Dominic was there.

She felt as if Dominic was there in the car beside her.

It rang again and this time it was her mum. Still, she ignored it.

Then it rang again as she arrived home and she sat at her computer before answering.

'Oh. Hi, Mum!'

'You didn't pick up.'

'I was driving.'

'Where are you?' she asked. 'I thought you'd gone down to the canteen.'

'I'm at home,' she said, as if she was breathing normally, as if home was the natural place she should be.

'Well, you need to get here!' Bridgette stared at her screensaver and tried to shut out the sound of her mother's panic. 'The doctors are here and they say Harry needs an operation. There's a space that's opened

up on the list and they want him to have an operation!'
she said again really loudly.

'What operation?'

'He has to have surgery on his ears, and if she doesn't
sign the consent, he'll go back on the list…' She could
hear the panic in her mother's voice. 'Bridgette, you
need to get here. You know what your sister's like—
Courtney can't make a decision. She's gone off!'

'It's a tiny operation, Mum. It could do him an awful
lot of good.'

'Bridgette, please, they've added him to the list this
evening. Courtney's going crazy!'

'Mum…' Bridgette looked into Dominic's eyes as
she spoke, and then into her own and wanted to be her
again, wanted to be the woman who smiled and laughed
and lived. 'It's up to Courtney to give consent. If not,
he can go on the waiting list and wait, but it would be a
shame, because his hearing is really bad.' She stood up.
'I've got to go, Mum. I've got things to do. Give Harry a
big kiss from his aunty Bridgette. Tell him that I'll bring
him in a nice present for being brave.' And she rang off.

She took the phone into the bathroom with her and
because she didn't have any bubble bath, she used shampoo, put on a load of washing while she was waiting
for the bath to fill and every time the phone rang, she
did not pick up.

And then she did her hair, straightened it and put on
blusher and lipstick too, even though she knew Dominic was on call and wouldn't be coming round. Then
when her phone finally fell silent, she tackled her bedroom, worked out how to use a stud finder and put up
the shelves that had been sitting in cardboard for way

too long. Then the phone bleeped a text and it was from Dominic.

She took a breath and read it.

Op went well—he's back on ward and having a drink. Home tomoz.

She felt the tension seep out of her.

Should I come in now?

She was quite sure what the response would be, that he'd tell her to stay put, that Courtney was there and to let her deal with it, but as she waited for his reply, there was a knock at the door and when her phone bleeped he didn't say what she'd thought he might.

No, stay put—your mum's with him.

She wanted to know what was happening so badly. She had this stupid vision it was him as, phone in hand, she opened the door.

Instead it was her father and Courtney.

CHAPTER FIFTEEN

It was a long night and he was glad when it hit six a.m. and there were just a couple of hours to go.

'Cot Four.' Karan, the night nurse, looked up from the baby she was feeding. 'I'll be there in a minute.'

'I'll be fine,' Dominic said, and headed in.

He took off his jacket, glanced again at Harry, who sitting there staring, and then proceeded to wash his hands. When he turned around, Harry was smiling. Dominic couldn't help himself from looking at the pull-out bed beside him, relieved to see that Betty was there.

He didn't know what had happened.

He'd heard the explosions from the fuse he'd lit when he'd asked for a favour from Raymond and a certain blue-eyed theatre nurse, but he'd been up and down between here and NICU and had never caught up as to what had really gone on.

He smiled back at Harry and then headed over to the cot opposite him, carefully examining the baby who was causing concern, pleased with her progress.

'How's Harry Joyce?' he asked Karan. He had every right to enquire as he was the paediatrician on call that night and Karan wouldn't know that he had stepped aside from the case.

'He's doing well.' Karan smiled. 'You could see the difference in him almost as soon as he came back from Theatre. He must have been struggling with his ears for a while. He's much more smiley and he's making a few more noises, even had a little dance in his cot. He's off home in the morning to the care of Mum.' She pulled out a notebook. 'Hold on a moment. Sorry, he's home with his aunt tomorrow. There was a big case meeting today apparently. Lots of drama.' She rolled her eyes. 'I haven't had a chance to read the notes yet.' She stood up and collected the folder and put it in front of him. 'Should make interesting reading.'

Karan walked back to the nursery to put down the baby she had been feeding and Dominic sat there, tempted to read the notes, to find out all that had gone on. It would be so easy to. 'So this is your last morning.' Tony stopped by the desk, just as Dominic went to open the folder. Tony had been up and used the parent showers before all the others did, was dressed and ready for when Abuela came in.

'It is,' Dominic said. 'I'm flying to Sydney this afternoon.'

'Well, thanks again.' Tony stifled a yawn.

'You must be exhausted.' It was Dominic who extended the conversation.

'Ah, but it's Saturday,' Tony said. 'I'm going home to sleep. That's if the twins and Esperanza let me.'

'You've got a lot on your plate,' Dominic said, but Tony just grinned.

'Better than an empty plate.'

Dominic stood up and shook Tony's hand and

when Tony had gone he stepped away from the notes.
Bridgette didn't deserve her ex reading up on her private
life. If he wanted to know, he should ask her.

CHAPTER SIXTEEN

'HARRY!' She took him into her arms and wrapped him in a hug, truly delighted to have him home. 'I've got a surprise for you.' And she carried him in to what had been her study as well as Courtney's room and spare room. The cot had been folded and put away (well, it had been neatly put away under Bridgette's bed till she hauled it to the charity shop on Monday) and the bed that had been under a pile of ironing now had a little safety rail, new bedding and a child's bedside light. There were new curtains, a new stash of bricks in a toy box and an intercom was all set up.

'You've been busy,' her mum said when she saw Harry's new bedroom. 'Isn't he a bit young for a bed?'

'Well, at least he can't climb out of it. I'll just have to make sure I close the bedroom door or he'll be roaming the place at night.'

'It looks lovely.' Betty smiled at her daughter. 'I'm sorry that we haven't been much help.'

'You have been,' Bridgette said, because she couldn't stand her parents' guilt and they had probably been doing their best.

'No,' her mum corrected. 'We've been very busy burying our heads in the sand, trying to pretend that everything was okay, when clearly it wasn't. We're going to be around for you much more, and Harry too.'

'And Courtney?' Bridgette watched her mother's lips purse. 'She needs your support more than anyone.'

'We're paying for rehab,' Betty said.

'It's not going to be an instant fix,' Bridgette said, but she didn't go on. She could see how tired her parents looked, not from recent days but from recent years. 'We can get through this, Mum,' Bridgette said, 'if we all help each other.'

'What about you, though?' It was the first time her father had really spoken since they'd arrived. 'What about that young man of yours, the one in Sydney?'

'Let's not talk about that, Dad.' It hurt too much to explore at the moment. It was something she wanted to examine and think about in private—when she had calmed down fully, when she was safely alone, then she would deal with all she had lost for her sister, again. But her father was finally stepping up, as she had asked him to, and not burying his head in the sand as he usually did—which was a good thing, though perhaps not right now.

'We need to discuss it, Bridgette.' He sat down and looked her square in the eye. 'We didn't know you were serious about someone.'

'It never really got a chance to be serious,' Bridgette said.

'We should have had Harry more.'

Yes, you bloody should have, she wanted to say, but that wasn't fair on them, because really it wasn't so much Harry who had got in the way; it had been her too—she hadn't wanted a relationship, hadn't wanted to let another close. 'Things will be different now,' Bridgette said instead.

'You could go away for the odd weekend now and then…' her dad said. And teeny little wisps of hope seemed to rise in her stomach, but she doused them— it was simply too late.

After her parents had gone, Bridgette made Harry some lunch and then cuddled him on the sofa. She did exactly what she'd tried not to—she let herself love him. Of course she always had, but now she didn't hold back. She kissed his lovely curls and then smiled into his sleepy eyes and told him that everything was going to be okay, that Mum was getting well, that she would always be here for him.

And she would be.

It was a relief to acknowledge it, to step back from the conflict and ignore the push and pull as to who was wrong and who was right—she wasn't young, free and single, she had a very young heart to take care of.

'You wait there,' she said to Harry as the doorbell rang. They were curled up, watching a DVD. Harry was nearly ready to be put down for his afternoon nap and Bridgette was rather thinking that she might just have one too.

'Dominic!' He was the last person she was expecting to see, though maybe not. She knew that he did care about her, knew he would want to know how she was.

He wasn't a bastard unfortunately. It would be so much easier to paint him as one—they just had different lives, that was all.

'I thought you had a gangster party to be at!'

'I've got a couple of hours till the plane.' He was dressed in a black suit. 'I've just got to put on a tie and glasses—Mum's sent me a fake gun, though I'd better not risk it on the plane.' His smile faded a touch. 'I wanted to see how the meeting had gone…'

'Didn't you hear?' Bridgette said, quite sure the whole hospital must have heard by now. 'Or you could have read the notes.' He saw her tight smile, knew that Bridgette, more than anyone, would have hated things being played out on such a public stage—it was her workplace, after all. She opened the door. 'Come in.'

He was surprised to see how well she looked, or perhaps *surprised* wasn't the right word—he was in awe. Her hair swished behind her as she walked, all glossy and shiny as it had been that first night, and he could smell her perfume. She looked bright and breezy and not what he had expected.

Back perhaps to the woman he had met.

'I didn't want to read the notes,' Dominic said, walking through to the lounge. 'Though I heard that Harry had come home with you…' His voice trailed off as he saw Harry lying on the lounge, staring warily at him. 'Hi, there, Harry.'

Harry just stared.

'What happened to the nice smile that you used to give me when I came on the ward?' Dominic asked, but Harry did not react.

'Do you want a drink?' Bridgette offered, though perhaps it was more for herself. She wanted a moment or two in the kitchen alone, just to gather her thoughts before they had to do what she had been dreading since the night they had first met—officially say goodbye. 'Or some lunch perhaps?' She looked at the clock. 'A late lunch.'

'I won't have anything,' Dominic said. 'I'll have

something on the plane and there will be loads to eat tonight. A coffee would be great, though.' It had already been a very long day. 'You've changed the living room.'

'I've given Harry his own bedroom,' Bridgette said, 'and I quite like the idea of having a desk in here.' And she could breathe as his eyes scanned the room, because, yes, she'd changed the screensaver again. Now it was a photo of Harry and his mum, a nice photo, so that Harry could see Courtney often.

'It looks nice,' he said as Bridgette headed out to the kitchen and Dominic stood, more than a little awkward, nervous by what he had to say. He wasn't used to nerves in the least—he always had a level head. He said what was needed and rarely any more. He took off his jacket and looked for somewhere to hang it, settling on the back of Bridgette's study chair. Turning around he saw Harry smile, half-asleep, lying on the sofa. He gave Dominic the biggest grin and then closed his eyes.

'What are you smiling at?' Bridgette asked Dominic as she walked back in the room carrying two mugs and saw him standing there grinning.

'Harry,' Dominic answered, still smiling. 'That nephew of yours really does love routine.' He saw a little flutter of panic dart across her eyes, realised that she thought perhaps he was there to tell her something. He understood she had an overactive imagination where Harry was concerned. 'He smiles when I take my jacket off. I've just realised that now. Whenever I came onto the ward at night he watched me and frowned and then suddenly he gave me a smile. I could never work out why.'

'It's what you do.' Bridgette grinned, because she'd noticed it too. 'Before you wash your hands. I don't think I've ever seen you examine a patient with your jacket on. Funny that Harry noticed,' she mused. 'I guess when your world's chaotic you look for routine in any place you can find it.'

'Well, it doesn't look very chaotic to me. You've done great,' Dominic said. He waited while she put Harry down for his very first nap in his big-boy bed— Bridgette surprised that he didn't protest, just curled up and went straight to sleep. She gently closed the door. 'So,' he asked when she came back in, 'how did the meeting go?'

'You really didn't read the notes?' She was a little bit embarrassed and awkward that he might be here to question her *plans* to follow him to Sydney, because even though she hadn't given his name, if Dominic had read the notes, the indication would be clear. 'Because I was just bluffing…'

'Bluffing?' Dominic frowned. 'About what?'

'Getting a life.' Bridgette gave a wry smile. 'Moving to Sydney.'

'You said that at the meeting?'

'Oh, I said that and a whole lot more,' Bridgette admitted. 'I did what you suggested. I spent the time before the meeting trying to work out rules I could live with. I said that he had to attend daycare, but I had to be able to take him to a doctor if needed and to take him for any procedures if Courtney wasn't available. I said that Mum and Dad had to help more if Courtney wasn't around…that I was through looking out for Courtney, that I was only on Harry side.'

'You said all that?' He put down his coffee and took her hand. 'Well done. How did Courtney take it?'

'I didn't stay to find out,' she said. 'I just left the

meeting. I hope you don't mind, but I said that I'd been seeing someone, that he lived in Sydney—it just made it seem more real to them. It made them believe that I would leave if I told them I had somebody who wanted me to go with them.'

'You did.'

And she'd no doubt cry about it later—but not now. 'Thank you,' she said. 'For getting him squeezed onto the list.' He gave a frown. 'I know you must have…'

'Well, I thought it might buy another night before she dropped her act, and when you came out of the meeting…' He looked at her, didn't want to tell her how hard it had been to step aside, to not be in that room, not as a doctor but sitting beside her. 'I figured she might drop it a little quicker if you weren't there to sort it out for her.'

'Well, it worked. She fell apart when she had to actually make a decision and it all came out. It isn't drugs—it's alcohol. She's just been slowly falling apart since I kicked her out.'

'It would have happened wherever she was,' Dominic said. 'It was probably going on here…'

And she nodded because, yes, it had been a bit.

And she thought of Harry's birthday that should have been about cordial and cake but instead her sister had chosen to party on—and so too had Paul.

'I hate what she did,' Bridgette said. 'I just couldn't have her stay after that.'

'Of course you couldn't.' Dominic thought for a moment, knew he had to be very careful with what he said. Certainly he was less than impressed with Courtney, but even if people didn't like it at times, he was always honest. 'But I think it's something you have to move on from. She's clearly made a lot of mistakes, but if you're going to be angry with anyone—' he looked at Bridgette, who so deserved to be angry '—then I think it should be with him.'

'It was both of them.'

'He took advantage.'

'Oh, and you never have—' She didn't get to finish.

'Never,' Dominic said. 'Not once. My sexual résumé might not be impressive to you, but…' He shook his head. 'Nope, what he did was wrong, and however awful your sister has been, I bet she's been trying to douse an awful lot of guilt about her treatment of you.'

Bridgette nodded. 'She's gone to rehab. It's three months and Mum and Dad are paying. She came over last night with Dad and said she was terrified of letting everybody down…which she may well do, so I'm not getting my hopes up, but I've made a decision to be here for Harry.' She saw him glance at his watch.

'Sorry, I'm rattling on…'

'It's not that. I have to leave in an hour. I can't miss that plane.' He took a deep breath. Really, he was finding this incredibly difficult—she seemed fine, better than fine, as if she wasn't missing him at all.

Wouldn't miss him.

But he would miss her.

Which forced him to speak on.

'What you said about Sydney, about having someone who wanted you there, you weren't exaggerating, Bridgette.' He took her hand and her fingers curled around his. Inside her, those little wisps of hope uncurled too, and it was so wonderful to see him, to have him sitting beside her, to know this was hard for him. 'I want this to work too. I just can't not be there for Chris,' he said.

'I was very unfair to you—it was ridiculous that I couldn't even get away for a single weekend, and it is about to change. I spoke to my parents this morning so maybe I can get away now and then, maybe I could come up on days off, or some of them.' She stared at her fingers being squeezed by his, and she wished he would jump in, would say that was what he wanted, but he let her speak on. 'And who knows what might happen in the future? Courtney might get well—'

'You're not going to leave Harry,' Dominic cut in. 'You might be able to convince them, but you'll never convince me. You're not going anywhere while Harry's so little.'

'No.' She could feel tears trickling down at the back of her throat and nose. She'd been so determined not to cry, to do this with dignity, to let him go with grace. She could see the second hand on his watch rapidly moving around, gobbling up the little time that they had left. 'No, I'm not going anywhere. Well, not long term.'

'And I don't think the odd weekend is going to suffice.'

'No,' she said, because it wouldn't be enough.

And they could talk in the time they had left, but what was the point? Bridgette realised there was no solution to be had, so instead of tears she gave him a smile, not a false one, a real one. And she put herself first for once, was completely selfish and utterly indulgent and just a little bit wild, because as he went to speak she interrupted him.

'Have we got time for a quickie before you go?'

'We need to talk,' Dominic pointed out.

'I don't need anything,' she cut in. 'I know what I want, though.'

And he wasn't going to argue with that.

He didn't know what he had expected to find when he came over, how he'd expected her to be when he'd knocked at the door, but as always she'd amazed him. Then, as she opened the bedroom door, she amazed him all over again.

'Wow.' As he walked into her bedroom he let out a low whistle. 'You've got a carpet!'

'I know!'

'I'm impressed.' He looked at the shelves and politely didn't comment about five holes she had made in the wall—because he wouldn't know how to find a stud either.

'Just you wait.' She was at his shirt as she spoke. He pulled off her T-shirt and undid her bra and it slowed things down undressing each other, so they stripped off for themselves and then Bridgette peeled back the duvet.

'You get first feel…'

'Of what?' he asked, hands roaming her body, but she peeled off his hands and placed them on the bedding.

'Of my million-thread-count sheets. I was saving them for best…'

Which he was, Bridgette knew that, because he lay on the sheets and wriggled around and made appreciative noises, and then he pulled her in and kissed her.

'I want to feel them now,' she said.

So she lay on the sheets and wriggled around and made appreciative noises too.

And then he kissed her again.

'Don't let me fall asleep after,' Dominic said.

'After what?' She frowned, naked in his arms. 'If you really think you can just come here and have sex…'

She made him laugh and she loved making him

laugh. She loved the Dominic others so rarely saw. When it was just the two or them, the austere, remote man seemed to leave—and he understood her humour and matched it. He made her laugh too, turned those cold black eyes into puppy-dog ones. 'I don't want sex, Bridgette. I just want to hold you.'

'Oh, no.' They were laughing so much they would wake up Harry.

'I just want to lie next to you…' he crooned.

'No.'

He straddled her.

'I just want to talk,' he said.

'No talking,' she begged.

It was a whole new realm for Dominic, like swimming in the ocean after a lifetime doing laps in a pool.

He did not know that you could laugh so much on a Saturday afternoon, that she could laugh even now as she lost him.

As she loved him.

It was a different kiss from any they had tasted before, a different feeling from any they had ever felt.

He kissed her slowly and more tenderly and *he* let himself love her—smothered her, physically, mentally, buried her and pressed her against her very best sheets. He wrapped his arms under her and drove into her till she wanted to scream, and she pressed her mouth to his chest and held on for dear life. She didn't know what the future held and she couldn't control it anyway, so she lived in the moment, and what a lovely moment it was. And she could cry afterwards and not be embarrassed or sorry.

It was a wonderful afternoon, and nothing like the one he had intended, the most delicious surprise. His head was spinning that she could love him like that when she considered it over between them.

'I've made some decisions too.' He took a deep breath, dived out of the pool and into the ocean, where it was rough and choppy but exhilarating and wild. 'When I went to resign this week, when I told them I wouldn't be back, I was offered a job.' He looked at her grey eyes that were for the first time today wary. 'Here.'

She felt little wisps of hope rising again, then she moved to douse them. They were guilty wisps. Surely this was wrong.

'I'm going to ring on Monday and take it.'

'You want to work in Sydney, though. Your family's there, your friends, Chris. You always wanted to work there. It's your goal.'

'Goals change,' Dominic said.

'What about your brother?'

'I'm not going to say anything to him yet,' Dominic said. 'It's his birthday.'

He shook his head, because he couldn't do it to Chris this weekend. 'Look, the job doesn't start for a month and I'm taking the time off. I'm not working. You and I will spend some proper time together, do some of that talking you so readily avoid, and we'll see how I go with Harry...'

'You could have told me!'

'I tried,' Dominic said. 'You didn't want to discuss it—remember? I'll be back on Monday and we can talk properly then.' He looked at his watch. 'I'm going to have to get going soon. This is one plane I can't miss.'

She lay in bed and stared up at the ceiling, tried to take in what he was saying. A month...

A month to get to know Harry, to see how they went,

and then… She was happy, happier than she had ever felt possible, but it felt like a test. Then he turned around and maybe she should compromise too.

'I could ask Mum and Dad to come over.' She was torn. 'If you want me to come tonight…'

'I think Harry needs a couple of nights in his new bed, don't you?'

And she was so glad that he understood.

'I have to get back.' He smiled. 'Would it wake Harry if I had a shower?'

'Don't worry about that.' And she had a moment of panic, because Harry was being golden and sleeping now, but what about at two a.m. when he decided to wake up, what about when it was six p.m. and her mother hadn't picked him up from crèche? How would Dominic deal with those situations? She wasn't sure she was ready for this, not convinced she was up to exposing her heart just to have Dominic change his mind. 'I'll get you some towels.'

'Could you pass my trousers?' he asked as she climbed out of bed. 'Oh, and can you get out my phone?' He snapped his fingers as she trawled through his pockets, which was something Bridgette decided they would work on. Sexy Spaniard he may be, and in a rush for his brother's party perhaps, but she didn't answer to finger snaps. 'I can't find it and don't snap your fingers again,' she warned him. 'Hold on, here it is.' Except it wasn't his phone. Instead she pulled out a little black box.

'That's what I meant.' He grinned. 'So, aren't you going to open it?'

Bridgette was honestly confused. She opened the box and there was a ring. A ring that looked as if they were talking about a whole lot more than a month.

'I thought we were going to take some time…'

'We are,' Dominic said. 'To get to know all the stuff and to work things out, but, compatible or not, there's no arguing from me.' He pulled her over to the bed. 'I love you.' He looked at her and to this point he still didn't know. 'And I hope that you love me?'

She had to think for a moment, because she had held on so firmly to her heart that she hadn't allowed herself to go there. And now she did. She looked at the man who was certainly the only man who could have taken her to his home that first night. She really was lousy at one-night stands, because she knew deep down she had loved him even then.

'If I say it,' she said, 'you can't change your mind.'

'I won't.' That much he knew. She was funny and kind and terribly disorganised too—there was nothing he might have thought he needed on his list for the perfect wife, but she was everything that was now required.

'How do you know?' she asked.

'I'm not sure…' Dominic mused. 'Chemistry, I guess,' he said.

'And Chris?' she said as he pulled her back to bed and put his ring on her finger. She realised the magnitude of what he was giving up.

'He'll be fine.' Dominic had thought about it a lot and was sure, because of something Tony had said. He should have thanked Tony, not the other way around, for far better a full plate than an empty one. He didn't want to be like his father, hitting golf balls into the sky at weekends, a perfect girlfriend waiting at home, with not a single problem. 'I'll go up at least once a month and he can come here some weekends. If I'm working you might have to…' He looked at her and she nodded.

'Of course.'

'We'll get there,' he said. 'You're it and I know you'll do just fine without me, but better with me.' He looked at eyes that weren't so guarded, eyes that no longer reflected hurt, and it felt very nice to be with someone you knew, but not quite, someone you would happily spend a lifetime knowing some more. 'And I'm certainly better with you.'

'Hey!' There was a very loud shout from down the hall. 'Hey!' came the voice again.

'Oh, no.' Bridgette lay back on the pillow as Harry completely broke the moment. 'Those bloody grommets. It's as if he's suddenly found his voice.'

Harry had found his voice and he knew how to use it! 'Hey,' Harry shouted again from behind his closed door. It was a sort of mixture between 'Harry' and 'Hello' and 'Have you forgotten me?'

'I'll get him.' Bridgette peeled back the sheet, liking the big sparkle on her finger as she did so.

'If you say you love me, I'll go and get him,' Dominic said, and pulled on his trousers, deciding he had to be at least half-respectable as he walked in on the little guy.

'If you go and it doesn't make you change your mind—' Bridgette grinned, knowing what he would find '—I'll say it then.'

It was the longest walk of his life.

He'd just put a ring on a woman's finger. Shouldn't they be sipping champagne, booking a restaurant, hell, in some five-star hotel having sex, not getting up to a baby?

But with him and Bridgette it was all just a little bit back to front and he'd better get used to the idea.

He pushed open the door.

'Hey!' Angry eyes met him, and so did the smell. Angry eyes asked him how dared he take so long, leave him sitting in this new bed that he wasn't sure how to get out of?

'This isn't how it's supposed to be, Harry,' Dominic said, because surely it should be a sweet, cherubic baby sitting there smiling at him, but it was an angry Harry with a full nappy. The newly engaged Dominic had to change the first nappy in his life and, yes, it was shocking, a real baptism of fire!

'Think of all the cruises I won't be going on,' Dominic said as he tried to work out all the tabs, 'all the sheer irresponsibility I'm missing…'

'Hey!' Harry said, liking his clean bottom and new word.

'Hey,' Dominic answered

And then he picked him up.

A bare chest, a toddler who was still a baby and a mass of curls against his chin, and it *was* inevitable—he didn't just love Bridgette, he loved Harry too. For the second time in twenty minutes he handed over his heart and it was terrifying.

He would never tell, but he thought he was crying. Maybe he was because Harry's fat hands were patting his cheeks. He could never tell Bridgette that he was terrified too.

That the phone might ring.

That there might be a knock on the door.

That Courtney might come back.

That this little guy might have to be returned too soon.

'I'll make this work.' He looked into the little grey eyes that had always been wary and saw the trust in them now. 'I will make this work,' Dominic said again, and his commitment was as solid as the diamond he had placed on Bridgette's finger—his promise to Harry would cut glass if it had to, it was that strong. 'It will all be okay.'

He walked back into the bedroom with a sweet-smelling Harry and did a double-take as he saw his previously sexy fiancée in bright orange flannelette pyjama bottoms and a T-shirt.

'Don't want him having flashbacks about his aunt in years to come,' Bridgette said.

And it was hard, because she was more a mother than the one Harry had.

'I'm just going to wash my hands.'

He was so tidy and neat. As he handed over Harry and headed to the bedroom, she worked something out. 'That's why he smiled,' Bridgette said. 'When you took your jacket off, he knew that you were staying.'

She looked at her nephew, at smiling grey eyes that mirrored her own, and it was easy to say it as Dominic walked back in the room.

'I love you.'

EPILOGUE

BRIDGETTE never got tired of watching a new life come into the world. It had been a glorious morning and had been a wonderful straightforward birth. Kate was watching from the bed, and Michael, the father, was standing over Bridgette as she finished up the weights and measurements, popped on a hat, wrapped up their son and handed him over—the perfect miracle, really.

'We're going to move you back to your room soon,' Bridgette told the new parents. 'I'll come and check on you later, but Jasmine is going to take over from me for a little while.'

'That's right.' Kate looked up from her baby. 'You've got your scan this morning. I'm glad he arrived in time and you didn't have to dash off.'

'I wouldn't have left you,' Bridgette said. 'I'd already rung down and told them I might not be able to leave.' She looked at the little pink squashed face and smiled. 'You have a very considerate baby.'

'You'll have one of your own soon.'

'Not that soon.' Bridgette gave an impatient sigh, because she really couldn't wait. 'I'm only nineteen weeks.' And then she checked herself, because she sounded just like any impatient first-time mum, and then she laughed because that was exactly what she was. She gave a small wink. 'Nineteen weeks and counting!'

She would breathe when she got to twenty-four weeks, she decided, no, twenty-five, she corrected, thinking of the difference those extra few days had made to Francesca. Francesca had been discharged the day Dominic had started his new job—home on oxygen but doing brilliantly. It had been a nice way to start, Dominic had said.

As she walked down to the canteen where she was meeting Dominic, she wondered if he'd be able to get away. She really didn't mind if he couldn't. It was a routine scan, after all, and he'd end up asking the sonographer way too many questions. Still, even if she would be fine without him, she smiled when she saw him sitting at the far end of the canteen, sharing lunch with Harry, and she realised he was going to make the appointment—it was better with him there.

'Hi, Harry.' She received a lovely kiss that tasted of bananas, and asked about his busy morning, because along with building bricks he'd done a painting or two, or was it three? He really had come on in leaps and bounds. 'Any news from Courtney?' Bridgette asked Dominic.

'I was about to ask you the same,' Dominic said. 'She seems to be taking ages. I thought it started at eleven.'

Courtney had an interview this morning at the hospital. She was attending college, and now that she had been clean for well over a year, she was applying for a job on the drug and alcohol unit. But as much as Bridgette wanted her sister to get the job and to do well, she was a little bit torn, not quite sure that Courtney was ready for such a demanding role. Courtney lived in Bridgette's old flat, paid a minimal rent and had been working hard in every area of her life. Although Bridgette was unsure about this job, she was also worried how Courtney would take it if she was turned down when she had such high hopes.

'We're about to find out,' Dominic said, and she looked up as Courtney made her way over.

'How did you go?' Bridgette asked.

'I didn't get it,' Courtney said, which seemed contrary to her smile as she kissed her little boy. 'They don't think I'm quite ready to work with addicts yet. I need more time sorting out myself and they said that there was another course I should think about, but—' she gave a very wide smile '—they were very impressed with me. Apparently there is a position as a domestic. The patients do a lot of the cleaning work, but I would be in charge of the kitchen, sort of overseeing things.' She pulled a face. 'And I have to do the toilets and bathrooms. It's three days a week for now and some weekends, but they'll also pay me to do the course.' She gave a nervous swallow. 'Really, it's like a full-time job.'

'Oh, my!' Bridgette beamed. 'It sounds perfect.' Then laughed. 'Except I can't really imagine you keeping things clean.'

'She's such a bossy landlady, isn't she, Harry?' Courtney said, and Bridgette admitted that, yes, maybe at times she was. 'I have to go to the uniform room and then down to HR. I'd better get him back.'

'We'll take Harry back to daycare,' Dominic said, rather than offered, because Harry was still eating. 'That way he can finish his lunch.'

He was very firm with Courtney, didn't play games

with her, didn't bend to any to her whims, and he didn't let Bridgette bend too far either.

Courtney breezed off and Dominic rolled his eyes. 'She's doing great and everything, but she's still the most self-absorbed person that I've ever met.' He let out a wry laugh. 'She didn't even wish you luck for your scan.'

'That's Courtney.'

With Harry's lunch finished, they headed back to daycare but at the last minute, as he handed Harry over to Mary, it was Dominic who changed his mind. 'Should we bring him?'

'To the ultrasound?' Bridgette frowned at Mary. 'Won't it upset him?'

'It might be a wonderful way to get him used to the idea,' Mary said. 'After all he's going to be like a big brother.'

'I guess,' Bridgette said, because Harry was going to be a brother to this baby, even if not in the conventional way... And that just about summed them up entirely. It was as if Harry had three parents. Even if Courtney was doing brilliantly, it hadn't been the smoothest of rides, and it was an ongoing journey. As Dominic had once pointed out, Harry deserved the extra ration of love and he got it, over and over—from his mum, from his aunt and her husband, from his grandparents too, who made a far more regular fuss of him.

So as Dominic held Harry, Bridgette lay on the bed and the ultrasound started. 'Are we going to find out?' She still couldn't decide if she wanted to know the sex or wanted the surprise.

'I am,' Dominic said, studying the screen closely, and she felt sorry for the sonographer with this brusque

paediatrician in the room. 'Don't worry, I won't let on.'
He wouldn't; Bridgette knew that much. He was the
best in the world at keeping it all in. It had taken ages
to work him out and she was still doing it, would be
doing it for the rest of her life no doubt—but it was the
most pleasurable job in the world.

She heard the clicks and the measurements being
taken and felt the probe moving over her stomach. She
looked over to where Dominic and Harry were closely
observing the screen and then she laughed because there
he was doing somersaults, a little cousin for Harry, and
a nephew for Chris, who would be the most devoted
uncle in the world.

'Everything looks normal.' The sonographer smiled
and then she spoke to Dominic. 'Did you want to have
a look?'

She saw him hover, could almost hear the ten million
questions whizzing around that brilliant brain, knew
he wanted to take the probe and check and check again
that everything was perfect, that everything was just
so, but with supreme effort Dominic gave a small shake
of his head.

'"Normal" sounds pretty good,' he said, 'and it's not
as if we'll be sending it back.'

Already their family was perfect.

* * * * *

UNLOCKING THE SURGEON'S HEART

BY
JESSICA MATTHEWS

First published in Great Britain 2012
by Mills & Boon, an imprint of Harlequin (UK) Limited.
Harlequin (UK) Limited, Eton House, 18-24 Paradise Road,
Richmond, Surrey TW9 1SR

© Jessica Matthews 2012

ISBN: 978 0 263 89177 5

Harlequin (UK) policy is to use papers that are natural, renewable
and recyclable products and made from wood grown in sustainable
forests. The logging and manufacturing process conform to the
legal environmental regulations of the country of origin.

Printed and bound in Spain
by Blackprint CPI, Barcelona

Dear Reader

I've always wanted to write a cancer survivor story because so many of us have had our lives touched by this disease, whether from personal experience or through the experience of a friend or family member. Finally I sensed it was time to tell the story that had been waiting patiently for its turn.

Facing a life-threatening disease takes a lot of courage, and that became the main character trait of my heroine, Christy. Her courage, however, comes at a high price, which means she needs a hero who will be strong when she needs strength, compassionate when she needs compassion, and dependable when she needs someone to depend on. Linc is her perfect partner—although Christy has a difficult time believing…

Fortunately, love conquers all. I hope you enjoy being a part of Christy and Linc's journey as they search for and find their own happy ending.

Until next time

Jessica

Jessica Matthews's interest in medicine began at a young age, and she nourished it with medical stories and hospital-based television programmes. After a stint as a teenage candy-striper, she pursued a career as a clinical laboratory scientist. When not writing or on duty, she fills her day with countless family and school-related activities. Jessica lives in the central United States, with her husband, daughter and son.

This book is dedicated to cancer survivors everywhere—especially my friend Carla Maneth, who so graciously shared her experiences and insights—and to the memory of those who fought hard but didn't win the battle—especially my mother and my father-in-law.

CHAPTER ONE

I<small>T WAS</small> a shame, really. A man as handsome as Lincoln Maguire should have a personality to match, shouldn't he? The good doctor—and he was more than good, he was *exceptional* when it came to his surgical expertise—was so completely focused on his work that he wouldn't recognize a light-hearted moment if one landed in the middle of his operating field.

Christy Michaels peered sideways at the man in question. His long, lean fingers danced across the keyboard as he clearly ignored the hospital staff's ideas and opinions regarding Mercy Memorial's part in Levitt Springs' upcoming Community Harvest Festival. Apparently, talk of craft booths, food vendors, and a golf tournament to benefit the cancer center and the local Relay for Life chapter didn't interest him enough to join in the conversation.

It wasn't the first time he'd distanced himself from the conversations swirling around him; he was the sort who came in, saw his patients, and left, usually with few people being the wiser. Today, though, his distant demeanor—as if these details were too unimportant for his notice—coupled with her own special interest in the center and the treatment it provided, irritated her.

"I have an idea," she blurted out, well aware that she didn't but it hadn't been for lack of trying. She'd been considering options—and discarding them—for weeks, because none had given her that inner assurance that "this was the one".

Yet as voices stilled and all eyes focused on her—except for one midnight-blue pair—she had to come up with something unusual, something noteworthy enough to shock Dr Maguire into paying attention. With luck, he might even come out of his own little world and get involved.

"Make it snappy, Michaels," Denise Danton, her shift manager, said as she glanced at her watch. "The festival committee meets in five minutes and it takes at least that long to walk to the conference room."

Acknowledging Denise with a brief nod, she began, "It's something we haven't done before."

One of the nurses groaned. "If you're going to suggest a bachelor auction, it's already been mentioned. Personally, I think we need a newer idea."

Darn it, but that *had* been her suggestion. Rather than admit defeat, she thought fast. "We could create our own version of *Dancing with the Stars*. Only we would call it *Dancing with the Doctors*."

Instantly, his hands slowed, and she was immensely pleased. And yet he didn't look away from the digital pages in front of him, so maybe he was only thinking about Mrs Halliday's chest tube and her antibiotic regimen.

"How would that work?" someone asked her.

She ad-libbed. "We'd sell tickets for the public to watch the doctors and their partners perform. People could vote for their favorite pair—making a donation for the privilege, of course—and at the end, one lucky team is crowned the winner and all proceeds benefit the hospital."

Denise looked thoughtful. "Oh, I like that. We'd have to strong-arm enough physicians to participate, though."

"I'm sure any of them would jump at the opportunity to raise money for a good cause. Right, Dr Maguire?" she asked innocently.

If she hadn't taken that moment to glance directly at the side of his face, she might have missed the weary set to his mouth as well as the barely imperceptible shadow on his skin that suggested his day had begun far earlier than hers. The wisps of walnut-brown hair appearing out from under his green cap were damp, and perspiration dotted the bridge of his chiseled nose. His scrub suit was wrinkled and his breast pocket had a frayed edge at the seam.

Funny thing, but she hadn't noticed he'd looked quite so frazzled when he'd sat in the chair.

Instantly, Christy felt guilty for distracting him. In hindsight, she realized it wasn't his scheduled surgery day, which meant he was obviously filling in for one of his partners. It also meant he was rushing to finish the paperwork so he could see his private patients. From the volume of cases he brought to the hospital, his waiting room was probably packed and growing more so by the minute.

"Sure, why not," he answered without any real emotion, his attention still focused on his computer screen.

"Okay, then," she said brightly, ready to leave him to

his work. "Denise, you can mention this at your meeting—"

"Dr Maguire," the other woman said boldly, "you wouldn't mind participating, would you?"

This time, his hands froze. To Christy's surprise and dismay, his dark blue gaze met hers instead of Denise's and she was sure she saw exasperation in those depths. He clearly held her responsible, not only for being interrupted but also for having to field Denise's request.

However, when he addressed Denise, his tone was as pleasant and even-tempered as ever. "I'll forego the spot to make room for someone who's more capable."

"Ability has nothing to do with it," Denise retorted. "This is all for fun and as Christy said, it's for a good cause."

"But—" he began.

"If you sign up, I just *know* more of the medical staff will be willing to join in," Denise coaxed. "And with you on the program, we'll sell tons of tickets. Just think how much we'll earn for the cancer center."

Christy groaned inwardly. He *would* be a big draw because she couldn't imagine anyone who wouldn't be willing to fork out money to see the straitlaced, cool, and collected Lincoln Maguire cut loose on the dance floor. More importantly, because it was a known fact that he didn't date, everyone would want to speculate about the lucky woman he'd chosen to be his partner.

His thoughts obviously ran along the same track because he shot a warning glare in her direction before he spoke to Denise. "You're giving me far too much credit—"

"Nonsense." She clapped her hands softly in her excitement. "This is going to be great. The committee will love this idea. I can't wait to tell them—"

"Stop right there," he ordered in his most authoritative voice.

No one moved. Christy didn't even breathe because she suddenly had a feeling of impending doom as he pinned her with his gaze.

"If you're penciling me on the list," he said firmly, "I have a couple of conditions. One, if you have more volunteers than you can accommodate, my name will be the first to be removed."

Denise frowned, but, apparently recognizing his tone brooked no argument, she nodded. "Okay. Not a problem."

"Second, in the event that doesn't happen—and I suspect someone will make sure that it doesn't," he added dryly, "Christy must agree to be my partner."

Everyone's heads turned toward her in a perfectly choreographed motion. Expressions ranged from surprise to curiosity and a few were also speculative.

"You want…what?" Christy asked hoarsely. He might be her best friend's brother-in-law, but that wasn't a solid connection to warrant such a request. After all, they'd only been at Gail and Tyler's house together on two occasions and they'd hardly spoken to each other.

"To be my partner."

This wasn't supposed to happen. "Why me?" she asked.

He raised an eyebrow. "This was your idea," he reminded her. "It's only fair that you participate, too."

He had a point, although if she had her choice, she'd pick someone who complemented her, not someone who was vinegar to her oil. While in the hospital they'd dealt with each other amicably over the past two years—he gave orders and she carried them out—but in the private atmosphere of Gail's home their differences had been highlighted. As a man who prided himself on control and self-restraint, she'd seen how he didn't appreciate her outspoken and sometimes impulsive nature.

Neither would she delude herself into believing he'd set his condition with romantic motives in mind. According to Gail, her brother-in-law had mapped out his life so carefully that he wasn't allowing for a wife until he was forty, and as he still had two or three years until then, his work was his mistress.

"Unless, of course, you object," he added smoothly, if not a trifle smugly, as if he *expected* her to refuse so she could provide his get-out-of-jail-free card.

She didn't blame him for thinking that. It was no secret she wasn't interested in a romance any more than he was, but while his excuse was because his work consumed his life, her reasons were entirely different.

However, he'd issued a challenge and she was living proof that she didn't back down from one. If dusting off her dancing shoes and practicing her two-step meant the workaholic, type A personality Dr Maguire would participate in a night of fun and frivolity, then she'd do it.

She shrugged. "Okay, fine with me."

"Good," Denise said. "It's settled."

"I don't know how settled this is." He sounded doubtful and hopeful at the same time. "Won't the committee, as a whole, have to approve the idea first?"

"Trust me, they're going to love the concept," the older woman assured him. "I can already think of fifty ways to promote the event and guarantee a brilliant turnout. Now, I'm off. Hold the fort while I'm gone, people, so that means everyone back to work!"

The crowd dispersed, but Christy hardly noticed. Dr Maguire—Linc, as Gail affectionately called him— sat in his chair, arms crossed, as he drilled her with his gaze.

A weaker woman would have quaked under his piercing stare, but she'd stared death in the face and Linc Maguire wasn't nearly as intimidating. Still, she felt a little uncomfortable as she waited for him to speak. From the way he worked his jaw and frowned periodically, he obviously had trouble verbalizing his thoughts.

"*Dancing with the Doctors*?" he finally asked, his expression so incredulous she wanted to laugh, but knew she shouldn't. "Was that the best you could do?"

She shrugged, relieved that he seemed more stunned than angry, at least at this point. "On short notice, yes. However, from everyone's response, the idea was a hit."

"It was something all right," he grumbled. "If I were you, I'd pray the committee thinks it's ridiculous and dreams up another plan."

"I don't think *Dancing with the Docs* is so bad," she protested. "You have to admit the concept is unusual. We've never done anything like this before."

"We haven't had an old-fashioned box supper or a kissing booth either," he pointed out. "It doesn't mean we should start now."

Unbidden, her gaze landed on his mouth. To her, it was perfect with the bottom lip just a little wider than the top. No doubt there was a host of other women who'd agree.

Oddly enough, it only seemed natural for her gaze to travel lower, down his neck to a sculpted chest that even the shapeless scrub top and white undershirt didn't disguise. His skin was tan, and dark hair covered his muscular arms, indicating that somewhere in his busy schedule he found time to work out on a regular basis.

Oh, my. And she was going to be in his arms, pressed against that chest, in front of hundreds of people? Maybe she *should* start praying the committee wouldn't be interested in her idea. Better yet, she could pray for enough physicians to volunteer so the team of Maguire and Michaels would be excused from the lineup.

She swallowed hard. "It's for a good cause," she said lamely.

"Tell yourself that when you're nursing a few broken toes," he mumbled darkly.

His expression reminded her more of a sullen little boy than a confident surgeon and it made her chuckle. "You don't dance?"

He shook his head. "Other than a slow shuffle? No."

She wasn't surprised. In her view, Lincoln Maguire was too controlled and tightly wound to ever do anything as uninhibited as gliding around a dance floor in step to the music. However, she was curious about his reasons.

"You surely practiced a few steps for your senior prom, didn't you?"

He blinked once, as if she'd caught him off guard. "I didn't go. The girl I'd asked turned me down."

Remorse hit her again. She hadn't intended to embarrass him, or trigger bad memories. "I'm sorry."

"I'm not," he said, matter-of-factly. "We were just

good friends and she was waiting for a buddy of mine to dredge up the courage to ask her himself. As soon as I knew her feelings leaned in his direction, I told him and the rest, as they say, is history. In fact, they celebrated their twelve-year anniversary this year."

"Talk about being versatile," she teased. "You're a surgeon *and* a matchmaker."

He grinned. "Don't be too impressed. They were the first and only couple I pushed together."

She was too caught up by the transformation his smile had caused to be embarrassed by her remark. He looked younger than his thirty-seven years and appeared far more approachable. His chiseled-from-granite features softened and he seemed more hot-blooded male than cold-hearted surgeon.

His smile was also too infectious for her not to return it in full measure. However, if she told anyone he had actually softened enough to smile, they'd never believe her.

Neither would anyone believe her if she told them they'd actually discussed something *personal* instead of a patient. As far as she knew, it was the first time such a thing had happened in the history of the hospital.

"I hate to break this to you," she said, "but a slow shuffle won't cut it when it comes to a competition."

"Only if your *Dancing with the Doctors* idea takes hold," he pointed out. "With luck, it won't and we'll both be off the hook."

She heard the hopeful note in his voice. "Trust me, the committee will love it. You may as well accept the fact you're going to dance before hundreds of people."

He frowned for several seconds before he let out a heavy sigh of resignation. "I suppose."

"And that means you're going to have to learn a few steps. A waltz, maybe even a tango or a foxtrot."

"Surely not." His face looked as pained as his voice.

"Surely so," she assured him. "It'll be fun."

He shot her a you've-got-to-be-kidding look before his Adam's apple bobbed. He'd clearly, and quite literally, found her comment hard to swallow.

"Tripping over one's feet in front of an audience isn't fun," he pointed out.

"That's why one learns," she said sweetly. "So we don't trip over our feet, or our partner's. Besides, I know you're the type who can master any skill that's important to you. Look at how well you can keyboard. Most docs are still on the hunt-and-peck method but you're in the same league as a transcriptionist."

"I'm a surgeon. I'm *supposed* to be good with my hands," he said, clearly dismissing her praise. Unbidden, her gaze dropped to the body part in question. For an instant she imagined what it would be like to enjoy this man's touch. Would he make love with the same single-minded approach he gave everything else in his life that he deemed important?

Sadly, she'd never know. She couldn't risk the rejection again. However, it had been a long time since she'd been in a relationship and he was handsome enough to make any girl dream of possibilities....

"Hands, feet, they all follow the brain's commands. 'Where there's a will there's a way'," she quoted.

He rubbed the back of his neck as he grimaced. "Are

you always full of helpful advice, Nurse Pollyanna?"
he complained.

Oh, my, but she'd just experienced another first—the
most taciturn physician on staff had actually *teased* her.
She was going to have to look outside for snow, which
never fell in the Midwest in August.

"I try." In the distance, she heard the tell-tale alarm
that signaled someone's IV bag had emptied. As if the
noise had suddenly reminded him of time and place,
he straightened, pulled on his totally professional demeanor like a well-worn lab coat, and pointed to the
monitor.

"Keep an eye on Mrs Hollings's chest tube. Call me
if you notice any change."

She was strangely disappointed to see the congenial
Lincoln Maguire had been replaced by his coolly polite
counterpart. "Will do."

Without giving him a backward glance, she rushed
to take care of John Carter's IV. He'd had a rough night
after his knee-replacement surgery and now that they'd
finally got his pain under control, he was catching up
on his sleep. She quickly silenced the alarm, hung a
fresh bag of fluid, then left the darkened room and
returned to the nurses' station. To her surprise, Linc
hadn't budged from his spot. He was simply sitting
there…as if waiting. For her, maybe? Impossible. Yet
it was a heady thought.

"One more thing," he said without preamble.

"What's that?" she asked, intending to head to the
supply cabinet on his other side in order to replenish
the supply of alcohol wipes she kept in her cargo pants
pocket.

He rose, effectively blocking her path. "I'll pick you up tonight."

Flustered by his statement, she made the mistake of meeting his blue-black gaze, which at her five-eight required some effort because he was at least six-three. It was a gaze that exuded confidence and lingered a few seconds too long.

"Pick me up?" she said. "What for?"

"You're going to Gail and Ty's for dinner, aren't you?"

"Yes," she began cautiously, "but how did you know?"

"Because they invited me, too."

Great. The first time Gail had hosted a dinner to include both of them, it had turned into a miserable evening. It had been obvious from the way Gail had steered the conversation that she'd been trying to push them together and her efforts had backfired. Lincoln had sat through the next hour wearing the most pained expression in between checking his watch every five minutes. To make matters worse, his attitude had made her nervous, so she'd chattered nonstop until he'd finally left with clear relief on his face. After that, Gail had promised never to put either of them through the misery of a private dinner again.

While the past few minutes had been pleasant, she wasn't going to believe that *this* dinner would end differently. Given his unhappiness over the fundraising idea, the results would be the same. It was inevitable.

"How nice," she said inanely.

"So I'll swing by and get you."

She bristled under his commanding tone. He might be able to expect his orders to be obeyed at the hospital, but this was *her* private life and she made her own decisions.

"Thanks, but don't go to the trouble. I'll drive myself."

"It's not inconvenient at all. Your house is on my way."

She stared at him, incredulous. She'd always believed he barely knew who she was, but he knew where she lived? How was that possible?

"Don't look so horrified," he said impatiently, as if offended by her surprise. "Gail gave me the address and suggested we come together."

Good old Gail. Her friend simply wouldn't stop in her effort to convince her to get back in the dating game, but to use her own brother-in-law when their previous encounter had turned into such a disaster? It only showed how determined—and desperate—her happily married buddy was.

"That's sweet, but I'd rather—"

"I'll pick you up at six," he said, before he strode away, leaving her to sputter at his high-handedness.

For an instant, she debated the merits of making him wait, then decided against it. Given their differing personalities, they'd clash soon enough without any effort on her part. There was no sense in starting off on a sour note. Besides, Gail had set dinner for six-thirty, which meant she'd timed her meal to be ready minutes later. If Christy flexed her proverbial muscles to teach Linc a lesson, she'd also make four people unhappy.

In a way, though, having him fetch her for dinner had that date-night feel to it. Although, she was quick to remind herself, just because it seemed like one on the surface—especially to anyone watching—it didn't mean it was *real*.

Wryly, she glanced down at her own chest, well aware of how deceiving appearances could be.

Linc strode up the walk to Christy's apartment, wondering if the evening would be as full of surprises as the day had been. He'd gone to the hospital as he did every morning, but today he'd been swept into the fundraising tide before he'd realized it. He couldn't say what had prompted him to force Christy into being his dance partner, but if she was going to drag him into her little schemes then it only seemed fair for her to pay the piper, too.

Of course, being her partner didn't pose any great hardship. She was sociable, attractive, and his thoughts toward her weren't always professional. He might even have allowed his sister-in-law to matchmake if Christy didn't have what he considered were several key flaws.

The woman was always haring off on some adventure or getting involved in every cause that came down the pike. While he'd been known to participate in a few adventures himself and had gotten involved in a cause or two of his own, he practiced restraint. Christy, on the other hand, seemed happiest when she flitted from one activity to another. She was like a rolling stone, intent on moving fast and often so she wouldn't gather moss.

His parents, especially his mother, had been like that. He, being the eldest, had always been left to pick up the pieces and he'd vowed he'd never put his children in a similar position.

No, Christy wasn't the one for him, even if she'd

captivated him with her looks and her charm. He simply needed a way to get her out of his system and the *Dancing with the Docs* idea seemed tailor-made to do just that. They'd spend time practicing and he'd learn just how unsuitable they were together. Then, and only then, he could forget about her and begin looking for the steady, dependable, down-to-earth woman he really wanted.

Your ideal woman sounds boring, his little voice dared to say.

Maybe so, he admitted, but there was nothing wrong with "boring". Perhaps if his parents had relegated their dream of becoming a superstar country music duo to the past where it had belonged, they wouldn't have driven that lonely stretch of highway halfway between here and Nashville at four a.m. They'd have been safe in bed, living long enough to see their children grow to adulthood.

As for tonight, he hadn't been able to coax the reason for their gathering from his sister-in-law or his brother, but it had to be important. After the last dinner-party fiasco between the four of them, only a compelling reason would have convinced Gail to repeat the experience.

Gail had been immensely disappointed that he and Christy hadn't clicked together like two cogs, but, as he'd later told her, Christy was everything he wasn't looking for in a romantic partnership. After all the upheavals in his life—his parents' deaths, school, work, college studies, raising siblings—he wanted someone who wasn't in search of the next spine-tingling, hair-raising adventure; someone stable, calm, and content. While it wasn't a bad thing that Christy's friendliness and sunny disposition attracted people like sugar called to ants, he wasn't interested in being one of a crowd of admirers.

Tonight he'd sit through dinner, learn what scheme Gail was up to now, spend the rest of the evening in Ty's den watching whatever sports event was currently televised, then drive Christy home. Dinner with Ty's family wasn't a red-letter occasion, but hanging with them was better than spending time alone.

He leaned on Christy's doorbell, but before the melodic chime barely began, he heard a deep-throated woof followed by thundering paws. Gail had never mentioned her friend owned a dog, so it was entirely possible he'd come to the wrong apartment.

His sister-in-law had told him apartment 4619, but given that the nine was missing from the house number above the porch light, he may have made an error in guessing his prize lay behind this particular door. However, the whimsical fairy stake poked into the pot of impatiens seemed to be the sort of yard ornament Christy would own.

As the footsteps—both human and canine—grew louder, he was already framing an apology for the intrusion when Christy flung open the door with one hand tucked under the black rhinestone-studded collar of a beautiful cream-colored Labrador.

He'd definitely come to the right place.

"Hi," he said inanely, aware he was out of practice when it came to picking up a date.

"Hi, yourself." Christy tugged the dog out of the way. "Come in, please."

He stepped inside and wasn't quite sure if he should look at her or the dog. He wasn't worried about Christy biting a hole in his thigh, though, so he focused on the animal and held out his hand for sniffing purposes. "Who is this lovely lady?"

"Her name is Ria," she said. "She's very protective of me, but she's really a sweetheart."

As expected, Ria sniffed his hand, then licked it, making Linc feel as if he'd passed doggy muster. "I can see that," he said.

She eyed her pet as Ria nudged Linc with her nose. "It appears you two are friends already."

"Dogs usually like me," he said. "Why, I'm not sure." His fondest memories involved pets, but after their family's golden retriever had died of old age when Linc had been sixteen, they'd never replaced him. As it had turned out, a few years later, his hands had been full trying to raising his younger siblings and attend college, without adding the responsibility of a canine.

"Animals are a far better judge of character than we are," she said. "However, Ria doesn't usually give her seal of approval so soon after meeting someone."

"Then I'm flattered." Then, because time was marching on, he asked, "Shall we go?"

Pink suddenly tinged her face. "I'm sorry, but I need a few more minutes."

He couldn't imagine why. She wore a red and white polka-dotted sundress with a matching short-sleeved jacket. Her bare legs were long and tanned and her toenails were painted a matching shade of red and one little toe had a silver ring encircling it.

Wisps of her short reddish-blonde hair framed her face most attractively and seemed to highlight her fine bone structure. From the freckles dancing across the bridge of her nose, she either didn't need makeup to create that warm glow or she only wore just enough to enhance her natural skin tone. He also caught a delightful whiff of citrus and spice that tempted him to lean into her neck and inhale deeply.

Certain she sensed his intense, and appreciative perusal, he met her gaze, hardly able to believe the non-hospital version of the dark-eyed Christy Michaels was so…gorgeous. As far as he was concerned, a few more minutes couldn't improve on the vision in front of him. The idea that he would spend his evening seated across from such delightful eye candy instead of poking inside someone's abdomen suddenly made him anticipate the hours ahead.

"You look great to me," he commented.

Apparently hearing the appreciation in his voice, she smiled. "Thanks, but Ria has carried off my sandals. She does that when she doesn't want me to leave, and now I'm trying to locate where she's stashed them. Would you mind checking around the living room while I go through my bedroom again?"

Ever practical and conscious of the time, he suggested, "You could wear a different pair."

"No can do," she said, plainly impervious to his suggestion. "They match this dress perfectly and nothing else I own will look quite right."

He wanted to argue that it was just the four of them and no one would notice much less care if her sandals coordinated with her dress, but she'd already disappeared down the hallway, leaving him to obey.

"Okay, Ria," he said to the Lab, "where's your favorite hiding place?"

Ria stared at him with a dopey grin on her face.

"No help from you, I see." Linc raised his voice. "Where does she normally hide her treasures?"

"Under the furniture," she called back, "or in her toy box."

Linc glanced around the great room and decided that Christy lived a relatively spartan existence. She didn't own a lot of furniture and other than a few silk flower arrangements scattered around, the surfaces were free of what he called dust-collectors, although none would pass the white-glove treatment.

Spartan or not, however, the room had that cluttered, lived-in feel. Decorative pillows were thrown haphazardly, a fuzzy Southwestern print afghan was tossed carelessly over one armchair, and women's magazines were gathered in untidy heaps on the floor.

Dutifully, he peeked under the floral-print sofa and found a few mismatched but brightly colored socks. Some were knee-length and others were just footies, but each one sported varying sizes of chew holes. Next, he moved to the matching side chair where he unearthed two pairs of silk panties—one black and one fire-engine-red—that couldn't claim more than a dollar's worth of fabric between them.

After adding the lingerie to his pile, he pinched the bridge of his nose and told himself to forget what he'd just seen and touched. Knowing her tastes ran along those kinds of lines, when he saw her on duty again, he'd have a difficult time keeping his mind off what might be underneath her scrub suit.

Shoot, why wait until then? His imagination was already running wild over what color underwear she was wearing under her sundress.

He carefully glanced around the room in search of something resembling a doggie toy box and found a wicker basket tucked on the bottom shelf of the bookcase in the corner filled with playthings that a canine would love. Resting on his haunches, he rummaged through a pile of half-chewed dog bones, several balls and Frisbees, a short rope, and an assortment of stuffed animals before he struck bottom.

"No shoes in here," he called out as he rose.

"Thanks for checking," she answered back.

His watch chimed the quarter-hour. "We really should be going."

"Just a few more minutes. I promise."

Because he had so little time for leisure reading, the books on her shelves drew his gaze next, and he took a few minutes to glance at the titles. Most of her paperbacks were romances with a few adventure novels sprinkled among them. He also ran across several cookbooks and a few exercise DVDs, but tucked among them were a few books that piqued his curiosity.

Chicken Soup for the Survivor's Soul. Life after Cancer. Foods that Fight. Staying Fit after Chemo.

Before he could wonder what had caused her interest in such topics, she returned to the living room, wearing a pair of strappy red high-heeled sandals that emphasized her shapely legs. "Sorry about the wait," she said breathlessly. "I found them in my laundry basket."

"Great. By the way, I ran across a few things you might have lost." He plucked his pile of treasures off the coffee table and handed them to her.

MILLS &
BOON ®

millsandboon.co.uk

Get an **EXCLUSIVE 15% OFF ORDERS**

when you order online today!

Simply enter the code **15JUN12** as you checkout and the discount will automatically be applied to your order. **BUT HURRY**, this offer ends on 30th June 2012.

All of the latest titles are available 1 MONTH AHEAD of the shops, **PLUS:**

- 🌹 **Titles available in paperback and eBook**

- 🌹 **Huge savings** on titles you may have missed

- 🌹 **Try before you buy** with Browse the Book

Shop now at **millsandboon.co.uk**

Her face turned a lovely shade of pink as she eyed the scraps on top. "I wondered where those had gone," she said, her chuckle quite pleasing to his ears. "I've blamed the washing machine all this time. Ria, you've been a bad girl."

Ria sank onto her belly and placed her head on her front paws.

"But I love you anyway," she said as she crouched down to scratch behind the dog's ears. "Now, behave while we're gone."

As she rubbed, Ria responded with a contented sigh and a blissful doggy smile before rolling over onto her back for a tummy rub. Obviously Christy had The Touch, and immediately he wanted to feel her fingers working their magic on *his* sore spots.

He tore his gaze from the sight, reminding himself that Christy wasn't his type even if she could engender all sorts of unrealistic thoughts. She was too perky, too lively, and too *everything*. Women like her weren't content with the mundane aspects of living. They wanted the constant stimulation of social activities, four-star shopping and exotic vacations. Staying home for popcorn and a movie would be considered slumming.

"Are we ready now?" he asked, conscious of his peevish tone when all he wanted to do was shake these wicked mental pictures out of his head.

She straightened. "Of course. Sorry to keep you waiting."

To his regret, the warm note in her voice had disappeared and he wondered what it would take to bring it back. If he walked into his brother's house with icicles hanging in the air, his sister-in-law would read him the

Riot Act. He didn't know why Gail was so protective of Christy, but she was.

Minutes later, Linc found himself on the sidewalk, accompanying her to his car. He couldn't explain why he found the need to rest his hand on the small of her back—it wasn't as if the sidewalk was icy and he intended to keep her from falling—but he did.

That small, politely ingrained action made him wonder if his plan to concentrate on his career should be revised. He was thirty-seven now and he had to admit that at times he grew weary of his own company. To make matters worse, lately, being around Gail and Ty made him realize just how much he was missing.

Now was one of those moments. Especially when he caught a glimpse of a well-formed knee and a trim ankle as he helped her into the passenger seat.

He might be physically attracted to Christy Michaels, but their temperaments made them polar opposites. He had enough drama in his life and when he came home at night, he wanted someone to share his quiet and peaceable existence, not someone who thrived on being the life of a party.

Opposites or not, though, he wasn't going to pass the drive in chilly silence. Given how much she obviously loved Ria, he knew exactly how to break the ice.

"After seeing your dog, I'm wondering if I should get one," he commented as he slid behind the wheel.

"They're a lot of work, but the companionship is worth every minute," she said. "Did you have a breed in mind?"

"No, but I'd lean toward a collie or a retriever. We

had one when I was a kid. Skipper died of old age, but we didn't replace him."

She nodded. "I can understand that. Bringing a new pet home can make you feel guilty—like you're replacing them as easily as you replace a worn-out pair of socks—when in actuality, you aren't replacing them because they'll always be a part of you, no matter what."

Spoken like a true dog lover, he thought, impressed by her insight.

"Why don't you have a dog now?" she asked.

"Isn't it obvious? A pet doesn't fit into my lifestyle."

"Oh." He heard a wealth of emotion—mainly disappointment—in the way she uttered that one word. It was almost as if she found him lacking when she should have been impressed by his thoughtfulness. After all, the poor mutt would be the one suffering from inattention.

"You're probably right," she added politely. "They do have a habit of ruining the best-laid plans."

The conversation flagged, and he hated that the relaxed mood between them had become strained once again. Wasn't there anything they could discuss without venturing into rocky territory? If he didn't do something to lighten the tension, they'd face an uncomfortable evening ahead of them. He'd already promised Gail he'd be on his best behavior, so he had to repair the damage before they arrived.

Recalling another subject in which she'd seemed quite passionate, he asked, "Any word on the festival fundraiser idea?"

"According to Denise, it's a go." To his relief, the

lilt in her voice had returned, although her revelation wasn't the news he'd wanted to hear.

"I was afraid of that."

"Still worried about dancing in front of people?"

"Not worried," he corrected. "Uncomfortable."

"As a surgeon, you should be used to being in the spotlight."

"Yes, but it isn't the same spotlight," he insisted. In the OR, he actually knew what he was doing and was at ease in his own skin. Sailing around a dance floor didn't compare.

"The problem is, my schedule for the next month is a killer and lessons are out of the question," he explained. "My partners are going on vacation and—"

"No one said you had to take lessons," she pointed out.

The motto he'd lived by was simple. *Anything worth doing was worth doing well.* If he was going to participate in this dancing thing, then he'd put forth his best effort.

"Whatever we do at the time of the competition will be fine with me," she added. "If you just want to stand and sway to the music, I'll be happy."

"You told me this morning it wouldn't be good enough," he accused.

She shrugged. "I changed my mind. I'm not participating to win a prize."

He didn't think the possibility of taking first place was her motive. She was simply one of those people who threw herself into whatever project caught her fancy, which was also why he disagreed with her remark about being happy. Christy had too much vim and vigor to be content with a lackluster performance. Even *he* wasn't satisfied and he was far less outgoing than she was.

All of which meant that he was going to have to carve out time in his schedule for lessons—lessons that involved holding this woman with her citrusy scent and skimpy underwear in his arms.

Merely picturing those moments was enough to send his blood tumbling through his body at a fast and furious rate. The things a man had to do for charity...

Christy had known her evening was off to a bad start when Ria hid her shoes. She'd hoped to find them before Linc arrived but, as luck would have it, she hadn't. Although he'd been polite about it, clearly the delay had taxed his patience and his perfectly timed schedule.

Yet she'd enjoyed the little courtesies he'd shown her. Being in the close confines of his vehicle, she'd been painfully aware of his fresh, clean scent to the point her throat went dry.

Of all the men in her circle of friends and acquaintances, why did *he* have to be the one who oozed sex appeal? After feeling his hand at her waist, she honestly didn't know how she'd survive an evening as his dance partner.

To make matters worse, Gail had seated her next to him at the dinner table and his arm had brushed against hers on several occasions as they'd passed the food.

Maybe she needed to call an escort service in order to calm those suddenly raging hormones, but her fear of rejection was too strong to risk it. If a man who'd supposedly loved her hadn't been able to handle her diagnosis and resultant treatment, who else could?

No, better that she hurry home after dinner, take Ria for a long run at the dog park until they were both too tired to do more than curl up on the sofa with a carton of frozen chocolate yogurt, a handful of dog treats, and a sappy movie on the TV screen.

Linc's voice forced her to focus on her surroundings. "Okay, you two. What's up? And don't tell me 'Nothing' because I know you both too well to believe otherwise."

Gail and Ty looked at each other with such an expression of love between them that Christy was half-jealous. Made a little uncomfortable by their silent exchange, she glanced at Linc and immediately noticed the similarities between the brothers.

They had the same bone structure, the same complexion, and the same shade of brown hair. Both Maguire males were handsome but, to her, Linc's features were far more interesting—probably because life had left its imprint on them. According to Gail, as the oldest brother, Linc had stepped into his parents' role after their deaths in a car accident when he was nineteen and he'd guided his younger siblings through their rocky teenage years. It was only logical that the sudden responsibility had formed him into the driven, purposeful man he was today.

Christy glanced at her dark-haired friend and saw the gentle smile on her face. "You're pregnant again?" she guessed.

Gail patted her husband's hand as she shook her head. "No. But maybe we can announce that when we get back."

"Get back? Where are you going?"

Ty answered his brother's question. "Paris."

Christy was stunned…and envious. It was one of the cities she'd put on the bucket list she'd created during her chemotherapy sessions. "Oh, how fun. I've always wanted to go there."

Linc didn't seem to share her excitement. "Paris? As in France? Or Paris, as in Texas?"

"France," Ty told him. "My company is opening an overseas branch and they want a computer consultant to be on site. They chose me."

Linc reached across the table to shake his brother's hand. "Congratulations. You've worked hard for this. I'm proud of you. How long will you be gone?"

Ty exchanged a glance with Gail. "Two months, give or take a few weeks, depending on how well the project progresses. Because Gail knows the secretarial ropes of our firm, my boss has offered to send her as my assistant."

Theirs had been an office romance and after Derek had arrived, Gail had cut her work status to part time.

"And the kids?" Christy thought of six-year-old Emma and eight-year-old Derek, who'd already been excused from the table to play outside with their friends. "What about them?"

Gail's expression turned hopeful. "That's why you're both here tonight. We wanted to ask a favor."

"Anything," she promptly replied.

"Would you and Linc be their guardians and take care of them while we're gone?"

CHAPTER TWO

CHRISTY was overwhelmed by their request but in her mind she didn't have any doubts as to her answer. She loved the Maguire children and she couldn't wait to step into a temporary mom role. Because of her diagnosis and the resultant treatment, she'd already resigned herself to the possibility that Ria might be the closest thing to ever having a child of her own, so the idea of acting as a fill-in mother was exciting.

She was also quite aware that Gail had chosen *her* out of all their friends and family to take on this responsibility. Okay, so they'd asked Linc, too, but he didn't really count. His work was his life and by his own admission his schedule for the next few weeks was packed. For all intents and purposes, she'd be on her own.

It was a heady thought.

It was also quite daunting.

She started to speak, but Gail forestalled her. "Christy, I know you'll immediately agree because it's in your nature to help out a friend. And, Linc, I know you'll accept because you're family, but before either of you commit yourselves, I want you to know *exactly* what you'd be letting yourselves in for. And if either of you have second thoughts, we won't be hurt or upset."

"Okay," Christy said, certain she wouldn't change her mind no matter what Gail and Ty told them. "We're listening."

"First, we'd expect you to live here because it will be best if Derek and Emma stick with the familiar."

Christy hadn't considered that, but Gail's plan made perfect sense. Living in their home wouldn't pose any hardship whatsoever. What it would require, though, was coordination between her schedule and Linc's to be sure they covered every hour of every day, and she was curious how Gail had ironed that small but important detail. No doubt, she'd learn the answer shortly.

"What about Ria?" she asked. "I'd hate to board her for that length of time."

"She's welcome, too," Ty answered. "In fact, I know the kids would be thrilled. They've been asking for a dog for some time, and looking after Ria will give them a taste of what pet ownership is about."

Satisfied by how easily that potential problem had been averted, Christy relaxed. She imagined her Labrador and the kids playing Frisbee in the large Maguire back yard and could hear the children's laughter interspersed with Ria's excited woofs. They'd have a great time.

"Second," Gail continued, "the fall term starts next week so the kids will already be in a routine before we leave the week after that. On the days Christy doesn't work, you'll have to take them to school and pick them up at four, which shouldn't pose a problem.

"The days you both work are little trickier as there's a two-hour window when Linc would be on his own. One of the neighborhood high-school girls—Heather—

can come by around six-thirty to fix breakfast and take them to school. She'll come sooner to cover that window if Linc's on call, but you'll have to let her know the night before.

"Then, at the end of the day, the kids can walk across the street to the church's after-school daycare until Christy's shift ends at five. The daycare is open until seven, so that works out well." She smiled. "Repeat as necessary."

"It sounds as if you've thought of everything," Christy said.

"We tried," Gail answered.

"Do Emma and Derek know you're asking me?" As Linc stiffened beside her, she corrected herself. "I mean *us*?"

"It was the only way they'd agree to being left behind," Gail admitted ruefully. "I suspect they think you'll cater to their every whim. I know what a pushover you are, Christy..." she softened her statement with a smile "...so I'm counting on you to be firm."

"Be firm," she repeated. "Got it."

"Don't kid yourself," Ty warned. "They'll push you to the max. You can't be the benevolent aunt and uncle. This isn't a weekend vacation."

"In other words, you expect us to give them a healthy breakfast, send them to bed on time, and eat dinner before dessert," Linc said.

His sidelong glance made Christy wonder if he'd mentioned those things purely for her benefit. Didn't he think she had an ounce of common sense? He obviously suspected she'd offer cookies and cake for breakfast, lunch, and dinner, and let them stay up as late as they pleased. While she didn't consider herself a rule-breaker, she also knew that every moment should be lived to its fullest. If a few rules had to be broken on occasion, then so be it.

Now that she'd raised the question in her mind, she took it a step further. Did he have the same lack of faith in her nursing skills as he obviously did in her parenting abilities? There hadn't been a single incident when he'd questioned her patient care, but she'd ask him when they were alone.

"We're asking a lot from both of you," Ty added, "but you were first on our list."

"I appreciate the vote of confidence," Christy said. "Count me in."

"Me, too," Linc added. "We only need to choose which days are yours and which are mine."

She nodded, although she would have preferred having Linc suggest that she be their sole caretaker while he filled in when his schedule allowed. Clearly, he wanted equal, or as near equal, time as possible.

Darn the man!

"Actually, we want you both to stay here," Gail said. "Together."

Christy met Linc's startled gaze and guessed that her own surprise mirrored his. "At the same time?" she asked redundantly.

Gail nodded. "That way, if Linc gets called out for a patient in the middle of the night, he won't have to worry about the kids because you're just down the hall. You two won't have to rearrange and juggle your own schedules, so it'll be less disruptive for everyone."

They wanted her to stay here, in their house, with

Linc? Christy had a difficult time wrapping her brain around that concept. While they were amicable enough to each other at the hospital, being together twenty-four seven meant they'd drive each other crazy within a week, and then where would the kids be? Most likely in the middle of a war zone.

What concerned her even more, though, was the simple question of how would she handle being in such close proximity to a guy she found so attractive? If seeing him in a scrub suit and interacting with him on a purely professional basis made her nervous and sent her imagination soaring, how would she manage if she saw that handsome smile, those broad shoulders on a regular, casual basis?

"This is how we want it," Gail said, as if she sensed Christy's reservations. "The kids will handle our absence better if they stay in their normal surroundings. That's not to say they can't spend a night or two elsewhere, but we'd feel better knowing they're in familiar territory and in the same homey, two-parent environment."

"We know it won't be easy for either of you because you're both so fiercely independent, so if it's a problem, we can ask someone else," Ty said.

Miss the opportunity to pamper Gail's kids? Not a chance. Yes, Linc would probably drive her crazy with his rigid, no-time-to-stop-and-smell-the-roses attitude, but she was an adult. She could handle the inevitable clashes.

On the other hand, Linc went to work early and stayed late. Chances were they wouldn't see each other until the kids went to bed. Afterward, they could each slink into their separate corners.

It was a workable plan, she decided. If it wasn't, she'd dream up a Plan B. Emma and Derek's well-being was what mattered, not her personal preferences.

"If you can handle the arrangements we've outlined—"

"Piece of cake," Christy said, although the idea of living under the same roof as Linc gave her some pause.

"Not a problem," Linc added. "We can learn to live with each other for a few weeks."

"Good. Then it's settled." Gail beamed. "You don't know what a relief this is for us."

As Christy glanced around the table, Gail was the only one who seemed remotely satisfied with the arrangement. She saw a combination of speculation and caution in Ty's eyes as he studied his brother. Linc's squared jaw and the chiseled lines around his mouth reflected resignation rather than enthusiasm. No doubt her reservations were clear on her face as well.

Living under the same roof was only a two-month gig or less, she consoled herself, and those six or eight weeks were nothing more than a single pebble along life's riverbed. She could endure *anything* for that length of time, because the benefits of being with Emma and Derek overshadowed the potential problems. If she could survive breast cancer, she could handle Lincoln Maguire's idiosyncrasies.

"I know what you're going to say." Ty held up his hands to forestall Linc's comments the moment the two of them were alone on the shaded back-yard patio, "but before you unload, hear me out."

Linc took a swig from his bottle of cold root beer. "I'm listening."

"You're upset we asked Christy to help you, but honestly our decision is no reflection on your parenting abilities. You've had the kids before and they came back raving about the great time they had. They love you and I know you love them."

He did. No matter how busy he was, he'd move heaven and earth for his niece and nephew. They were his family, and even if he wasn't in any hurry to have one of his own, those bonds were still important to him.

"I can't imagine a single scenario you can't handle by yourself with your eyes closed and one hand tied behind your back," Ty added loyally.

"Thanks for the vote of confidence."

"After all," Ty continued, "you kept us on the straight and narrow when you were hardly out of your teenage years yourself. Joanie and I weren't angels either, if I recall. I'm sure there were times when you wanted to tear out your hair, and ours, too, but you didn't. When you finally decide to focus on your personal life instead of your professional one, you're going to be a great dad."

Linc recognized Ty's strategy. "You can stop heaping on the praise, pip-squeak," he affectionately told his brother. "In the middle of all that, I know there's a 'but'."

Ty grinned sheepishly. "I never could fool you for long, could I? The thing is, we're talking two months. You don't have the usual nine-to-five job, and we had to think of a contingency plan for the times you work late, go in early, or get called out in the wee hours, because we don't expect you to put your doctor business on hold for us."

Linc shifted in his chair, suddenly uncomfortable at hearing how lonely his life sounded, even if the description was uncannily accurate.

"I'll confess that sharing the responsibility with another person bothered me," he admitted soberly, "but your way is best for the kids' well-being. I even see your point about asking us to stay here *together.*"

He saw the logic behind their request, but he didn't like it, especially now that he'd seen those small scraps of silk Christy called underwear. How was he supposed to focus on the youngsters when a picture of her wearing a pair of those and just a smile kept popping into his head at the most inopportune times?

He might not find fault with her nursing skills, but taking care of patients wasn't the same as maintaining a home and looking after the needs of two children on a round-the-clock basis.

Did she even know how to boil water? If the stories circulating about her were to be believed—and he didn't dispute them because he'd heard her share some of them herself—she rarely sat still long enough for such mundane things. Canoeing down the Amazon, skydiving in California, white-water rafting in Colorado, cross-country motorcycle trips and a few laps around the Daytona 500 speedway were only part of her repertoire of experiences.

Lessons from Martha Stewart or Rachel Ray weren't on the list.

Her culinary skills aside, he hoped she had more redeeming qualities than being Gail's friend who was the life of every party and who owned a dog that Emma and Derek loved. As far as he was concerned, they could have handled the nights he was on call on a case-by-case basis, but if this was how his brother wanted it, then he would suffer in silence.

"I'm glad you're being a good sport about this," Ty said. "And when you feel your control slipping over the edge, think of your circumstances as some of the medicine you forced down our throats as kids." He grinned. "It tastes terrible going down, but in the end it cures what ails you."

Two weeks later, Christy made a point to hang around the nurses' station to lie in wait for Linc. Ever since their dinner with Gail and Ty, he'd slipped in and out of their unit like a wraith. She knew he was extra-busy right now, with one of his partners on vacation, but she wasn't completely convinced that he wasn't avoiding her as well.

As of tonight they'd more or less be living together and she had a few issues she wanted to iron out before they actually became roomies, but those would have to wait. Her patient, Jose Lopez, a recent ruptured appendix case, concerned her.

Her patience paid off. Linc strode in shortly before eight looking more handsome than a man who had spent his day with sick people had a right to. His yellow polo shirt stretched across his shoulders and his hair had a damp curl as if he'd just got out of the shower.

He didn't walk with a cocky swagger but carried himself with a quiet confidence that suggested no problem was too big for him to solve. She certainly hoped so because today she had one.

She immediately cornered him before he could disappear into a patient room.

"I don't like the way Jose, Mr Lopez, looks," she said without preamble.

"Okay," he said with equanimity. "What's his complaint?"

"He doesn't have one, as such."

He lifted one eyebrow. "You aren't giving me much to go on. A diagnosis of 'He doesn't look right' isn't strong enough to justify a battery of tests."

Her face warmed under his rebuke. Other physicians would have attributed her impression as that proverbial gut feeling no one could afford to ignore, but clearly Lincoln Maguire didn't believe in intuition. He only wanted cold, hard evidence. As far as she was concerned, he'd answered her private question about what he thought of her nursing savvy.

"I realize that," she said stiffly, her spine straight, "which is why I've been watching him. He doesn't complain about pain as such, but he finally admitted he has a few twinges because I've caught him rubbing his chest. According to the nursing notes, he received an antacid for heartburn several times during the night."

"You don't think heartburn is a possibility?" he asked.

"No," she said bluntly, "but only because I think his skin color is off."

He retrieved the chart on the computer and began perusing the notes. "How are his oxygen sats?"

"On the low end of normal."

"Shortness of breath?"

She shook her head. "He said his chest sometimes feels a little tight, but that's all."

He stared thoughtfully at the computer before meeting her gaze. "It could be anything and it could be nothing."

"I know, which is why I wanted to ask you to check him thoroughly."

He hesitated for a fraction of a second before he shrugged. "Okay. Duly noted. I'll see what I can find."

She'd been half-afraid he'd dismiss her concerns, so she was grateful to hear of his intentions to follow through. And because she was relieved to pass the burden onto his shoulders, she chose to make small talk as they strode toward the room. "Are you ready for tonight?"

"I am," he said. "Do you need help taking anything over to Ty's house?"

"Not now," she said. "I'm only moving some clothes and a few books. What I don't bring now, I can always get later."

"Fair enough." He strode into Lopez's room and the subject was closed.

Christy watched and listened as Linc checked his patient, seeming much more congenial with Jose than with her, but, then, a lot of the nurses had said he was far more personable with his patients than with the staff. She took some comfort in that because she'd begun to wonder if he was only uncomfortable around her.

"I hear you're having a few chest twinges," Linc mentioned as he pulled out his stethoscope and listened to Jose's heart and lung sounds.

"Some. It's happening more often than it did yesterday, though. Sometimes I cough for no reason," the forty-year-old replied. Jose was of average height, but between his wife's reportedly fantastic cooking and his years as a stonemason, he was built like the bricks he laid for a living. "Do you think it's the hospital food? Maybe it's giving me the heartburn." His tanned, leathery face broke into a smile.

Linc laughed. "If you're hinting that you want me to give Francesca permission to bring you some of her famous enchiladas, you'll be disappointed."

"It was worth a try, Doc."

Christy watched the friendly exchange, stunned by how Linc's smile made him seem so…*normal*. Clearly, the man did have moments when he wasn't completely focused on his work, but she'd gone on countless rounds with him over the past year and had never heard such a heartfelt sound. She would have remembered if she had. Somehow, she sensed the two of them had more than a simple doctor-patient relationship, which only made her curious as to what connection a blue-collar worker like Jose had with the highly successful general surgeon.

He flung the stethoscope around his neck. "A few more days and you can eat her cooking to your heart's content. Meanwhile, though, I want to check out these little twinges and the cough you're having. We're going to run a few tests so be prepared for everything from X-rays and EKGs to blood work."

Jose's expression sobered. "You think it's my heart?"

"Not necessarily. If your chest feels tight and you're noticing a cough, pneumonia is a concern," he said, "so I'm going to try and discover what's going on. As you said, you may only have heartburn but, to be thorough, we're going to check out everything. Okay?"

His confidence was reassuring because Jose's face relaxed. It was obvious why Linc's patients loved him, and why he was so very busy.

"Are you having any pain in your legs?" Linc asked.

Jose wrinkled his face in thought. "I had a charley horse earlier in my right calf, but it's gone now."

Linc immediately flung back the sheet and checked his legs. "We'll look into that, too," he said, sounding unconcerned, "and as soon as I get those results, we'll let you know what we've found. Okay?" He patted Jose's shoulder before he left.

Outside Lopez's room, Christy immediately pounced. "Then I was right. You found something."

"Not really," he admitted.

"Oh." Her good spirits deflated.

"Are you sure his condition has changed in the last twenty-four hours?"

She knew what her intuition was telling her and she wasn't going to back down. "He said himself he has a cough and his chest feels tight," she reminded him. "Now he has a muscle spasm in his leg. Those are new symptoms."

He looked thoughtful for a moment. "Okay," he said decisively. "I want a chest X-ray, a Doppler exam on his legs, and blood drawn for a blood count, a cardiac panel and a D-dimer test."

She recognized the latter as one used to diagnose the presence of a blood clot. "Do you suspect a PE?" She used the shorthand for pulmonary embolism.

"I suspect a lot of things, but in the interest of ruling

out as much as we can we'll add that to the list of possibilities. I also want a CT scan of his lungs and if the results are inconclusive, I want a VQ scan."

The CT scan was a quick way to detect a blood clot, but not every clot was detected using this procedure, which meant the next step was the VQ scan. The two-part ventilation-perfusion procedure used both injected and aerosolized radioactive material to show the amount of blood and air flowing through the lungs. Naturally, if the patterns were abnormal, intervention was required.

"I'll get right on it," she said.

"And call me ASAP with those results," he ordered in the brisk tone she knew so well.

As Christy placed the various orders into the computer system, she was hoping the tests would show something to support her nagging intuition, although she hoped it would be something relatively uncomplicated.

Several hours later the results were in. Shortly after Christy phoned him with the radiologist's report, Linc appeared on the unit. Asking for her to join him, he marched directly into his patient's room.

"Jose," he said briskly, "I have news on your tests."

Jose nodded his salt-and-pepper head. "I had a feeling something was wrong when they stuck me in that fancy X-ray machine," he said. "How bad is it?"

"You have a very small blood clot in your leg and a small one in your lung, which isn't good," Linc said bluntly.

"But you can fix it. Right?"

Christy recognized the hope and the uncertainty on the man's face. She knew exactly how he felt.

"This is where I give you the good news," Linc said kindly. "I'm going to start you on a variety of blood thinners and other drugs that will work to dissolve the clots so they don't break off and plug a major vessel. It'll take time—you won't be cured overnight—but eventually you should be fine."

Jose leaned head back against the pillows in obvious relief.

"The other good news is that you had a nurse who was on the ball so we could catch the problem early," Linc said as he eyed Christy. "A lot of patients aren't that fortunate."

"And I should be fine?" Jose repeated, clearly wanting reassurance that the final outcome would be positive.

"Yes."

After a few more minutes of discussing Jose's treatment plan, they left. Outside the room Linc pulled her aside. "Increase his oxygen and keep a close eye on him. I want to know if there's a change, no matter how slight."

"Okay."

"Tomorrow, we'll—" he began.

"It's Saturday," she reminded him. "I'm off duty. Emma and Derek, remember?"

He looked surprised, as if for a minute he'd forgotten what day it was. "Then I'll see you tonight," he said.

"Before or after dinner?"

"Before, I suppose. Why?"

She was flying high on her success, so she couldn't hold back from teasing him. "Just checking to see if I can serve dessert as the appetizer or not."

His eyes narrowed ever so slightly. "You're kidding, aren't you?"

"Of course I am," she responded pertly. "Contrary to what you might think, I can exercise self-control and I do use the gray matter between my ears from time to time."

His eyes suddenly gleamed with humor. "I stand corrected. Either way, though, I'll be at the house in time to take Gail and Ty to the airport."

She received the distinct impression that he would move heaven and earth to do so. It also occurred to her that he might be as reluctant to see his brother leave as his niece and nephew were.

"Okay, we'll save you a piece of cake."

"Do that. By the way, good work with Lopez today."

His unexpected praise only added to her high spirits. "Thanks."

"See you tonight," he said, before he turned on one heel and left.

She stared at his backside until he rounded the corner, startled by how *husbandly* he'd sounded. Suddenly she realized that not only would she see him tonight, she'd see him *every* night thereafter, too.

It also meant that every night he'd drop the trappings of his profession and she wouldn't have the barrier of the doctor-nurse relationship to keep her wicked imagination in check. He'd appear as a normal guy—one who mowed the grass, took out the trash, left dirty dishes in the sink, and woke up every morning with his hair mussed and a whiskery shadow on his face.

Anticipation shivered down her spine.

* * *

She was being completely unreasonable.

Linc walked into the kitchen of Gail and Ty's house with his small entourage and fought to keep his voice even-tempered. It had been a long day in his practice and seeing off his younger brother to another country for two months—*Paris*, no less—had been far more emotionally draining than he'd expected. He'd left his twenties behind ages ago and was a highly respected surgeon, yet he felt as lost as he had when he'd moved Ty into his first apartment.

Ty might not need him in that big-brother-knows-best role, but it was still hard to accept whenever the fact hit him between the eyes. No, he wanted to veg out with nothing more mentally or emotionally taxing than a game of checkers with Derek or a tea party with Emma, but if Christy had her way, it wouldn't happen.

"Going out to dinner when Gail has a refrigerator full of food waiting for us is unnecessary," he pointed out. "Need I also remind you it's Friday night?" Which meant every restaurant was packed and would be for quite a while.

"I know it's Friday and I agree that eating out isn't *necessary*," she said with a hint of steel underneath her sweet tone, "but it would be *fun*."

He rubbed his face. *Fun* was going to become a four-letter word if every activity had to be measured against that standard. "We have all weekend for fun."

She rubbed the back of her neck in a frustrated gesture and drew a deep breath. "I realize that," she finally said, "but look at those two. Don't you think they need something as a pick-me-up *now*, rather than tomorrow?"

He glanced at Derek and noticed his slumped posture

in the straight-backed chair, his ball cap pulled low as he rested his chin on his propped arm. Emma sat beside him and occasionally wiped her eyes and sniffled as her thin shoulders shook. Christy's Lab stood between the two, gazing at one then the other, as if trying to decide which one needed her comfort more.

They made a dejected picture, which was only understandable. They'd just driven home from the airport after saying goodbye to their parents and the reality of the situation had hit them hard.

"I agree they're down in the dumps, but a fast-food hamburger won't make them feel better."

"You might be surprised." She clapped her hands. "Hey, kids, how does a picnic sound? Ria needs a spin around the dog park and while she's running around with her buddies, we'll enjoy our dinner in the great outdoors."

A picnic, at seven o'clock at night, with dark clouds rolling in and rain in the forecast, wasn't Linc's idea of fun. While the kids didn't seem overly enthusiastic with her suggestion, interest flickered in Derek's eyes and Emma's shoulders stopped shaking as she gazed expectantly at Christy. Apparently Ria recognized the word *park* because her ears suddenly perked and her tail wagged.

"Then it's settled," she declared, although as far as Linc was concerned she'd simply made an executive decision. Because he knew they had to do something drastic or the entire evening would remain miserable for everyone, he let it stand. "Everyone can make his or her own sandwich and then we're off."

Before Linc could wonder where the dog park actually was, Christy had emptied the refrigerator and created an assembly line of fixings. "Who wants to be first?" she asked.

The two children rushed to her side and began assembling their sandwiches with her help. Linc hovered in the background, ready to kill the idea if the kids gave him the slightest bit of encouragement.

They didn't. In fact, he would never have thought the idea of a picnic would have turned the mood around so quickly. Ordinary sandwiches suddenly became gourmet delights under Christy's tutelage. Every now and then a tasty nugget would fall and an ever-vigilant Ria would snap up the evidence.

He noticed Derek had made himself a man-sized meal while Emma's dinner was a dainty mix of meat, cheese, and pickles sliced into four perfect triangles. Christy, he'd noticed, used a special roll and included lots of lettuce and tomato as well as thinly sliced cucumbers, avocado, and black olives on a thin layer of slivered turkey.

She glanced at him with a raised eyebrow. "You'd better start assembling or you'll end up without."

"Yours looks so good, maybe you can make an extra," he said hopefully.

"Sorry. Dinner tonight is self-service." She slid the package of rolls in his direction. "He who doesn't fix his own doesn't eat."

"Yeah, Unca Linc," Emma said as she speared olives onto her fingers and began eating them. "You have to get in the spirit. Ria and I are gonna play catch with her Frisbee. Wanna play with us?"

"We'll see," he said as he opened a roll and piled on

his ingredients. Just before he was ready to position the top part of the bun, Christy held up a shaker.

"What's that?" he asked.

"A little extra flavor," she said. "Garlic, onion, and few other spices. Want to try some?"

Three people's gazes rested on him and each one reflected open curiosity, as if they were expecting him to refuse. Was he that predictable?

"Sure, why not?" he said. "Tonight's a night to throw caution to the wind and have fun. Who cares about bad breath? Right, kids?"

"Right," they echoed.

Yet as he watched Christy pop a slice of avocado into her kissable mouth, he realized there was an advantage to having garlic breath. He wouldn't be tempted to do something immensely stupid on their first night together.

Soon they were on their way with food and bottled drinks in the ice chest, a few blankets, Ria's toys and water bowl. By the time they'd arrived at the dog park, Christy had led them in a noisy rendition of "B-I-N-G-O" that made his ears hurt.

"Aren't you going to sing?" Christy asked him when the group stopped momentarily for breath.

He couldn't stop a smile, neither did he want to because the excitement had become infectious. "First you roped me into dancing, and now you expect me to become a vocalist? A man has to draw the line somewhere," he said, pretending affront.

"Spoilsport." She obviously didn't take offense because she chuckled, then immediately led them in the next stanza.

As he looked into the back seat in the rearview mirror, hearing Emma and Derek's laughter was far better than seeing them with sad faces, so he didn't have the heart to tell them to tone down the noise level.

He also didn't have the heart to scold them for eating only half of their food because they were in such a rush to play with Ria before the rain fell.

"They're going to be starving later," he said as Christy wrapped up their sandwiches.

"Probably," she agreed, "but their sandwiches will keep. How's your dinner?"

He polished off his last bite before grabbing a bunch of red grapes. "Delicious."

"Then we should do this more often."

"Maybe," he said, unwilling to commit.

"Food always tastes better eaten outside."

He glanced around the park, noting that several other families had taken advantage of the picnic tables. "Oh, I don't know," he mused, thinking of ants and flies and a host of other associated nuisances, not to mention spilled drinks and sticky hands. "It isn't always a great experience."

She chuckled. "Let me guess. Your idea of eating outside is gobbling down a bagel or a burger while you're stuck in traffic."

It was uncanny how accurately she could read him and they'd hardly spent any time together. How much of his soul would she see by the end of two months? "Yeah," he admitted.

"That doesn't count. You have to soak up the ambience of your surroundings. Allow nature's scents of pine and honeysuckle and lavender to mingle with the aroma of the food." She inhaled. "That's what dining outdoors is all about."

As she closed her eyes, he had the strangest urge to trace the line of her jaw with his fingertips and kiss away the fleck of avocado on the corner of her mouth. He also wanted to see if her strawberry-blonde hair was as soft as it looked, discover if she'd fit against his body as perfectly as he imagined.

Giving in to temptation wasn't a wise thing to do. He simply had to deny that sudden attraction because if he didn't, it would only create more problems in the long run. They were only two people who shared the responsibility of two kids for a few weeks. Nothing more, nothing less.

And yet her soft skin beckoned and his fingers itched to explore...

A sudden crack of thunder told him the storm would arrive soon. Immediately, he rose. "Come on, kids. Time to load up and head for home."

As the children scampered back to their picnic table, with Ria keeping pace, he was once again grateful to see smiles on their faces.

"They really needed this, didn't they?" he mused as he helped Christy pack up the ice chest.

"Of course they did. Otherwise they would have moped all evening."

"Bedtime still could be rocky," he warned.

"Probably," she admitted, "but why do you think I wanted them to chase Ria? I predict they'll be too tired to think much about their parents being gone."

"And if they do?"

"Then we give them something to look forward to

tomorrow. Before they know it, one day will slide into another and the weeks will fly by."

She was right. His whole life had been about staying busy and the years had blended together. Other than a few milestones to mark the passage of time, including his birthday, one month wasn't any different than the next.

"I hope you're right. In any case, your picnic idea was brilliant."

She laughed. "Oh, my. Two compliments in one day. You aren't feverish, are you?"

As she placed her palm on his forehead, his heart immediately pounded to a double-time beat. He was hot all right, but it had nothing to do a virus and everything to do with her.

CHAPTER THREE

"TELL me the story of the princess again, Unca Linc," Emma demanded.

"We read Penelope's tale already," he told her.

"Not hers. I want to hear the one you have in your head."

Christy smiled at the sight of the six-year-old, wearing her frilly pink nightgown, snuggled under Linc's left arm, while Derek, clad in camouflage pj's, lounged on the chair's opposite arm.

What struck her most with the scene was how comfortable Linc appeared. His smiles were wide and his touch gentle as he tousled Derek's damp hair and tickled Emma's ear.

How had she ever thought him cold and unfeeling?

"Aw, Emma, not again," Derek moaned. "I want to hear the knight story and how he killed the dragon and slept under the stars with his trusty steed, Thunder."

"Trusty steed?" Christy chimed in as she perched on the edge of the sofa. "Oh, I want to hear about him, too."

Linc cast an exasperated glance at her. "It's late and you know the rule, one make-believe story per night. Which story did I tell last time?"

"Emma's," Derek said.

"Mine," Emma reluctantly admitted.

"Then it's Derek's turn." He gave Emma a hug meant to console her. "I'll tell the princess story tomorrow."

"Okay," she said in a long-suffering tone. "I'll wait until then."

"That's my girl," he praised. "Let's see, how does it start again?"

"Once upon a time," Derek prompted.

"Ah, yes. Once upon a time there was a young knight who was left in charge of his parents' castle while they went to visit the king. It would be a long journey so to help the knight, the baron and his wife left behind two trusty advisors to guide the young man in case problems should arise."

Christy listened to the story unfold, finding herself as riveted as the children. He'd just reached the part about the baron's son finding a wounded doe when his cell phone jangled.

His warm tone disappeared as he took the call and his professional persona became fully evident. She hoped the reason for the interruption was minor, but when he clicked off his phone, she sensed their family interlude had ended.

"I have to go, kiddos," he apologized affectionately. "So I'll finish the story with 'To be continued'."

Apparently this wasn't the first time a story had been cut short under similar circumstances because the children didn't argue. They simply flung their arms around his neck and kissed him. "'Night, Uncle Linc," they chimed in unison before they slid off his lap. "See you in the morning."

As soon as the two disappeared down the hall, Christy asked, "Problems, I take it?"

He nodded. "Jose is having severe pain in his other leg. I don't know how long I'll be."

That wasn't good news. In spite of being heavily dosed on blood thinners, Jose could still be developing blood clots.

"I didn't realize you were on call."

"I'm not, but Jose asked for me."

Which meant he wouldn't refuse to go to the hospital, she realized. "I hope everything goes okay for him."

His eyes seemed uncommonly tired as he paused in his path to the door. "Me, too."

Christy hated that his already long day had just been extended. She made a mental note to keep the children as quiet as mice tomorrow morning so he could sleep late. In any case, who would have thought Gail's scenario would have played out so soon? As much as she would have liked to split the parenting duties, sharing them was turning out to be for the best.

As she'd predicted earlier, both Derek and Emma had fallen asleep almost immediately after she'd tucked them in and kissed them goodnight.

She was ready for bed herself, but she and Linc hadn't discussed their sleeping arrangements. Commandeering the master bedroom on her own seemed presumptuous on her part. Although the luxury of Gail and Ty's king-sized bed was enticing, her sense of fair play dictated that Linc deserved the perk. His tall frame would fit so much better there than on the daybed in the guest bedroom. His late and/or early comings and goings would disrupt the household less if he had immediate access to a private bathroom.

Christy turned down her bed, unpacked her clothes, lined her bottles of pills and vitamins on the top of her dresser next to her doctors' appointments cards, tidied the kitchen and let Ria out for her last toilet break of the evening. An hour had passed and Linc still hadn't returned.

She patted on her weekly facial mask, took a long, leisurely shower, slipped on her pink breast cancer awareness Minnie Mouse sleep shirt, then slathered on body moisturizer while Ria watched from her spot on the floor.

Still no Linc.

Afraid that poor Jose was in serious shape, she decided to wait for news. She convinced Ria to lie on her pallet in the living room, then curled up in the easy chair Linc had vacated earlier with one of the paperback books she'd brought from her personal library.

She didn't realize she'd begun dozing until Ria's low grumble startled her awake. As soon as the back door opened, her pet bolted upright and dashed into the kitchen like an enthusiastic puppy rather than a fierce protector.

Clearly, Linc was home.

She padded after her to find Linc rummaging in freezer for ice. Stifling her yawn, she asked, "How did things go?"

"Good." He filled his plastic tumbler with water and took a long swig of his drink.

"What happened?"

"Jose developed a DVT in his other leg."

She translated his shorthand into "deep vein thrombosis", which shouldn't have happened given all the medication they'd given him earlier in the day. "And?"

"I called in Howard Manning and he inserted a Greenfield filter into his vena cava to stop the clot from entering his lung."

"How's he doing?"

"Fine for now. He'll be monitored closely for a while."

Christy noted the lines of exhaustion on his face and his weary-looking gaze when he glanced at her. While her shirt was perfectly modest and covered as much of her body as regular clothing, she was quite aware they were still only pajamas.

"You should be asleep," he said as he finished off the drink.

"I think I was."

"You didn't have to stay up."

"I wanted to hear about Jose. I also didn't want Ria to think you were a burglar and sound the alarm, but she obviously knew who you were because she didn't."

As if aware of the hour and disappointed by the lack of attention his humans were paying her, the dog gave a wide, noisy yawn, then turned around and headed for her rug.

"I also couldn't go to bed because we hadn't worked out our sleeping arrangements. I was afraid you'd either stumble around and wake everyone or spend the night in a chair."

"Right now, a chair sounds like heaven."

"Well, there's a bed waiting for you." Aware of how suggestive her comment sounded, she hurried to explain. "I took the spare room. The master bedroom is all yours."

He rubbed his eyes as he nodded. "I should be chivalrous and argue, but maybe tomorrow when I'm not beat."

"Argue all you want, but I've already unpacked my stuff. Do you have to go in early or can you sleep late?"

His smile was small and lopsided. "It's my weekend off, so I don't need an alarm clock."

"Then I'll keep the kids extra-quiet while we eat breakfast."

"It's not necessary. A few hours and I'll be good as new. Wake me in time to help."

"Okay," she said, only because she didn't want to argue with him at two a.m. At some point they would have to discuss job duties and meal planning, but not now. "Will you go to the hospital this weekend to check on Jose?"

He nodded. "I'll drop by late morning or early afternoon."

She knew he wasn't on call this weekend, which made her curious about his plans. "Do you give all of your patients the royal treatment? I don't think any of them would fault you for taking a night or a weekend off and passing their care off to one of your partners."

He refilled his tumbler and drank deeply again. "Probably not, but Jose isn't just a patient. I've known him and his wife for about five years."

"As a patient?"

He shook his head. "I met him when I hired him to build an outdoor fireplace. Because he was eager for the job, he'd work on evenings and weekends when I was at home, and his wife sent along some of her cook-ing." He grinned. "I think she used me to clean out her leftovers, but I didn't mind. Everything was delicious. Eventually, I got to know their family and when the old-est son expressed an interest in medicine, Jose asked if Emilio could job-shadow me for a week before he started college."

"And you did," she guessed.

He chuckled. "Yeah. Now he's in his final year of medical school." A note of pride filled his voice.

She was half-surprised by his story, and yet, after seeing him interact with his niece and nephew, she wasn't. Obviously he was a completely different per-son around the people who'd been lucky enough to enter his charmed circle of friends and family. Oddly enough, she realized that she wanted to be included.

Not because she had any romantic designs on him, she hastened to tell herself. Even if her ex, Jon, hadn't blasted the stars out of her eyes, getting that close to a guy wouldn't happen before she got the all-clear on her five-year check-up. It would take someone special to deal with the baggage she carried and she honestly didn't think there was a man alive who could.

"Does he know about his father?"

"I called him this evening. Francesca was too rattled to make sense and I knew Emilio would have a lot of questions." Suddenly he yawned. "Sorry about that."

Immediately, she felt guilty for keeping him from his well-deserved and much-needed sleep. "I'm the one who's sorry. If I hadn't stayed up to ask about Jose, you'd already be in bed asleep. So, go on." She made a shooing motion. "I'll get the lights and lock up."

"Okay, but in the morning you and I need to sort out a few details," he began.

"I'll be here," she promised. Then, looking around, she asked, "Where's your suitcase?"

He snapped his fingers. "I left my duffel bag in the car."

"I'll get it while you hop in the shower."

She expected him to argue, but he simply nodded. "Thanks. It's on the back seat."

When she returned with his bag in hand, she was surprised to hear dead silence. She knocked softly on the master bedroom's door and when she didn't hear an answer, she assumed it was safe to enter.

However, as she peeked inside, she found him lying fully clothed on top of the king-sized bed.

She wanted to wake him so he could change into something more comfortable than his dress clothes and crawl under the covers, but the lines of exhaustion on his face stopped her. The medical residents she'd encountered during her nursing career had learned to fall asleep as soon as they were horizontal, regardless of what they were wearing, and Linc obviously hadn't given up those old habits.

Knowing she couldn't leave him as he was, she tugged off his shoes and placed them side by side on the floor beside his bag. Determined to protect his rest as much as she could, she reassured herself the curtains were tightly pulled and the alarm clock was turned off. By the time she tiptoed to the door and flicked off the overhead light, an occasional soft snore punctuated the silence.

She smiled. Until now, she would have sworn that

a man as tightly in control as Linc was wouldn't allow his body to do anything as ordinary as snore. It would be interesting to see how many of her other preconceived opinions he'd disprove over the coming weeks, although she hoped he wouldn't.

Learning that Lincoln Maguire was a great guy underneath his staid exterior would only lead to heartbreak.

Linc woke to the most delicious aroma—coffee. He sniffed the air again, trying to catalog the other scent that mingled with his beloved caffeinated breakfast blend. It reminded him of...

Waffles. His eyes popped open and it took him a few seconds to realize he wasn't in his own bed. Memories of last night crashed down and he immediately checked the bedside alarm clock.

Eleven-thirty. No wonder the sun was peeking around the edges of the heavy drapes. He couldn't remember the last time he'd slept that late, although he vaguely remembered waking at one point to use the bathroom and shed his clothes before he crawled between cool, fresh-smelling sheets.

He also didn't recall the last time he'd awakened to the aroma of a delicious meal. Although he didn't expect her to prepare his breakfast, he hoped she'd prepared extra for him this morning. As he swung his bare legs over the bed's edge, his stomach rumbled in agreement.

Raking a hand through his hair, he rose, stepped into his previously discarded pants, and followed his nose.

Derek and Emma were seated at the kitchen table and Christy stood in front of the stove, clad in a pair of above-the-knee light blue plaid cotton shorts that showed off her delightfully long legs and a matching blue button-down shirt. Both children had powdered sugar dusting their faces, syrup smeared around their mouths and milk mustaches.

Emma saw him and her eyes lit up. "Christy?" she asked in a loud whisper. "Can we use our regular voices now?"

"Not until you're uncle is awake," she whispered back.

"But he is," she declared in a normal tone. "Morning, Unca Linc."

Christy turned, spatula in hand, and her eyes widened before a big smile crossed her face. "Good morning," she said as her gaze pointedly remained above his neck. "The coffee's ready if you are."

He nearly smiled at her discomfiture, then decided it wouldn't win him any brownie points. "You read my mind. Thanks. Can I pour you a cup, too?"

She shook her head. "I'm not a coffee drinker."

"Really?" he asked as he poured his own mug. "I thought everyone who worked in the medical profession mainlined the stuff."

"I used to, but I switched to herbal tea. It's better for you."

"Probably, but you can't beat a bracing cup of coffee to jump-start the day." He watched her flip a perfectly made waffle out of the iron and dust it with powdered sugar. "That smells good."

She chuckled. "Are you hinting you'd like one?"

He was practically drooling, but he was too conscious of his morning scruffiness to agree. His face itched, he needed a shave and a shower, and his teeth felt furry. He definitely wasn't presentable for the dining table.

"I should clean up first."

"Probably," she agreed, "but this waffle is ready and the griddle's still hot if you'd like seconds." Her gaze traveled up and down his full length, making him even more aware of his half-dressed appearance. "Judging from the way you look, the kitchen will be closed before you come back, so I suggest you eat first and shower later."

He got the sneaking impression that once she unplugged the waffle iron she wouldn't plug it in again. How had he ever thought her easygoing and malleable? She had a steely spine that he'd never seen and certainly hadn't expected.

"I should put on a shirt," he began.

Once again, she avoided his gaze. "Suit yourself, but, whatever you do, I promise to sit downwind."

"Mom never lets Dad eat at the table without a shirt," Derek said, "but if Uncle Linc can, can I?"

This time Christy looked at him helplessly, her gaze sliding from his pectorals to his face and back again. "Well," she began, "these are extenuating circumstances—"

"If those are your mom's rules, then they'll be ours, too," Linc said firmly. "I'll be right back."

The lure of the waffle was too great and the slices of ham too appetizing to do more than grab yesterday's wrinkled shirt and slip it on. He'd only buttoned the middle two buttons before he was back in the kitchen and sliding into an empty chair.

If Christy noticed his speedy return, she didn't comment. Instead, she simply set his plate in front of him, passed the meat platter and returned to the stove.

Linc dug in. He was hungry enough to be grateful for the hospital's bland cafeteria food, but he was pleasantly surprised to discover Christy's meal actually melted in his mouth. When she delivered a second waffle as perfect as the first one, he could only utter a long sigh of appreciation.

"These are delicious," he said as he drenched it with maple syrup.

"Surprised?" She took the chair beside him and began sectioning her grapefruit.

"A little," he admitted. "Where did you learn to cook like this?"

"My mom. She owns an exclusive little gourmet restaurant in Seattle and she sends recipes for me to try before she adds them to her menu."

"Then that explains all the fancy food in the fridge."

Confusion spread across her face. "Fancy food?"

"You know. The organic milk, the fruit and vegetables I can't identify."

She smiled. "I don't consider organic food as being fancy. As for the unidentifiable stuff, I try new things to see if I'll like them." She motioned to his plate. "Speaking of new things, how would you rate this recipe?"

"It's a keeper." The cuckoo suddenly popped out of his door and chirped twelve times. "I didn't realize it was noon. Did you guys sleep late, too?" he asked.

"We've been up for *hours*." Derek drained his milk glass and wiped his mouth with his forearm until

Christy cleared her throat and he sheepishly swiped at it with his napkin.

"Hours and *hours*," Emma added. "Christy said we had to be quiet, so we ate our breakfast on the patio."

"Isn't this breakfast?" he asked.

"This is lunch," Christy corrected. "Breakfast was at eight and consisted of cold cereal, fresh strawberries, pineapple, and toast."

"Whole wheat," Derek mumbled with disgust.

She chuckled and Linc was entranced by the sound. "With all the jelly you slathered on, you couldn't taste or see that I didn't use white bread."

Emma obviously didn't care because she continued her play-by-play account of the morning. "Then we took Ria for a walk around the block so he could get 'quainted with the dog smells in the neighborhood. After that, we watered Mama's flowers and weeded and before we knew it, Christy said it was time to eat again. I think she's almost as good a cook as Mama is, don't you?"

He'd been put on the spot by a mere six-year-old. No matter how he answered, he was going to have one female in the household unhappy. Christy obviously saw his dilemma because her eyes twinkled with humor. He wouldn't receive any help from that quarter....

"Almost," he agreed loyally, as he exchanged a smile with Christy that said otherwise.

"We'll wait for you in the cafeteria," Christy told Linc a few hours later as he parked in the physicians' parking lot. They'd decided to spend the afternoon running errands, including driving to his house to pick up a few of what he referred to as "necessities", but on the way he'd wanted to run in and check on Jose.

"I won't be long, I promise."

"Yeah, right," she said, unable to hide her skepticism.

"You don't believe I can get away in a reasonable amount of time?"

"Only if you went incognito," she said.

"I thought I was," he said. "No one will expect to see me looking like this."

"Like this" meant dressed in a polo shirt, cargo shorts, and a pair of sandals. It wasn't his usual garb, so he'd cause quite a stir when the staff saw him. She spoke from experience because she still couldn't believe this was the same man who'd sat at the kitchen table a few hours ago looking scruffy and bleary-eyed.

A little water and a shave could do amazing things.

As great as he looked now, though, her first image of him was indelibly etched in her brain. His muscles had flexed and rippled under his skin just from the simple act of pouring his own cup of coffee. As much as she'd enjoyed seeing those wide shoulders as nature intended, it was a good thing Derek had piped up when he had. She might have done something really stupid, like set off the smoke alarm or drool in her grapefruit.

Nope, if more women saw the sight she'd been privileged to see, cardiology offices would be standing room only.

"They won't, but if you're going to be longer than thirty minutes, give me a call, will you?"

"Okay, but, whatever you do, don't load them up with a bunch of sugar and junk food."

She paused, momentarily hurt by his remark. "Do

you honestly think I'll turn them loose at the candy machine?"

He shifted uncomfortably in the seat. "I think you'd spoil them if you had the chance," he began slowly.

"And you wouldn't, I suppose."

"Once in a while, I do," he admitted, "but—"

Aware of two sets of little ears in the back seat, she lowered her voice and clenched her fingers into a tight fist as she interrupted, "But you think I'll do it all the time."

"Maybe not all—"

"Why else would you remind me?"

He shut off the engine, then gripped the steering wheel with both hands. "I only meant—"

She cut him off once again. "I know what you meant." She didn't know why his lack of faith both-ered her, but it did. Yes, they'd only been joint par-ents for less than twenty-four hours, but where had he gotten the idea she'd let Emma and Derek run amok, nutrition-wise? And if he thought she'd turn a blind eye to their eating habits, what did he think she'd do when making other decisions?

"All I can say is, if you're that worried, you'd better finish your business as quickly as possible so you can supervise what they choose for a snack," she said stiffly.

"I am *not* worried," he said.

"You are, so you may as well admit it." As she turned to face the children, she pasted on a smile and injected a lighter note into her voice. "Okay, gang. Let's go!"

While the two scrambled out of their seat belts, he grabbed her arm. "I'm not worried," he repeated.

"Of course not," she said politely. "My mistake."

Then, shaking free, she hopped out of the car and herded her two charges into the hospital like an over-protective mother hen.

When she directed them to the stairwell, Derek complained, "Can't we take the elevator? Uncle Linc is."

"We'll take it on the way up," she prevaricated, unwilling to see for herself or admit that sharing such close confines at the moment was more than she could handle.

With luck, an hour or so of mindlessly watching the fish swim around the aquarium would restore her good mood.

Linc had major damage control facing him. For a man who was normally efficient at stating his thoughts, he'd missed the mark today. He'd hurt Christy with his thoughtless remark—that had been evident and he deeply regretted doing so.

To make matters worse, in trying to explain, he'd practically told her that she was a pushover when it came to Derek and Emma and he knew she wasn't. Christy's mere glance this morning had convinced Derek to use his napkin instead of his sleeve and if she could do that, she'd be immune to any cajolery they might try.

He checked Jose's chart and slipped into his room to visit for about fifteen minutes. Satisfied by his progress, he strode toward the bank of elevators, ready to leave. As he punched the "Down" button, he wondered if he should kill time elsewhere in the hospital. If he arrived in the cafeteria too soon, Christy would assume he'd hurried to check on her.

The point was he *was* in a hurry, but not for that particular reason. If anyone saw him, he could easily get embroiled in a patient case and he had too many other things to do this afternoon—*family* things—that wouldn't allow it. His objective also included getting to know Gail's best friend because there seemed to be more to her than had previously met his eye.

On the other hand, Christy seemed like a forgiving sort, so perhaps during their time apart she'd decided to cut him some slack.

He strode into the near-empty cafeteria and saw Emma and Derek peering into the giant aquarium in the far corner of the dining hall.

"Hi, guys. Are you enjoying the fish?" he asked.

"I like the spotted ones," Emma declared as she pointed to one. "Do you know what kind of fish he is?"

Linc referred to the chart posted above the aquarium. "A Dalmation Molly."

Emma giggled. "She looks like a fire-truck dog, doesn't she?"

"She does," he agreed, then asked, "Where's Christy?"

"She's over there with that guy." Derek inclined his head in her direction.

Linc glanced at the corner in question and saw her with a fellow he recognized as one of the physical therapists. From their wide smiles and the laughter drifting across the room, both appeared entirely too comfortable with each other for Linc's taste.

"He's got the hots for her," Derek said with a typical eight-year-old boy's disgust.

Linc had arrived at the same conclusion and was instantly envious. His reaction was completely illogical, but when he saw the guy scoot his chair closer and fling his arm over her shoulder to draw her close enough to whisper in her ear, he felt an envy he hadn't noticed before.

"See?" Derek said with satisfaction. "Maybe we should warn Christy that he wants to get in her—"

Derek's blunt description finally registered and Linc cut off the boy's sentence. "Whoa there, buddy. Does your mother know you're a teenager in an eight-year-old body?"

A blush crept across Derek's face, which suggested his mother probably didn't know the extent of her son's education. "I watch TV," he defended.

"Really?" Linc raised an eyebrow. "Before I ask what sort of programs you're viewing and if your mother knows you are, we aren't going to say a word to Christy. We don't want to embarrass her."

He, on the other hand, was jealous.

The boy shrugged. "If you say so, but it's still true. He held out her chair for her, got her a refill, and keeps putting his arm around the back of her chair and leaning in close. I think he might be her boyfriend."

A boyfriend. Linc hadn't considered the possibility that Christy might have her own reasons for not wanting to share the house with him. Living under someone else's roof with another guy, no matter how innocent it might be, could certainly strain a relationship.

On the other hand, although he didn't socialize with the staff, he'd picked up enough tidbits from conversations around him to know the gossip currently circulating on the grapevine. He'd never heard her name linked to anyone else's. If he had, he would have remembered.

On the other hand, her relationship might be new enough that it hadn't become the latest news yet. Or, as Derek had said, this Masterson fellow might still be trying—

"He isn't," Emma interrupted with childlike certainty.

Linc's mind was too focused on Derek's report of Masterson's activities to follow Emma's train of thought. "He isn't what?"

"Her boyfriend. I heard Mama telling her that she needs to get one, but Christy only laughed and said she'd think about it after her next pet. Do you think she's going to get another dog? I hope she finds a little one next time. One you can carry in your purse."

Linc was totally confused. A boyfriend was contingent on Christy's new pet? Emma had obviously missed a few important details.

"How long ago did you hear your Mom and Christy talking?" he asked. If their conversation had taken place months ago, Christy could easily have found someone since then to play that role, new pet or not.

"A few days before Mama and Daddy left. Oh, look." Once again, she pointed to the tank. "Those two fish are *kissing*." She giggled.

He glanced at the tank and saw two fish with their mouths pressed together. The fish clearly didn't spend their days swimming aimlessly around their environment. Once again, he referred to the posted list of names and photos.

"They're called Kissing Gourami," he reported.

"Do you think they like each other, Unca Linc?" Emma asked.

"Don't be silly." Derek rolled his eyes. "Fish don't like each other like people do."

"How do you know?" Emma's eyes flashed. "You don't know everything just 'cause you're older than me. If it's a boy fish and a girl fish, they could, *too*, like each other—"

"Enough," Linc said firmly. "We aren't going to argue here. We'll research the subject on the internet when we get home."

To his surprise and delight, Christy joined them at the tank. "Actually, those two aren't getting along right now," she said.

"They aren't? But they're acting like they do," Emma protested.

"They're a peaceful species, but the males fight over their territory like other animals. When they do, they press their mouths together."

The little girl frowned as if trying to puzzle over how such a move could be a sign of aggression. "They don't have much room to fight over," she remarked, her attention riveted to the pair in question.

"I don't know how large they consider their territories," Christy replied. "Maybe one raced the other to the food and he was a sore loser. Or maybe one cut in front of the other while they were swimming."

"I get it," Linc said, humored by her story. "They're having the aquatic equivalent of road rage. And I thought I had an active imagination."

Emma tugged on his shorts pocket. "What's road rage?"

"It's when one driver gets angry with another driver and they get into an argument."

"Oh."

"The point is, Em," Christy interrupted, "it doesn't take much for guys of any species to find a reason to flex their muscles."

He had a feeling she'd directed her last comment to him.

"Yeah, but they fight by kissing?" Derek shuddered. "Yuck."

Christy grinned. "You don't like the idea of locking lips with the guy you want to punch?"

"No way."

While Derek and Christy discussed the more acceptable forms of dealing with conflict, Linc realized that her former companion had disappeared. "Is Masterson's coffee break over?"

"Dan had only stopped in for his usual afternoon soda and ran into us. He's on the *Dancing with the Docs* committee and was trying to convince me to volunteer."

"Did he? Convince you, that is?"

She shook her head. "I told him my days were full enough as it is with being a participant, but I'd save him a dance."

Linc felt an unreasonable desire to remind her that she would be busy dancing with *him*, but he didn't. He did, however, make a mental note to carve out time for lessons the week after next. By then, his partners would have returned from their respective vacations and he could implement a less hectic schedule in the weeks ahead.

"As enjoyable as it is to stay and chat about the fish or the upcoming festival, we have plenty to see and do today," she said.

"You're right. We should leave," he agreed. After tossing the empty cracker wrappers and milk cartons into a bin, Linc ushered the group to the elevator. As they were making their ascent, curiosity drove him to ask, "Emma said you might be getting another dog?"

She smiled. "Afraid not. Ria is all I can handle for now." She touched her finger to the tip of the little girl's nose. "Whatever gave you that idea, Em?"

"We were wondering if that guy you were with was your boyfriend. I said he wasn't 'cause you told Mama you'd get one after your next pet and you still just have Ria."

Linc had expected her to laugh in her usual melodic way—the way that made him smile whenever he heard the sound. He wasn't prepared to see her face turn pale and her hand shake as she touched her throat.

Something had driven the color out of her face. He didn't understand what, but he intended to find out.

CHAPTER FOUR

CHRISTY tried to remember the details of her conversation with Gail and wondered how much Emma had heard. She opted to pretend ignorance. "Trust me. I don't intend to replace Ria or give her a doggy brother or sister. Okay?"

"Then you won't ever have a boyfriend?"

Emma had no idea how painful her innocent question was. "Someday. If I find the right guy," Christy answered lightly, although she had her doubts. In her experience, the good ones were already taken.

Suddenly aware of Linc's speculative gaze, she wondered why the elevator suddenly slowed to a crawl. "I'm too busy for a fella right now anyway." She brushed a lock of unruly hair off Emma's forehead. "I'm looking after my favorite kids, remember?"

Fortunately, they'd arrived on the main floor at that particular moment. As soon as the stainless-steel doors opened, she edged her way through the space so fast she was the first one out.

"What's next on our agenda?" she asked, hoping Linc hadn't noticed her too-bright tone. A quick glance showed an impassive expression so she relaxed, certain she'd successfully dodged that uncomfortable situation.

"My place," he said.

It came as no surprise that Linc lived in an upper-middle-class neighborhood. His sprawling, ranch-style house stood in the middle of a well-manicured lawn. Hostas and other shade-loving perennials circled the large maple trees and a mixture of petunias, marigolds, and other annuals she didn't recognize filled the flower bed next to the front entrance.

"When do you find the time to work outdoors?" she asked as they walked inside.

"I have a yard service," he confessed. "I also have a housekeeper who drops in every three weeks, although there isn't much for her to do."

She didn't expect there would be. The man spent most of his life at the hospital.

"Can we go to the back yard and play, Uncle Linc?" Derek asked.

"Sure," he told them, "but don't get too involved because we won't be staying long."

"Okay." The children scampered through the house and a few seconds later an unseen door slammed.

"What are we getting?" Christy asked, trying not to be awed by his house and failing. The home was built with an open floor plan similar to hers, but his living room also had a gorgeous red-brick fireplace in one corner. His décor included a lot of woodwork and deep accent colors in blues, greens, and browns, which gave a very relaxing atmosphere.

"My single-cup coffeemaker," he said as he skirted the island on his way to the end of the counter where the appliance in question was located. "You don't drink coffee, so it seems a waste to make an entire pot for the one cup I drink on my way to the office."

"True." She glanced around again. "This is absolutely lovely."

"You like it?" he asked.

"Very much. If I lived here, I'd have a tough time leaving to go to work."

She heard childish laughter and screams of delight, so she moved to the French doors that opened onto the patio. There, she looked outside into the most beautiful back yard she could imagine.

An outdoor fireplace and a bricked-in grill formed the wall on the west side of the patio and protected the table and chairs from the setting sun. On the east side, a couple of cushioned lounge chairs were grouped together with a small end table in between.

Beyond that, a pair of large oak trees stood like sentinels in the fenced yard. A tree house was nestled in one and a tire swing hung from a huge branch in the other. A gym with a climbing rope and a slide stood off to one side and both Emma and Derek were crawling over it like agile monkeys.

"This is fantastic!" she exclaimed. "Did you or a previous owner create all this?"

He joined her at the door, his smile wide with well-deserved pride. "Ty and Jose did most of the physical labor, but I helped."

"It's amazing," she remarked, awed by his thoughtfulness for his niece and nephew. She was also extremely aware of his proximity as she could almost feel the heat radiating off his body and the most delightful masculine scent surrounded her. "I suppose you don't call this 'spoiling' your niece and nephew?"

He shook his head. "I call it self-preservation. Gail and Ty always designate one night a month as their date night, so I began hosting sleepovers at my place. Sometimes they stretched into a full weekend. After one visit of hearing 'We're bored, Unca Linc,' and 'Can we go to the park and play on the swings' every five minutes, I decided it would be easier on all of us if they had something special to play on here. So I commissioned everything you see."

"I'm very impressed." And she was. He might be single-minded about his work, but he didn't completely ignore his family, as she'd first thought.

"Impressed enough to forgive me for my comment this afternoon?"

She had to think a minute to remember. "Oh, that. I'd already forgotten."

"Really?" he asked. "You were rather upset."

She shrugged. "At the time I was. As a general rule, I try to look at what happened in terms of the big picture and usually nothing is so bad that it's worth making a fuss about. Although it takes me a bit longer to reach that point when my feelings are hurt, eventually I get there."

"That's a very healthy attitude to have."

Facing one's mortality had a tendency to change one's perspective. "Thanks."

"I didn't mean to hurt your feelings."

She fell silent. "I accept your apology, but the question is do you trust me to exercise good judgment with Derek and Emma? If you don't, I'd like to know now."

"I don't *distrust* you," he said slowly. "Old habits simply die hard and as the responsible person in my family, it seemed like I was always reminding my siblings to do one thing or another. My parents left me in charge a lot, and by the time they died, it had become second nature. 'Don't forget your lunch money. Pick up a loaf of bread on your way home from school. Start the laundry when you get home.'"

"Ah, the controlling type."

"If by controlling you mean trying to keep everything organized and running smoothly, then yes."

"I'm surprised you took on that responsibility by yourself."

He grinned. "I did, and I didn't. My grandmother was still alive and she wanted Ty and Joanie to move in with her, but Gram was already showing signs of senile dementia and had a heart problem. Taking care of two teenagers would have completely done her in. The three of us voted to move her in with us. She felt useful and we unobtrusively kept an eye on her."

"That's amazing."

He shrugged. "It was the best solution at the time and in hindsight I'm glad we made that decision because a year later she died in her sleep."

"I'm sorry," she murmured.

"She was a great gal. She tended to deliver last-minute instructions every time anyone left the house—young or old, it didn't matter—and I suppose I picked up that habit early on."

"How did Ty and your sister handle those *little reminders*?"

"We had our moments, but they listened." His grin

was a beautiful sight to see. "Or at least they pretended to listen."

"So is that what I should do?" she teased. "Pretend to hang on your every word until your ego can't fit through doorways?"

"It's a pleasant thought, but I'd rather have honesty."

"Honesty I can do."

As they exchanged a smile, she felt as if they'd reached a milestone. Sharing the responsibility of the children didn't seem quite as frustrating as she'd once thought. Maybe, just maybe, they could get through the next two months without feeling as if she were tiptoeing through a minefield.

Oh, they were certain to clash; it was inevitable because he was the type of man who grabbed the horns of leadership. He was used to being the guy with the answers and had been for most of his life. Becoming a surgeon had only reinforced his independence. To him, decisions weren't by group consensus and consequently he expected people to follow his directives without question.

She, on the other hand, believed in hearing both sides and weighing all the pros and cons before arriving at a solution. To her, flexibility and family relationships were far more important than schedules and to-do lists. Life was simply too precarious not to enjoy it to the fullest.

"I'll try to be more sparing with my reminders," he added, "but in case I forget, don't take them personally."

"Okay, as long as you understand I don't handle 'control' very easily."

He chuckled. "I suspected as much. Now that we've cleared the air, we should discuss our free time."

"Free time?"

"Yeah. If you ever want to go out with Masterson—"

"I don't," she said firmly. "He's a great guy, but…" she wasn't ready to bare her soul, so she relied on her standby excuse "…the sparks aren't there."

"Are you sure? He certainly has them."

"Were you *spying* on me?"

He held up his hands. "I'm only repeating what Derek said."

The knowledge that an eight-year-old boy saw the very fire she'd been trying to extinguish was disconcerting.

"The point is, whether you want to go out with him or anyone else, I'm sure Gail and Ty don't expect either of us to forego dating for the next two months. We need to create a schedule."

Another schedule. How in the world did the man keep track of them all? She pictured his daily calendar and imagined a block of time designated as 'Christy's date', and inwardly smiled.

She didn't know if he was fishing or being kind, but admitting she didn't have a romantic interest and only went out with her girlfriends or colleagues for an occasional beer at the end of a long week made her seem… sad and pathetic. She'd endured enough of people's well-meant sympathy over the past four-plus years and she especially didn't want any from Lincoln Maguire.

"Your suggestion is noted," she said instead. "I'll give you plenty of notice when I have plans. What about you? Is there a lady friend in your life that I should work around?"

"Not really. I have met someone, though. No, I take that back. We've been passing acquaintances for a while, but lately I'm seeing her a little differently."

The idea that another woman had attracted his attention was unsettling, which was a completely illogical response. Just because her pulse did that stupid skittery thing when he was around and just because they were living together under the most innocent of terms for the sake of two minors didn't mean she had a right to be possessive. A man who thrived on control and preferred having everything in its place wouldn't be interested in a woman who walked a tightrope between being cured of cancer and having a relapse.

"Anyone I know?" she asked, realizing her offhanded question was as painful as poking herself in the eye.

"I'd rather not name names at this point."

She didn't know what was worse—knowing the woman's identity or being left to speculate. "Okay, but if you ever ask her out—"

"You'll be the first to know."

His promise brought little comfort because the green-eyed monster had perched on her shoulder.

Linc had hoped Christy would be more forthcoming about her personal life when he'd mentioned creating a date-night schedule, but she hadn't. Hearing she didn't feel the sparks with Masterson had come as some relief, but Masterson wasn't the only guy sniffing around her. She attracted single fellows like grape jelly attracted orioles, although, as far as he could tell, she didn't encourage them.

No doubt they responded to her ready smile and open friendliness, which he completely understood. He lingered longer on her nursing unit than he did elsewhere in the hospital because lately, even if he only spent a few minutes with her and they never discussed anything except patient care, being with her seemed to rejuvenate him.

It was an odd observation. She was unconventional and impulsive—two traits he hadn't been looking for in his ideal significant other because he wasn't about to have *his* children live through the same upheaval and uncertainty he had—but apparently, like the other eligible males in the hospital, he was drawn to her because of them.

For the first time he began to wonder if steady and dependable was really what he wanted. After all, he'd met a multitude of steady, dependable women and yet he hadn't bothered to get to know any of them. Was it possible that deep down, in spite of his avowal otherwise, he wanted the excitement that his parents had enjoyed as they'd pursued their dream together?

Maybe he did, but he'd certainly go about achieving it in a different way, and he certainly wouldn't do so by placing an unreasonable burden on his children. Surely there was a happy medium? He simply had to find it.

In the meantime, though, he'd solve the riddle of the "pet" comment Emma had overheard because his instincts said there was more to that particular story than Christy had divulged.

To his surprise, the pieces which hadn't fit suddenly slid into place later that evening.

"Unca Linc, I need you."

Emma's loud whisper pulled his attention away from his latest *Lancet* journal as he sat in the recliner with his feet raised. "What's up, Em?" he asked in a normal voice.

"Shh," she whispered, holding a finger to her lips. "I don't want Christy to hear. I need you. *Now*." She motioned frantically for him to join her.

The worry on her elfin features convinced him to follow. As soon as he reached her side, she pulled him into the hallway that led to the bedrooms.

"What's up?" he whispered back.

"I'm in a bit of a pickle," she admitted, "but I can't 'splain yet. Christy will hear."

He smiled at her turn of a phrase because it sounded like something his sister-in-law frequently said. "She's outside."

Emma's shoulders heaved. "Oh, good."

"So what's this pickle you're in?" he asked, trying to not smile when Emma was clearly distressed.

She stopped outside Christy's room and the story poured out of her. "I know we're not s'posed to go into rooms when we're not invited, but Ria and I were playing and Ria ran in here and I came after her. She was jumping and I was trying to stay out of her way but we both bumped into the dresser and Christy's stuff rolled off and some of the bottles fell off the back and I can't get them out!" Her voice rose. "Now Christy's going to be mad at us and she won't let me play with Ria or talk to Mama and Daddy when they call tonight and I just gotta talk to them! Please, Unca Linc. You hafta help me."

With that, she burst into tears.

Linc's mouth twitched with a smile, but laughing at Emma's worries wouldn't allay his niece's fears. Instead, he crouched down and hugged her.

"None of this is as bad as you think," he consoled, wiping away her tears with his thumbs. "We'll get the bottles and set them back on top of the dresser. No harm done."

Emma sniffled.

"Were they big bottles or little ones?" he asked.

"Little. Mama gets the same ones when she's sick."

She must have knocked over prescription bottles. "Okay. Give me two minutes and everything will be just like it was."

"But she'll know I came into her room without her permission," she hiccupped, "and then I'll be punished. So will Ria."

The Labrador sat on her haunches next to the bed, her usual doggy smile absent, as if she recognized the gravity of the situation.

"You may get scolded, but Christy wouldn't stop you from talking to your mom and dad."

"You don't think so?" Her watery blue-gray eyes stared into his. "What we did was wrong."

"Yes, it was, but not allowing you to talk to your mom and dad would be mean, and deep down you know she isn't mean." He paused. "Am I right?"

She nodded and the worried wrinkle between her eyes lessened.

"I'll move the dresser, we'll find her things and put them back the way they were. Now, don't cry. Okay?"

She swiped her nose and nodded. "Okay."

Linc pivoted the dresser far enough to locate the missing prescription containers. After retrieving them, he moved the furniture so the legs matched the same carpet depressions as they had previously. Satisfied he'd hidden the evidence of the mishap, he placed the two he'd rescued at the end of the row of her other medications and neatly stacked the appointment cards.

Noticing that she'd positioned each bottle so the labels faced outward, he lined his in the same manner, half-surprised that someone as young and obviously healthy as Christy required so much medication. As he turned away, he caught one drug name out of the corner of his eye and his blood immediately ran cold.

Tamoxifen.

Although he didn't prescribe it for his patients, he knew exactly what it was used for—the treatment of certain types of breast cancer.

The books on her shelf now made sense, as did the row of pill bottles and vitamins, her organic hormone-free milk, and the refrigerator full of fresh vegetables and low-fat dairy products.

It also made her guiding philosophy of life understandable. After battling cancer, there weren't many other problems too big to face and definitely not many worth getting upset over.

But, oh, how he hated to think of what she'd gone through, both physically and emotionally.

"Unca Linc." Emma tugged on his pants. "Are you done? We should go."

"You're right, we should." He ushered her out of the room and closed the door firmly behind him, wishing he could block off his new-found knowledge as easily.

"There you two are," Christy said with relief as she and Derek met Linc and Emma in the living room. "It's almost time for Gail and Ty to call. Linc, can you power up the laptop?"

While he obeyed, she addressed the children. "Let me look at you and make sure you're both presentable."

She stood them side by side and cast a critical eye on them. The clean clothes they'd changed into an hour ago were still clean. Emma's hair was neatly combed, but Derek's definitely needed a bit of straightening. She couldn't do it properly so she simply smoothed the unruly locks with her fingers.

"Gail and Ty aren't expecting them to look their Sunday best," Linc teased her. "They know these two. If they're too neat, Gail will accuse us of replacing her kids with someone else's."

"I don't want them to think we're neglecting—"

"Trust me, they won't. As long as they're not bleeding, a little dirt and stray hair won't faze Gail and Ty." He pushed a few keys, then set the laptop on the coffee table in front of the youngest Maguires, who were bouncing with excitement on the sofa. "Here we go."

At seven o'clock on the dot, thanks to a wireless internet connection and a webcam, Gail and Ty appeared on the computer screen and the conversation began.

Christy moved into the background and listened as the children talked about their recent activities and Gail mentioned a few of the sights they'd seen. She and

Linc gave a short statement about how well things were going and eventually, after a promise for a follow-up call on Thursday and a tearful goodbye, he closed the connection.

"Can we do that again?" Emma asked.

"On Thursday," Christy told her.

"I want to talk before then."

Arranging a time to coordinate with school events, homework, dance lessons, and soccer practice had been tough, so everyone had agreed to plan their calls near the children's bedtime. Unfortunately, with the seven-hour time difference, it meant Gail and Ty they had to call at three a.m. local time, which explained why they'd looked a little bleary-eyed.

"I know you do, but your mom and dad have to wake up in the middle of the night to talk to us. They can't do that every day."

"But I didn't tell Mama about the caterpillar I saw and Daddy doesn't know about my loose tooth."

"I'll help you email them," Linc offered. "How does that sound?"

Emma frowned, her bottom lip quivering as if she wouldn't need much encouragement to break into a wail.

He tugged on the little girl's earlobe. "Did you lose your smile? You'd better find it quick because you'll need it for school tomorrow. You don't want your teacher calling me and saying that Emma Maguire is being grumpy today, do you?"

"No."

"Good. Now, run and get ready for bed." He glanced

at Christy. "Whose turn is it tonight? The princess or the knight?"

"The princess," Emma stated firmly. With Linc's one, innocently phrased question, eagerness replaced her downcast expression.

Christy was impressed by the way he'd turned his niece's ill-humor completely around. Was his success born out of experience or did he have an innate gift for handling children? Given his past, she suspected a combination of both were responsible.

"Okay, then. Off you go. The longer it takes you to get ready for bed, the shorter the story will be."

The two dashed off and Christy felt Linc's gaze. "What's wrong?" she asked.

"Nothing. I just wondered if you felt better now."

"I've felt fine all evening," she said, puzzled. "Why?"

"You were as fidgety as the kids. I assumed you were nervous."

She sank onto the sofa, surprised he'd noticed. "I was. I wanted everything perfect so Gail wouldn't worry about them or wonder if they'd made the right decision when they asked me, *us*, to watch them."

"Trust me, she saw two happy, healthy kids who were coping with their parents' absence quite well."

"I'm glad you think so."

"I do."

"Unca Linc!" Derek called from his bedroom. "We're ready!"

Laughing, he rose. "Now, if you'll excuse me, my fans await."

For a few minutes Christy listened to Linc's deep voice as he began his story. She couldn't hear the words, but she heard the tone and it touched her in ways she hadn't expected.

Idly, she wondered how Linc would deal with a diagnosis such as hers if delivered to *his* wife or girlfriend. Would he decide, as Jon had, that he hadn't bought a ticket for that particular movie and wasn't interested in doing so? Or would he see her through the entire process—the surgery, the chemo, more surgery, the endless waiting for test results?

She suspected he wouldn't leave his significant other hanging in similar circumstances. A man who'd taken on the care of his younger siblings as well as his grandmother while barely in his twenties wouldn't walk away from a woman he loved.

On the other hand, after taking on so many responsibilities at such a young age, he obviously wasn't interested in tying himself down because he was in his late thirties and didn't seem interested in changing his marital status. His career *was* both wife and mistress, so imagining him in Jon's place was pointless.

Life was what it was and fate had given her a fellow whose love hadn't been strong enough to face the challenges that had presented themselves. In hindsight, she was grateful to have discovered his character flaws before their relationship had become legal.

As for the future, self-preservation ruled the day. She wouldn't allow any man to get close until she received her five-year all-clear report. Without that medical reassurance, it wouldn't be fair to dump such a heavy burden on a guy. Waiting until then would also save her the trouble of dealing with heartache in addition to cancer, round two.

Aware of the hour, Christy tidied the living room, sent Ria outside for her last trip outdoors, then delivered her own share of goodnight hugs and kisses to Derek and Emma. For some reason, though, when they both turned away to leave Emma's bedside, the little girl clung to Linc and whispered in his ear.

"You should tell her," she heard him say.

"Please?" the little girl begged.

"Okay. I'll do it, but next time you have to 'fess up yourself."

"Thanks, Unca Linc."

Curious about what Emma considered so terrible that her uncle had to divulge it on her behalf, Christy held her questions until she'd called in Ria and they were both relaxing on the living-room sofa with the television volume turned low.

"What couldn't Emma tell me about?" she asked as she sipped on her cup of herbal tea.

"She went into your room today."

Considering all of her medications, vitamins, and supplements, which might pique a child's curiosity, Christy panicked. "She didn't swallow anything, did she? Ria didn't eat—"

"No, nothing like that."

She relaxed. "Good."

"Apparently Emma has this horrible fear you'd be furious if you knew she went into your room. She believes she's facing a fate worse than death and asked me to beg for mercy on her behalf."

Christy smiled at Linc's wry tone. "I told them I had things in my room that could make them or Ria sick, so it would be best if they didn't go inside unless I gave them permission." She didn't intend to explain what those things were; she simply hoped Linc would accept her simplified explanation as the kids had.

"Emma understands that, which was why she was worried."

"Out of curiosity, how did she end up there, anyway?"

"She and Ria were playing and somehow the two of them ended up in your room. In their exuberance, some of the bottles on your dresser rolled off. Nothing broke, so you shouldn't worry about that."

"Then no harm done, I'm sure," she said lightly.

"The problem was," he continued, "a few vials rolled behind and she couldn't reach them."

"Thanks for telling me. I would have wondered why some had disappeared. Before I go to bed I'll—"

"The lost have been found. I put the vials on top of your dresser with the others."

She swallowed hard. "You...did?" Then she plastered a wide smile on her face and pretended nonchalance. "How nice of you. Thanks."

"You're welcome."

At first, she believed she'd skated through that awkward moment with ease, but the compassion she saw on his face said otherwise. He might not ask questions—it would be rather forward of him to do so—but whether he did or didn't, his eyes held a *knowing* look that hadn't been present before.

Of the pills he'd retrieved, only one would have generated the curiosity and sympathy in his gaze—the one easily recognizable as a cancer treatment.

If she didn't say a word, she sensed he'd drop the

subject, but it seemed cowardly not to address the obvious. It would become the elephant in the room they both tried to ignore and she would analyze his every remark and every glance for a hidden meaning.

She could handle anything from him except pity.

No, she didn't want that. Better to face the situation head-on.

"You know, don't you?" she asked.

CHAPTER FIVE

You know, don't you? Christy's question echoed in Linc's head and he paused to debate the merits of pretending ignorance. However easy it might seem in the moment, honesty had been and always would be the best policy.

Her eyes held resignation, as if she hated that her secret had been revealed, and he softened his own gaze. "I wasn't being curious. I didn't intend to read the label, it just happened."

From the way Christy visibly hunched her shoulders in an effort to draw inside herself, Linc knew he'd thrown her off balance. He had plenty of questions, but there were times to speak and times to listen. At the moment, listening seemed to be the most appropriate course of action.

Had anyone else told him news of this sort, he would have reacted in a most clinical, detached manner. With Christy, however, his detachment had flown out the window.

Sensing her mental turmoil, he scooted closer to lend his comfort and encouragement. She stiffened in his one-armed hug as if she didn't want to accept his support, but gradually the tension in her body eased.

Silence hung in the air as she continued to cradle her teacup, but Linc waited.

"You're probably wondering why I never told you," she began.

"Not really." At her startled glance, he explained. "I'm not your physician or…" He wanted to say *your lover* but caught himself. "Or more than a casual acquaintance, so I understand why you haven't shared your personal issues with me. I assume Gail knows?"

"We hadn't shared too many yoga classes before I told her. One doesn't keep many secrets from the ladies at the gym," she said wryly. "For the record, though, my having breast cancer doesn't diminish my ability to look after Derek and Emma."

"Of course not," he answered quickly, to soothe her obvious fears that somehow he'd find her lacking. It also made sense as to why she'd been so worried about the children's appearance for tonight's internet call and had driven herself frantic to make everything perfect. She wanted to prove she could handle the job.

"Good, because for the time being I'm perfectly healthy."

His mental cogs clicked together. "Then Emma wasn't far off the mark, was she? The pet she'd heard you mention was a PET *scan*, not a four-legged animal."

She nodded, a small smile curving her vulnerable mouth. "Yes. My five-year check-up is due a few days after Gail and Ty return, so you don't have to worry about—"

He snagged onto the time frame she'd divulged. "Five years?"

"I was twenty-four when I was diagnosed, which

gives me the dubious honor of being one of those rare young people who develop breast cancer. Mine was a particularly aggressive type, so I opted for a double mastectomy."

Knowing what he did about the drug she was taking, her tumor had also been estrogen-receptor positive, which meant estrogen fueled the cancer. Tamoxifen would stop production of the hormone so the abnormal cells couldn't multiply.

"Speaking from a medical standpoint, you made a wise decision."

She shrugged. "It was the only one I *could* make. Because you're curious, as are most men, all this…" she motioned to her chest "…is courtesy of a skilled plastic surgeon and reconstruction."

Admittedly, he enjoyed seeing those curves and fantasizing about them, but he considered himself more of a leg man. Picturing her long legs and those miles of smooth skin wrapped around his waist was one strong image that would keep him awake at night. "I'm not most men."

She grew thoughtful. "You're not, are you?"

He wasn't sure if she was paying him a compliment or not. "As for worrying about your ability to look after Derek and Emma, I'm not. I merely wanted to say that whatever you need to do, whenever you need to do it, we'll handle the logistics."

"Thanks, but for now I only need to swallow my pills, eat right, and take care of myself, which is what every other person on the planet should do."

"True." Thinking of his upcoming week, he leaned forward. "About the taking-care-of-yourself part, one of my colleagues is still on vacation. I won't be able to pull my share of the load until next weekend so unfortunately you'll have to carry the extra burden. After that, things should settle down considerably."

In light of Christy's revelation, he'd make sure he was available after that. Although he sensed she wouldn't appreciate being treated as gently as if she were blown glass, he'd make a point to stay alert and step in whenever she needed extra help. Gail and Ty really had been smart to ask them to share parenting duties. They'd obviously foreseen areas of potential problems and had prepared for them. Now it was his turn to do the same.

"Thanks for the warning," she said.

"Meanwhile, I don't want you to physically do more than you should. You don't have to be Super-Aunt. No one is holding you to an impossible standard, least of all me."

He'd expected her to appreciate his support, but instead she bristled. "I'm quite capable of taking care of the kids, maintaining the house, and doing my job at the hospital. This is precisely why I don't blurt out my history to everyone I meet. People tend to wrap me in cotton wool and treat me like an invalid, but I'm *not*."

"Of course you aren't," he said, realizing she'd misinterpreted his intent. "I was trying to be considerate. That's all. I don't want you to be afraid I'll complain if I come home and find dishes in the sink."

Her hackles seemed to drop. "Sorry. I get a little defensive sometimes. It really bugs me when I'm told I can't or shouldn't do something because I had cancer."

So many things now made sense, from her can-do, full-steam-ahead attitude to the myriad daring activities that most people would shun. "Offends your over-developed sense of independence, does it?"

Color rose in her face. "It does," she admitted. "That's why…"

When she stopped in midsentence, he filled in the blanks. "That's why you go skydiving, white-water rafting, and all the other physically challenging hobbies you're known for."

Her eyes widened. "How did you know?"

"It was a logical assumption. Anyone trying to prove themselves usually chooses a task that most people wouldn't dream of doing."

"I haven't done anything *that* bizarre or unusual," she pointed out. "Lots of people go white-water rafting."

"Sure, but skydiving?"

"Okay, so that's not quite as popular, but my little excursions are my way to celebrate a good medical report. Some people reward themselves with chocolate. I work on my bucket list."

He was relieved to know she wasn't a thrill-seeker, as he'd thought; she was only working her way through a list of experiences. He instantly felt small for misjudging her motives.

"So what's on tap for this year?" he asked. "Bungee-jumping? Swimming with sharks? Diving for sunken treasure?"

"My list consists of things I want to do before I kick the proverbial bucket, not the things that would kill me in the process," she said wryly. "The first two you mentioned are definitely out, although…" she tapped her mouth with her forefinger "…the sunken treasure idea has possibilities, provided I find time to learn how to scuba dive."

He chuckled. "I stand corrected. So what's left?"

"A trip to Paris. Walking on a glacier. Yodeling in the Swiss Alps. Watching my nieces and nephews graduate from college. They're younger than Derek and Emma—my sister has two boys and my brother has two girls and a boy. It'll be a while until I can cross off that entry and I intend to be around until I do."

He smiled at her determination and applauded her for it. "Do they live around here?"

"They live in the Seattle area near my mom. My family wasn't happy when I moved to the Midwest, but they understood."

He suspected she'd relocated as a way to assert her independence. However, it didn't take much imagination to picture the resistance Christy had encountered when she'd announced her plans to leave the bosom of her family. He'd spent weeks trying to convince his own sister to accept the promotion her company had offered here in Levitt Springs, but she'd wanted to strike out on her own, too. He would have preferred having her only fifteen minutes away instead of ninety, but she had to live life on her terms, not his. In the grand scheme of things, however, she was relatively close and he could bridge the distance with a mere hop and a skip.

"Then your family was your support group?" he asked.

"I don't think I would have kept going if not for them and my friends. They drove me to doctors' appointments and chemo sessions when I couldn't, loaded my refrigerator with chicken soup, and took me shopping at Victoria's Secret when my reconstruction was completed. They were the greatest. Everyone should have support like I did."

That explained the scrappy underwear he'd found. Unfortunately, being reminded of her lingerie made him wonder what color she was wearing today.

Yanking his mind off that dead-end track, he noticed one significant absence in her list of supportive people. "Assuming you had a boyfriend, where was he in all this?"

She let out a deep sigh of apparent resignation. As if recognizing her mistress's inner turmoil, Ria padded to the sofa and rested her jaw on Christy's knee. She scratched the dog's ears and met his gaze. "He took off."

He wasn't surprised; he'd seen enough in his own practice to know that some people simply couldn't handle illness, whether it was their own or their spouse's, but the idea of leaving someone under those circumstances was beyond his ability to comprehend.

"What happened?"

"Jon seemed to accept my diagnosis through the talk of lumpectomies, chemotherapy, losing my hair, et cetera, until the word 'mastectomy' was mentioned. When 'double' was added to the table as the best course of action, even though he knew I planned to undergo reconstruction so I'd have my figure back by Christmas, he freaked out."

"So he left."

"Not immediately. The final straw came when he learned I'd need hormone suppression therapy for at least five years and my ovaries might or might not wake up and be ready to work. He wanted kids of his own, through the usual method and not through special medical means, so he wished me luck, kissed me goodbye, and I never saw or heard from him again."

In his disgust Linc muttered an expletive that would have shocked the most hardened longshoreman.

She burst out laughing, clapping her hands over her mouth as her eyes twinkled the entire time. "My, my, Dr Maguire. I'd scold you for your language but those are my sentiments exactly."

He grinned. "It's nice to know we're on the same page." After a brief hesitation he spoke again. "He's the reason you won't date until your next scan, isn't he?"

"I date," she protested mildly. "Just not often and it's never serious. I make that plain from the beginning."

"Do you explain why?"

She looked at him with a measure of horror. "Of course not. Actually, that's not quite true. I'd gone out with someone before I moved to Levitt Springs two years ago."

Instinctively, he knew this story wouldn't have a happy ending either, but knowledge was power and he wanted the facts so he knew exactly what demons she was fighting. "What happened?"

"Nothing. I shared everything I've told you—maybe not quite *everything*…" her smile was rueful "…but Anthony knew about my cancer and the surgeries. We had a wonderful evening."

She paused and he sensed a "but" was coming.

"After he took me home, I never heard from him again," she finished.

He cursed under his breath and she smiled. "It wasn't that bad," she told him. "We only went out once. When

I realized he wouldn't call, I was disappointed but not crushed. After that, I moved here and decided to keep my tale to myself. Some women tell everyone they meet about their cancer experience and I understand why they do. The more women realize it could happen to them—at any age—the better, but for me, I want people to see me for who I am, not for what I've gone through in the past or might in the future."

"Aren't you selling us short? You shouldn't assume all men are as weak-willed and lacking in character as those two."

"I know," she admitted, "but I can't take the risk. If a particular relationship is meant to be, it'll happen at the right time, under my terms."

He hated that she'd lumped all men in the same category, himself included. "When did Ria appear on the scene?"

"After Jon disappeared to find the new love of his life, my brother brought me a puppy. She was beautiful, happy, and loved the water, so I named her Ria. She also had the biggest paws, which made me afraid she was part horse, but in the end she was my best friend and was there whenever I needed a warm body to hold on to."

Once again, he had an uncommon urge to hunt down this Jon character and do him bodily harm. As special as Ria was, Christy should have had a real person holding her during those dark days and nights. In fact, he wished he'd known her at the time because he couldn't imagine leaving her. A person didn't desert the one he loved.

Yet he was glad this guy had decamped, otherwise *he* might never have met her. The possibility of living the rest of his life without her waltzing into it drove the air out of his lungs like a fist to his solar plexus.

"Now you know my whole sordid tale," she said lightly, "and why fundraising for the cancer center and the Relay for Life organization is important to me."

"You could be the hospital's poster child for the event," he pointed out.

"I could, but I won't. I'll leave that to someone else." She grinned. "I'm going to be too busy getting my dance partner up to speed for the competition."

"Speaking of which, did you have to drag *me* into your plan?" he said in mock complaint.

"I did," she stated innocently, although her eyes sparkled with humor. "You always walk into the unit so completely focused on nursing notes and lab reports that I decided you should get involved on a more personal level."

"I'm involved," he protested mildly. Being conscious of her fragrance and the softness of her skin, he could think of at least one other activity in which he'd like to involve himself. "I write a check and it comes out of my *personal* bank account."

One of her eyebrows arched high. "Writing a check is nice, but it isn't *participation*."

"Well, thanks to you, I'm participating now," he complained good-naturedly.

She giggled. "You are, aren't you?"

While his apprehension about sailing around the floor in front of a group of people hadn't faded, it seemed small and insignificant when compared to Christy's challenges. Spending an evening in the company of a woman who embraced life to the degree that she did wouldn't be the royal pain in the backside that he'd first thought. Perish the thought, but, to borrow her phrase, it would probably be…fun.

"I'm warning you, though. After this week, when I don't have to cover so many extra shifts, we're going to start practicing," he said firmly. "And I do mean *practice*."

A small wrinkle formed between her eyebrows. "I was only teasing about getting my dance partner up to speed."

"You have may have been teasing, but I'm not."

"Need I remind you this is only a friendly event? No one is expecting you to be Patrick Swayze."

"If they are, they'll be sorely disappointed, but if something is worth doing—and you keep telling me it is," he added wryly, "then we're going to do it well."

As he saw her smile, he asked, "What's so funny?"

The grin disappeared, but the humor remained in her eyes. "Nothing," she said innocently. "If you want to practice, we'll practice."

The cuckoo suddenly chirped eleven times, which caught Linc by surprise. He wondered where the hours had gone, but he'd been so engrossed in Christy's story that he hadn't noticed how quickly the evening had passed.

"I'd better start the dishwasher before I forget." She rose out of his loose embrace. "Then I'm turning in."

As he followed suit, his arm felt empty and almost unnatural, as if his body sensed what his mind could not—that she belonged there. Not just for a few minutes or over the course of a conversation, but for years and years.

Perhaps it was time he reconsidered a few points he'd etched in stone. The ideal woman he'd hoped to find— the one with steady, dependable traits—suddenly didn't seem quite as attractive she had a few weeks ago. Being with Christy had made his nameless, faceless future wife seem so…colorless, so black and white.

He now wanted color in his life.

Out of habit, he checked the front door to be sure the deadbolt was thrown, and armed the alarm system.

It was such a husbandly sort of thing to do, he decided as he waited for her to return so he could turn off the lights. Yes, he knew she could flick the switch as easily as he could, but he'd reverted back to his early days when his family had been together. He had always been the last to go to bed because, as the man of the house, he'd accepted the responsibility of securing their home for the night. Old habits, as he'd told Christy, definitely died hard because he'd fallen back into them as if it were only yesterday.

He heard the water running into the dishwasher, then the rhythmic swish as it circulated, but she still hadn't reappeared. Wondering what had delayed her, he meandered into the kitchen and found her with her hands planted on the counter, head down.

"Is something wrong?" he asked.

She straightened immediately and turned toward him, but he saw the too-forced smile. "Why do you ask?"

"You looked as if you were a few hundred miles away."

Her smile was small. "I suppose I was," she said slowly. "For years I haven't thought about some of the things I shared tonight. I'd pushed Jon and the incident with Anthony completely out of my mind, but remembering the way it was...now my emotions are a little tangled."

He didn't believe she had pushed those two experiences out of her head as much as she thought she had. The fact that she intended to hold any fellow at arm's length until she passed her magical five-year date proved that both men's rejections continued to color her relationships.

"Understandable," he said, "but I'm honored you opened up to me. For the record, though, if you hadn't have volunteered the information, I wouldn't have pressed."

"The story was bound to come out sooner or later. You can't share a house with someone and keep any secrets," she said ruefully. "I trust, though, you'll hold everything in confidence? It's not that I don't want anyone in Levitt Springs to know, but I'd rather tell people in my own time and in my own way."

"I won't say a word."

"Thanks."

He sensed the absence of her normally confident air and he felt somewhat responsible. If he'd pretended ignorance about the pills, denied any knowledge of what he'd seen, she wouldn't be reliving the sting of her ex-boyfriend's rejection.

Impulsively, feeling as if he needed to comfort her as he would a distraught Emma, he covered the distance and drew her against him. "Jon was, and still is, an ass," he murmured against her hair. "For that matter, so is Anthony."

She shook in his arms and he didn't know if she was laughing or crying until she spoke. Then he heard the hoarse, tell-tale quiver in her voice. "They are."

"You're better off without them."

"I am," she agreed.

"Jon definitely didn't deserve you."

"He didn't."

She sounded as if she was repeating the arguments she'd used before. He pulled away just enough so he could tip up her chin and stare into her chocolate-brown eyes. "A fellow with any brains would be happy to call you his, cancer diagnosis or not."

She licked her bottom lip before squeezing out a weak smile. "Thanks for the thought."

His gaze landed on her mouth and he instantly realized she was definitely *not* Emma by any stretch of his imagination. He had an uncontrollable urge to determine if her lips would fit his as well as her body did, and if they tasted as delicious as he suspected. Before he could restrain himself, he bent his head and kissed her.

It was a chaste kiss, one meant to console, but not only did that contact pack a powerful punch, it also ignited a hunger inside him.

Gradually, he increased the pressure, waiting for her to respond to his lead, and to his utter delight she did. He caressed her back, carefully encouraging her to lean closer until he finally felt her weight settle against him. Little by little, he inched one hand toward her bare shoulder. Entranced by the smooth skin, he trailed his fingers along the bones before stopping at the hollow of her throat.

He'd run his fingers along the skin of countless patients, but his touch had been clinical as he'd felt for lumps, bumps, and other signs of illness. This time it was different. This time his sensitive fingertips noticed softness while his nose picked up the fresh, floral scent that was pure Christy.

Stopping was impossible; it seemed crucial to catalogue every inch of her, although he was cautious of what he suspected were her well-defined boundaries. But her skin was warm and his five senses conspired against his good sense until his fingers traveled an inch lower and she suddenly pulled away.

Puzzled, he stared at her, wondering if he'd touched a tender spot, but as he glanced at the point where his hand had roamed on her sternum, he mentally kicked himself for his insensitivity. Clearly, she thought he intended to stray deeper into what she considered forbidden territory.

"I should go to bed," she said, her voice breathy as if she'd been jogging for a mile. "Goodnight."

"Goodnight," he answered to her back as she fled. His night, however, couldn't end with him in his current state. He'd work off his tension in Ty's basement weight room and if that didn't resolve his problem, a cold shower would come next.

All because of the sixty seconds she'd spent in his arms.

Christy spent the next twenty-four hours scolding herself for overreacting to Linc's touch. His gentle caresses hadn't been inappropriate and yet she'd jumped like a frightened virgin.

The truth was she'd enjoyed being in his arms far

more than she'd dreamed possible. He was solid and warm and comforting, which gave her such a deep sense of safety—almost as if she was being protected from the latest of life's impending storms. More than that, though, he reminded her of a steady rock she could lean on whenever the need arose.

In spite of all that, she'd jumped away from him like a startled rabbit, she thought with disgust.

She might have apologized, but she didn't see him at all on Monday, although she knew he had come home because he'd left a glass in the sink and a scribbled note on the counter, asking her to pick up his clothes at the dry cleaner's. *Please*, he'd underlined in thick, bold strokes.

On Tuesday, she saw him at the hospital, but other than a quick "How are the kids?" their conversation had been limited to the status of his patients.

She didn't see him at all on Wednesday, but once again she'd found a note. This time he'd stated how much he'd liked the oatmeal cookies she'd left for him. She'd seen his distinctive scrawl before and thought nothing of it, but his personal message—his compliment—brightened her day. Because she was off duty and intended to spend her hours on household chores and laundry, she needed that bright spot.

Since the kids were in school, she vowed to tackle household projects. She cleaned furiously, debating for the longest time if she should go into Linc's room in case he'd think she was invading his privacy. Finally, after she'd cleaned bedrooms and the community bathroom, she caved in to her own arguments. The man hardly had time to breathe, so he certainly wasn't going to spend his free hours dusting and scrubbing the tub. As neat as he was, he wouldn't notice she'd been in his domain, anyway.

She, however, certainly did. The masculine scent of his bath soap hovered in the bathroom and clung to his towels. Even his bed sheets retained his personal fragrance.

He left more than his scent behind, though. She found other clues that fit the man she knew him to be. The unmade bed suggested he'd been called out early, but even the rumpled bedding testified to Linc's control. A faint indentation of his head on the pillow and one corner of the sheet pulled out from under the mattress hinted that he wasn't a restless sleeper—probably because when he finally closed his eyes, he was too exhausted to move.

Idly, she wondered what he'd be like to sleep with. Would he snuggle up close, like Ria did when it was cold outside, or stick to his side of the bed? Would he pull her toward him or move to the center to meet her?

As she caught herself in her own daydream, she chuckled with embarrassment and was grateful that he wouldn't walk in and discover her locked within her own wicked imagination.

She stripped the bed, forcing a clinical detachment to complete the job.

His full laundry hamper presented another problem. It seemed a horrible waste of water to ask him to launder his things separately—again, when would he even have time?—so she gathered his washables and added them to her other loads, all the while trying not to no-

tice how wifely it felt for his T-shirts and unmention-
ables to mingle with her own.

Determined to keep her thoughts occupied, she
dusted and scrubbed and vacuumed until Ria fled the
house for the quiet safety of the back yard. She left
nothing unturned, and had even gone into Ty's basement weight room where she'd found a few dirty towels. By the time Emma and Derek were out of school,
the place was spotless and she was literally exhausted.

They strolled to the park to exercise Ria and came
home at dinnertime, but once again Linc didn't put in an
appearance. She didn't see him until the next day at the
hospital and then she was certain it was only because
Thursday was his normal scheduled surgery day. One
of his patients had just been wheeled to a room after
waking up in Recovery and Linc had walked in to talk
to the man's wife, wearing his green scrubs.

After they'd dealt with the usual order of patient
business, he pulled her aside. "When can you get away
for lunch?"

"It's hard to say," she admitted. "We're swamped
today."

"Make time."

She was tired enough to bristle at his demand—between keeping up with two busy children, a house, and
working a short-staffed twelve-hour shift, she now understood why her working-mother colleagues had fragile tempers by the end of the week—but she had to eat
and if she didn't take a break soon, her feet would revolt.

"Maybe by one or so," she began.

"Okay. I'll see you then."

He strode away before she could recover from her

surprise. As far as the gossip mill had reported, the man rarely took time for himself between his surgical cases and when he did, he usually ate on the run. Could it be he was finally loosening up and becoming more approachable? She smiled at the thought.

Yet as she watched him pause to talk to a pharmacist, then laugh at whatever she'd said, her self-satisfaction dimmed as an unreasonable combination of curiosity and jealousy flooded over her.

Was this the woman he'd mentioned he'd wanted to get to know? If so, then her plan to convince him to enjoy life's simpler pleasures might drive him into another woman's arms.

It was silly of her to consider the possibility. After all, she didn't have any illusions that she was his type.

But, oh, it was nice to dream...

Linc's work schedule for the week hadn't been that unusual for him, but throughout the day—especially during the evenings—he'd caught himself wondering what Christy and the kids might be doing. Knowing that he was missing out had made him impatient at times and he'd earned a number of startled glances from his staff who obviously wondered what had twisted his surgical gloves into a knot.

Each night as he came home he half hoped Christy would be waiting for him, as she had on that first night. Logically, he knew he was expecting too much. Ten-thirty or eleven was late for someone who went to work at five a.m. Not being accustomed to keeping up with two active children, she probably ended her day as soon as Emma and Derek did.

Illogically, he still hoped.

Whenever he walked into a quiet house, those hopes deflated, although he was pleased by her gesture of leaving the kitchen light blazing so he wouldn't stumble in the dark in the somewhat unfamiliar surroundings.

While she might not physically make an appearance, he felt her presence in other ways—a plate of food in the refrigerator, a pan of frosted brownies on the stove, clean towels in Ty's weight room. Only one thing could have topped them all—if he'd been able to slip into her bed instead of his.

With great relief, he saw his hectic week finally drawing to a close. He could hardly wait another day to talk to her in person instead of through hastily scribbled notes left on the kitchen counter. Yes, he'd seen her a few times at the hospital, but they'd both been coming and going, so conversation had been limited to medical issues.

Today, though, he'd decided to make a change. Before his last case, he'd shocked his surgery staff when he'd announced a thirty-minute break between patients, but he didn't care that he'd wrecked his own routine. He only knew he couldn't wait until Friday night or Saturday morning to see Christy again, and maybe... steal another kiss.

In fact, he couldn't remember the last time he'd been this eager to meet someone. His job had meant so much to him that it had consumed his existence until most of the personal side of his life had faded away. He'd become somewhat aware of the situation—his time with his brother's family had pointed out what he was missing—but he hadn't discovered a compelling reason to change the habits he'd formed.

Christy had provided it.

A week ago, he'd believed she wasn't right for him with her daring, impulsive approach to life. Oh, he'd been drawn to her like a hapless bug flew toward light, but, given enough opportunity, he was certain he'd eventually purge her from his system. Now, a mere seven days later, it was the last thing he wanted.

His attitude was odd, really. They'd spent more time apart than together, and yet everything he'd seen, everything he'd heard, and everything he'd done only whetted his appetite for more.

The good news was, "more" hung right around the corner.

He returned to the surgery floor at the appointed hour with five minutes to spare, then waited for her to swap an IV fluid bag that had run low. He chafed at the delay, but he was only minutes away from having her to himself, relatively speaking, so he hid his impatience by accessing several lab reports while he listened for her footsteps.

When she returned breathlessly, as if she'd hurried on his account, her smile was worth the wait.

In the cafeteria, he steered her toward a table for two in the corner near the aquarium. Aware of the curious glances directed toward them, he simply ignored everyone and focused on Christy.

"You look tired," he said without preamble as she poured her low-fat dressing over her chef's salad.

"Is it that obvious?" she asked ruefully.

He shrugged as he dug into his roast beef special. "Only to me. You aren't doing too much, are you?"

"Probably, but that's how it works," she quipped. "To be honest, you're looking a little frayed around the edges, too. You aren't the only one with keen powers of observation."

"Apparently not," he answered dryly, surprised she'd picked up the signals others had overlooked. He immediately wondered what else she'd deduced about him. If she had any idea of how easily she triggered a surge in his testosterone level, she'd probably lock herself in her bedroom and never come out.

"I don't know where I'm busier—here at work or at home with the kids. We haven't had a dull moment."

"I've seen the calendar Gail left for us. Next week will be better."

"I don't see how. Between soccer practice two nights and a Cub Scout meeting—"

"I'll be available to help," he interrupted. "The load won't fall completely on you. I'm sorry it did this week, but it won't happen again."

"Don't apologize. A doctor's life doesn't run on a schedule. If it's any consolation, the kids have missed you."

"I've missed you all, too. How did the internet call go last night? No tears when it was all over?"

"A few, but not many. Emma's having a ball, sending emails. You created a monster when you created her own account and showed her how to send letters. I think she's singlehandedly trying to fill her mom's in-box."

"Maybe we should limit her to one or two a day."

"Keeping her too busy to think about sending a message would be better. Forbidding her to contact Gail will only make her more homesick and she'll dwell more on her parents' absence than she should."

He considered her comment. "You're probably right."

"Don't worry. She'll get past this. We simply need to be patient."

"How did you get to be so wise with kids?"

She tipped her bottle of lemonade and drank deeply. "I learned a lot from watching my brother and sisters interact with their children. How about you?"

"My parents constantly reminded me that as the oldest I had to look out for the younger siblings no matter where we were or what we were doing. I'm afraid I wasn't always tactful," he said wryly.

"Ah, you were the bossy older brother."

"Afraid so. I suppose I had more of a dictatorial style, but I think that came from being left in charge so often. My mom had a fantastic voice and a dream to make it big in the country-music scene, so my dad hauled us all over so she could perform and it was my job to keep the little ones busy. As soon as I turned thirteen, they left the three of us at home."

"What did you do to occupy the time?"

"Board games, cards, whatever. You name it, we played it. If I had a dime for every round of *Chutes and Ladders* or *Sorry*, I'd be a wealthy man," he said wryly. "In any case, our main goal was to be awake when our parents came home."

"Were you successful?"

He shook his head. "No. Joanie would usually conk out around eleven, Ty would fall asleep at midnight, and one was my limit."

"Did they do that often? Leave you home alone?"

"Every Saturday night."

"That must have been tough."

He considered for a moment. "It wasn't as tough as it was frustrating. The little kids needed their attention, not mine. I knew my parents loved us, but at times I resented how easily they left us to chase their own dreams."

And that, he knew, was the main reason why he hadn't been in any rush to look for Mrs Right. Although his job guaranteed there would be times when he'd be gone at night, just as his parents had been, he wanted the mother of his children to be a mother twenty-four seven, not just when it was convenient.

"Regardless of their actions, they must have done something right," she said softly. "You and Ty both turned into responsible adults."

They had, hadn't they? he thought.

"Your story does explain why you take life so seriously," she remarked. "Didn't you ever do anything just for fun?"

"Sure. I hung out with my buddies on Friday nights after football and basketball games. Band kids had to stick together."

"Marching band?"

"I was quite the trumpet player in my day," he said proudly.

"Can you still play?"

"I doubt it." He grinned. "Fortunately for you, I sold my trumpet so we'll never know. By the way, the house looks great. You've been busy."

"I'm surprised you could see a difference. You haven't been home much."

He couldn't tell if she was peeved by his absence or surprised that he was aware of his surroundings even if he came home during the wee hours. He grinned. "You'd be surprised at what I notice. Speaking of which, I don't expect you to clean my room or do my laundry."

"I'm sure you didn't, but I couldn't very well let your room turn into a pigsty, could I? Gail would kill me."

"Actually, she'd kill *me*," he said wryly. "Regardless, I don't want you taking on more than you need to. I'll ask my housekeeper to add us to her list and—"

"You'll do no such thing." Her voice was firm. "I'm perfectly capable of performing a few chores."

"It isn't a matter of capabilities." He had to tread lightly because he hated to offend her independent spirit. "It's a matter of having enough hours in the day."

"We'll make time. If everyone pitches in, cleaning won't take long at all. 'Many hands make light work,' my mother always says."

"Yes, but, as far as I'm concerned, paying a housekeeper is money well spent."

"I'm sure it is, but I wouldn't feel right if you footed the bill. We're in this together, remember, and, as far as I'm concerned, it's an unnecessary expense."

Her light tone didn't disguise the steel in her voice. He wanted to continue to argue his point, but his gaze landed on the fraying edge of her scrub top's neckline. Nurses might be paid well these days, but thanks to the associated expenses of her illness he suspected money was still tight.

Although he wanted this to be his contribution to the

household, he didn't press the issue. "Okay, we'll do it your way. For now," he tacked on his proviso.

"Fair enough."

"So you know, if I had my choice as to what I'd like you to do—cook or clean—I'd choose cooking. What are the odds of getting another batch of those cookies?"

She laughed, clearly amused by his hopeful tone. "That depends on when Derek is scheduled to provide treats for another soccer game."

"Ah, that explains why I couldn't find any more. You gave them away."

She finished her salad. "I did, but you liked them, did you?"

"The best oatmeal cookies I ever tasted."

"Somehow I never saw you as having a sweet tooth."

"I do, which is why I work out three or four times a week. I'm surprised you haven't heard me in the basement."

"You actually exercise when you get home?" She sounded incredulous.

"Sometimes," he admitted. "Lifting weights helps me work out the kinks if I've been in surgery all day. Sometimes I'm too keyed up to go to sleep, so pumping iron helps."

"Wow. I usually stare mindlessly at the television when I'm exhausted. I'm impressed you're that...disciplined."

"Impressed enough to make another batch of cookies?"

She giggled. "Okay. I'll let you get lucky this weekend."

If she didn't catch the double entendre of her own

words, he certainly did. As he glanced at the aquarium and saw those same fish kissing again, he realized his craving went beyond mere cookies. He wanted another taste of Christy and he wanted it as soon as possible.

Getting that taste wouldn't be easy. Underneath her bubbly personality and a layer of friendliness lurked a skittish woman who'd been hurt by someone she'd trusted.

It would be up to him to prove that he was someone she could trust.

CHAPTER SIX

BY FRIDAY, Christy knew she was in trouble. Dredging up the old memories of Jon had fueled her determination to prove that just because she'd had cancer, she was still capable of doing everything any other woman could do. As a result, she'd pushed herself too hard and was paying the price with her nauseous stomach and the headache behind her eyes. She should have been at home because it was her day off, but someone had called in with a family emergency, so as soon as Christy had sent the kids to school, she'd reported to work.

She would have rather spent the day in bed.

There was one silver lining to this dark cloud—she'd arrived on duty after Linc had already made his rounds, otherwise he would have taken one look at her and with the tell-tale twitch in his cheek to indicate his unhappiness he would have insisted she return home. Naturally, she would have had to disobey his command on principle. She was still her own woman and made her own decisions even if, in this case, he was right.

Fortunately, her supervisor had also arranged for a second-shift nurse to come early, so Christy was able to leave as soon as Derek and Emma's school day ended.

She swallowed several anti-inflammatories and painkillers, and soldiered on through the rest of the afternoon—even making Linc's requested cookies—but by dinner's end her own food refused to stay in her stomach and she finally had to face facts. Her body had reached its limit.

"Are you guys ready for bed?" she asked, hoping she sounded brighter than she felt.

Derek was horrified. "We never go to bed at seven, even on school nights. Fridays is our night to stay up late 'cause Mom wants us to sleep in on Saturdays."

"Yeah," Emma chimed in. "It is."

"Then you do sleep late on Saturdays?" Christy asked, because so far they hadn't.

Derek's grin was sheepish. "Sometimes, but if we don't and Mom or Dad aren't awake, we know not to bother them."

Thank you, Gail, for training them properly, she thought with some relief. "I'd suggest you snooze as long as you can. We have a full day tomorrow."

Derek was suspicious. "Doing what?"

She had no idea, but surely Linc had a plan. "I have to discuss it with your uncle first," she prevaricated.

"We can watch a movie now, can't we?" Derek asked.

"Yeah." Emma's head bobbed enthusiastically. "Mom lets us on a Friday."

She hated to park them in front of the television, but common sense told her that Gail and Ty allowed them to watch their movies if the size of the children's collection was any indication. As for leaving them alone, she also knew their parents didn't hover over them every second. They were school-aged children, not toddlers who required constant supervision.

"Okay, but after that, it's bedtime."

"Sure." Emma peered at her. "You don't look so good, Christy. Are you sick?"

She managed a smile. "A little. I'm going to lie down, but I want you to get me if you need anything. Anything at all. Is that understood?"

"Sure."

"And don't eat all the cookies. Save some for your uncle."

"We will," the two said in unison.

"Don't forget to wake me in half an hour or when your uncle arrives, whichever comes first."

"We will."

As the opening credits appeared on the screen, Christy dropped onto her bed. Ria padded in and curled against her in her usual, I'm-here-for-you-because-I-know-you-don't-feel-well position.

Christy patted the dog's head in gratitude for her faithfulness before she promptly closed her eyes and tried to relax.

"All I need are thirty minutes," she murmured aloud. "Just thirty minutes and I'll be ready to go. Linc will never know I couldn't keep up. How much trouble can two kids cause while watching a movie, anyway?"

Linc was more than ready to be home. His hospital patients were stable, including the emergency splenectomy case, and, barring a car accident, he should have a quiet evening ahead of him.

He strode into the house at seven forty-five, expecting to see three smiling faces eager to enjoy the remaining daylight. Instead, he walked into a kitchen that resembled a disaster area, with stacks of dirty pots and pans, spilled juice, and a popcorn trail that led into the living room.

Before he could wrap his head around the unusual scene, Emma came running and launched herself into his arms.

"Unca Linc's home!"

"Hi, sprout. How are you?" he asked as he settled her on his hip.

"I'm fine. Christy's sick."

Emma's revelation explained the mess. Immediately, he tried to recall what bug was making the rounds now, and came up blank. "She is? Was she sick all day?"

Emma shrugged. "Just since dinner. She's in bed so you hafta be quiet. Derek and I are watching a movie. We missed you, Unca Linc." She flung her arms around his neck and hugged him.

Not for the first time in his life, Linc was envious of his brother. This was what Ty came home to every night, not an empty house with a radio or television for company.

This, he decided—coming home to a wife and kids and even an occasional mess—was what he wanted, too. Preferably sooner rather than later.

"We missed you."

"I missed you, too." He prodded for information. "What's wrong with Christy?"

"I think it's her stomach because I heard her throwing up. She told us to wake her when you came home. Do you want me to get her?"

"That's okay. I'll check on her myself," he told her as he lowered her until her feet touched the floor.

"Christy left a plate for you in the 'frigerator," Emma offered helpfully, before she headed for the living room. "I'm gonna watch the rest of our movie."

Whatever Christy had served definitely smelled delicious and from the looks of the pots and pans on the stove, she'd served spaghetti. Although he wanted to dig into his own serving, he chose to wait until he discovered what was wrong with Christy.

He strolled through the living room, past the two children, who were engrossed in their movie, and stopped at Christy's door. When she didn't answer his knock, he peeked inside and saw her lying in bed with a watchful Ria at her side.

"Christy?" he asked softly.

She stirred. "Linc?"

"It's me," he assured her. "I hear you're not feeling well."

"I'm okay. Dinner's in—"

"The refrigerator. Emma told me." He strode in and stood next to her bed, worried that whatever had hit her had laid her so low and so quickly.

"I still need to clean the kitchen." She grimaced as she tried to rise.

"The kitchen can wait. Do I need to phone your doctor? Call in a prescription?" He imagined all sorts of possible causes and treatments—some dire, some run-of-the-mill—as he gently placed his hand on her forehead. Her skin felt cool, which eased his worries to some degree.

"No. Please, no. It's nothing."

He disagreed. "What's wrong? Stomach flu?" He'd

already ruled out a chest cold because she breathed easily and her nose wasn't running.

"No, just overtired."

"Overtired?" His momentary panic eased. "I thought you agreed to pace yourself."

"I know, and I tried, but I felt so wonderful and thought I could do it all, so I did. Unfortunately, pushing my limits caught up to me today." She met his gaze for an instant before she closed her eyes. "I know you want to, so go ahead and scold."

She sounded defeated as well as sick, so he opted for mercy. "I'll wait until you're feeling better," he teased. "It's tough to kick a man—or woman—when she's already down."

"Thanks. Just give me another hour or so. I'll feel better by then. Honest."

Linc doubted it. Her face was too pale and the circles under her eyes too dark for him to believe a mere hour's nap would solve her problems, but he didn't intend to argue with her.

"Okay," he said evenly. "Can I get you something in the meantime? Hot tea? Aspirin?"

"I'm fine, thanks, although I'd appreciate it if you could let Ria outdoors. She hasn't had a bathroom break for a while."

"Will do." He snapped his fingers. "Come, Ria. Outside?"

Ria perked her ears as if she wanted to obey, but from the way she glanced at Christy, then back at him, she was torn between obeying nature's call and comforting her mistress.

"Come on, girl," he coaxed. "Take care of business and you can join Christy again."

Reluctantly, Ria rose, stretched, then gracefully leaped off the bed. Linc opened the patio door and as soon as Ria returned from a trip to her favorite bush, she ignored the tasty popcorn trail and disappeared into Christy's bedroom.

Certain the animal was now cuddled against her owner, Linc had one thought as he microwaved his dinner.

He was jealous of a dog.

After he'd eaten, washed the dishes, changed into a pair of comfortable gym shorts and an old T-shirt, he carried in a cup of tea prepared the way she liked it—with one teaspoon of honey—and stayed with her until she drank it.

He spent the rest of the evening watching movies, playing a few hands of *Go Fish* and *Old Maid* with Derek and Emma, and checking on Christy.

"I'm going to float away," she grumbled as he helped her sit so she could drink another cup of tea.

"Better that than getting dehydrated," he said cheerfully. As soon as she'd emptied most of the cup and lay down again, he returned to the living room and found both children fighting to stay awake.

For the next hour he oversaw their bedtime ritual and read the obligatory two stories, with an extra book for good measure.

"Christy said we had big plans for tomorrow," Derek mentioned as he crawled between the sheets. "What are we doing?"

Linc thought fast. "We'll see how she feels," he

hedged, "but I thought we could spend the day at my house. My weeds are probably knee-high by now."

"Can I ride the mower with you?" Derek asked, his tired eyes brimming with excitement.

"Maybe," he said. "Now go to sleep and we'll talk about it in the morning."

Outside Christy's room, he paused in indecision, but a noise in the kitchen drew him there instead. He found Christy leaning against the counter, a cupboard door open, as if she'd been trying to retrieve a glass but hadn't quite managed it.

"How are you feeling?" he asked.

She straightened with obvious effort. "Better. I came to wash the dishes, but everything's done."

Because she sounded almost irritated, he fought back a smile. "It gave me something to do while the kids finished their movie."

"Where are they?"

"In bed, ready to wake up at the crack of dawn for a fun-filled, action-packed day at the Maguire house." He motioned to the cupboard. "Can I get you something?"

"Water, please."

He filled a glass and placed it beside her.

"You should have left the dishes for me," she said in between sips. "I said I'd—"

"Yes, I know, but I didn't mind," he said calmly. "There weren't that many, so it didn't take long. I didn't even get dishpan hands. See?" He held up his hands to show her.

To his surprise, then dismay, a few tears trickled down her face and she swiped them away with her fingertips. Oh, man. She was *crying*.

"Hey," he protested. "Washing a few pots and pans isn't anything to get upset over."

"I'm not." She sniffed.

From where he was standing, she certainly seemed as if she was. "If you're not upset," he said carefully, "then what's wrong?"

"I'd wanted everything to be perfect when you finally came home."

"It was," he assured her. At her skeptical glance, he corrected himself. "Maybe not *perfect*, but it was close."

"No, it wasn't."

"Hey, the kids were fed and my dinner was waiting for me. Having only a few dirty dishes waiting was pretty darned good, in my opinion."

"That's not the point. I—"

"If you were afraid I'd find fault, I apologize. You don't have to impress me, Christy, because I've been impressed since our first weekend."

She met his gaze, her smile wan. "How could you be?"

"Trust me. I am."

Her expression revealed her skepticism. "I truly wanted to amaze you with what I could do and how well I could keep up, but I'd really wanted to convince myself." She raked her hair with one hand. "And I failed."

She'd caught him off guard. "You wanted to impress yourself? Why?"

"After thinking about Jon the other night, I realized that all this time I've been trying to prove him wrong— that my cancer treatments wouldn't make me less of a woman than any other. That I could still juggle the same things every other woman juggles in her life, even if I lacked a few body parts and didn't have the same hormones swimming around my system. He'd never know if I'd succeeded or not, but *I* would know the truth." She paused and her shoulders drooped. "I'm beginning to think he was right."

Furious with Jon's insensitivity and angry at himself for dredging up enough of the past to rob her of her confidence, he held her by her shoulders. "Absolutely do *not* mention or think about that man's narrow-mindedness again. You've done a remarkable job when it comes to balancing work and children and a house. Do not *ever* suggest or even *think* otherwise. Got that?" he ground out.

She blinked several times before she nibbled on her bottom lip.

He squeezed her shoulders and gave her a slight shake. "Did you hear what I said?"

"I heard. But—"

He gentled his hold as well as his voice. "You have nothing to prove to me or to anyone else, and I don't want you to try." He nudged her chin upward with his index finger so her gaze could meet his. "You're tired and aren't feeling well, so it's easy to let your imagination and your fears run wild, but, honestly, no one in this house has any reason to complain about what you have or haven't done, least of all me. I'm the one who's been absent without leave for the past five days."

She hesitated, her face pensive as if she was giving his words some thought. "So you're saying I should complain about you?"

"If it'll make you feel better, yes."

Her chuckle was weak but, nonetheless, it was still a chuckle. "I'll pass."

"Good, because I'm not sure my fragile ego could take it. For the record, there's no shame in recognizing one's limitations and delegating accordingly. If we could manage everything ourselves, we wouldn't need each other, would we?"

Her downcast expression suddenly turned thoughtful. "I suppose not."

"Good. Now, finish your water and hop into bed where you belong. Tomorrow will roll around soon enough and I have a few plans on how we'll spend the day."

She nodded, but didn't move. Instead, her gaze continued to rest on him until he felt almost uncomfortable.

"Do I have spaghetti sauce on my chin?" he joked.

"No, but this is the first time I think I've ever seen you so passionate about something. Normally, you're so…so *controlled*."

"People respond better if their surgeon is controlled and doesn't rant and rave like a lunatic when he's aggravated," he said lightly.

"You can be passionate without being out of control. Watching you express your emotion is…comforting, I guess. You seem so much more…*natural*. I like seeing you less formal."

He could think of many other ways to show her just how passionate he could be, but now wasn't the time and the kitchen wasn't the place. It was, however, reassuring to realize he didn't have to hide his innermost feelings around her. He could relax and be himself, such as he was.

"You'll see my emotional side more often in the coming weeks after we all start to get on each other's nerves," he said in a dry tone. "In the meantime, you need your rest."

"I'm tired but I'm not sleepy. Does that make sense?"

"It makes perfect sense," he said as he led her toward her room, "but I'll tell you what I tell the kids. Get ready for bed and by the time you're finished, you'll change your mind."

He turned down her sheets while she slipped into the bathroom, then returned to the living room where he sprawled on the sofa and debated if he needed another trip to Ty's weight room before he called it a day, too.

However, when she appeared wearing her sleepshirt that hit her midthigh, every part of his body seemed to notice just how long her legs were. "Do you need anything?" he asked her, hoping his voice didn't sound as hoarse as it did to his own ears.

"Stay with me," she said.

He froze, certain his hearing had suddenly and inexplicably failed. "Stay?" he echoed as surprise paralyzed his lungs for a few seconds.

"Talk to me until I fall asleep," she said. "Please?"

He simply rose and followed her like a lemming. He couldn't explain why he obeyed—perhaps it was the plea in her voice and on her face. Perhaps he was just a glutton for punishment. Whatever the reason, he knew he couldn't refuse.

As he watched the slight sway of her trim hips, he decided that he deserved a sainthood for what he was about to do. His discomfort increased as she crawled into bed with her nightshirt riding dangerously high over her delightful backside, and he hardly noticed Ria standing at the foot of the bed, watching what her humans would do next.

The instant Christy scooted across the full-sized bed that was hardly large enough for her and patted the spot beside her, he immediately lost his ability to breathe or swallow. He'd expected to sit beside the bed, not share it.

"Please?" she asked.

Considering how she'd nearly jumped out of her skin when he'd touched her the other day, her request seemed out of character. Only able to arrive at one reason for her change of heart, he narrowed his eyes to study her with a physician's objectivity. Her pupils appeared normal, but he still had to wonder if she was acting under the effects of a drug or suffering from some sort of chemical reaction.

"What have you taken?" he asked, suspicious.

"Over-the-counter stuff," she said. "Why?"

Telling her that he thought she was high on drugs wouldn't win him any brownie points.

"No reason," he said, resigned to a very long workout after she'd dozed off.

"I know I'm asking a lot of you but, as comforting as Ria is, our conversations are one-sided. If you don't want to, though…"

He wanted to, and if she knew how badly he wanted it, she'd have locked her door before he'd come inside. However, he must have paused too long to answer because she suddenly sat up and wrapped her arms around her knees in a protective gesture.

"Forget it," she said. "I shouldn't have asked. I knew better, but I'd hoped you were comfortable enough…"

Once again, he mentally kicked himself. She'd seen his hesitation as a sign of distaste when in reality he was simply trying to keep his body under control.

"Trust me, I want to be here, beside you," he said as he lowered his weight onto the bed. "If you knew how much, though, you'd rethink your request."

Idly, he noticed Ria had disappeared but the tell-tale sound of her scratching her pallet as if making her nest told him the animal had accepted his place in Christy's bed.

Christy hadn't responded. Thinking she might be reconsidering her request, he glanced at her and saw her eyes wide with disbelief. "Really?" She hesitated, her teeth worrying her lower lip, "You're not just saying that because you feel sorry—"

"Sweetheart, right now I'm feeling a lot of things and 'sorry' isn't on that list." He held out his left arm as an open invitation and she slowly curled against him.

It was heaven. It was hell. He persevered as she wriggled to find a comfortable position with her head resting on his shoulder and her body plastered against his. He inhaled sharply, but that, too, was a mistake because her sweet scent filled his nostrils.

Hoping conversation would focus his attention on subjects other than her physical presence and how great she felt in his arms, he asked, "What should we talk about?"

"I don't care. Whatever you like."

He wanted to point out that she was the one who'd requested conversation, but didn't. He simply had to think of this as being similar to sitting beside Derek or Emma as he read or told bedtime stories.

Unfortunately, the circumstances weren't the same; they didn't compare in any way, shape, or form.

"Okay," he said, casting about for a place to start. "Do you always get physically ill when you're over-tired?"

"No. I wasn't like this B.C., before chemo. I keep hoping it'll fade, but it hasn't. Normally, I do a better job of pacing myself, but taking care of Derek and Emma is like a dream come true. I was like the Energizer Bunny. I kept going and going and going."

"Why? You have two months to fill Gail's shoes."

"Two months in which to pack a lifetime of moth-ering," she corrected. "If I never have kids of my own, I have to store up the memories when I borrow some-one else's."

"You don't know that you won't ever be a mother."

"I also don't know if I will."

"No one has guarantees," he pointed out. "I hate to break it to you, but you're like the rest of us. Fertility for anyone isn't a given. If it were, there wouldn't be specialty clinics all over the country."

"Hmm. I never thought of it like that. But you have to admit the odds of my hormones staying on a perma-nent sabbatical are much greater."

"People beat the odds every day. However, if you don't…" he shrugged "…there are a host of other ways to have a family. Your real problem is that you worry too much."

She snickered. "I do, don't I? So tell me, why don't you let anyone see your emotions and the passion in-side you?"

It took him a minute to follow her conversation shift

because she'd started rubbing her fingers against his heart and the contact was doing crazy things to his nerve endings. He placed his hand over hers to stop the gentle torment as he spoke.

"People trust me with their lives. They want to feel confident about the person who's cutting them open and messing around with their insides. Patients prefer a surgeon who is cool, calm, and collected under fire, not one whose emotions are constantly on display."

"I suppose you're right." She burrowed deeper against him and sighed like a contented kitten, which effectively sent a fresh surge of blood into his groin.

"I know I am."

Her words came slower, which made him think she was finally starting to doze. A few seconds later, she spoke again.

"Why aren't you married by now?"

"I haven't found the right woman," he answered.

"Have you been looking?"

"Not seriously," he admitted.

"Why not?"

There was something about the darkness that made it easier to share things he only admitted to himself. "I had this idea to wait until I was forty."

"Forty? Gracious. Your life will be half-over."

He grinned at her affronted tone. For a woman who wrung every minute of joy from her day, he was surprised she had such a glass-half-empty attitude. Then again, if he'd endured what she had, aware that any day could be his last, hindsight would paint those years as wasted, too. As he'd already pointed out, life didn't come with guarantees.

Unsettled by his epiphany, he went on to explain. "I suppose I wanted my future spouse to be settled in her career like I was, wanting the same things I did when it came to raising a family. I'd met a few women who'd interested me, but there always seemed to be something missing."

"No passion?"

Was that it? Possibly. Probably. Whatever the reason, he'd never felt compelled to pursue them. Christy, however, was the exception.

"What about the lady you told me about?"

"Which lady?"

"You know. The one you said you wanted to get to know."

He had to think a minute to remember…and when he did, he was grateful the room was too dark for her to see his grin. "Oh, *that* woman."

"So, Romeo, are you going to ask her out?" Her body tensed, as if bracing herself for his answer.

"Definitely."

Because it was dark, he sensed rather than saw her disappointment. "That's nice," she answered, although her words lacked sincerity.

He wanted to believe she was jealous; he certainly hoped so because it meant she had feelings for him. His for her were certainly multiplying at an exponential rate.

"What's she like? Is she pretty?"

"I think she's beautiful, but I get the impression she wouldn't agree."

"What attracted you to her? I'll bet she has a great body. Doesn't have a single scar either."

Once again, he heard her mournful tone. "She has

scars, but I'm a surgeon so they don't bother me. I think of them as badges of courage."

"Oh, what a great description. What else can you tell me about her?"

"She's sweet." As she snorted at that remark, he continued, "And kind. She'd do anything for her friends. She loves kids and is definitely a dog person."

She sighed. "She sounds perfect."

"Oh, she has her flaws, but to me no one else compares."

"Where will you take her on your first date?"

"I haven't decided yet. Where would you suggest?"

"My choice would be Grant's Point," she said, her voice growing softer. "It's a very peaceful, romantic spot. You can reach out and touch the stars while you hear the wind whisper through the trees and smell the pines. There's no place better."

If memory served him, the landmark was a famous place for couples to visit. Local folklore suggested the majority of Levitt Springs' population had been conceived on that overlook. Regardless, if the hill was Christy's choice, he'd take her there.

However, she seemed to be speaking from experience and he hated the idea of another guy taking her there, even if only for a platonic let's-see-the-local-hotspots trip.

"You've been there before?"

"Ria and I drove there one night and watched the stars come out. It was great. You and your lady friend will enjoy it."

He was uncommonly pleased to hear Ria had been her date. "I'm positive we will."

"If you want, she can take my place as your dance partner." Her reluctance was evident, as if she didn't want to extend the offer but good manners demanded it.

"I'm happy with the partner I have."

"If you change your mind…"

"I won't," he assured her.

"Thank you."

He wondered what she was thanking him for—for not changing his mind or for being happy to have her as his partner. Maybe it was simply because he wasn't rejecting her in favor of another woman.

For a long minute he only heard her gentle breathing and he thought she'd finally fallen asleep, but before he could move a muscle, she spoke again.

"I'm sorry for jumping out of my skin the other night when you touched me." She slurred her words and he wondered if she realized she was speaking.

"It's okay. I understand."

"It's not okay. I wanted you to do what you did, but—"

"But what?"

"I don't feel anything," she said flatly. "Men expect a woman to respond, but I can't because they aren't feeling *me*. If you don't mind, I need your help."

Clinically he understood her dilemma, but personally he sensed a minefield had appeared in front of him. He could only hope she wouldn't remember this conversation in the morning. "Help with what?"

"Help me so I don't jump next time," she said. "We could practice."

He swallowed hard. "Practice?"

Her nod felt as if she was nuzzling his shoulder with her nose. "That way, if I ever meet a fellow and he—"

The idea that she wanted him to condition her to handle another man's touch nearly made him growl with frustration. As uninhibited as her exhaustion had made her, if she'd asked to begin now, *he* would be the one jumping out of his skin, not to mention her bed. Although he was male enough to be grateful she had asked *him* for help.

"Sorry, but that isn't something we should do. You'll have to wing it when the time comes."

Once again, she sighed. "You're right. Your girlfriend wouldn't understand, would she?"

For lack of anything else to say, he resorted to, "No, she wouldn't."

"You know something?" She slurred her words. "I was prepared to dislike you, but you're a very nice man."

He grinned like a loon. "I'm glad you think so."

"It's too bad, though."

"Oh?" he asked.

"Because it wouldn't take much for me to fall in love."

His breath froze in his lungs. "Would that be so terrible?" he asked softly.

"Not terrible," she murmured. "It would be wonderful. Not a good idea, though."

"Why not?" he asked.

One minute of silence stretched into two, then into five, but she didn't answer. He wanted to nudge her awake so she could reply to his question, but he was reasonably certain she wouldn't remember what she'd said.

He, however, wouldn't forget.

Another five minutes went by. With great regret, Linc eased out from under her, covered her bare legs with a sheet, then tiptoed from the room.

He'd never imagined the evening would end with the two of them engaging in pillow talk. If another woman had said she could fall in love with him, he would have run for the nearest exit, but hearing Christy admit those feelings only reinforced his determination to hold on to her in any way he could.

Aware of his lingering arousal, he headed once again to the basement. At the rate he was going, he'd develop a bodybuilder's physique before Ty and Gail returned.

CHAPTER SEVEN

"I THINK Jose is well enough to go home, don't you?" Linc said to Christy after he'd reviewed Jose's chart five days later.

"He's doing remarkably well," she agreed. "He's complaining about the food again, so he's definitely feeling better." Between the filter that had been surgically inserted and medication adjustments, his most recent tests showed the clot in his leg was nearly dissolved.

Linc clicked a few final computer keys before he logged off the terminal. "I'll break the news to him while you get things rolling."

"Will do."

He scooted his chair away from the counter. "You have a sitter for tonight, right?"

"Heather's coming over at seven," she told him. Heather was the sixteen-year-old high-school girl who came early on the mornings Christy had to work and oversaw Derek and Emma getting ready for school. Sometimes Linc was still there, but more often than not he'd left early, too, so Heather's presence was a godsend.

"Although I still don't understand why we need a sitter while we practice a dance routine," she grumbled good-naturedly. "Derek and Emma won't bother us."

He raised an eyebrow. "If they don't, it would be a first," he said wryly.

"I agree they're rather clingy, but they're still adjusting."

"I understand that, but even if by some miracle they would give us an hour to ourselves, I'd rather not risk it. Constant interruptions aren't conducive to learning what we need to learn. The competition is only six weeks away."

As if she needed reminding. She'd fielded more questions about being Linc's partner, and from some of the comments she'd overheard, most were surprised to hear of his participation. Speculation and curiosity had increased ticket sales, as she'd suspected would happen. She only hoped Linc hadn't heard those same rumors because, knowing his determination to excel, he'd insist on incorporating a more advanced routine than necessary.

"Regardless, everything is set for tonight," she said.

"Great." With that, he rose and headed to Jose's room.

Less than a minute later, one of the other nurses, Rose Warren, strode into the nurses' station, looking over her shoulder with eyes wide and her jaw slack.

"I can't believe it," she remarked to Christy. "Did you see him?"

"See who?" Christy answered as she pulled the appropriate discharge forms and patient home-care instructions from various folders.

"Dr Maguire." Rose stared in the direction she'd come. "The man *smiled* at me."

Christy grinned. "How absolutely terrible."

"I wonder what's happened? I mean, he's always been courteous but he's never gone out of his way to be friendly."

"Yes, he has," she protested mildly.

"To you, maybe. To the rest of us, he's just…*polite*."

Was Rose right? Christy thought for a moment and suspected there was some truth to her observation, but if Linc spoke to her more often than anyone else, it was only because most of the staff didn't bother including him in their conversations. Granted, they'd probably tried at one point and his usual monosyllabic answers had eventually convinced them to stop trying, but she'd been undaunted. She'd always forced him into a discussion that didn't involve treatment plans or patient symptoms and over the two years she'd known him they'd progressed to single sentences. Now, though, he didn't wait to speak until spoken to, which was quite an achievement, in her opinion.

"He's a very quiet, reserved person," she countered, "but once you get to know him, he's a great guy."

"Well, whatever you're doing to put the smile on his face, keep it up."

She wasn't doing anything in particular, although she had to admit that ever since Linc had sat with her while she'd fallen asleep, she'd caught him staring at her with the most amazing twinkle in his eyes. She must have said something amusing, but she couldn't remember what it must have been. She recalled asking him why he hadn't married, as well as a host of other questions regarding the woman he wanted to get to know. In a fuzzy corner in her memory she thought she'd apologized for jumping out of her skin when he'd touched her, and had told him why, but the rest was a blur between reality and a dream.

However, when she pressed him for details, he simply smiled, which made her wonder if she'd talked in her sleep.

It was probably best if she didn't know what she'd said while her defenses had been down because she'd never be able to face him again.

"I wonder if he's seeing someone," Rose said thoughtfully.

The idea gave her a moment's pause, but unless he carved out time in his already busy days, she couldn't conceive how it might be possible. Although she wasn't trying to keep him from his lady friend, she was, however, pleased that he'd devoted his evenings to her and the children.

"Could be," she said in a noncommittal tone.

Rose's dark eyes grew speculative. "Aren't the two of you looking after his brother's family while they're out of the country?"

"Yes."

"How's that working out?"

Christy was nothing if not circumspect. "Fine. You know how it is with kids, there's hardly time to breathe."

Once again, Rose glanced in the direction he'd disappeared. "If a love interest hasn't lightened his mood, then being around you must have done the trick."

Linc *had* spent far more time at home than she'd initially expected. While he still had definite ideas about how and when things should be done, he'd also been more willing to compromise than she'd dreamed possible.

"Unless…" Rose stared at Christy thoughtfully "…you two are having a romance."

Christy fought the warmth spreading up her neck and into her face. "Don't be ridiculous. He's just getting into the spirit of the hospital fundraiser," she prevaricated. "Have you bought your tickets yet?"

"I have. Dean and I are looking forward to a night out." She grinned. "Even if we have to spend it with the same people we work with."

"Oh, the sacrifices one must make."

"Where are you going on your vacation this year?" Rose asked. "Let me guess. You're running the bulls."

Christy laughed. "Sorry, that's in July and I've missed it for this year."

"Maybe you can do one of those Ironman events."

"I'm not in shape for it."

"You're not in shape for what?" Linc's voice interrupted.

"An Ironman event," Christy explained. "You know—those endurance events that involve swimming, biking, and a marathon run."

"We were discussing ideas for her annual adventure," Rose added helpfully. "She's already missed running with the bulls, but I suppose she could always do something wild like climbing Mount Everest."

"Sorry," Christy answered cheerfully, noting how Linc had suddenly tensed. "Too cold."

Rose turned to Linc. "Do you have any suggestions for her, Doctor?"

A predatory gleam appeared in his eyes as he met Christy's gaze and the heat she saw caused all her nerve endings to tingle.

"Not off the top of my head," he said. "But I'll give the subject some thought."

Hearing that Christy was looking for a new adventure activated a fiercely protective streak he hadn't noticed before. He didn't want her choosing a dangerous pastime and he certainly didn't want her getting her thrills in the company of some other guy, no matter how innocent the circumstances might be.

As for suggesting an exciting activity, he had an idea and it had driven him to the weight bench on several occasions. It involved the two of them, alone on a deserted island and surrounded only by the sun, sand, and the sea. Unfortunately, the rest of his mental picture wasn't suitable to mention to a relative stranger and he was certain Christy wasn't ready to hear it either.

Some things a man had to keep to himself until the proper moment.

However, he'd planned an adventure of another sort for this very evening—Christy didn't know about it, yet—and he spent most of his afternoon keeping close tabs on the clock. If his office staff thought he was unusually eager to leave, they were too polite to comment.

At six forty-five, after promising Derek and Emma that he'd make up for missing their bedtime story, Linc promptly ushered Christy into his car. Tonight was their first private dance lesson and he couldn't decide if he was dreading the experience or looking forward to it. He hoped the instructor would be as good as his billing because he didn't want to disappoint Christy with his two left feet.

He passed the street leading to her apartment, then

turned in the opposite direction from his house when she spoke.

"Linc," she said carefully, "I thought we were going to practice a dance routine."

"We are."

"Then where are we going?"

He made a right turn. "I've scheduled private lessons for us at the You Can Dance studio."

Her jaw visibly dropped. "However did you manage that? They're booked for weeks in advance and that's just for a *group* lesson. I can't imagine what one would have to do for a private session."

"Yeah, well." He shrugged. "It's who you know. In my case, one of my patients is a relative and he put in a good word for me."

"I should be angry with you," she said without heat. "First you announce at dinner that your housekeeper will come by every week and now you've arranged for private dance lessons? What's next? A caterer?"

He chuckled at her obvious frustration. "Catering is definitely out, but we have a dance routine to perfect," he reminded her, "and that won't happen overnight. So, to be sure we have time to devote, it only makes sense for Paullina to take on a few of our housekeeping chores. It isn't a reflection on you, I swear."

She fell silent and he hoped she was weighing the benefits and not preparing to present new arguments. "Okay," she conceded, "but the minute we don't need her—"

Gail and Ty would be home. However, he didn't want to mention, or think about, the day when their familial interlude would end. In the meantime, whether he turned into an overnight dance sensation or not, he intended to practice his steps with Christy as often as possible until he had another legitimate reason—one she would accept—to hold her in his arms.

"She'll be gone. I promise." He parked in a space in front of the studio's entrance. "Shall we see what Mario and Carmen can do for us?"

Mario and Carmen were a Cuban husband-and-wife team in their mid-thirties and they greeted them with wide smiles.

"What would you like to dance for your competition?" Mario asked in his distinctive Spanish accent.

Linc shared a glance with Christy. "We're open to suggestions."

"Then we will show you various types of dance and you can choose which one speaks to you."

As the couple demonstrated everything from the tango to mambo, the Viennese waltz to a foxtrot, with a fluidity that Linc envied, he began to wonder what he'd gotten himself into. Christy obviously sensed his concern, because she'd threaded her arm through his in a most comforting manner.

Halfway through the session, Carmen started the music for "The Time of My Life". As he watched the pair perform the steps Patrick Swayze had made famous, he knew what he wanted. The sparkle in Christy's eyes and her tight grip on his arm suggested she agreed.

"A good choice," Mario said when Linc announced their decision. "I'm afraid some of the steps might be too much for you to learn in such a short time. The lift, for instance."

"Then modify it for us," Linc said, "because that, or something similar, is what we want."

Mario grinned. "Ah, I like to see determination. That is good because you must work hard. We will meet only twice a week, but you will practice every day."

Linc had anticipated the order and was looking forward to it. "We will."

The lessons began. Ten minutes into the session, Mario pulled him aside.

"You are trying too hard, *amigo*. You wish to impress the lady, no?"

Frustrated by his missteps that made it difficult for Christy to follow, Linc rubbed his face with both hands. "Am I that obvious?"

"Only to me," Mario assured him. "Don't think about what you're feet are doing. This is a song of love between you and your partner and has nothing to do with people out there." He swept out his arm toward an imaginary audience. "As you express your feelings, you will relax and move with the confidence of a man who has a prize that many others want but cannot have."

He recognized the truth in his instructor's comments, but he hadn't earned the prize either.

Mario must have seen something on Linc's face because he smiled. "Ah, so that's how it is. You are not certain you've won."

Linc shrugged sheepishly. "No."

"But you are here and they are not, so that gives you an advantage, does it not?" He paused. "She is a beautiful woman."

Linc didn't hesitate. "She is."

Mario winked. "And do you not think so many men will be envious of you?"

He grinned. "Probably."

"Then be confident that for this moment she is yours and only yours. When you move securely in that knowledge, your feet will go where they need to and she will follow."

Yours and only yours.

He liked the sound of that. Furthermore, he suddenly realized that he wanted far more than only a moment. He didn't know how or when it had happened, but he wanted weeks, months, and *years* with her. He also wanted the clock to begin now, not later after her check-up.

"Shall we try again?" Mario asked.

He drew a bracing breath. "Okay. Let's do this."

The instructor clapped his hands. "Good. Then we begin."

By the end of the session Linc was exhausted and he was certain Christy's head was spinning from all the turns they'd practiced, but as soon as he'd put Mario's advice into play, he'd felt himself become more sure-footed.

Mario pulled him aside as they were leaving. "Well done. I can see your confidence growing, no? Perhaps when you return you will be the teacher and I will be the student?"

Linc laughed. "I appreciate the thought, but that would take a miracle."

Mario smiled, his teeth white in his tanned face. "Stranger things have happened, no? Now, go home and practice. We will see your progress at the next session."

* * *

"Linc," Christy cried three nights later as she collapsed on the sofa after another set of spins. "No more. Please."

Linc grinned. "You aren't wimping out on me now, are you? What happened to the woman who's looking for an adventure?"

"She's tired and if she turns one more time, she's going to do something horrible, like deposit her dinner on your feet." She rubbed her midsection in an effort to calm her stomach.

He sank onto the cushions beside her. "Poor baby. I have been working you hard, haven't I?"

"To put it mildly. You haven't forgotten this is just a friendly competition, have you?"

"No, but anything worth doing..."

"Is worth doing well." She finished his saying because if she'd heard it once, she'd heard it a hundred times. "Now I understand how you became such a brilliant surgeon. You give new meaning to the word 'single-minded.'"

"Thanks. I think."

"You're welcome. The good news is that Mario and Carmen should be pleased when we see them tomorrow night."

"They certainly should be," he said, sounding pleased with himself. "We're positively awesome."

She had to admit, they were. Of course, Mario and Carmen had only assigned them a few steps to perfect, but they had learned those well. While she'd always had a good sense of rhythm, Linc had completely surprised her. He moved so naturally to the music, she couldn't believe she'd ever thought him stilted and straitlaced.

"You never did say why Mario pulled you aside," she said, curious.

"He gave me a pep talk. He said I was trying too hard."

"You were." She'd seen him struggling and she'd found his determination endearing. She'd also been tempted to suggest they try something less complicated, but Carmen had stopped her.

"Men are simple creatures," she'd said. *"They give gifts to the ones they care about. He wants to do this for you, so you must not deny him the chance."*

Now, three days later, the notion that he might care about her made her smile with delight. On the other hand, when she wasn't reveling in those female feelings, she was having a panic attack. She didn't want to fall in love with him, even though she feared she'd already marched halfway down that path.

Besides, Carmen must have misread Linc's signals because someone else had already captured his eye. If Linc seemed determined to master this particular dance, proving that he could was his only motivation.

She pinched her thumb and forefinger together. "By then, I was this close to suggesting we stick to a simple waltz."

"Won't happen," he said firmly. "I'd already made up my mind."

Once he'd reached a decision, she knew nothing short of an act of God would convince him to change his mind. "What exactly did Mario say to get you to relax?"

"That I'd be the envy of every man watching, so I might as well enjoy myself. Those weren't his exact words, but they're close."

Certainly the women in the audience would feel the same about her, she thought. It was inevitable as she would have the most handsome man in the hospital at her side.

"By the end of the evening, you'll be on every single woman's radar," she said lightly.

"Won't matter," he said firmly. "There's only one on mine."

She ignored the instant pain she felt. "When *are* you going to ask out this paragon of virtue?"

"Soon."

"How soon?"

"You seem awfully concerned about my dating habits."

"Only because I don't want to stand in the way of true love," she quipped. "Derek and Emma have been invited to a sleepover on Friday night. Why don't you taking her out then? With the kids gone, I wouldn't slap a curfew on you."

He laughed. "Good idea. I could arrange a date." He paused. "What will you do?"

She didn't want to think about the long hours she'd face in her apartment, but whether he brought his date here or to his own house, she definitely wouldn't stick around to meet her.

"Girl things," she answered promptly, thinking she was overdue for a facial and a long bubble bath complete with candles, soft music, and a romance novel.

"I see. Then I'll plan my evening."

"Yes, do." She pasted a smile on her face, painfully aware of unreasonable jealousy gripping her soul.

* * *

Christy touched the homemade beer-and-cucumber mask she'd applied to her face and decided it was time to wash off the residue. As Friday night activities went, indulging in a facial wasn't high on the excitement meter, but her pores said it was long overdue. Although her great-grandmother's recipe probably didn't have any real scientific basis for giving a peaches-and-cream complexion, knowing she was one of a long line of women in her family to engage in the ritual was comforting.

Tonight, more than ever, she needed to feel as if she weren't alone.

Puréeing the cucumbers and blending in the other ingredients had also given her something to concentrate on other than Linc's date.

Ever since she'd dropped off the children at their friends' house—fortunately Derek and Emma's buddies were a brother and sister—her thoughts had drifted in a most fruitless direction. It was too easy to create a mental minute-by-minute scenario of Linc's evening.

He *should* spend time with the woman who'd caught his eye, she told herself fiercely. She *should* be happy because he'd finally realized his work was a cold-hearted mistress and was seeking one of flesh and blood. If she'd convinced him to stop postponing his plans for his personal life, then she should pride herself for nudging him along.

Vowing to find a constructive activity, she'd tried to read two different books, but neither held her interest.

She'd lounged on her postage-stamp-sized balcony to enjoy the fall weather and the last few rays of direct sunlight in the quietness, but even nature conspired against her. Birds called to their mates, crickets answered each other's chirps, and the distant sound of children laughing only emphasized her loneliness.

She'd also considered whipping up a batch of cookies, but couldn't because her cupboards were literally bare. Although running into Linc and his date at the grocery store was highly unlikely, she didn't want to risk it.

For a woman who didn't want romance, who was positive she hadn't found a man strong enough to cope with her uncertain future, she was acting completely ridiculously.

She shook off her gloom with great force of will and planned the rest of the evening. As soon as she finished her beauty treatment and slipped on her running shoes, she would take Ria for a romp around the park. By the time they came home, she'd be too tired to imagine what Linc might or might not be doing.

Not knowing was part of her problem, she decided with some irritation. She'd pressed him for details about his prospective girlfriend and his itinerary, aware that asking was similar to probing a sore tooth, but he'd been remarkably uncommunicative.

"I'll leave it up to her," had been his reply, so she'd finally held her questions. Yet she hadn't stopped wondering...

She hoped his mystery woman deserved him.

The doorbell—and Ria's answering barks—interrupted her thoughts. She was inclined to ignore her unexpected visitor, but Ria bounded into the bathroom and began barking in her familiar follow-me style.

"Okay, okay," she grumbled as she patted her face

dry, hoping she'd removed all traces of crustiness and didn't smell as if she'd fallen into a distillery vat.

Ria nudged her toward the stairs and stood beside Christy as she unlocked the door.

The man on the stoop caught her by surprise. "Linc!" she exclaimed. "What are you doing here?"

"May I come in?"

"Certainly." She stepped aside, both happy and puzzled that he'd dropped by. "Where's your date? Or should I ask *when* is your date?"

His grin was broad as his gaze traveled down her entire body. A second later, he flicked at a dried flake on her T-shirt. "I came to pick her up, but I'd say she isn't ready."

Her heart pounded and she couldn't breathe. "You came for *me*? But…"

"You're my date." His mouth curled with amusement. "Now, run along and get dressed. I'll occupy Ria's attention so she won't hide your shoes."

Shock, as well as suspicion that she'd somehow misunderstood, had rooted her feet to the floor. "You mean…*I'm* your mystery woman?"

He nodded.

"*I'm* the woman you want to get to know?"

"Yes."

Although her spirits wanted to soar into the stratosphere, she held a tight rein on them. "I don't understand. I thought you cared about…"

"Someone else?" he supplied helpfully.

She hesitated. "Well, yes."

"You were wrong. There isn't anyone else. *You're*

the one I care about—the one I want to spend my evening with."

She wanted to cry tears of joy as well as frustration. "You shouldn't want that—"

"Of course I should," he interrupted. "You're a kind, generous, thoughtful woman and every bachelor I know would trade places with me in an instant."

"It's a nice thought, but—"

"Whatever has happened in the past or will happen in the future doesn't matter. The current moment is what we have, so we're going to focus on it. The real question is, have you eaten yet or…" he leaned closer to sniff "…have you been drinking your dinner?"

Her face warmed. "I suspect the ingredients in my great-grandmother's facial recipe were chosen for their, shall we say, *medicinal* qualities." She grinned. "According to Grandma Nell, her mother faithfully applied her facial every Saturday night. Her private time probably included sampling the ingredients while she pampered her skin."

He chuckled. "I don't blame her. Life was hard a hundred years ago and she probably deserved a beer or two at the end of her week."

She smiled. "It makes for an interesting story, doesn't it?" Then, because she didn't want to think about not having descendants who could pass on the tale, she changed the subject. "As for dinner, I haven't eaten."

"Good, because I'm starved. Now, put on your glad rags and let's go."

She should protest, and she was inclined to do so, but she didn't. Perhaps she held back because he acted more like a friend than a guy who was seriously intent on a commitment. Maybe it was only because she was relieved she didn't have to share him with anyone else. She was certainly flattered he'd asked *her* when he could have chosen from a host of eligible women.

It was also far too easy to remind herself she was mere weeks away from her five-year check-up and the end of her self-imposed moratorium on romantic relationships. She could go out, keep the mood light, and just enjoy being in the company of a handsome fellow.

The more she considered, the more enticing an evening of Linc's undivided attention sounded.

"Casual, I assume?" she asked, eyeing his jeans and noticing how fantastic he looked in denim and a cotton shirt.

"Whatever's comfortable," he agreed. "Keep in mind it'll be cool after dark."

She changed in record speed, although she was so excited it took her three tries to successfully brush on her mascara and apply lip gloss.

"I'm ready," she said breathlessly when she emerged fifteen minutes later, wearing her favorite low-cut jeans, a sleeveless white cotton shell and her favorite pearl earrings.

He held out his arm. "Then shall we?"

Before she could pat Ria one final time, he snapped his fingers. "Let's go, Ria."

The dog raced to the door while Christy stared at him. "We're taking her with us?"

"Not to dinner. We'll drop her off at my place on the way. She can chase rabbits and hunt squirrels while we're gone."

"She could stay here. She's used to being alone."

"She could," he agreed, "but wouldn't you rather let her run in a huge yard instead of relegating her to a tiny apartment? Do you really want to deprive her of one of our rare days of nice weather?"

She couldn't refute his argument, although he obviously intended to end up at his place at some point. Was he giving her the opportunity to spend the night by ensuring she couldn't use Ria as an excuse to refuse?

He must have read her mind because he pulled her close. "Before you get all righteous and accuse me of having an ulterior motive, I want you to remember this. However long our night lasts, whether it ends at ten o'clock or in the wee hours, nothing will happen that both of us aren't ready for."

She knew he wouldn't push her beyond her comfort zone—he wasn't the sort who notched his bedposts— but nevertheless she had to ask. "You won't be disappointed if we have an early night?"

His smile was tender as he cupped her face. "I'm a guy. Of course I'd be disappointed, but tonight isn't about me. Tonight is for you."

He was being so sweet, she wanted to cry. More than that, though, she wanted him to kiss her. He obviously wanted it too because he bent his head and she felt his breath brush against the bridge of her nose. Unfortunately, in that split second before his lips met hers, Ria barked impatiently.

He grinned and instead of the lingering kiss he'd been so obviously prepared to give, he delivered a swift peck on her cheek. "We're being paged, so hold that thought."

She did.

CHAPTER EIGHT

"Thanks for letting me share your dinner," Christy said as ninety minutes later they left Rosa's Italian Eatery, the mom-and-pop restaurant he favored for its authentic cuisine and intimate dining atmosphere.

"You're welcome." He'd never divided his dinner with a date before, but Christy had eyed his chicken and eggplant parmesan with such curiosity that he'd given her a sample. In the interest of fairness, she'd shared a taste of her vegetable lasagna and before he knew it, they'd split both meals between them.

"How long have you known Rosa and her husband?" she asked.

He thought for a minute. "Several years. I first met them when their sixteen-year-old son, Frank Junior, had been in a car accident. After I put him back together, Rosa insisted on showing her gratitude by catering a meal for my office staff. The food was fabulous and now, if I want Italian food, her place is at the top of my list."

She stopped in her tracks and he felt her gaze. "You really amaze me," she said.

He grinned, pleased she was seeing him as a good

guy and not of the same ilk as the infamous Jon. "Why? Because I prefer eating at great places?"

"No, because your patients aren't just patients. The ones I've met have always spoken highly of you, and I'd assumed it was because of your surgical skills and the stories of how, no matter how busy you are, you find time to see someone who needs you."

"I try," he admitted, "but I have a few favorites, as I'm sure you do, too."

"Yes, but, unlike you, I don't usually see them again."

They'd reached the car and because Linc had been keeping tabs on the weather, he noticed a bank of clouds building in the west.

"Looks like the weatherman might be right about the rain," she commented.

"That's what I was afraid of."

"Oh? You don't want the moisture? For shame, Dr Maguire. Don't let the farmers hear you utter such blasphemy," she teased.

"I don't want it *tonight*," he corrected. "I need nice weather for what I had planned."

"Then you *did* organize your evening," she accused good-naturedly. "You told me you were allowing your date to plan your activities."

He grinned. "I did, more or less. She told me what she'd like to do and I took her suggestions to heart."

"I didn't give you any suggestions."

"If I recall, you mentioned Grant's Point."

Her face lit up like the mall's Christmas tree. "Is that where we're going? I can't believe you remembered."

"You'd be amazed at what I remember," he said lightly. In fact, he remembered a lot more than she thought he did. "The only problem is…" he pointed to the sky "...we won't have much time out there before we get wet."

"Bummer."

"Yeah, but if you're okay with waiting, we'll save that excursion for next time." It was a subtle mention of his intention to take her out again, and he waited for her reply.

"I'd like that."

Hiding his satisfaction over her response, he helped her into the car, then walked around to the driver's side.

So far, everything was turning out better than he'd hoped. He'd worried how Christy would react when he arrived on her doorstep unannounced and had half expected her to refuse to go at all. She'd seemed determined to shun a personal relationship until she'd reached the magical date she'd set, which was why he'd used the just-friends approach.

However, his ultimate goal was to show her that friendship would never be enough. For himself, he already wanted more because he didn't want to return to his previous life when everything he did revolved around his work. He wanted his days—his future—revolving around her because he couldn't imagine facing a day without her.

A short time later, Linc escorted Christy into his house and once again she was filled with a sense of belonging, as if she "fit" in this house. If she'd had the finances, not to mention the time and strength, to maintain a place like his, she'd buy it. Her feelings had nothing to do with the owner.

Oh, who was she kidding? She enjoyed being around Linc whether they were at the hospital, Gail and Ty's house, or his place. If the truth were told, she enjoyed being with him far more than she should at this point in her life.

She paused in front of the patio door. "I'll get Ria so we can go."

"How about a glass of wine first?"

She hesitated. Returning to her empty house wasn't nearly as attractive as staying here with Linc, but, given how easily she was falling for him, it wasn't wise to stay.

"I bought this bottle specifically for our star-gazing," he coaxed. "We may not be able to see too many stars from my patio, but we can't let it go to waste."

Rather than argue that a sealed bottle of wine would keep indefinitely, she gave in because deep down she wanted to stay and pretend she possessed a future as secure as any other twenty-eight-year-old woman's. "One glass, on the patio, please."

If she'd refused, she was certain he would have been chivalrous and obliged, but his broad smile suggested her answer had pleased him. He grabbed two wine glasses and the bottle he'd brought in from the car then accompanied her outdoors.

As soon as she stepped outside and called for Ria, the Lab raced toward them, only to stop abruptly in front of Linc and nudge his leg in an apparent attempt to receive his personal attention, too.

He laughed as he tucked the wine bottle under one arm, then obliged. He'd obviously found the right spot because the dog extended her neck as if to encourage him to shower his attention over a much larger area.

"Don't I get a hello?" she asked her pet lightly, disappointed Ria had transferred her allegiance to Linc so quickly.

Ria wagged her tail and continued to lean into Linc's touch.

"Apparently not," he said. "You know I can find the right spots, don't you, girl?"

"Yes, well, you're going to spoil her with those magic fingers of yours." Remembering his touch on several occasions, she wished she was on the receiving end instead of her dog. "Ria," she asked, "are you almost ready to go home?"

A rabbit darted across the yard and slipped through a small opening in the wooden fence. Ria gave a sharp woof before bounding to the same corner to nose the ground where her prey had escaped.

"I think her answer was 'No'," Linc said as he handed her an empty glass, then popped the cork on the bottle.

"You do realize she'll be willing to spend hours in your yard?"

He grinned. "She's a dog. Of course she will."

"Yes, but we shouldn't wear out our welcome."

"You won't," he assured her. "If the weather hadn't interfered with my original plan, she'd be spending hours doing what she's doing now."

"Yes, but—"

"Do you have something special to do when you get home?"

"No," she said slowly. "But—"

"But nothing," he said as he poured both glasses half-full. "We may have postponed our Grant's Point trip, but the evening is still ours. *And*..." he emphasized the word "...I have a Plan B."

"Which is?" She sipped her wine.

"We haven't practiced our dance steps today," he reminded her.

"No, we haven't, but one day won't matter."

He lifted an eyebrow. "Speak for yourself, my dear."

She smiled at his grumble. "Mario was quite impressed with you at our last lesson."

"And I want him to stay that way. Or are you trying to get me in trouble with the teacher?"

She laughed. "I can't believe you ever got in trouble at school."

"Contrary to what you might think, I had my moments of infamy. Unfortunately, my stories can't leave this property. They would ruin the 'perfect son' standard I projected to Ty and my sister." He grinned.

She laughed. "I promise. What did you do?"

"Nothing malicious. Mostly stuff like hiding red pens on test days, rearranging the books on the teacher's desk, hiding the dry-erase markers in another classroom so she couldn't post assignments on the board."

"Did your ploys work?"

"Once," he admitted, "but my teachers were a wily bunch. They kept extra red pens and markers in their file cabinets. If one disappeared, they simply pulled another one from their stash or borrowed from another instructor." He smiled. "But my tactics gave us a few minutes' reprieve and to an eight-year-old a few minutes' delay was a coup."

"Did you go to school in Levitt Springs?"

He shook his head. "We grew up about three hours from here. Fortunately, my hometown had a college, so I earned my undergrad degree while Ty and my sister finished high school. After that, we went our separate ways. I began med school, Ty and Joanie entered different colleges and Gran had died by then, so splitting up was inevitable. We kept in touch with weekly phone calls, though."

"How did you and Ty both land in Levitt Springs?"

"Ty had gotten a job with an architecture firm here after he finished his education. Eventually, after I'd completed my surgery residency, I looked for a place to go. I'd narrowed my job offers down to two—one in St. Louis and one here."

"And you chose Levitt Springs."

"My niece and nephew swayed my decision," he admitted. "They don't have grandparents, so it seemed important to give them a doting uncle. I would have moved to be near my sister, too, but she's a buyer for a department-store chain and spends most of her life on the road."

"A win-win situation for everyone," she remarked.

"It is," he agreed. "Being surrounded by family after all those years of only getting together for Memorial Day or Christmas is wonderful. Of course, I'm busy enough that I don't see Ty and his kids as often as I'd like, but we manage to get together at least once a week, even if only for an hour or so."

"Family means a great deal to you," she guessed.

"It does. Although I've watched the kids before on weekends, filling in for Ty makes me eager to have a Derek and Emma of my own."

In another lifetime she would have been thrilled to hear him confirm that his philosophy mirrored hers.

However, her future was too uncertain to rejoice in those similarities.

She drained her glass because she couldn't think of a suitable reply.

"More wine?" he asked.

"No, thanks. Our steps are difficult enough without having impaired coordination."

He rose to click a button on his iPod player. The music began and he smiled at her. "Shall we start?"

Regardless of what her future held, her heart skipped with excitement as she set her glass on the end table and walked into his outstretched arms. "Of course."

For the next thirty minutes she turned and twirled, conscious of his strength as he caught her. Occasionally he stepped on her toes or she stepped on his but as time went on, those incidents occurred less and less.

Finally, they'd managed to make it through the first half of their routine without a single misstep.

"Are we getting good or was that a fluke?" she teased him.

"I vote we try once more," he told her.

So he started the music once again.

To Christy's delight, they repeated their steps perfectly, ending with a final spin that required him to catch her.

For a long minute he simply held her against him, making her aware of how his labored breathing matched hers.

The patter-patter of rain on the roof punctuated the silence and the fresh, clean scent it brought mingled with Linc's masculine fragrance. He exuded warmth, and while that was pleasant, as the air suddenly carried a coolness she hadn't noticed before, she was more impressed by his strength and rock-solidness.

In that instant Linc no longer seemed like a friendly dance partner. He was an attractive, virile man in the prime of his life.

She should push herself away, but she couldn't. The intensity in his gaze was too mesmerizing and savoring this moment too important for her to move.

"That was awesome," he murmured.

"Oh, yes." She didn't know if her breathlessness was due to physical exertion or from being in his arms. She was playing with fire, but it had seemed like for ever since she'd felt as carefree and as attractive as she did at this moment.

It was also a bittersweet moment. She hated to be realistic with romance simmering in the air but she had to control her attraction because these feelings could never grow. Not yet, anyway, and, depending on her doctor's findings, maybe never.

"I suppose we should stop practicing while we're ahead," she said lightly. "End the session on a high note, so to speak."

"Probably."

Yet for the next sixty seconds he didn't release her and she didn't push the issue. The moment would end soon enough and she wanted to enjoy it for as long as it lasted.

"It's raining," she commented inanely, wishing she could go back to her carefree youth when the C word only applied to other people. "We should call Ria and go inside."

"I'd rather kiss you," he said.

Her gaze landed on his mouth and although her small voice cautioned her about the wisdom of it, she raised her chin to meet his lips in a kiss so fierce her toes curled and her inner core ached.

"We shouldn't do this," she murmured when he gentled his mouth and inched his way to the sensitive area behind her ear.

"Of course we should."

Her mind barely registered his words, she was too consumed with the sensation of being pressed against his entire length to make sense of them.

Suddenly he pulled away just enough to meet her gaze. The hunger in his expression warmed her down her to her toes. "Have you thought about what we'll do after Gail and Ty return?"

"The Fall Festival is the same day," she pointed out. "The next afternoon I leave for Seattle so I can be bright-eyed and bushy-tailed for my doctor's appointment on that Monday. With a hectic schedule like that, I haven't thought past that weekend."

"We should," he said.

Instinctively, she sensed he was referring to a topic she'd been purposely avoiding. "I imagine we'll go back to the way things were before," she said lightly. "We'll see each other a few times a week at the hospital."

"I don't think so. Too much has changed."

He had a point. Between their shared parenting responsibilities and the dance competition, whenever she saw him on her unit, she treated him differently. Oh, she still gave him the respect he deserved, but now she joked and teased and asked personal questions that she'd never had the courage to ask before. He'd also loosened up enough to join in staff conversations without prompting. Rose hadn't been the only person who'd noticed the change.

"You're right. Things are different. In fact, *you're* so different that several single women have mentioned they'd love to go out with you. If you like, I can give you their names."

She struggled to make the offer because she felt rather possessive about him, but she had no right to that particular feeling. Yes, she'd dragged him out of his shell and convinced him to stop putting his professional career ahead of his personal life, but those lessons would simply prepare him for the woman of his dreams. When he found her and eventually had his own Derek and Emma, and maybe even a Nick or a Beth, she could take pride in the role she'd played.

"You're pulling my leg, right?"

"Not at all. Theresa in Respiratory Therapy, Monica in the Recovery Room, and—"

His hold around her waist tightened. "Their names don't matter because every one of them will be disappointed. Maybe you didn't hear me when I came by your house. I want to spend my time with you—no one else."

It was a wonderful thought and her heart did a happy dance, but the implications scared her. He was asking too much, too soon. "That's sweet of you to say, but—"

"I know you're worried about your upcoming appointment but, whatever happens, I'm not going anywhere. I'll be with you every step of the way."

Christy stiffened, and Linc sensed her mental withdrawal. Any second she'd bolt, and he imperceptibly tightened his hold. She felt too good right where she was and he wanted to show her both literally and figuratively that he wouldn't let her go without a fight.

There would be no turning back.

He could have said nothing and let the days roll by, but she needed to know that *this* time she wouldn't face her future with only Ria as her companion. His intentions were to prove he had more staying power and more strength of character than the other jerks who had walked into—and out of—her life.

Moisture glistened in her eyes and she blinked rapidly. "I know you mean well, but please don't make any promises."

"I already have."

"I won't hold you to them," she warned.

"Are you giving me an escape clause?"

"Someone has to."

"Do you really think I'm the sort of guy who runs at the first sign of trouble?"

Her shoulders slumped before she shook her head. "No, but it's too risky to say what you might do when or if the situation changes."

He disagreed, but she wouldn't change her opinion in the space of this conversation. "Okay." He spoke evenly. "We'll continue our discussion after your appointment, but I happen to believe we have a future. Don't let fear hold you hostage."

For a long minute she didn't move, until finally she nodded ever so slightly. "I'll try."

Pleased by his small victory, he stepped forward and lightly brushed her cheekbone with his lips. "That's all I ask."

* * *

At times over the next three weeks Christy wondered if she'd imagined that particular conversation because Linc never referred to it again. However, every now and then she'd catch him studying her, sometimes with curiosity and sometimes with a speculative gleam, but no matter what she saw in his eyes, he always smiled his lazy grin that turned her insides to mush. She tried to do as he'd asked—to think about a life after she received her five-year medical report—and it was easy when he was nearby. In the wee hours of the night, however, when darkness had closed in and she had only Ria to hold her fears at bay, it wasn't. Fortunately, those instances didn't happen often. She was simply too busy trying to stay on top of their schedule and keep the household running smoothly to reflect past the upcoming weeks.

Time, however, was marching on and the kitchen calendar reflected it. Emma had circled the date of her parents' return with a red magic marker and, thanks to the huge black Xs she marked in the squares at the end of each day, Christy could count the remaining white spaces at a glance.

There were fourteen of them.

Her time of sharing the house with Linc and playing a mother's role was drawing to a close, so she savored every moment, including those less than idyllic times…

"Christy." Derek raced into the kitchen while she was finishing the dinner dishes. "Emma keeps bugging me. She won't stay out of my room."

"He took my doll's car," Emma wailed, "and I know he's hiding it under his bed. I want it back."

"I didn't take it. It's probably buried under all your doll junk." His disgust was obvious.

"My stuff is *not* junk." Emma's lower lip quivered.

"Is, too."

"Is not."

"Guys," Christy warned. "Both of you, calm down."

"He called my stuff *junk*." Emma was clearly affronted. "I don't make fun of his toys." She poked a finger in her brother's chest. "Take that back."

"Will not. And quit touching me."

He shoved his sister and Emma began weeping. "You're being mean. I want my mommy! She'd make you be nice to me!"

Christy abandoned her task to hold the little girl as she sobbed on her shoulder. "Oh, sweetie, your mom will be home in two weeks. That's only fourteen days. Don't forget about tonight being our phone call night. You don't want your mom and dad to see you with red eyes and a runny nose, do you?"

Emma sniffled.

"You're just being a baby," Derek complained in a typical big-brother voice.

"Am not!"

"Stop, you two," Christy scolded. "We'll straighten this out in a few minutes."

Linc had been outside watering the shrubs and walked in as Christy delivered her warning.

"What's going on?" he asked.

Emma pointed a finger at her brother. "He started it."

"Did not."

"Quiet. Both of you," Linc ordered. "Will someone tell me what's going on?"

"Emma can't find her doll's car and she thinks Derek took it," Christy explained.

"I didn't," Derek insisted.

"Did, too!"

Linc held up his hands. "There's only one way to solve this. We'll look for the car right now."

"It's in Derek's room," Emma informed them.

"Is not."

Christy exchanged a glance at Linc over their heads and shrugged. "They've been like this all afternoon."

"Off you go to your rooms," he commanded as he pointed. "I'll be there in a minute."

As each child stormed to their private corners, Linc paused. "All this drama is over a lost car?"

"That convertible is very important to Em," Christy said with a smile. "The main problem is they both miss their parents. She reacts with tears and Derek hides his feelings behind aggression."

"I didn't realize. Everything was going so smoothly I'd hoped we'd passed that stage."

"We did, but two months can seem like for ever to a child. A time out for both is in order, I think." A distant door slammed and Christy smiled. "Do you want to deal with that or should I?"

"I will," he said.

He returned less than ten minutes later. "The mystery of the missing car is solved."

"Where was it?"

"Under Emma's bed. She'd decided the space was the perfect place for a 'garage' and forgot. She apologized to Derek, so life is good."

"Will you be able to handle them by yourself tomorrow?"

"Considering they'll be in school most of the day, I'd say so," he said wryly, "but I've been thinking. I could go with you."

His offer surprised her because when she'd mentioned her upcoming trip a week ago, he'd simply nodded. "I'm flying to Seattle for the usual battery of tests, not open-heart surgery. Don't you have patients to see?"

"None that couldn't wait until next week," he said. "I've been rearranging my schedule, just in case."

"You have?" She could hardly believe he'd go to the trouble. "Whatever for? You'd go crazy sitting in waiting rooms all day."

He grinned. "Probably, but I'd do it. For moral support."

She wanted to cry at his thoughtfulness. "Thanks, but my mom has planned to spend the day with me. She's used to the routine."

"Good, because I don't want you to be alone," he stated firmly.

It seemed strange to have someone other than her own family fuss over her. His concern gave her a warm, fuzzy feeling that was far better than hot cocoa and a warm blanket on a cold winter night.

"I won't be," she assured him. "This way is best for the kids, too. After tonight's outburst, they need you, not a sitter."

"Maybe, but I still don't understand why you want to travel so far for your tests, only to turn around in another two weeks to visit your doctor. We run the same procedures here, you know."

His voice and expression revealed his frustration quite clearly and she tried to explain her reasons. "This seems silly, but all my records are there and I'd like to have the same people looking at my scans. As crazy as it sounds, they've given me good reports and I don't want to jinx myself."

He fell silent for a few seconds before he finally nodded. "If that's what you need for peace of mind, then that's what you should do."

She was half-surprised he didn't try to convince her otherwise. "You aren't going to tell me I'm being illogical and superstitious?"

"I could," he admitted, "but having faith in one's medical team is crucial to a patient's recovery. If you aren't ready for someone else to run your tests, you shouldn't. Otherwise, whatever the outcome, you'll always question the results."

"Thanks for understanding."

"What I don't like is how you're going to be exhausted when you return."

"It's sweet of you to worry, but I'll be fine."

He frowned. "I don't see how you will be. You're taking the red-eye flight in the morning, spending the entire day being poked, prodded and scanned, then jetting back late at night. At least stay a little longer and fly home Saturday."

"I scheduled my flights months ago. I can't change them now without huge penalties."

"Screw the penalties. I'll pay the difference."

"I can't have you do that. Honestly, I'll be fine." She grinned. "Keep the light on for me, okay?"

"I'll do better than that. I'll be waiting up."

CHAPTER NINE

CHRISTY kissed her mother on the cheek as soon as she met her at the baggage claim the next morning. "Hi, Mom. It's great to see you."

"You, too, hon," her mother said. At a very young-looking fifty-four, Serena Michaels was dressed fashionably smart in spite of the early hour and their final destination. Although Christy had told her repeatedly that no one expected her to look as if she was heading for a photo shoot instead of a day at the hospital, her mother had disagreed.

"If you look great, you'll feel great, too," had been her mantra, so Christy had taken a few special pains herself. Instead of wearing blue jeans and a T-shirt, she'd worn a comfortable pair of dress slacks, one of her favorite designer shirts, and a matching sweater.

"Did you have a good flight?"

"No problems," she answered cheerfully, preparing for the inevitable question that would come next.

"How are you feeling?"

She'd trained herself over the years to not worry about cancer invading again if she didn't feel well, but her mother hadn't learned the same lesson. She still needed the reassurance that as long as her daughter felt healthy, then it must be so.

"Never better," Christy answered. "I really appreciate you taking the time away from the restaurant today."

"Of course I'd take the day off," Serena assured her as she ushered her to the parking garage. "We may as well use the time in between your tests to catch up. I want to hear all about your side job as a live-in nanny and this dance competition you've told me about."

While Christy filled in the details, she soaked up the ambience of the city. She'd grown up here, and while it was home, it also wasn't. Oddly enough, she felt more rooted in Levitt Springs and she wondered if Linc had made the difference.

Throughout the day Christy shared story after story between her sessions of blood draws, PET and bone-density scans, and every other test her physician had ordered. She didn't realize Linc had figured prominently in every tale until her mother commented.

"You've talked about this Linc a lot lately. Is he someone new?"

"I've been acquainted with him since I moved to town, but I didn't really *know* him until we began taking care of his brother's children."

"He sounds like a special fellow," Serena remarked.

"He is. He even offered to rearrange his patient schedule to come with me today."

A knowing smile appeared on her mother's face. "He's that taken with you, is he?"

"He seems to be, but…" she hesitated "…I'm not sure it's wise."

"Why not? You're healthy, attractive, and—" Serena stopped short. "You've told him about your history, haven't you?"

"Yes, Mother."

"The news didn't scare him away?"

"It should have," she said honestly, still amazed by his tenacity, "but it hasn't so far."

Serena's eyes glowed with happiness and she leaned over to hug her. "You're going to keep him, aren't you?"

"A relationship isn't that simple for me, Mom. There are long-term consequences to consider."

"He's a physician, Christy. Of course he knows the consequences."

"I'm just trying to protect him from making a mistake he'll regret, especially if my ovaries never wake up and he can't have the son or daughter he wants."

"I may not be in the medical profession, but even I know there are plenty of ways around that particular problem. Do you love him?"

Christy pondered for a moment. Her feelings for Linc were much stronger and deeper than those she'd felt toward Jon, but she wasn't ready to admit she was in love.

"I care about him," she said simply. "More than I'd expected I would. Probably even more than I should, which is why I can't be certain he really knows what he's getting into. Yes, he has all the medical knowledge, but I'm not sure his heart knows what he's getting into."

"You want to protect him."

Linc had called her tactic "giving him an escape clause". However anyone described it, her mother had pegged her correctly.

"Yes."

"You can be right about so many things, but in this

you're wrong. Call your excuse for what it is, daughter. You're not trying to protect him as much as you're trying to protect yourself."

Christy mentally argued against that notion throughout the day, but by the time she was back on the plane and flying home, she finally conceded her mother's assessment might have merit.

She'd always thought she was being altruistic by spelling everything out early in her relationships. Full disclosure early on was in everyone's best interests because if a fellow couldn't deal with her situation, she'd rather learn it early in a relationship. Maybe she *was* only protecting herself, but her method worked.

With Linc, however, it hadn't. He wasn't reacting true to form.

I'll be with you every step of the way, he'd told her. She wanted to believe him, but she couldn't take that leap of faith. He was the one man who, if he ever changed his mind and walked away, would devastate her to the point where she'd never recover.

As the evening dragged on and bad weather delayed her flight, one thought kept her going—she was heading home.

As the hours ticked by, Linc found it more and more difficult to wait patiently for Christy's return. Every light in the main part of the house blazed because he wanted her to see the beacon as soon as she turned onto their street.

He'd expected her at nine and wished he could have met her at the airport, but he couldn't leave Derek and Emma unattended. He'd tried phoning her, but his call had gone straight to her voice mail. A check on her flight status via the internet told him she'd been delayed due to bad weather. He might have wished the airline had cancelled the flight so she wouldn't endure such a long travel day, but he wanted her safe at home and he wouldn't rest until she was.

Finally, he heard the distinctive sound of the garage door mechanism and his shoulders slumped with relief.

"You made it," he said inanely as he greeted her with a heartfelt hug and a brief kiss.

"Finally," she muttered. Her body drooped with apparent exhaustion, her smile seemed forced, and she leaned on him as if the sheer act of standing required more energy than she could summon. She made no effort to leave his embrace, which suited him just fine.

"It's past midnight. I can't believe you waited up for me. You didn't have to, but I'm glad you did."

He grinned. Those few words made the hours of impatience worth it. "I said I would. I couldn't go back on my word, could I?" he said lightly, hoping she'd see this incident as another example of his trustworthiness. "I couldn't sleep anyway until you got home."

She chuckled. "I'll bet you stayed awake when Ty or your sister went out, too."

"Sometimes," he admitted, although waiting for his siblings didn't compare to waiting for Christy. Not knowing where she was or what might be happening had made it impossible to close his eyes. The saying "Ignorance is bliss" didn't apply where Christy was concerned.

He changed the subject. "How did your tests go?"

"Like they usually do. I didn't do a thing except lie

on the X-ray tables or sit in chairs. Machines and the staff did all the work."

"Are you tired?" he asked, already knowing the answer.

"Very. You'd think, though, after sitting or lying down all day, I wouldn't be."

"It's a good thing tomorrow is Saturday," he told her. "The kids and I will watch cartoons so you can sleep late."

"That isn't necessary," she began.

"Yes, it is," he insisted. "I'm repaying the favor."

As a sign of her exhaustion, she capitulated. "Okay, but no later than nine," she warned. "Derek has a soccer game at eleven and I have a few things to do before then."

"Nine a.m.," he repeated. "Can I get you anything now? A cup of herbal tea? A glass of water?"

"No, thanks."

"Okay, then. Pleasant dreams."

"You, too," she murmured, before disappearing into her room.

As he performed his final walk-through of the house for the night, his own exhaustion tugged at him and he realized he was ready for the day to end. Now, though, it could, because Christy had come home.

Christy didn't report to work until Tuesday, but the thought of what Linc and the children had done for her this past weekend still brought a smile to her face. Promptly at nine a.m. on Saturday, Emma had knocked on her door and Linc had barged in, carrying a breakfast tray. The plate had contained several misshapen

pancakes, a small bowl of fresh strawberries and blue-
berries, and a cup of her favorite herbal tea prepared
specially for her by Emma.

The day had been declared a "Coddle Christy" day
and the trio had done so with great enthusiasm. She'd
been encouraged to do nothing but eat and sleep and
although she'd been certain she didn't need a nap, she'd
found herself snoozing in Linc's lounge chair when
they'd gone to his house to water his flowers.

His thoughtfulness had given her a few bittersweet
moments because their time of sharing a house would
be ending soon. While it wouldn't be long before she'd
only have her memories to sustain her, what fun it was
to create them.

Her good mood faded, however, as Linc pulled her
and her supervisor, Denise, into a treatment room during his morning rounds and closed the door.

"I want Christy to look after Mrs Connally this
week," he informed Denise in his typical, authoritative physician's voice.

Shocked by his request, Christy listened with a combination of horrified surprise, embarrassment, and
anger at his high-handedness. "I appreciate your request, Doctor," the charge nurse said diplomatically,
"but I can't honor it. If I allowed the doctors to pick and
choose which nurses would look after their patients, I'd
have a staffing nightmare."

"It's in Mrs Connally's best interests for Christy to
be her nurse," he argued. "Have I ever asked for a favor
before?"

"Well, no, but I can't establish a precedent. If the

other doctors—or the nurses—learned I gave you a special favor, I've have a mutiny on my hands."

"Who has to know?" he said. "This is strictly between the three of us."

"I realize the medical staff each has his or her favorite nurses, but I work hard to spread the difficult cases around. Christy already has several. I can't load her with one more."

"Then pass one of hers to someone else."

"I could, but why do you want her for this particular case?" Denise asked, ever blunt. "I have more experienced nurses—"

"This woman and her family need Christy right now."

"I don't understand."

"You don't have to. However, I know what I'm talking about."

Denise frowned. "I'm sorry, but if you want me to bend the rules, I need a good reason to do so. Why is Christy the only nurse who can take care of your post-mastectomy patient?"

Christy's anger and embarrassment faded as the reasons were painfully obvious. To Linc's credit, he didn't divulge her story but simply reiterated his stance.

"Because I believe she is," he said. "Let's leave it at that, shall we?"

Seeing Denise's mulish expression, Christy knew her supervisor wouldn't give in. Linc wasn't trying to draw attention to her but he must be concerned about his patient to ask for such an unusual favor.

"I can explain," she addressed her supervisor quietly. "I had a double mastectomy myself."

Denise's argumentative expression vanished and she looked as shocked as if the floor had disappeared underneath her feet. "You?"

"Yeah. About five years ago."

"My patient needs to see she can still have a full and happy life," Linc added. "Because of her personal experience, Christy can show her that in a way few others can."

Denise let out a deep breath. "Okay. You've been reassigned. Tanya can take Mr Wiseman." She paused, peering over her reading glasses. "You should have told me about this before now."

She shrugged. "I've told a few of my patients if they've had similar surgeries, but I didn't necessarily want it to be common knowledge."

"You do realize I'll take advantage of your experience in the future, don't you?"

Christy nodded. "Yes, ma'am."

"Then it's settled." Denise addressed Linc. "Are you satisfied, Doctor?"

He worked his mouth in an obvious attempt to hide a grin. "Absolutely."

"Good." Denise strode from the room, leaving Christy alone with Linc.

"I'm sorry for putting you on the spot," he began, "but Renee Connally is having a difficult time coping with her diagnosis. She's forty years old, has three children, and is convinced her life is over."

"Is it?" she asked.

"The cancer is invasive, but we caught it early and her sentinel lymph nodes are clear. You were the first person I thought of who might convince her that she can get past this. I'm sorry I outed you."

"The news was bound to break sooner or later," she said, "but don't worry about it. Meanwhile, I'll talk to her."

"Thanks," he said. "The sooner you get her to look positively at her future, the better."

Christy found Renee dozing, her husband in the chair beside her bed. As soon as she walked in, the woman opened her eyes.

"I'm Christy and I'll be taking care of you," she said calmly. "Are you staying ahead of your pain?"

"For the most part."

Christy chatted about non-consequential topics while she checked Renee's drain and offered to teach her how to maintain it as soon as Renee was able. After discussing a few other physical issues with her, Christy said cheerfully, "Doctor says we have to get you moving, so I'm going to bump your hubby from his chair. You can sit there for a while."

As her husband jumped up, Renee shook her head. "I'd rather not. There isn't any point, is there?"

"Of course there is. Lying in bed won't help you return to your normal life."

"That's the point. My life isn't normal any more, is it?"

"Not by your old standards, but whatever treatment you face won't last for ever. You're facing a tough period, to be sure, but you can get past this. You have to, for your children's sakes."

"I know you mean well, but save your Pollyanna

attitude for someone else. You have no idea what I'm going through."

"Actually, I do," she said bluntly. "I had a double mastectomy five years ago and I'm proof that life goes on." She pulled up a nearby folding chair and began to tell her story.

By the end of the week, Christy was pleased with Renee Connally's progress. She had begun to take an active interest in her own nursing care and her entire outlook seemed much improved.

She'd also learned something from Renee and her husband as well. As she watched her walk the hallway with his help and sometimes caught the two of them in the room with their heads together, she came to a startling conclusion.

Jon hadn't loved her.

Oh, he'd been good company and they'd got along well, but true love had staying power. When the going got tough, love allowed two people to endure. It didn't encourage one person to abandon the other.

I'm not going anywhere.

Linc's words resurfaced in her memory. For the first time she began to believe it was possible—that there *were* men who stood by their wives and girlfriends during difficult times. That fellows like Jon were the exception, not the rule.

Unfortunately, her revelation came at a time when she had to shelve her personal concerns and focus on the job at hand. Gail and Ty were due home on Saturday and Christy had a million things to do before they arrived. Not only was the dance competition on her mind but she wanted everything in the house to be in perfect order, from the housework to the laundry. To that end, she created lists of chores for everyone until Linc complained as loudly as the children.

Naturally, Derek and Emma were wild with anticipation.

"We should visit the park so Ria can run off their energy, shouldn't we?" Linc said on Wednesday evening.

"I think so," she said ruefully. "The sad thing is, they're like Energizer Bunnies. Poor Ria is so tired her tail drags most of the time."

"After Saturday, Ria can resume her quiet life." He paused. "If their flight is delayed again for any reason, we'll cut it close to get to our event on time."

"We'll manage. If nothing else, we'll leave their car and they can drive themselves home."

"Let's hope we don't have to. Derek and Emma would be crushed if they weren't able to greet their parents as soon as they land."

Christy didn't understand what had caused the airline to bump Gail and Ty to a later flight, but she was relieved to have the extra hours' reprieve. Truth was, she wasn't looking forward to returning to her quiet little apartment after being a part of a boisterous family atmosphere.

"I've been spoiled the past two months," Linc commented.

"Spoiled? How?"

"As crazy as it sounds, I liked having all the commotion when I came home at night. It'll take time to get used to peace and quiet again."

"I agree." She grinned. "Maybe we can borrow Derek and Emma for the occasional weekend."

"It's a deal," he said.

Suddenly both children raced through the house, doors slamming, with Ria barking at their heels as they rushed into the back yard.

Linc visibly winced. "I was going to ask if you wanted to run through our dance routine again, but we'd better save that for later. Unless you think we don't need the practice."

She hated the idea of never dancing with him again, so she intended to make the most of her opportunities.

"'Practice makes perfect,'" she quoted. "I'll pencil you into my schedule after the kids are in bed for the night."

"I can't wait."

Neither, it seemed, could she.

On Saturday at two, Linc herded his group through the airport to the baggage claim where they waited for Gail and Ty to arrive. According to the monitors, their flight would land in a few minutes, so they still had plenty of time to wait. Linc would have preferred spending the extra hour at the house, but every five minutes Derek or Emma had asked, "Can we leave yet?"

Although he'd miss the time with the children, Linc was glad his brother would be home again. He looked forward to giving Christy his full attention.

"Are you okay?" he asked her as they milled around the open area along with others who were also waiting for their friends and family to appear.

"Sure. Why wouldn't I be?"

He suspected the reason went far beyond her desire to create a perfect homecoming. She'd been in her element taking care of Derek and Emma and she was probably sad because her opportunity would end within the next few minutes. Little did she know, though, that he intended to keep her busier than ever.

"You look a little stressed," he hedged.

"Too much on my mind, I guess. Oh, look." She pointed to the group of passengers descending on them. "They're here."

As both children broke away to run toward their parents, Linc remained at Christy's side, his arm slung around her waist. From the way she swiped at the corner of her eyes, he knew his brother's family reunion bothered her more than she let on.

He remained rooted to the spot, determined to show her that no matter the situation, she could lean on him.

"My word, Christy!" Gail exclaimed as she walked into her house a short time later. "This place looks better than when I left."

Christy laughed at her friend's awe. "I wouldn't go that far, but everyone worked hard to get ready for you. We also went grocery shopping and stocked the refrigerator so you won't have to fight the stores for a few days until you recover from jet lag."

"You've thought of everything," Gail marveled. "So tell me quick while the men are unloading the suitcases—how did things go with you and Linc?"

"Great."

Her gaze narrowed. "You're not just saying that, are you?"

"No, I'm not. In fact, things went much better than I'd ever dreamed they would. You were right. He really is a great guy. In fact, I'll probably miss having him around on a daily basis, dirty socks and all," she finished lightly.

Gail eyed her carefully. "Oh, my gosh. You've fallen in love with him, haven't you?"

Christy wanted to deny it, but she couldn't—not to her dearest friend. She didn't know when it had happened, but it had. "I think so," she said.

"How does he feel?"

She smiled. "He says he isn't going anywhere."

Gail clapped her hands and crowed. "I *knew* you two were meant for each other. This is absolutely *wonderful*."

"No, it isn't," she said flatly. "We have so many potential problems ahead of us. It wouldn't be fair to ask him to face those when he doesn't have to."

"Don't you think he's already weighed the pros and cons? He's an adult and can make his own decisions," Gail informed her. "He doesn't need you to think for him."

"I know, but how can I be sure he won't change his mind when the going gets rough?"

"Some things you have to take on faith."

Unfortunately, when it came to something this important, her faith was practically non-existent.

"Are you worried about your doctor's appointment? Is that why you can't think reasonably?"

"I'm concerned, not worried, and I *am* thinking reasonably."

The sympathy in Gail's eyes suggested that she didn't

agree. "You've been feeling okay, haven't you? You don't have any symptoms that you're not telling me about?"

"No symptoms and, yes, Mother, I've been feeling fine. Thanks for asking."

"I'm sounding mother-hen-ish, aren't I?"

"A little, but I know you mean well." She hugged her friend. "I'm glad you're back," she said sincerely, because she *had* missed her. "Thanks again for the opportunity to look after your kids. We had a wonderful time and I'll never forget it."

"I'm glad. We couldn't have enjoyed ourselves as much as we did if we weren't confident Derek and Emma were taken care of."

Linc walked in with a suitcase in each hand, his brother behind him equally laden. "I hate to rush away without hearing about your time in France, but Christy and I have a fall festival to attend."

Gail snapped her fingers. "That's right. The dance competition is tonight. I'd forgotten."

"We haven't, because, oh, by the way, we're going to win." Linc grinned.

Christy laughed. "Spoken like an overconfident surgeon. Seriously, though, we're quite good."

"I left four tickets on the counter if you decide you'd like to watch our performance," Linc informed his brother and sister-in-law. "We're the very last couple on the schedule, so it'll be close to nine o'clock. After that, the disc jockey will provide music and open the dance floor to everyone."

After a quick round of goodbyes, Christy allowed Linc to escort her and Ria to her car. Her suitcases were already in the trunk and as soon as he opened the passenger door, Ria bounded inside.

"I guess this is it," she said.

"Only for now," he said firmly. "I'll pick you up at your house in two hours. That will give you time to rest before our big evening."

"You mean time to get nervous?"

"You aren't nervous, are you? This can't be coming from the woman who assured me this fundraiser was all in the spirit of fun."

"I lied," she said promptly.

"Surely my fearless partner—the same lady who jumps out of airplanes and rides the rapids—isn't suffering from cold feet, is she?"

"As crazy as it sounds, yes."

"Silly woman," he said with obvious affection. "Win or lose, we're going to be great."

She eyed him carefully. "Somehow I'd always imagined that I'd give *you* the pep talk tonight. Are you the same Lincoln Maguire who had to be coerced into participating?"

"One and the same, but we've practiced until we could both dance our steps in our sleep and sometimes I have. If we trip or miss a step, we've already practiced that, too." He grinned. "We'll recover."

His humor was infectious. "We will, but why don't I save time and meet you at the convention center?"

"I seem to remember having this same discussion once before," he said sternly, although the twinkle in his eye minimized the sting, "but now, like then, my answer is no. We're partners. We'll arrive and leave together."

His description made her realize how badly she

needed him to understand what a partnership with her would mean. Somehow she had to make certain he looked at a future through regular lenses and not rose-colored glasses. However, she'd save that discussion for later.

She gave in. "If that's what you want to do."

"It is. Now, drive home safely, and I'll see you soon."

She couldn't stop her pulse from leaping with anticipation, although she knew tonight's dance competition might only be the beginning of the end.

CHAPTER TEN

LINC strode into his house and hardly noticed the quiet. He was too busy replaying the last few hours they'd spent together. From the moment they'd got into the car and headed to the airport, he'd sensed Christy's mental withdrawal. At first, he'd thought it was because she simply didn't want to say goodbye to the kids, but his gut warned that it went much deeper. She intended to distance herself from *him*, probably out of an altruistic notion that she would save him from himself.

He wasn't going to let her because he intended to stick to her like glue. The only way she'd get away from him would be if she moved to another city, and he wasn't averse to following her. In the space of a few weeks he'd come to the point where he wanted her to be a part of his every day. He didn't want some steady, dependable sort, although Christy was all that and more. He wanted the Christy who fearlessly faced life with joy and grace because…

Because he loved her.

The realization hit him hard, but it was true. He loved her, and he'd do anything within his power for her, just as his father had done for the love of *his* life. As he looked at his childhood with new eyes the weight of his old resentments dropped off. He couldn't let the day end without telling Christy how he felt.

She'd probably tell him he was mistaken or try to convince him of her shortcomings, but she didn't understand the most important thing. He needed her just as she was.

They were by no means late and, in fact, had arrived at the convention hall a little early, but Christy was amazed by the crowd of people who'd already gathered.

"You're at table five, near the front," the woman at the check-in desk informed them. "Enjoy yourselves and good luck with the competition. We have a packed house tonight."

The news didn't come as any surprise. Christy had suspected people would come in droves and it was nice to know she'd been right.

"Let's find our table before we mingle," Linc said in her ear because the noise level already made hearing difficult.

"Good idea," she said, conscious of his hand on the small of her back as they wound their way through the tables and groups of people. The skirt of her red silky dress, purchased specifically for tonight's occasion because it flared and flowed in the right places, swung provocatively over her sashaying hips. The spaghetti-strapped bodice was covered in glittery sequins and would sparkle like diamonds under the spotlight. The garment fit perfectly and although Linc's hand didn't stray from the base of her spine, her skin sizzled under the heat of his fingers.

She'd proved her mother's belief about clothing, she

decided. She felt as sensational as the dress, and Linc's admiring gaze when he'd arrived at her house had told her it had been money well spent.

Linc had earned her admiring gaze, too. She'd seen him wearing scrubs, casual work attire as well as work-out clothes, but, as wonderfully as he filled out those garments, he was positively awesome in his black tuxedo pants and the long-sleeved dress shirt he wore open at his neck.

Christy meandered past various groups and mingled with others, conscious of Linc remaining at her side. She was surprised he didn't veer off to visit with his own friends and colleagues and leave her to her own devices. Instead, if he wanted to speak to someone, he'd grab her hand and drag her along. If she saw someone and headed toward them, he followed.

The truth was she was thrilled he didn't leave her. At this moment they were a couple. A pair.

Partners.

I'm not going anywhere, he'd told her on several occasions, and since then he hadn't. For the first time she began to believe that it might be true—that he wouldn't leave her when or if the going got rough.

By the end of the hour the hall was packed and they took their seats at the same table as several of Linc's partners and their wives.

Janice Martin, a distinguished lady in her mid-sixties, who was seated on Christy's left, leaned close. "I'm pleased you convinced Linc to participate in this event. The man is too young to work twenty-four seven. He needed an interest outside the hospital and I'm delighted you gave him one."

"Thank you, but it was more a case of bullying him into it rather than persuading him to volunteer."

Janice patted her arm. "However you managed this miracle, I'm glad you did. Why, he looks like a new man."

Christy glanced at Linc, who was chatting with Dale Zorn, a cardiologist, on his right. The version of the Lincoln Maguire beside her bore little resemblance to the man she'd known a few weeks ago. That fellow had been tense, extremely focused, and didn't smile. Now his face was animated and his body relaxed, as if he didn't have a care in the world.

"Being a temporary father to his nephew and niece had a lot to do with his transformation," she told Janice.

"Ah, yes. My husband told me you two were look-ing after his brother's kids. How did you enjoy being parents?"

How could she possibly describe the best experi-ence in recent memory? "I had the time of my life," she said simply.

As soon as she'd voiced those words, she realized how appropriate it had been for Linc to choose that particular song for their dance routine. It was a fitting end to their two months together.

Selfishness suddenly reared its head. Because of all the potential obstacles facing them, ending their relationship might be for the best, but every fiber of her being warned that it would be a mistake—one she would regret for the rest of her days. Truth was, she wanted what the Connallys had—a partnership that saw them through the good times as well as the bad.

Their partnership was more than a simple agreement between two people. Love had knit them together; love had made the difference—the same type of love she felt for Linc.

Then you know what you have to do, her little voice chided her. *Take the risk.*

She wanted to ponder her choices and replay all of her what-if scenarios, but the master-of-ceremonies interrupted her thoughts as he began the event. Linc turned to her. "Nervous?"

"A little. You?"

"Never better."

For the next thirty minutes Christy and the rest of the guests were entertained by the various teams who performed. Some were good, others fair, still others were perfectly awful or downright hilarious, but through it all she was conscious of Linc's arm resting on the back of her chair, his hand curled around her shoulder.

She simply couldn't imagine going back to the way things had been before. In the hours prior to tonight's event, her apartment had seemed so sterile and lifeless and the thought of facing that existence day after day was too horrible to imagine.

She wanted to be with Linc, morning, noon, and night. She wanted him to tease her about how she squeezed her toothpaste, rave over her meals, and pamper Ria as much as she did. She needed him in more ways than she could ever list, and she needed him like she needed air to breathe, because she loved him.

So focused was she on her epiphany, she hardly noticed he'd moved until he whispered into her ear, his breath warm against her neck. "We're next."

She nodded. The butterflies in her stomach suddenly

settled as she resolved to express her feelings during their song. She realized how diligently he'd been working to convince her to trust him and now seemed the perfect opportunity to show him what lay in her heart. The words would come later, when they were alone.

The performance ended, although Christy had been so focused on her private thoughts she hadn't paid attention to her competition. After the applause died down, the MC announced their names.

Linc grabbed her hand and led her to the dance floor. Before he left her to stand alone center stage, he squeezed her fingers and winked.

She laughed at his irreverence while he moved to stage right. The crowd fell silent as the familiar melody began.

Christy allowed the music to wash over her, paying careful attention to the lyrics as she poured out the emotions that matched those expressed in the song.

Through the basic grind that brought a few catcalls, then the flamenco, various dips and spins, the spectators faded into nothingness as she focused on Linc.

He clearly did the same because his gaze had locked on hers. Easily, effortlessly, she glided through the steps. As the music drew to a close, the final spin brought her into Linc's embrace.

Barely conscious of the thundering applause, she only had eyes for Linc. He traced her jaw, then bent his head and kissed her in such a lingering manner that her toes tingled and the crowd went wild.

As the announcer came to the microphone, Linc broke contact and they made their way back to their table. Christy's heart pounded as much from his kiss as from the exertion and she felt so marvelous she was certain her feet didn't touch the floor. People nodded to her as they clapped while others pounded Linc on his back for a job well done.

"Okay, folks. Based on the amount of applause, I think it's easy to tell which team is our winner. Dr Lincoln Maguire and his lovely partner, Christy Michaels!"

The hired DJ began a music set and encouraged everyone to participate. The mood in the building was high and from the numbers of couples who took to the dance floor, they'd been energized by Christy and Linc's performance.

"Do you want to stay?" Linc asked her.

She hesitated, trying to read him and failing. "Would you mind if we didn't?"

His slow grin was the answer she wanted. "Not at all."

Although Linc graciously accepted everyone's congratulations on their way out, he chafed at the delay. He wanted to simply toss Christy over his shoulder and walk through the throng, but he'd already pushed his limits when he'd kissed Christy in front of five hundred spectators. People he knew and those he didn't remarked on his memorable performance, although he didn't know if they'd been impressed by his dancing ability or because he'd kissed his partner with such fervor.

Either way, the first *Dancing with the Docs* event would go down in hospital history.

"Would you like to come inside?" she asked as he pulled into a parking space outside her apartment.

"I'd like that." His gut warned him that something

monumental would take place and, if his suspicions were correct, it wouldn't be good.

"My selection is limited tonight," she said as she headed for her kitchen. "Would you like water or wine?"

The wine could wait until they had something to celebrate. "Water, please." As she handed him a glass and they headed into the living room, he asked, "What's on your mind? And don't say 'Nothing' because I can read you too well."

"Okay." She placed her glass on the coffee table before she sank onto her sofa. "Here's the deal.

"This afternoon, I'd contemplated how we should go our separate ways."

He nodded. "I suspected as much."

"It seemed the right thing to do. You want things out of life that I might not be able to give you—two point five kids, a minivan, becoming soccer parents, and the potential to celebrate a fiftieth anniversary, to name a few.

"My mother told me I was trying to protect myself from being hurt, and deep down I was. I'd done a good job, too, until you came along," she said wryly, "but you wiggled through my defenses and I did the unthinkable. I fell in love with you."

After bracing himself for the worst, relief swept through him to the point he couldn't speak.

Her mouth trembled as she met his gaze. "Whatever happens next is up to you."

Rather than act on her cue to leave if he so desired, he drew her against him. "I'm not going anywhere."

"You're sure? Think long and hard about your decision," she warned.

"I already have. I love you too much to be intimidated by the obstacles we might face."

Tears glistened in her eyes. "Oh, Linc."

"You should know that I'd anticipated this conversation ever since you left Gail and Ty's. In fact, I'd intended to seduce you if that's what it took to persuade you of my sincerity."

She chuckled. "Wow."

"In fact, I may do it anyway." With that, he kissed her.

When Christy finally came up for air, she scooted away. "Before we take this to its logical conclusion, I want everything perfectly clear between us. My cancer could return. Derek and Emma might never have a cousin or two. We could—"

"Whatever happens, I'm going into our relationship with both eyes open," he assured her. "Do I need to sign your list in blood or is my word good enough?"

She smiled. "Your word is enough," she said simply.

"Good. While we're tossing out worst-case scenarios, I could develop a life-threatening disease in five, ten or twenty years. I had mumps as a child and could be sterile. What if I walk into the hospital parking lot and a runaway car runs me down? Could you deal with *my* issues if they ever happen?"

His points made her realize she might be making more out of her worries than necessary. "Yes. However, there's one more thing for you to consider."

"Christy," he said kindly, "whatever your concern, it isn't as important as you think it might be. I love you for the woman you are."

"That's sweet of you to say, but I want to give you

one last chance to change your mind. You may not need to see this, but I need to show you."

She led him into her bedroom and turned her back toward him. "Unzip me, please. I can't reach."

"This is completely unnecessary."

"I don't agree. Just do it."

As soon as he tugged down the zipper, she turned around to face him. Slowly, carefully, she let the gown drop to the floor.

"I want you to see exactly what you're getting," she said softly. "If you're repulsed—"

She held her breath and watched his expression as he gazed at her manmade curves. She saw interest and awe, but not disgust, and she finally allowed herself to breathe.

He traced her collarbone with a feather-light touch before trailing his fingers down her breastbone. Meeting her gaze without flinching or hesitation, he suddenly pulled her against his chest and covered her back with his hands.

"I see the most beautiful woman in the world."

Although logic said otherwise, she was thrilled he thought so. "Will you stay with me tonight?"

He nodded. "On two conditions."

She raised an eyebrow. "And they are?"

"One, I won't leave until morning. In fact, I won't leave until it's time for our flight."

Surprised by his comment, she asked, "Do you want to come along?"

"Nothing could keep me away. In fact, I bought my ticket two weeks ago. I had planned to go with you, one way or another."

If she'd needed final proof that he would stick by her, no matter what, he'd just provided it.

"What's the second condition?"

"That you agree to marry me. I want you to know beyond all doubt that I won't be influenced by the outcome of your appointment."

Although she'd suspected as much, until now she'd been afraid to believe. "I know you will," she said simply. "And, yes, I'll be your wife."

His grin instantly stretched across his face before he stepped back and began unbuttoning his shirt. "Good. Now that we've addressed those minor details, I want to make love with you."

She wanted to cry with happiness and all she could do was nod her agreement.

"I hope you got a nap this afternoon," he added, "because we won't be sleeping most of the night."

Christy helped with his buttons, enjoying the feel of his hard chest beneath her fingers. "Is that so?"

"Oh, yes," he assured her, before he stepped out of his trousers and drew her against him once again. "It's a promise."

Christy sat in her oncologist's private office with Linc beside her as they waited for Dr Kingston to walk in. He'd conducted his exam in his usual noncommittal manner and after he'd finished, he'd suggested she join him in his office as soon as she'd dressed.

She pulled on her clothes in record time.

As she sat in front of the doctor's desk, outwardly she was calm, but inwardly she was a bundle of nerves.

"Whatever he tells us, we'll deal with it," Linc assured her as he held her hand in his strong one.

She managed a smile. "I know, but—"

"Think optimistically," Linc told her.

The door swung wide and Dr Kingston entered. He was tall, thin, and reminded her of an oversized scarecrow, but his eyes were full of compassion. He also seemed older than she remembered, but she supposed his job was more difficult and more stressful than most.

"Sorry for the delay," he said in a kindly voice that matched his expression. "I had to take a phone call."

Christy introduced Linc, then waited for the oncologist to open her chart on his desk.

"You're doing well?" he asked. "Still enjoying your job?"

"Oh, yes."

"My wife insists I need to take a vacation. Maybe we should travel to the Midwest. I haven't been in the area in years."

"It's a wonderful part of the country," she agreed, fighting her impatience.

"I imagine it is. But, then, you aren't here to listen to my vacation plans, are you?" Without waiting for her response—which was a good thing because she suddenly couldn't breathe—he opened her folder. "Ah, yes. I remember now. Your results came in a week ago."

"And?" she asked, her palms suddenly moist.

He leaned back in his chair and steepled his fingers. "Your scans are clear. No sign of any abnormalities."

Christy's shoulders slumped and tears came to her eyes as Linc hugged her.

"Your tumor marker levels haven't changed either,

so I'd say you passed your five-year check-up with fly-ing colors."

"Thank you," she choked out.

He smiled. "I'll be happy to take the credit because I don't often have the opportunity to deliver good news. Out of curiosity, though, I know you celebrate your anniversary with an adventure. What did you plan for this year?"

Christy looked at Linc and smiled at him with all the love in her heart. "A wedding."

* * * * *

A sneaky peek at next month...

Medical Romance™

CAPTIVATING MEDICAL DRAMA—WITH HEART

My wish list for next month's titles...

In stores from 6th July 2012:

☐ Sydney Harbour Hospital: Marco's Temptation
— Fiona McArthur

& Waking Up With His Runaway Bride — Louisa George

☐ The Legendary Playboy Surgeon

& Falling for Her Impossible Boss — Alison Roberts

☐ Letting Go With Dr Rodriguez — Fiona Lowe

& Dr Tall, Dark...and Dangerous? — Lynne Marshall

Available at WHSmith, Tesco, Asda, Eason, Amazon and Apple

Just can't wait?

Special Offers

Every month we put together collections and longer reads written by your favourite authors.

Here are some of next month's highlights— and don't miss our fabulous discount online!

On sale 15th June

On sale 15th June

On sale 6th July